THE STROLLING SAINT

THE
STROLLING SAINT

BEING THE CONFESSIONS OF THE HIGH
AND MIGHTY AGOSTINO D'ANGUISSOLA,
TYRANT OF MONDOLFO AND LORD OF
CARMINA IN THE STATE OF PIACENZA

BY

RAFAEL SABATINI

AUTHOR OF
SAINT MARTIN'S SUMMER,
MISTRESS WILDING,
SCARAMOUCHE, Etc.

NEW YORK
GROSSET & DUNLAP
PUBLISHERS

PRINTED IN THE U.S.A.

CONTENTS

BOOK I

THE OBLATE

BOOK II

GIULIANA

BOOK III

THE WILDERNESS

BOOK IV
THE WORLD

THE STROLLING SAINT

BOOK I: THE OBLATE

.·.

CHAPTER I

NOMEN ET OMEN

IN seeking other than in myself — as men will — the causes of my tribulations, I have often inclined to lay the blame of much of the ill that befell me, and the ill that in my sinful life I did to others, upon those who held my mother at the baptismal font and concerted that she should bear the name of Monica.

There are in life many things which, in themselves, seeming to the vulgar and the heedless to be trivial and without consequence, may yet be causes pregnant of terrible effects, mainsprings of Destiny itself. Amid such portentous trifles I would number the names so heedlessly bestowed upon us.

It surprises me that in none of the philosophic writings of the learned scholars of antiquity can I find that this matter of names has been touched upon, much less given the importance of which I account it to be deserving. Possibly it is because no one of them ever suffered, as I have suffered, from the consequences of a name. Had it but been so, they might in their weighty and impressive manner have set down a lesson on the subject, and so relieved me — who am all-conscious of my shortcomings in this direction — from the necessity of repairing that omission out of my own experience.

Let it, then, even at this late hour, be considered what a subtle influence for good or ill, what a very mould of character may lie within a name.

To the dull clod of earth, perhaps, or, again, to the truly strong-minded nature that is beyond such influences, it can matter little that he be called Alexander or Achilles; and once there was a man named Judas who fell so far short of the noble associations of that name that he has changed for all time the very sound and meaning of it.

But to him who has been endowed with imagination — that greatest boon and greatest affliction of mankind — or whose nature is such as to crave for models, the name he bears may become a thing portentous by the images it conjures up of some mighty dead who bore it erstwhile and whose life inspires to emulation.

Whatever may be accounted the general value of this premiss, at least as it concerns my mother I shall hope to prove it apt.

They named her Monica. Why the name was chosen I have never learnt; but I do not conceive that there was any reason for the choice other than the taste of her parents in the matter of sounds. It is a pleasing enough name, euphoniously considered, and beyond that — as is so commonly the case — no considerations were taken into account.

To her, however, at once imaginative and of a feeble and dependent spirit, the name was fateful. Saint Monica was made the special object of her devotions in girlhood, and remained so later when she became a wife. The "Life of Saint Monica" was the most soiled and fingered portion of an old manuscript collection of the life histories of a score or so of saints that was one of her dearest possessions. To render herself worthy of the name she bore, to model her life upon that of the sainted woman who had sorrowed and rejoiced so much in her famous offspring, became the obsession of my mother's soul. And but that Saint Monica had wed and borne a son, I do not believe that my mother would ever have adventured herself within the bonds of wedlock.

How often in the stressful, stormy hours of my most unhappy youth did I not wish that she had preferred the virginal life of the cloister, and thus spared me the heavy burden of an existence which her unholy and mistaken saintliness went so near to laying waste!

I like to think that in the days when my father wooed her, she forgot for a spell in the strong arms of that fierce Ghibelline the pattern upon which it had become her wont to weave her life; so that in all that drab, sackcloth tissue there was embroidered at least one warm and brilliant little wedge of colour; so that in all that desert waste, in all that parched aridity of her existence, there was at least one little patch of orchard, fragrant, fruitful, and cool.

I like to think it, for at best such a spell must have been brief indeed. And for this I pity her — I, who once blamed her so very bitterly. Before ever I was born it must have ceased; whilst still she bore me she put from her lips the cup that holds the warm and potent wine of life, and turned her once more to her fasting, her contemplations, and her prayers.

That was in the year in which the battle of Pavia was fought and won by the Emperor. My father, who

had raised a condotta to lend a hand in the expulsion
of the French, was left for dead upon that glorious
field. Afterwards he was found still living, but upon
the very edge and border of Eternity; and when the
news of it was borne to my mother, I have little doubt
but that she imagined it to be a visitation — a punishment upon her for having strayed for that brief
season of her adolescence from the narrow flinty path
that she had erst claimed to tread in the footsteps of
Holy Monica.

How much the love of my father may still have
swayed her I do not know. But to me it seems that in
what next she did there was more of duty, more of
penitence, more of reparation for the sin of having
been a woman as God made her, than of love. Indeed,
I almost know this to be so. In delicate health as she
was, she bade her people prepare a litter for her, and
so she had herself carried into Piacenza, to the
Church of Saint Augustine. There, having confessed
and received the Sacrament, upon her knees before a
minor altar consecrated to Saint Monica, she made
solemn vow that if my father's life was spared she
would devote the unborn child she carried to the
service of God and Holy Church.

Two months thereafter word was brought her that
my father, his recovery by now well-nigh complete,
was making his way home.

On the morrow was I born — a votive offering, an
oblate, ere yet I had drawn the breath of life.

It has often amused me to conjecture what would
have chanced had I been born a girl — since that
could have afforded her no proper parallel. In the circumstance that I was a boy, I have no faintest doubt

but that she saw a Sign, for she was given to seeing
signs in the slightest and most natural happenings. It
was as it should be; it was as it had been with the
sainted Monica in whose ways she strove, poor thing,
to walk. Monica had borne a son, and he had been
named Augustine. It was very well. My name, too,
should be Augustine, that I might walk in the ways of
that other Augustine, that great theologian whose
mother's name was Monica.

And even as the influence of her name had been my
mother's guide, so was the influence of my name to
exert its sway upon me. It was made to do so. Before
I was able to read, the life of that great saint — with
such castrations as my tender years demanded —
was told me and repeated until I knew by heart its
every incident and act. Later his writings were my
school-books. His "De Civitate Dei" and "De Vita
Beata" were the paps at which I suckled my earliest
mental nourishment.

And even to-day, after all the tragedy and sin and
turbulence of my life, that was intended to have been
so different, it is from his "Confessions" that I have
gathered inspiration to set down my own — although
betwixt the two you may discern little, indeed, that is
comparable.

I was prenatally made a votive offering for the
preservation of my father's life, for his restoration to
my mother safe and sound. That restoration she had,
as you have seen; and yet, had she been other than
she was, she must have accounted herself cheated of
her bargain in the end. For betwixt my father and
my mother I became from my earliest years a subject
of contentions that drove them ever farther asunder

and set them at last in enmity the one against the
other.

I was his only son, heir to the noble lordships of
Mondolfo and Carmina. Was it likely, then, that he
should sacrifice me willingly to the seclusion of the
cloister, whilst our lordship passed into the hands of
our renegade, Guelphic cousin, Cosimo d'Anguissola
of Codogno?

I can picture his outbursts at the very thought of
it; I can hear him reasoning, upbraiding, storming.
But he was as an ocean of energy hurling himself
against an impassive rock of obstinacy. My mother
had vowed me to the service of Holy Church, and she
would suffer tribulation and death so that her vow
should be fulfilled. And hers was a manner against
which that strong man, my father, never could prevail. She would stand before him white-faced and
mute, never presuming to return an answer to his
pleading or to enter into argument.

"I have vowed," she would say, just once; and
thereafter, avoiding his fiery glance, she would bow
her head meekly, fold her hands, the very incarnation
of long-suffering and martyrdom.

Anon, as the storm of his anger crashed about her,
two glistening lines would appear upon her pallid
face, and her tears — horrid, silent weeping that
brought no trace of emotion to her countenance —
showered down. At that he would fling out of her
presence and away, cursing the day in which he had
mated with a fool.

His hatred of these moods of hers, of the vow she
had made which bade fair to deprive him of his son,
drove him ere long to hatred of the cause of it all. A

Ghibelline by inheritance, he was not long in becoming an utter infidel, at war with Rome and the Pontifical sway. Nor was he one to content himself with passive enmity. He must be up and doing, seeking the destruction of the thing he hated. And so it befell that upon the death of Pope Clement (the second Medici Pontiff), profiting by the weak condition from which the papal arm had not yet recovered since the Emperor's invasion and the sack of Rome, my father raised an army and attempted to shatter the ancient yoke which Julius II had imposed upon Parma and Piacenza when he took them from the State of Milan.

A little lad of seven was I at the time, and well do I remember the martial stir and bustle there was about our citadel of Mondolfo, the armed multitudes thronging the courtyard of the fortress that was our home, or drilling and manœuvring upon the green plains beyond the river.

I was all wonder-stricken and fascinated by the sight. My blood was quickened by the brazen notes of their trumpets, and to balance a pike in my hands was to procure me the oddest and most exquisite thrills that I had known. But my mother, perceiving with alarm the delight afforded me by such warlike matters, withdrew me so that I might see as little as possible of it all.

And there followed scenes between her and my father of which hazy impressions linger in my memory. No longer was she a mute statue, enduring with fearful stoicism his harsh upbraidings. She was turned into a suppliant, now fierce, now lachrymose; by her prayers, by her prophecies of the evil that must attend his ungodly aims, she strove with all her poor, feeble might to turn him from the path of revolt to which he had set his foot.

And he would listen now in silence, his face grim and sardonic; and when from very weariness the flow of her inspired oratory began to falter, he would deliver ever the same answer.

"It is you who have driven me to this; and this is no more than a beginning. You have made a vow — an outrageous votive offering of something that is not yours to bestow. That vow you cannot break, you say. Be it so. But I must seek a remedy elsewhere. To save my son from the Church to which you would doom him, I will, ere I have done, tear down the Church and make an end of it in Italy."

And at that she would shrivel up before him with a little moan of horror, taking her poor white face in her hands.

"Blasphemer!" she would cry in mingled terror and aversion, and upon that word — the "Amen" to all their conferences in those last days they spent together — she would turn, and, dragging me with her, all stunned and bewildered by something beyond my understanding, she would hurry me to the chapel of the citadel, and there, before the high altar, prostrate herself and spend long hours in awful sobbing intercessions.

And so the gulf between them widened until the day of his departure.

I was not present at their parting. What farewells may have been spoken between them, what premonitions may have troubled one or the other that they were destined never to meet again, I do not know.

I remember being rudely awakened one dark morn-

ing early in the year, and lifted from my bed by arms
to whose clasp I never failed to thrill. Close to mine
was pressed a hot, dark, shaven hawk-face; a pair of
great eyes, humid with tears, considered me passionately. Then a ringing voice — that commanding
voice that was my father's — spoke to Falcone, the
man-at-arms who attended him and who ever acted
as his equerry.

"Shall we take him with us to the wars, Falcone?"

My little arms went round his neck and tightened
there convulsively until the steel rim of his gorget bit
into them.

"Take me!" I sobbed. "Take me!"

He laughed for answer, with something of exultation in his voice. He swung me to his shoulder, and
held me poised there, looking up at me. And then he
laughed again.

"Dost hear the whelp?" he cried to Falcone. "Still
with his milk-teeth in his head, and already does he
yelp for battle!"

Then he looked up at me again, and swore one of
his great oaths.

"I can trust you, son of mine," he laughed.
"They'll never make a shaveling of you. When your
thews are grown it will not be on thuribles they'll
spend their strength. Be patient yet awhile, and we
shall ride together, never doubt it."

With that he pulled me down again to kiss me, and
he clasped me to his breast so that the studs of his
armour remained stamped upon my tender flesh after
he had departed.

The next instant he was gone, and I lay weeping, a
very lonely little child.

But in the revolt that he led he had not reckoned upon the might and vigour of the new, Farnese Pontiff. He had conceived, perhaps, that one pope must be as supine as another, and that Paul III would prove no more redoubtable than Clement VII. To his bitter cost did he discover his mistake. Beyond the Po he was surprised by the Pontifical army under Ferrante Orsini, and there his force was cut to pieces.

My father himself escaped and with him some other gentlemen of Piacenza, notably one of the scions of the great House of Pallavicini, who took a wound in the leg which left him lame for life, so that ever after he was known as Pallavicini il Zopo.

They were all under the Pope's ban, outlaws with a price upon the head of each, hunted and harried from State to State by the papal emissaries, so that my father never more dared set foot in Mondolfo, or, indeed, within the State of Piacenza, which had been rudely punished for the insubordination it had permitted to be reared upon its soil.

And Mondolfo went near to suffering confiscation. Assuredly it would have suffered it but for the influence exerted on my mother's and my own behalf by her brother, the powerful Cardinal of San Paulo in Carcere, seconded by that Guelphic cousin of my father's, Cosimo d'Anguissola, who, after me, was heir to Mondolfo, and had, therefore, good reason not to see it confiscated to the Holy See.

Thus it fell out that we were left in peace and not made to suffer from my father's rebellion. For that, he, himself, should suffer when taken. But taken he never was. From time to time we had news of him. Now he was in Venice, now in Milan, now in Naples;

but never long in any place, for his safety's sake. And then one night, six years later, a scarred and grizzled veteran, coming none knew whence, dropped from exhaustion in the courtyard of our citadel, whither he had struggled. Some went to minister to him, and amongst these there was a groom who recognized him.

"It is Messer Falcone!" he cried, and ran to bear the news to my mother, with whom I was at table at the time. With us, too, was Fra Gervasio, our chaplain.

It was grim news that old Falcone brought us. He had never quitted my father in those six weary years of wandering until now that my father was beyond the need of his or any other's service.

There had been a rising and a bloody battle at Perugia, Falcone informed us. An attempt had been made to overthrow the rule there of Pier Luigi Farnese, Duke of Castro, the Pope's own abominable son. For some months my father had been enjoying the shelter of the Perugians, and he had repaid their hospitality by joining them and bearing arms with them in the ill-starred blow they struck for liberty. They had been crushed in the encounter by the troops of Pier Luigi, and my father had been among the slain.

And well was it for him that he came by so fine and merciful an end, thought I when I had heard the tale of horrors that had been undergone by the unfortunates who had fallen into the hands of Farnese.

My mother heard him to the end without any sign of emotion. She sat there, cold and impassive as a thing of marble, what time Fra Gervasio — who was my father's foster-brother, as you shall presently learn more fully — sank his head upon his arm and wept like a child to hear the piteous tale of it. And whether from force of example, whether from the memories that came to me so poignantly in that moment of a fine strong man with a brown, shaven face and a jovial, mighty voice, who had promised me that one day we should ride together, I fell a-weeping too.

When the tale was done, my mother coldly gave orders that Falcone be cared for, and went to pray, taking me with her.

Oftentimes since have I wondered what was the tenor of her prayers that night. Were they for the rest of the great turbulent soul that was gone forth in sin, in arms against the Holy Church, excommunicate and foredoomed to Hell? Or were they of thanksgiving that at last she was completely mistress of my destinies, her mind at rest, since no longer need she fear opposition to her wishes concerning me? I do not know, nor will I do her the possible injustice that I should were I to guess.

CHAPTER II

GINO FALCONE

WHEN I think of my mother now I do not see her as she appeared in any of the scenes that already I have set down. There is one picture of her that is burnt as with an acid upon my memory, a picture which the mere mention of her name, the mere thought of her, never fails to evoke like a ghost before me. I see her always as she appeared one evening when she came suddenly and without warning upon Falcone and me in the armoury of the citadel.

I see her again, a tall, slight, graceful woman, her oval face of the translucent pallor of wax, framed in a nun-like coif, over which was thrown a long black veil that fell to her waist and there joined the black unrelieved draperies that she always wore. This sable garb was no mere mourning for my father. His death had made as little change in her apparel as in her general life. It had been ever thus as far as my memory can travel; always had her raiment been the same, those trailing funereal draperies. Again I see them, and that pallid face with its sunken eyes, around which there were great brown patches that seemed to intensify the depth at which they were set and the sombre lustre of them on the rare occasions when she raised them; those slim, wax-like hands, with a chaplet of beads entwined about the left wrist and hanging thence to a silver crucifix at the end.

She moved almost silently, as a ghost; and where

she passed she seemed to leave a trail of sorrow and sadness in her wake, just as a worldly woman leaves a trail of perfume.

Thus looked she when she came upon us there that evening, and thus will she live forever in my memory, for that was the first time that I knew rebellion against the yoke she was imposing upon me; the first time that our wills clashed, hers and mine; and as a consequence, maybe, was it the first time that I considered her with purpose and defined her to myself.

The thing befell some three months after the coming of Falcone to Mondolfo.

That the old man-at-arms should have exerted a strong attraction upon my young mind, you will readily understand. His intimate connection with that dimly remembered father, who stood secretly in my imagination in the position that my mother would have had Saint Augustine occupy, drew me to his equerry like metal to a lodestone.

And this attraction was reciprocal. Of his own accord old Falcone sought me out, lingering in my neighbourhood at first like a dog that looks for a kindly word. He had not long to wait. Daily we had our meetings and our talks, and daily did these grow in length; and they were stolen hours of which I said no word to my mother, nor did others for a season, so that all was well.

Our talks were naturally of my father, and it was through Falcone that I came to know something of the greatness of that noble-souled, valiant gentleman, whom the old servant painted for me as one who combined with the courage of the lion the wiliness of the fox.

He discoursed of their feats of arms together; he described charges of horse that set my nerves a-tingle, as in fancy I heard the blare of trumpets and the deafening thunder of hooves upon the turf. Of escalades, of surprises, of breaches stormed, of camisades and ambushes, of dark treacheries and great heroisms did he descant to fire my youthful fancy, to fill me first with delight, and then with frenzy when I came to think that in all these things my life must have no part, that for me another road was set — a grey, gloomy road at the end of which was dangled a reward which did not greatly interest me.

And then, one day, from fighting as an endeavour, as a pitting of force against force and astuteness against astuteness, he came to talk of fighting as an art.

It was from old Falcone that first I heard of Marozzo, that miracle-worker in weapons, that master at whose academy in Bologna the craft of swordsmanship was to be acquired, so that from fighting with his irons as a beast with its claws, by sheer brute strength and brute instinct, man might by practised skill and knowledge gain advantages against which mere strength must spend itself in vain.

What he told me amazed me beyond anything that I had ever heard, even from himself, and what he told me he illustrated, flinging himself into the poses taught by Marozzo that I might appreciate the marvellous science of the thing.

Thus was it that for the first time I made the acquaintance — an acquaintance held by few men in those days — of those marvellous guards of Marozzo's devising; Falcone showed me the difference be-

tween the mandritto and the roverso, the false edge
and the true, the stramazone and the tondo; and he
left me spellbound by that marvellous guard appro-
priately called by Marozzo the Iron Girdle — a low
guard on the level of the waist, which on the very
parry gives an opening for the point, so that in one
movement you may ward and strike.

At last, when I questioned him, he admitted that
during their wanderings, my father, with that reck-
lessness that alternated curiously with his caution,
had ventured into the city of Bologna notwithstanding that it was a papal fief, for the sole purpose of
studying with Marozzo; that Falcone himself had
daily accompanied him, witnessed the lessons, and
afterwards practised with my father, so that he had
come to learn most of the secrets that Marozzo
taught.

One day, at last, very timidly, like one who, whilst
over-conscious of his utter unworthiness, ventures to
crave a boon which he knows himself without the
right to expect, I asked Falcone would he show me
something of Marozzo's art with real weapons.

I had feared a rebuff. I had thought that even old
Falcone might laugh at one predestined to the study
of theology, desiring to enter into the mysteries of
sword-craft. But my fears were far, indeed, from having a foundation. There was no laughter in the
equerry's grey eyes, whilst the smile upon his lips was
a smile of gladness, of eagerness, almost of thankfulness to see me so set.

And so it came to pass that daily thereafter did we
practise for an hour or so in the armoury with sword
and buckler, and with every lesson my proficiency

with the iron grew in a manner that Falcone termed
prodigious, swearing that I was born to the sword,
that the knack of it was in the very blood of me.

It may be that affection for me caused him to over-
rate the progress that I made and the aptitude I
showed; it may even be that what he said was no
more than the good-natured flattery of one who loved
me and would have me take pleasure in myself. And
yet when I look back at the lad I was, I incline to
think that he spoke no more than sober truth.

I have alluded to the curious, almost inexplicable
delight it afforded me to feel in my hands the balance
of a pike for the first time. Fain would I tell you
something of all that I felt when first my fingers
closed about a sword-hilt, the forefinger passed over
the quillons in the new manner, as Falcone showed
me. But it defies all power of words. The sweet seduction of its balance, the white gleaming beauty of
the blade, were things that thrilled me with something
akin to the thrill of the first kiss of passion. It was
not quite the same, I know; yet I can think of nothing else in life that is worthy of being compared
with it.

I was at the time a lad in my thirteenth year, but I
was well-grown and strong beyond my age, despite
the fact that my mother had restrained me from all
those exercises of horsemanship, of arms, and of
wrestling by which boys of my years attain development. I stood almost as tall then as Falcone himself
— who was accounted of a good height — and if my
reach fell something short of his, I made up for this by
the youthful quickness of my movements; so that
soon — unless out of good-nature he refrained from

exerting his full vigour — I found myself Falcone's match.

Fra Gervasio, who was then my tutor, and with whom my mornings were spent in perfecting my Latin and giving me the rudiments of Greek, soon had his suspicions of where the hour of the siesta was spent by me with old Falcone. But the good, saintly man held his peace, a matter which at that time intrigued me. Others there were, however, who thought well to bear the tale of our doings to my mother, and thus it happened that she came upon us that day in the armoury, each of us in shirt and breeches at sword-and-target play.

We fell apart upon her entrance, each with a guilty feeling, like children caught in a forbidden orchard, for all that Falcone held himself proudly erect, his grizzled head thrown back, his eyes cold and hard.

A long while it seemed ere she spoke, and once or twice I shot her a furtive comprehensive glance, and saw her as I shall ever see her to my dying day.

Her eyes were upon me. I do not believe that she gave Falcone a single thought at first. It was at me only that she looked, and with such a sorrow in her glance to see me so vigorous and lusty, as surely could not have been fetched there by the sight of my corpse itself. Her lips moved awhile in silence; and whether she was at her everlasting prayers, or whether she was endeavouring to speak but could not for emotion, I do not know. At last her voice came, laden with a chill reproach.

"Agostino!" she said, and waited as if for some answer from me.

It was in that instant that rebellion stirred in me.

Her coming had turned me cold, for all that my body was overheated from the exercise and I was sweating furiously. Now, at the sound of her voice, something of the injustice that oppressed me, something of the unreasoning bigotry that chained and fettered me, stood clear before my mental vision for the first time. It warmed me again with the warmth of sullen indignation. I returned her no answer beyond a curtly respectful invitation that she should speak her mind, couched — as had been her reproof — in a single word of address.

"Madonna?" I challenged, and emulating something of old Falcone's attitude, I drew myself erect, flung back my head, and brought my eyes to the level of her own by an effort of will such as I had never yet exerted.

It was, I think, the bravest thing I ever did. I felt, in doing it, as one feels who has nerved himself to enter fire. And when the thing was done, the ease of it surprised me. There followed no catastrophe such as I expected. Before my glance, grown suddenly so very bold, her own eyes drooped and fell away as was her habit. She spoke thereafter without looking at me, in that cold, emotionless voice that was peculiar to her always, the voice of one in whom the founts of all that is sweet and tolerant and tender in life are forever frozen.

"What are you doing with weapons, Agostino?" she asked me.

"As you see, madam mother, I am at practice," I answered, and out of the corner of my eye I caught the grim approving twitch of old Falcone's lips.

"At practice?" she echoed, dully as one who does

not understand. Then very slowly she shook her sorrowful head. "Men practise what they must one day perform, Agostino. To your books, then, and leave swords for bloody men, nor ever let me see you again with weapons in your hands if you respect me."

"Had you not come hither, madam mother, you had been spared the sight to-day," I answered with some lingering spark of my rebellious fire still smouldering.

"It was God's will that I should come to set a term to such vanities before they take too strong a hold upon you," answered she. "Lay down those weapons."

Had she been angry, I think I could have withstood her. Anger in her at such a time must have been as steel upon the flint of my own nature. But against that incarnation of sorrow and sadness, my purpose, my strength of character were turned to water. By similar means had she ever prevailed with my poor father. And I had, too, the habit of obedience which is not so lightly broken as I had at first accounted possible.

Sullenly then I set down my sword upon a bench that stood against the wall, and my target with it. As I turned aside to do so, her gloomy eyes were poised for an instant upon Falcone, who stood grim and silent. Then they were lowered again ere she began to address him.

"You have done very ill, Falcone," said she. "You have abused my trust in you, and you have sought to pervert my son and to lead him into ways of evil."

He started under that reproof like a fiery stallion under the spur. His face flushed scarlet. The habit of

obedience may have been strong in Falcone too; but
it was obedience to men; with women he had never
had much to do, old warrior though he was. Moreover, in this he felt that an affront had been put upon
the memory of Giovanni d'Anguissola, who was my
father and who went nigh to being Falcone's god.
And this his answer plainly showed.

"The ways into which I lead your son, Madonna,"
said he in a low voice that boomed up and echoed in
the groined ceiling overhead, "are the ways that were
trod by my lord his father. And who says that the
ways of Giovanni d'Anguissola were evil ways lies
foully, be he man or woman, patrician or villein, pope
or devil." And upon that he paused magnificently,
his eyes aflash.

She shuddered under his rough speech. Then answered without looking up, and with no trace of anger
in her voice:

"You are restored to health and strength by now,
Messer Falcone. The seneschal shall have orders to
pay you ten gold ducats in discharge of all that may
be still your due from us. See that by night you have
left Mondolfo."

And then, without changing her deadly inflection,
or even making a noticeable pause, "Come, Agostino," she commanded.

But I did not move. Her words had fixed me there
with horror. I heard from Falcone a sound that was
between a growl and a sob. I dared not look at him,
but the eye of my fancy saw him standing rigid, pale,
and self-contained.

What would he do, what would he say? Oh, she
had done a cruel, a bitterly cruel wrong. This poor

old warrior, all scarred and patched from wounds that
he had taken in my father's service, to be turned
away in his old age, as we should not have turned
away a dog! It was a monstrous thing. Mondolfo
was his home. The Anguissola were his family, and
their honour was his honour, since as a villein he had
no honour of his own. To cast him out thus!

All this flashed through my anguished mind in one
brief throb of time, as I waited, marvelling what he
would do, what say, in answer to that dismissal.

He would not plead, or else I did not know him;
and I was sure of that, without knowing what else
there was that must make it impossible for old Falcone to stoop to ask a favour of my mother.

Awhile he just stood there, his wits overthrown by
sheer surprise. And then, when at last he moved, the
thing he did was the last thing that I had looked for.
Not to her did he turn; not to her, but to me, and he
dropped on one knee before me.

"My lord!" he cried, and before he added another
word I knew already what else he was about to say.
For never yet had I been so addressed in my lordship
of Mondolfo. To all there I was just the Madonnino.
But to Falcone, in that supreme hour of his need, I
was become his lord.

"My lord," he said, then. "Is it your wish that I
should go?"

I drew back, still wrought upon by my surprise;
and then my mother's voice came cold and acid.

"The Madonnino's wish is not concerned in this,
Messer Falcone. It is I who order your departure."

Falcone did not answer her; he affected not to hear
her, and continued to address himself to me.

"You are the master here, my lord," he urged. "You are the law in Mondolfo. You carry life and death in your right hand, and against your will no man or woman in your lordship can prevail."

He spoke the truth, a mighty truth which had stood like a mountain before me all these months, yet which I had not seen.

"I shall go or remain as you decree, my lord," he added; and then, almost in a snarl of defiance, "I obey none other," he concluded, "nor pope nor devil."

"Agostino, I am waiting for you," came my mother's voice from the doorway.

Something had me by the throat. It was Temptation, and old Falcone was the tempter. More than that was he — though how much more I did not dream, nor with what authority he acted there. He was the Mentor who showed me the road to freedom and to manhood; he showed me how at a blow I might shiver the chains that held me, and shake them from me like the cobwebs that they were. He tested me, too; tried my courage and my will; and to my undoing was it that he found me wanting in that hour. My pity for him went near to giving me the resolution that I lacked. Yet even this fell short.

I would to God I had given heed to him. I would to God I had flung back my head and told my mother — as he prompted me — that I was Lord of Mondolfo, and that Falcone must remain since I so willed it.

I strove to do so out of my love for him rather than out of any such fine spirit as he sought to inspire in me. Had I succeeded I had established my dominion, I had become arbiter of my fate; and how much of misery, of anguish, and of sin might I not thereafter have been spared!

The hour was crucial, though I knew it not. I stood at a parting of ways; yet for lack of courage I hesitated to take the road to which so invitingly he beckoned me.

And then, before I could make any answer such as I desired, such as I strove to make, my mother spoke again, and by her tone, which had grown faltering and tearful — as was her wont in the old days when she ruled my father — she riveted anew the fetters I was endeavouring with all the strength of my poor young soul to snap.

"Tell him, Agostino, that your will is as your mother's. Tell him so and come. I am waiting for you."

I stifled a groan, and let my arms fall limply to my sides. I was a weakling and contemptible. I realized it. And yet to-day when I look back I see how vast a strength I should have needed. I was but thirteen and of a spirit that had been cowed by her, and was held under her thrall.

"I . . . I am sorry, Falcone," I faltered, and there were tears in my eyes.

I shrugged again — shrugged in token of my despair and grief and impotence — and I moved down the long room towards the door where my mother waited.

I did not dare to bestow another look upon that poor broken old warrior, that faithful, lifelong servant turned thus cruelly upon the world by a woman whom bigotry had sapped of all human feelings and a boy who was a coward masquerading under a great name.

I heard his gasping sob, and the sound smote upon my heart and hurt me as if it had been iron. I had failed him. He must suffer more in the knowledge of my unworthiness to be called the son of that master whom he had worshipped than in the destitution that might await him.

"My lord! My lord!" he cried after me despairingly.

On the very threshold I stood arrested by that heart-broken cry of his. I half turned.

"Falcone . . ." I began.

And then my mother's white hand fell upon my wrist. "Come, my son," she said, once more impassive.

Nervelessly I obeyed her, and as I passed out I heard Falcone's voice crying:

"My lord, my lord! God help me, and God help you!"

An hour later he had left the citadel, and on the stones of the courtyard lay ten golden ducats which he had scattered there, and which not one of the greedy grooms or serving-men could take courage to pick up, so fearful a curse had old Falcone laid upon that money when he cast it from him.

CHAPTER III

THE PIETISTIC THRALL

THAT evening my mother talked to me at longer length than I remember her ever to have done before.

It may be that she feared lest Gino Falcone should have aroused in me notions which it was best to lull back at once into slumber. It may be that she, too, had felt something of the crucial quality of that moment in the armoury, just as he must have perceived my first hesitation to obey her slightest word, whence came her resolve to check this mutiny ere it should spread and become too big for her.

We sat in the room that was called her private dining-room, but which, in fact, was all things to her save the chamber in which she slept.

The fine apartments through which I had strayed as a little lad in my father's day, the handsome lofty chambers, with their frescoed ceiling, their walls hung with costly tapestries, many of which had come from the looms of Flanders, their floors of wood mosaics, and their great carved movables, had been shut up these many years.

For my mother's claustral needs sufficient was provided by the alcove in which she slept, the private chapel of the citadel in which she would spend long hours, and this private dining-room where we now sat. Into the spacious gardens of the castle she would seldom wander; into our town of Mondolfo never.

Not since my father's departure upon his ill-starred rebellion had she set foot across the drawbridge.

"Tell me whom you go with, and I will tell you what you are," says the proverb. "Show me your dwelling, and I shall see your character," say I.

And surely never was there a chamber so permeated by the nature of its tenant as that private dining-room of my mother's.

It was a narrow room in the shape of a small parallelogram, with the windows set high up near the timbered, whitewashed ceiling, so that it was impossible either to look in or to look out, as is sometimes the case with the windows of a chapel.

On the white space of wall that faced the door hung a great wooden Crucifix, very rudely carved by one who either knew nothing of anatomy, or else — as is more probable — was utterly unable to set down his knowledge upon timber. The crudely tinted figure would be perhaps half the natural size of a man; and it was the most repulsive and hideous representation of the Tragedy of Golgotha that I have ever seen. It filled one with a horror which was far, indeed, removed from the pious awe which that Symbol is intended to arouse in every true believer. It emphasized all the ghastly ugliness of death upon that most barbarous of gallows, without any suggestion of the beauty and immensity of the Divine Martyrdom of Him Who in the likeness of the sinful flesh was alone without sin.

And to me the ghastliest and most pitiful thing of all was an artifice which its maker had introduced for the purpose of conveying some suggestion of the supernatural to that mangled, malformed, less than human representation. Into the place of the wound made by the spear of Longinus, he had introduced a strip of crystal which caught the light at certain angles — more particularly when there were lighted tapers in the room — so that in reflecting this it seemed to shed forth luminous rays.

An odd thing was that my mother — who looked upon that Crucifix with eyes that were very different from mine — would be at pains in the evening when lights were fetched to set a taper at such an angle as was best calculated to produce the effect upon which the sculptor had counted. What satisfaction it can have been to her to see reflected from that glazed wound the light which she herself had provided for the purpose, I am lost to think. And yet I am assured that she would contemplate that shining effluence in a sort of ecstatic awe, accounting it something very near akin to miracle.

Under this Crucifix hung a little alabaster font of holy-water, into the back of which was stuck a withered, yellow branch of palm, which was renewed on each Palm Sunday. Before it was set a praying-stool of plain oak, without any cushion to mitigate its harshness to the knees.

In the corner of the room stood a tall, spare, square cupboard, capacious but very plain, in which the necessaries of the table were disposed. In the opposite corner there was another smaller cupboard with a sort of writing-pulpit beneath. Here my mother kept the accounts of her household, her books of recipes, her homely medicines, and the heavy devotional tomes and lesser volumes — mostly manuscript — out of which she nourished her poor starving soul.

Amongst these was the "Treatise of the Mental Sufferings of Christ" — the book of the Blessed Battista of Varano, Princess of Camerino, who founded the convent of Poor Clares in that city — a book which even in early life seemed to me of a blasphemous presumption and fired the train of my first misgivings.

Another was "The Spiritual Combat," that queer yet able book of the cleric Scupoli — described as the "aureo libro," dedicated "Al Supremo Capitano e Gloriosissimo Trionfatore, Gesu Cristo, Figliuolo di Maria," and this dedication in the form of a letter to Our Saviour, signed, "Your most humble servant, purchased with Your Blood." [1]

Down the middle of the chamber ran a long square-ended table of oak, very plain like all the rest of the room's scant furnishings. At the head of this table was an armchair for my mother, of bare wood without any cushion to relieve its hardness, whilst on either side of the board stood a few lesser chairs for those who habitually dined there. These were, besides myself, Fra Gervasio, my tutor; Messer Giorgio, the castellan, a bald-headed old man long since past the fighting age and who in times of stress would have been as useful for purposes of defending Mondolfo as Lorenza, my mother's elderly woman, who sat below him at the board; he was toothless, bowed, and decrepit, but he was very devout — as he had need to be, seeing that he was half dead already — and this counted with my mother above any other virtue. [2]

[1] This work, which achieved a great vogue, was first printed in 1589. Clearly, however, manuscript copies were in existence earlier, and it is to one of these that Agostino here refers.

[2] *Virtu* is the word used by Agostino, and it is susceptible to a wider

The last of the four who habitually sat with us was Giojoso, the seneschal, a lantern-jawed fellow with black, beetling brows, about whom the only joyous thing was his misnomer of a name.

Of the table that we kept, beyond noting that the fare was ever of a lenten kind and that the wine was watered, I will but mention that my mother did not observe the barrier of the salt. There was no sitting above it or below at our board, as, from time immemorial, is the universal custom in feudal homes. Beyond doubt she had abolished it as an act of humility, although this was a subject upon which she never expressed herself in my hearing.

The walls of that room were whitewashed and bare. The floor was of stone overlaid by a carpet of rushes that was changed no oftener than once a week.

From what I have told you, you may picture something of the chill gloom of the place, something of the pietism which hung upon the very air of that apartment in which so much of my early youth was spent. And it had, too, an odour that is peculiarly full of character, the smell which is never absent from a sacristy and rarely from conventual chambers; a smell difficult to define, faint and yet tenuously pungent, and like no other smell in all the world that I have ever known. It is a musty odour, an odour of staleness which perhaps an open window and the fresh air of heaven might relieve but could not dissipate; and to this is wed, but so subtly that it would be impossible to say which is predominant, the slight, sickly aroma of wax.

translation than that which the English language affords, comprising as it does a sense of courage and address at arms. Indeed, it is not clear that Agostino is not playing here upon the double meaning of the word.

We supped there that night in silence at about the hour that poor Gino Falcone would be taking his departure. Silence was habitual with us at meal-times, eating being performed — like everything else in that drab household — as a sort of devotional act. Occasionally the silence would be relieved by readings aloud from some pious work, undertaken at my mother's bidding by one or another of the amanuenses.

But on the night in question there was just silence, broken chiefly by the toothless slobber of the castellan over the soft meats that were especially prepared for him. And there was something of grimness in that silence; for none — and Fra Gervasio less than any — approved the unchristian thing that out of excess of Christianity my mother had done in driving old Falcone forth.

Myself, I could not eat at all. My misery choked me. The thought of that old servitor whom I had loved being sent a wanderer and destitute, and all through my own weakness, all because I had failed him in his need, just as I had failed myself, was anguish to me. My lip would quiver at the thought, and it was with difficulty that I repressed my tears.

At last that hideous repast came to an end in prayers of thanksgiving whose immoderate length was out of all proportion to the fare provided.

The castellan shuffled forth upon the arm of the seneschal; Lorenza followed at a sign from my mother, and we three — Gervasio, my mother, and I — were left alone.

And here let me say a word of Fra Gervasio. He was, as I have already written, my father's foster-brother. That is to say, he was the child of a sturdy peasant-woman of the Val di Taro, from whose lusty, healthy breast my father had suckled the first of that fine strength that had been his own.

He was older than my father by a month or so, and as often happens in such cases, he was brought to Mondolfo to be first my father's playmate, and later, no doubt, to have followed him as a man-at-arms. But a chill that he took in his tenth year as a result of a long winter immersion in the icy waters of the Taro laid him at the point of death, and left him thereafter of a rather weak and sickly nature. He was, however, quick and intelligent, and was admitted to learn his letters with my father, whence it ensued that he developed a taste for study. Seeing that by his health he was debarred from the hardy, open life of a soldier, his scholarly aptitude was encouraged, and it was decided that he should follow a clerical career.

He had entered the order of Saint Francis; but after some years at the Convent of Aguilona, his health having been indifferent and the conventual rules too rigorous for his condition, he was given licence to become the chaplain of Mondolfo. Here he had received the kindliest treatment at the hands of my father, who entertained for his sometime playmate a very real affection.

He was a tall, gaunt man with a sweet, kindly face, reflecting his sweet, kindly nature; he had deep-set, dark eyes, very gentle in their gaze, a tender mouth that was a little drawn by lines of suffering, and an upright wrinkle, deep as a gash, between his brows at the root of his long, slender nose.

He it was that night who broke the silence that

endured even after the others had departed. He spoke at first as if communing with himself, like a man who thinks aloud; and between his thumb and his long forefinger, I remember that he kneaded a crumb of bread upon which his eyes were intent.

"Gino Falcone is an old man, and he was my lord's best-loved servant. He would have died for my lord, and joyfully; and now he is turned adrift to die to no purpose. Ah, well!" He heaved a deep sigh, and fell silent, whilst I — the pent-up anguish in me suddenly released to hear my thoughts thus expressed — fell soundlessly to weeping.

"Do you reprove me, Fra Gervasio?" quoth my mother, quite emotionless.

The monk pushed back his stool and rose ere he replied.

"I must," he said, "or I am unworthy of the scapulary I wear. I must reprove this unchristian act, or else am I no true servant of my Master."

She crossed herself with her thumb-nail upon the brow and upon the lips, to repress all evil thoughts and evil words — an unfailing sign that she was stirred to anger and sought to combat the sin of it. Then she spoke, meekly enough, in the same cold, level voice.

"I think it is you who are at fault," she told him, "when you call unchristian an act which was necessary to secure this child to Christ."

He smiled a sad little smile. "Yet, even so, it were well you should proceed with caution and with authority; and in this you have none."

It was her turn to smile, the palest, ghostliest of smiles, and even for so much she must have been

oddly moved. "I think I have," said she, and quoted,
"'If thy right hand offend thee, hack it off.'"

I saw a hot flush mount to the friar's prominent
cheek-bones. Indeed, he was a very human man
under his conventual robe, with swift stirrings of
passion which the long habit of repression had not yet
succeeded in extinguishing. He cast his eyes to the
ceiling in such a glance of despair as left me thoughtful. It was as an invocation to Heaven to look down
upon the obstinate, ignorant folly of this woman who
accounted herself wise and who so garbled the Divine
teaching as to blaspheme with complacency.

I know that now; at the time I was not quite so
clear-sighted as to read the full message of that
glance.

Her audacity was as the audacity of fools. Where
wisdom, full-fledged, might have halted, trembling,
she swept resolutely onward. Before her stood this
friar, this teacher and interpreter, this man of holy
life, profoundly learned alike in the humanities and
the divinities; and he told her that she had done an
evil thing. Yet out of the tiny pittance of her knowledge and her little intellectual sight — which was no
better than a blindness — must she confidently tell
him that he was at fault.

Argument was impossible between him and her.
Thus much I saw, and I feared an explosion of the
wrath of which I perceived in him the signs. But he
quelled it. Yet his voice rumbled thunderously upon
his next words.

"It matters something that Gino Falcone should
not starve," he said.

"It matters more that my son should not be

damned," she answered him, and with that answer
left him weaponless, for against the armour of a crass-
ness so dense and one-ideaed there are no weapons
that can prevail.

"Listen," she said, and her eyes, raised for a
moment, comprehended both of us in their glance.
"There is something that it were best I tell you, that
once for all you may fathom the depth of my purpose
for Agostino here. My lord his father was a man of
blood and strife . . ."

"And so were many whose names stand to-day
upon the roll of saints and are its glory," answered
the friar with quick asperity.

"But they did not raise their arms against the Holy
Church and against Christ's Own most holy Vicar, as
did he," she reminded him sorrowfully. "The sword
is an ill thing save when it is wielded in a holy cause.
In my lord's hands, wielded in the unholiest of all
causes, it became a thing accursed. But God's anger
overtook him and laid him low at Perugia in all the
strength and vigour that had made him arrogant as
Lucifer. It was perhaps well for all of us that it so befell."

"Madonna!" cried Gervasio in stern horror.

But she went on quite heedless of him. "Best of all
was it for me, since I was spared the harshest duty
that can be imposed upon a woman and a wife. It was
necessary that he should expiate the evil he had
wrought; moreover, his life was become a menace to
my child's salvation. It was his wish to make of
Agostino such another as himself, to lead his only son
adown the path of Hell. It was my duty to my God
and to my son to shield this boy. And to accomplish

that I would have delivered up his father to the papal emissaries who sought him."

"Ah, never that!" the friar protested. "You could never have done that!"

"Could I not? I tell you it was as good as done. I tell you that the thing was planned. I took counsel with my confessor, and he showed me my plain duty."

She paused a moment, whilst we stared, Fra Gervasio white-faced and with mouth that gaped in sheer horror.

"For years had he eluded the long arm of the Holy Father's justice," she resumed. "And during those years he had never ceased to plot and plan the overthrow of the Pontifical dominion. He was blinded by his arrogance to think that he could stand against the hosts of Heaven. His stubbornness in sin had made him mad. Quem Deus vult perdere . . ." And she waved one of her emaciated hands, leaving the quotation unfinished. "Heaven showed me the way, chose me for Its instrument. I sent him word, offering him shelter here at Mondolfo where none would look to find him, assuming it to be the last place to which he would adventure. He was to have come when death took him on the field of Perugia."

There was something here that I did not understand at all. And in like case, it seemed, was Fra Gervasio, for he passed a hand over his brow, as if to clear thence some veils that clogged his understanding.

"He was to have come?" he echoed. "To shelter?" he asked.

"Nay," said she quietly, "to death. The papal emissaries had knowledge of it and would have been here to await him."

"You would have betrayed him?" Fra Gervasio's voice was hoarse, his eyes were burning sombrely. "Your husband?"

"I would have saved my son," said she, with quiet satisfaction, in a tone that revealed how incontestably right she conceived herself to be.

He stood there, and he seemed taller and more gaunt than usual, for he had drawn himself erect to the full of his great height — and he was a man who usually went bowed. His hands were clenched, and the knuckles showed blue-white like marble. His face was very pale and in his temple a little pulse was throbbing visibly. He swayed slightly upon his feet, and the sight of him frightened me a little. He seemed so full of terrible potentialities.

When I think of vengeance, I picture to myself Fra Gervasio as I beheld him in that hour. Nothing that he could have done would have surprised me. Had he fallen upon my mother then, and torn her limb from limb, it would have been no more than from the sight of him I might have expected.

I have said that nothing that he could have done would have surprised me. Rather should I have said that nothing would have surprised me save the thing he did.

Whilst a man might have counted ten stood he so — she seeing nothing of the strange transfiguration that had come over him, for her eyes were downcast as ever. Then, quite slowly, his hands unclenched, his arms fell limply to his sides, his head sank forward upon his breast, and his figure bowed itself lower than was usual. Quite suddenly, quite softly, almost as a man who swoons, he sank down again into the chair from which he had risen.

He set his elbows on the table, and took his head in his hands. A groan escaped him. She heard it, and looked at him in her furtive way.

"You are moved by this knowledge, Fra Gervasio," she said, and sighed. "I have told you this — and you, Agostino — that you may know how deep, how ineradicable is my purpose. You were a votive offering, Agostino; you were vowed to the service of God that your father's life might be spared, years ago, ere you were born. From the very edge of death was your father brought back to life and strength. He would have used that life and that strength to cheat God of the price of His boon to me."

"And if," Fra Gervasio questioned almost fiercely, "Agostino in the end should have no vocation, should have no call to such a life?"

She looked at him very wistfully, almost pityingly.

"How should that be?" she asked. "He was offered to God. And that God accepted the gift, He showed when He gave Giovanni back to life. How, then, could it come to pass that Agostino should have no call? Would God reject that which He had accepted?"

Fra Gervasio rose again. "You go too deep for me, Madonna," he said bitterly. "It is not for me to speak of my gifts save reverently and in profound and humble gratitude for that grace by which God bestowed them upon me. But I am accounted something of a casuist. I am a doctor of theology and of canon law, and but for the weak state of my health I should be sitting to-day in the chair of canon law at the University of Pavia. And yet, Madonna, the things you tell me with such assurance make a mock of everything I have ever learnt."

Even I, lad as I was, perceived the bitter irony in which he spoke. Not so she. I vow she flushed under what she accounted his praise of her wisdom and divine revelation; for vanity is the last human weakness to be discarded. Then she seemed to recollect herself. She bowed her head very reverently.

"It is God's grace that reveals to me the truth," she said.

He fell back a step in his amazement at having been so thoroughly misunderstood. Then he drew away from the table. He looked at her as he would speak, but checked on the thought. He turned, and so, without another word, departed, and left us sitting there together.

It was then that we had our talk; or, rather, that she talked, whilst I sat listening. And presently as I listened, I came gradually once more under the spell of which I had more than once that day been on the point of casting off the yoke.

For, after all, you are to discern in what I have written here, between what were my feelings at the time and what are my criticisms to-day, in the light of the riper knowledge to which I have come. The handling of a sword had thrilled me strangely, as I have shown. Yet was I ready to believe that such a thrill was but a lure of Satan's, as my mother assured me. In deeper matters she might harbour error, as Fra Gervasio's irony had shown me that he believed. But we went that night into no great depths.

She spent an hour or so in vague discourse upon the joys of Paradise, in showing me the folly of jeopardizing them for the sake of the fleeting vanities of this ephemeral world. She dealt at length upon the love of God for us, and the love which we should bear to Him, and she read to me passages from the book of the Blessed Varano and from Scupoli to add point to her teachings upon the beauty and nobility of a life that is devoted to God's service — the only service of this world in which nobility can exist.

And then she added little stories of martyrs who had suffered for the faith, of the tortures to which they had been subjected, and of the happiness they had felt in actual suffering, of the joy that their very torments had brought them, borne up as they were by their faith and the strength of their love of God.

There was in all this nothing that was new to me; nothing that I did not freely accept and implicitly believe without pausing to judge or criticize. And yet, it was shrewd of her to have plied me then as she did; for thereby, beyond doubt, she checked me upon the point of self-questioning to which that day's happenings were urging me, and she brought me once more obediently to heel and caused me to fix my eyes more firmly than ever beyond the things of this world and upon the glories of the next which I was to make my goal and aim.

Thus came I back within the toils from which I had been for a moment tempted to escape; and what is more, my imagination fired to some touch of ecstasy by those tales of sainted martyrs, I returned willingly to the pietistic thrall, to be held in it more firmly than ever yet before.

We parted as we always parted, and when I had kissed her cold hand I went my way to bed. And if I knelt that night to pray that God might watch over poor errant Falcone, it was to the end that Falcone might be brought to see the sin and error of his ways and win to the grace of a happy death when his hour came.

CHAPTER IV

LUISINA

OF the four years that followed little mention need be made in these pages, save for one incident whose importance is derived entirely from that which subsequently befell, for at the time it had no meaning for me. Yet since later it was to have much, it is fitting that it should be recorded here.

It happened that a month or so after old Falcone had left us there wandered one noontide into the outer courtyard of the castle two pilgrim fathers, on their way — as they announced — from Milan to visit the Holy House at Loreto.

It was my mother's custom to receive all pilgrim wayfarers and beggars in this courtyard at noontide twice in each week to bestow upon them food and alms. Rarely was she, herself, present at that almsgiving; more rarely still was I. It was Fra Gervasio who discharged the office of almoner on the Countess of Mondolfo's behalf.

Occasionally the whines and snarls of the motley crowd that gathered there — for they were not infrequently quarrelsome — reached us in the maschio tower where we had our apartments. But on the day of which I speak I chanced to stand in the pillared gallery above the courtyard, watching the heaving, surging human mass below, for the concourse was greater than usual.

Cripples there were of every sort, and all in rags;

some with twisted, withered limbs, others with mere
stumps where limbs had been lopped off; others again
— and there were many of these — with hideous
running sores, some of which no doubt would be
counterfeit — as I now know, and contrived with
poultices of salt — for the purpose of exciting charity
in the piteous. All were dishevelled, unkempt, ragged,
dirty, and verminous. Most were greedy and wolfish
as they thrust one another aside to reach Fra Gervasio, as if they feared that the supply of alms and
food should be exhausted before their turn arrived.
Amongst them there was commonly a small sprinkling
of mendicant friars, some of these, perhaps, just the
hypocrite rogues that I have since discovered many
of them to be, though at the time all who wore the
scapulary were holy men in my innocent eyes. They
were mostly — or so they pretended — bent upon
pilgrimages to distant parts, living upon such alms as
they could gather on their way.

On the steps of the chapel Fra Gervasio would
stand — gaunt and impassive — with his posse of
attendant grooms behind him. One of the latter,
standing nearest to our almoner, held a great sack of
broken bread; another presented a wooden, trough-
like platter filled with slices of meat, and a third dis-
pensed out of horn cups a poor, thin, and rather sour
but very wholesome wine, which he drew from the
skins that were his charge.

From one to the other were the beggars passed by
Fra Gervasio, and lastly came they back to him, to
receive from his hands a piece of money — a copper
grosso, of which he held the bag himself.

On the day of which I write, as I stood there gazing

down upon that mass of misery, marvelling, perhaps, a little upon the inequality of fortune, and wondering vaguely what God could be about to inflict so much suffering upon certain of His creatures, to cause one to be born into purple and another into rags, my eyes were drawn by the insistent stare of two monks who stood at the back of the crowd with their shoulders to the wall.

They were both tall men, and they stood with their cowls over their tonsures, in the conventual attitude, their hands tucked away into the ample sleeves of their brown habits. One of this twain was broader than his companion and very erect of carriage, such as was unusual in a monk. His mouth and the half of his face were covered by a thick brown beard, and athwart his countenance, from under the left eye across his nose and cheek, ran a great livid scar to lose itself in the beard towards the right jaw. His deep-set eyes regarded me so intently that I coloured uncomfortably under their gaze; for accustomed as I was to seclusion, I was easily abashed. I turned away and went slowly along the gallery to the end; and yet I had a feeling that those eyes were following me, and, indeed, casting a swift glance over my shoulder ere I went indoors, I saw that this was so.

That evening at supper I chanced to mention the matter to Fra Gervasio.

"There was a big bearded Capuchin in the yard at alms-time to-day —" I was beginning, when the friar's knife clattered from his hand, and he looked at me with eyes of positive fear out of a face from which the last drop of blood had abruptly receded. I checked my inquiry at the sight of him thus suddenly disordered, whilst my mother, who, as usual, observed nothing, made a foolish comment.

"The little brothers are never absent, Agostino."

"This brother was a big brother," said I.

"It is not seemly to make jest of holy men," she reproved me in her chilling voice.

"I had no thought to jest," I answered soberly. "I should never have remarked this friar but that he gazed upon me with so great an intentness — so great that I was unable to bear it."

It was her turn to betray emotion. She looked at me full and long — for once — and very searchingly. She, too, had grown paler than was her habit.

"Agostino, what do you tell me?" quoth she, and her voice quivered.

Now here was a deal of pother about a Capuchin who had stared at the Madonnino of Anguissola! The matter was out of all proportion to the stir it made, and I conveyed in my next words some notion of that opinion.

But she stared wistfully. "Never think it, Agostino," she besought me. "You know not what it may import." And then she turned to Fra Gervasio. "Who was this mendicant?" she asked.

He had by now recovered from his erstwhile confusion. But he was still pale, and I observed that his hand trembled.

"He must have been one of the two little brothers of Saint Francis on their way, they said, from Milan to Loreto on a pilgrimage."

"Not those you told me are resting here until tomorrow?"

From his face I saw that he would have denied it

had it lain within his power to utter a deliberate false-hood.

"They are the same," he answered in a low voice.

She rose. "I must see this friar," she announced, and never in all my life had I beheld in her such a display of emotion.

"In the morning, then," said Fra Gervasio. "It is after sunset," he explained. "They have retired, and their rule . . ." He left the sentence unfinished, but he had said enough to be understood by her.

She sank back to her chair, folded her hands in her lap and fell into meditation. The faintest of flushes crept into her wax-like cheeks.

"If it should be a sign!" she murmured raptly, and then she turned again to Fra Gervasio. "You heard Agostino say that he could not bear this friar's gaze. You remember, brother, how a pilgrim appeared near San Rufino to the nurse of Saint Francis, and took from her arms the child that he might bless it ere once more he vanished? If this should be a sign such as that!"

She clasped her hands together fervently. "I must see this friar ere he departs again," she said to the staring, dumbfounded Fra Gervasio.

At last, then, I understood her emotion. All her life she had prayed for a sign of grace for herself or for me, and she believed that here at last was something that might well be discovered upon inquiry to be the answer to her prayer. This Capuchin who had stared at me from the courtyard became at once to her mind — so ill-balanced in these matters — a supernatural visitant, harbinger, as it were, of my future saintly glory.

But though she rose betimes upon the morrow, to see the holy man ere he fared forth again, she was not early enough. In the courtyard whither she descended to make her way to the outhouse where the two were lodged, she met Fra Gervasio, who was astir before her.

"The friar?" she cried anxiously, filled already with forebodings. "The holy man?"

Gervasio stood before her, pale and trembling. "You are too late, Madonna. Already he is gone."

She observed his agitation now, and beheld in it a reflection of her own, springing from the selfsame causes. "Oh, it was a sign, indeed!" she exclaimed. "And you have come to realize it, too, I see." Next, in a burst of gratitude that was almost pitiful upon such slight foundation, "Oh, blessed Agostino!" she cried out.

Then the momentary exaltation fell from that woman of sorrows. "This but makes my burden heavier, my responsibility greater," she wailed. "God help me bear it!"

Thus passed that incident so trifling in itself and so misunderstood by her. But it was never forgotten, and from time to time she would allude to it as the sign which had been vouchsafed me and for which great should be my thankfulness and my joy.

Save for that, in the four years that followed, time flowed an uneventful course within the four walls of the big citadel — for beyond those four walls I was never once permitted to set foot; and although from time to time I heard rumours of doings in the town itself, of the affairs of the State whereof I was by right of birth the tyrant, and of the greater business of the big world beyond, yet so trained and schooled was I that I had no great desire for a nearer acquaintance with that world.

A certain curiosity did at times beset me, aroused not so much by the little that I heard as by things that I read in such histories as my studies demanded I should read. For even the lives of saints, and Holy Writ itself, afford their student glimpses of the world. But this curiosity I came to look upon as a lure of the flesh, and to resist. Blessed are they who are out of all contact with the world, since to them salvation comes more easily; so I believed implicitly, as I was taught by my mother and by Fra Gervasio at my mother's bidding.

And as the years passed under such influences as had been at work upon me from the cradle, influences which had known no check save that brief one afforded by Gino Falcone, I became perforce devout and pious from very inclination.

Joyous transports were afforded me by the study of the "Life" of that Saint Luigi of the noble Mantuan House of Gonzaga — in whom I saw an ideal to be emulated, since he seemed to me to be much in my own case and of my own estate — who had counted the illusory greatness of this world well lost so that he might win the bliss of Paradise. Similarly did I take delight in the "Life," written by Tommaso da Celano, of that blessed son of Pietro Bernardone the merchant of Assisi, that Francis who became the Troubadour of the Lord and sang so sweetly the praises of His Creation. My heart would swell within me and I would weep hot and very bitter tears over the narrative of the early and sinful part of his life, as we may weep to see a beloved brother beset by deadly perils. And greater, hence, was the joy, the exultation, and finally the sweet peace and comfort that I gathered from the tale of his conversion, of his wondrous works, and of the Three Companions.

In these pages — so lively was my young imagination and so wrought upon by what I read — I suffered with him again his agonies of hope, I thrilled with some of the joy of his stupendous ecstasies, and I envied him the signal mark of Heavenly grace that had imprinted the stigmata upon his living body.

All that concerned him, too, I read: his "Little Flowers," his "Testament, The Mirror of Perfection"; but my greatest delight was derived from his "Song of the Creatures," which I learnt by heart.

Oftentimes since have I wondered and sought to determine whether it was the piety of those lauds that charmed me spiritually, or an appeal to my senses made by the beauty of the lines and the imagery which the Assisian used in his writings.

Similarly I am at a loss to determine whether the pleasure I took in reading of the joyous, perfumed life of that other stigmatized saint, the blessed Catherine of Siena, was not a sensuous pleasure rather than the soul-ecstasy I supposed it at the time.

And as I wept over the early sins of Saint Francis, so too did I weep over the rhapsodical "Confessions" of Saint Augustine, that mighty theologian after whom I had been named, and whose works — after those concerning Saint Francis — exerted a great influence upon me in those early days.

Thus did I grow in grace until Fra Gervasio, who watched me narrowly and anxiously, seemed more at ease, setting aside the doubts that earlier had tormented him lest I should be forced upon a life for which I had no vocation. He grew more tender and loving towards me, as if something of pity lurked within the strong affection in which he held me.

And, meanwhile, as I grew in grace of spirit, so too did I grow in grace of body, waxing tall and very strong, which would have been nowise surprising but that those nurtured as was I are seldom lusty. The mind feeding overmuch upon the growing body is apt to sap its strength and vigour; besides which there was the circumstance that I continued throughout those years a life almost of confinement, deprived of all the exercises by which youth is brought to its fine flower of strength.

As I was approaching my eighteenth year there befell another incident, which, trivial in itself, yet has its place in my development and so should have its place within these confessions. Nor did I judge it trivial at the time — nor were trivial the things that followed out of it — trivial though it may seem to me to-day as I look back upon it through all the murk of later life.

Giojoso, the seneschal of whom I have spoken, had a son, a great raw-boned lad whom he would have trained as an amanuensis, but who was one of Nature's dunces out of which there is nothing useful to be made. He was strong-limbed, however, and he was given odd menial duties to perform about the castle. But these he shirked where possible, as he had shirked his lessons in earlier days.

Now it happened that I was walking one spring morning — it was in May of that year '44 of which I am now writing — on the upper of the three spacious terraces that formed the castle garden. It was but an indifferently tended place, and yet, perhaps, the more agreeable on that account, since Nature had been allowed to have her prodigal, luxuriant way. It is true that the great boxwood hedges needed trimming, and that weeds were sprouting between the stones of the flights of steps that led from terrace to terrace; but the place was gay and fragrant with wild blossoms, and the great trees afforded generous shade, and the long rank grass beneath them made a pleasant couch to lie on during the heat of the day in summer. The lowest terrace of all was in better case. It was a well-planted and well-tended orchard, where I got many a colic in my earlier days from a gluttony of figs and peaches whose complete ripening I was too impatient to await.

I walked there, then, one morning quite early on the upper terrace immediately under the castle wall, and alternately I read from the "De Civitate Dei" which I had brought with me, alternately mused upon the matter of my reading. Suddenly I was disturbed by a sound of voices just below me.

The boxwood hedge, being twice my height and fully two feet thick, entirely screened the speakers from my sight.

There were two voices, and one of these, angry and threatening, I recognized for that of Rinolfo — Messer Giojoso's graceless son; the other, a fresh young feminine voice, was entirely unknown to me; indeed, it was the first girl's voice I could recall having heard in all my eighteen years, and the sound was as pleasantly strange as it was strangely pleasant.

I stood quite still, to listen to its expostulations.

"You are a cruel fellow, Ser Rinolfo, and Madonna the Countess shall be told of this."

There followed a crackling of twigs and a rush of heavy feet.

"You shall have something else of which to tell Madonna's beatitude," threatened the harsh voice of Rinolfo.

That and his advances were answered by a frightened screech, a screech that moved rapidly to the right as it was emitted. There came more snapping of twigs, a light scurrying sound followed by a heavier one, and lastly a panting of breath and a soft pattering of running feet upon the steps that led up to the terrace where I walked.

I moved forward rapidly to the opening in the hedge where these steps debouched, and no sooner had I appeared there than a soft, lithe body hurtled against me so suddenly that my arms mechanically went round it, my right hand still holding the "De Civitate Dei," forefinger enclosed within its pages to mark the place.

Two moist dark eyes looked up appealingly into mine out of a frightened but very winsome, suntinted face.

"O Madonnino!" she panted. "Protect me! Save me!"

Below us, checked midway in his furious ascent, halted Rinolfo, his big face red with anger, scowling up at me in sudden doubt and resentment.

The situation was not only extraordinary in itself, but singularly disturbing to me. Who the girl was, or whence she came, I had no thought or notion as I surveyed her. She would be of about my own age, or, perhaps, a little younger, and from her garb it was plain that she belonged to the peasant class. She wore a spotless bodice of white linen, which but indifferently concealed the ripening swell of her young breast. Her petticoat, of dark red homespun, stopped short above her bare brown ankles, and her little feet were naked. Her brown hair, long and abundant, was still fastened at the nape of her slim neck, but fell loose beyond that, having been disturbed, no doubt, in her scuffle with Rinolfo. Her little mouth was deeply red and it held strong young teeth that were as white as milk.

I have since wondered whether she was as beautiful as I deemed her in that moment. For it must be remembered that mine was the case of the son of Filippo Balducci — related by Messer Boccaccio in the merry tales of his "Decamerone" [1] — who had come to years of adolescence without ever having beheld womanhood, so that the first sight of it in the streets of Florence affected him so oddly that he vexed his sire with foolish questions and still more foolish prayers.

So was it now with me. In all my eighteen years I had by my mother's careful contriving never set eyes upon a woman of an age inferior to her own. And — consider me foolish if you will, but so it is — I do not think that it had occurred to me that they existed, or else, if they did, that in youth they differed materially from what in age I found them. Thus I had come to look upon women as just feeble, timid creatures, overprone to gossip, tears, and lamentations, and good for very little that I could perceive.

[1] In the Introduction to the Fourth Day.

I had been unable to understand for what reason it
was that San Luigi of Gonzaga had from years of
discretion never allowed his eyes to rest upon a
woman; nor could I see wherein lay the special merit
attributed to this. And certain passages in the "Confessions" of Saint Augustine and in the early life of
Saint Francis of Assisi bewildered me and left me
puzzled.

But now, quite suddenly it was as if revelation had
come to me. It was as if the Book of Life had at last
been opened for me, and at a glance I had read one of
its most dazzling pages. So that whether this brown
peasant girl was beautiful or not, beautiful she seemed
to me with the radiant beauty that I attributed to the
angels of Paradise. Nor did I doubt that she would
be as holy; for to see in beauty a mark of divine favour is not peculiar only to the ancient Greeks.

And because of the appeal of this beauty — real or
supposed — I was very ready with my protection,
since I felt that protection must carry with it certain
rights of ownership which must be very sweet and
were certainly desired.

Holding her, therefore, within the shelter of my
arms, where in her heedless innocence she had flung
herself, and by very instinct stroking with one hand
her little brown head to soothe her fears, I became
truculent for the first time in my new-found manhood, and boldly challenged her pursuer.

"What is this, Rinolfo?" I demanded. "Why do
you plague her?"

"She broke up my snares," he answered sullenly,
"and let the birds go free."

"What snares? What birds?" quoth I.

"He is a cruel beast," she shrilled. "And he will lie to you, Madonnino."

"If he does I'll break the bones of his body," I promised in a tone entirely new to me. And then to him — "The truth now, poltroon!"

At last I got the story out of them: how Rinolfo had scattered grain in a little clearing in the garden, and all about it had set twigs that were heavily smeared with viscum; that he set this trap almost daily, and daily took a great number of birds whose necks he wrung and had them cooked for him with rice by his silly mother; that it was a sin in any case to take little birds by such cowardly means, but that since amongst these birds there were larks and thrushes and plump blackbirds and other sweet musicians of the air, whose innocent lives were spent in singing the praises of God, his sin became a sacrilege.

Finally I learnt that coming that morning upon half a score of poor fluttering terrified birds held fast in Rinolfo's viscous snares, the little girl had given them their liberty and had set about breaking up the springes. At this occupation he had caught her, and there is no doubt that he would have taken a rude vengeance but for the sanctuary which she had found in me.

And when I had heard, behold me for the first time indulging the prerogative that was mine by right of birth, and dispensing justice at Mondolfo like the lord of life and death that I was there.

"You, Rinolfo," I said, "will set no more snares here at Mondolfo, nor will you ever again enter these gardens under pain of my displeasure and its consequences. And as for this child, if you dare to molest

her for what has happened now, or if you venture so
much as to lay a finger upon her at any time and I
have word of it, I shall deal with you as with a felon.
Now go."

He went — straight to his father, the seneschal,
with a lying tale of my having threatened him with
violence and forbidden him ever to enter the garden
again because he had caught me there with Luisina —
as the child was called — in my arms. And Messer
Giojoso, full of parental indignation at this gross
treatment of his child, and outraged chastity at the
notion of a young man of churchly aims, as were
mine, being in perversive dalliance with that peasant-
wench, repaired straight to my mother with the tale
of it, which I doubt not lost nothing in the repeti-
tion.

Meanwhile I abode there with Luisina. I was in no
haste to let her go. Her presence pleased me in some
subtle, quite indefinable manner; and my sense of
beauty, which, always strong, had hitherto lain dormant within me, was awake at last and was finding
nourishment in the graces of her.

I sat down upon the topmost of the terrace steps,
and made her sit beside me. This she did after some
demur about the honour of it and her own unworthiness, objections which I brushed peremptorily aside.

So we sat there on that May morning, quite close
together, for which there was, after all, no need, seeing that the steps were of a noble width. At our feet
spread the garden away down the flight of terraces to
end in the castle's grey, buttressed wall. But from
where we sat we could look beyond this, our glance
meeting the landscape a mile or so away with the

waters of the Taro glittering in the sunshine, and the Apennines, all hazy, for an ultimate background.

I took her hand, which she relinquished to me quite freely and frankly with an innocence as great as my own; and I asked her who she was and how she came to Mondolfo. It was then that I learnt that her name was Luisina, that she was the daughter of one of the women employed in the castle kitchen, who had brought her to help there a week ago from Borgo Taro where she had been living with an aunt.

To-day the notion of the Tyrant of Mondolfo sitting — almost coram populo — on the steps of the garden of his castle, clasping the hand of the daughter of one of his scullions, is grotesque and humiliating. At the time, the thought never presented itself to me at all, and had it done so it would have troubled me no whit. She was my first glimpse of fresh young maidenhood, and I was filled with pleasant interest and desirous of more acquaintance with this phenomenon. Beyond that I did not go.

I told her frankly that she was very beautiful. Whereupon she looked at me with suddenly startled eyes that were full of fearful questionings, and made to draw her hand from mine. Unable to understand her fears, and seeking to reassure her, to convince her that in me she had a friend, one who would ever protect her from the brutalities of all the Rinolfos in the world, I put an arm about her shoulders and drew her closer to me, gently and protectingly.

She suffered it very stonily, like a poor fascinated thing that is robbed by fear of its power to resist the evil that it feels enfolding it.

"O Madonnino!" she whispered fearfully, and sighed. "Nay, you must not. It . . . it is not good."

"Not good?" quoth I, and it was just so that that fool of a son of Balducci's must have protested in the story when he was told by his father that it was not good to look on women. "Nay, now, but it is good to me."

"And they say you are to be a priest," she added, a remark in which I could discern no sense at all.

"Well, then? And what of that?" I asked.

She looked at me again with those timid eyes of hers. "You should be at your studies," said she.

"I am," said I, and smiled. "I am studying a new subject."

"Madonnino, it is not a subject whose study makes good priests," she rejoined, and puzzled me again by the foolish inconsequence of her words.

Already, indeed, she began to disappoint me. Saving my mother — whom I did not presume to judge at all, and who seemed a being altogether apart from what little humanity I had known until then — I had found that foolishness was as natural to women as its bleat to a sheep or its cackle to a goose; and in this opinion I had been warmly confirmed by Fra Gervasio. Now here in Luisina I had imagined at first that I had discovered a phase of womanhood unsuspected and exceptional. She was driving me to conclude, however, that I had been mistaken, and that here was just a pretty husk containing a very trivial spirit, whose companionship must prove a dull affair when custom should have staled the first impression of her fresh young beauty.

It is plain now that I did her an injustice, for there was about her words none of the inconsequence I imagined. The fault was in myself and in the profound ignorance of the ways of men and women which went hand in hand with my deep but ineffectual learning in the ways of saints.

Our entertainment, however, was not destined to go further. For at the moment in which I puzzled over her words and sought to attach to them some intelligent meaning, there broke from behind us a scream that flung us apart, as startled as if we had been conscious, indeed, of guilt.

We looked round to find that it had been uttered by my mother. Not ten yards away she stood, a tall black figure against the grey background of the lichened wall, with Giojoso in attendance and Rinolfo slinking behind his father, leering.

CHAPTER V

REBELLION

THE sight of my mother startled me more than I can say. It filled me with a positive dread of things indefinable. Never before had I seen her coldly placid countenance so strangely disordered, and her unwonted aspect it must have been that wrought so potently upon me.

No longer was she the sorrowful spectre, white-faced, with downcast eyes and level, almost inanimate tones. Her cheeks were flushed unnaturally, her lips were quivering, and angry fires were smouldering in her deep-set eyes.

Swiftly she came down to us, seeming almost to glide over the ground. Not me she addressed, but poor Luisina; and her voice was hoarse with an awful anger.

"Who are you, wench?" quoth she. "What make you here in Mondolfo?"

Luisina had risen and stood swaying there, very white and with averted eyes, her hands clasping and unclasping. Her lips moved; but she was too terrified to answer. It was Giojoso who stepped forward to inform my mother of the girl's name and condition. And upon learning it her anger seemed to increase.

"A kitchen-wench!" she cried. "Oh, horror!"

And quite suddenly, as if by inspiration, scarce knowing what I said or that I spoke at all, I answered

her out of the store of the theological learning with
which she had had me stuffed.

"We are all equals in the sight of God, madam
mother."

She flashed me a glance of anger, of pious anger
than which none can be more terrible.

"Blasphemer!" she denounced me. "What has
God to do with this?"

She waited for no answer, rightly judging, perhaps,
that I had none to offer.

"And as for that wanton," she commanded, turning fiercely to Giojoso, "let her be whipped hence
and out of the town of Mondolfo. Set the grooms
to it."

But upon that command of hers I leapt of a sudden
to my feet, a tightening about my heart, and beset by
a certain breathlessness that turned me pale.

Here again, it seemed, was to be repeated —
though with methods a thousand times more barbarous and harsh — the wrong that was done years
ago in the case of poor Gino Falcone. And the reason
for it in this instance was not even dimly apparent to
me. Falcone I had loved; indeed, in my eighteen
years of life he was the only human being who had
knocked for admission upon the portals of my heart.
Him they had driven forth. And now, here was a
child — the fairest creature of God's that until that
hour I had beheld, whose companionship seemed to
me a thing sweet and desirable, and whom I felt that
I might love as I had loved Falcone. Her, too, they
would drive forth, and with a brutality and cruelty
that revolted me.

Later I was to perceive the reasons better; and

much food for reflection was I to derive from realizing that there are no spirits so vengeful, so fierce, so utterly intolerant, ungovernable, and feral as the spirits of the devout when they conceive themselves justified to anger. All the sweet teaching of Charity and brotherly love and patience is jettisoned, and by the most amazing paradox that Christianity has ever known, Catholic burns heretic, and heretic butchers Catholic, all for the love of Christ; and each glories devoutly in the deed, never heeding the blasphemy of his belief that thus he obeys the sweet and gentle mandates of the God Incarnate.

Thus, then, my mother now, commanding that hideous deed with a mind at peace in pharisaic self-righteousness.

But not again would I stand by as I had stood by in the case of Falcone, and let her cruel, pietistic will be done. I had grown since then, and I had ripened more than I was aware. It remained for this moment to reveal to me the extent. Besides, the subtle influence of sex — all unconscious of it as I was — stirred me now to prove my new-found manhood.

"Stay!" I said to Giojoso, and in uttering the command I grew very cold and steady, and my breathing resumed the normal.

He checked in the act of turning away to go upon my mother's hideous errand.

"What's this?" cried my mother, intuitively perceiving my intent. "So you gainsay my orders?"

"That no," I assured her. "Of course you will give Madonna's order to the grooms, Ser Giojoso, as you have been bidden. But you will add from me that if there is one amongst them dares to obey it and to lay

be it so much as a finger upon Luisina, him will I kill
with these two hands."

Never was consternation more profound than that
which I flung amongst them by those words. Giojoso
fell to trembling; behind him, Rinolfo, the cause of all
this garboil, stared with round big eyes; whilst my
mother, all aquiver, clutched at her bosom and looked
at me fearfully, but spoke no word.

I smiled upon them, towering there, conscious and
glad of my height for the first time in my life.

"Well?" I demanded of the seneschal. "For what
do you wait? About it, sir, and do as my mother has
commanded you."

He turned to her, all bent and grovelling, arms out-
stretched in ludicrous bewilderment, every line of
him beseeching guidance along this path so suddenly
grown thorny.

"Ma — madonna!" he stammered.

She swallowed hard, and spoke at last.

"Do you defy my will, Agostino?"

"On the contrary, madam mother, as you have
heard, I am enforcing it. Your will shall be done;
your order shall be given. I insist upon it. But it
shall lie with the discretion of the grooms whether
they obey you. Am I to blame if they turn cowards?"

Oh, I had found myself at last, and I was making a
furious, joyous use of the discovery.

"That . . . that were to make a mock of me and my
authority," she protested. She was still rather help-
less, rather breathless and confused, like one who has
suddenly been hurled into cold water.

"If you fear that, madam, perhaps you had better
countermand your order."

"Is the girl to remain in Mondolfo against my wishes? Are you so . . . so lost to shame?" A returning note of warmth in her accents warned me that she was collecting herself to deal with the situation.

"Nay," said I, and I looked at Luisina, who stood there so pale and tearful. "I think that for her own sake, poor maid, it were better that she went, since you desire it. But she shall not be whipped hence like a stray dog."

"Come, child," I said to her, as gently as I could. "Go pack, and quit this home of misery. And be easy. For if any man in Mondolfo attempts to hasten your going, he shall reckon with me."

I laid a hand for an instant in kindliness and friendliness upon her shoulder. "Poor little Luisina," said I, sighing. But she shrank and trembled under my touch. "Pity me a little. They will not permit me any friends, and who is friendless is, indeed, pitiful."

And then, whether the phrase touched her, so that her simple little nature was roused and she shook off what self-control she had ever learnt, or whether she felt secure enough in my protection to dare proclaim her mind before them all, she caught my hand, and, stooping, kissed it.

"O Madonnino!" she faltered, and her tears showered upon that hand of mine. "God reward you your sweet thought for me. I shall pray for you, Madonnino."

"Do, Luisina," said I. "I begin to think I need it."

"Indeed, indeed!" said my mother very sombrely.

And as she spoke, Luisina, her fears reawakened, turned suddenly and went quickly along the terrace, past Rinolfo, who in that moment smiled viciously, and round the angle of the wall.

"What . . . what are my orders, Madonna?" quoth the wretched seneschal, reminding her that all had not yet been resolved.

She lowered her eyes to the ground, and folded her hands. She was by now quite composed again, her habitual sorrowful self.

"Let be," she said. "Let the wench depart. So that she goes we may count ourselves fortunate."

"Fortunate, I think, is she," said I. "Fortunate to return to the world beyond all this — the world of life and love that God made and that Saint Francis praises. I do not think he would have praised Mondolfo. Indeed, I doubt if God had a hand in making it as it is to-day. It is too . . . too arid."

Oh, my mood was finely rebellious that May morning.

"Are you mad, Agostino?" gasped my mother.

"I think that I am growing sane," said I very sadly.

She flashed me one of her rare glances, and I saw her lips tighten.

"We must talk," she said. "That girl . . ." And then she checked. "Come with me," she bade me.

But in that moment I remembered something, and I turned aside to look for my friend Rinolfo. He was moving stealthily away, following the road Luisina had taken. The conviction that he went to plague and jeer at her, to exult over her expulsion from Mondolfo, kindled my anger all anew.

"Stay! You there! Rinolfo!" I called.

He halted in his strides, and looked over his shoulder, impudently.

I had never yet been paid by any the deference that was my due. Indeed, I think that among the grooms and serving-men at Mondolfo I must have been held in a certain measure of contempt, as one who would never come to more manhood than that of a cassock.

"Come here," I bade him, and as he appeared to hesitate I had to repeat the order more peremptorily. At last he turned and came.

"What now, Agostino?" cried my mother, setting a pale hand upon my sleeve.

But I was all intent upon that lout, who stood there before me shifting uneasily upon his feet, his air mutinous and sullen. Over his shoulder I had a glimpse of his father's yellow face, wide-eyed with alarm.

"I think you smiled just now," said I.

"Heh! By Bacchus!" said he impudently, as who would say: "How could I help smiling?"

"Will you tell me why you smiled?" I asked him.

"Heh! By Bacchus!" said he again, and shrugged to give his insolence a barb.

"Will you answer me?" I roared, and under my display of anger he dared to look at me with truculence, and thus exhausted the last remnant of my patience.

"Agostino!" came my mother's voice in remonstrance; and such is the power of habit that for a moment it controlled me and subdued my violence.

Nevertheless I went on: "You smiled to see your spite succeed. You smiled to see that poor child driven hence by your contriving; you smiled to see your broken snares avenged. And you were following after her, no doubt to tell her all this and to smile again. This is all so, is it not?"

"Heh! By Bacchus!" said he for the third time, and at that my patience gave out utterly. Ere any could stop me I had seized him by throat and belt and shaken him savagely.

"Will you answer me like a fool?" I cried. "Must you be taught sense and a proper respect of me?"

"Agostino! Agostino!" wailed my mother. "Help, Ser Giojoso! Do you not see that he is mad?"

I do not believe that it was in my mind to do the fellow any grievous hurt. But he was so ill-advised in that moment as to attempt to defend himself. He rashly struck at one of the arms that held him, and by the act drove me into a fury ungovernable.

"You dog!" I snarled at him from between clenched teeth. "Would you raise your hand to me? Am I your lord, or am I dirt of your own kind? Go, learn submission." And I flung him almost headlong down the flight of steps.

There were twelve of them and all of stone with edges still sharp enough, though blunted here and there by time. The fool had never suspected in me the awful strength which until that hour I had never suspected in myself. Else, perhaps, there had been fewer insolent shrugs, fewer foolish answers, and, last of all, no attempt to defy me physically.

He screamed as I flung him; my mother screamed; and Giojoso screamed.

After that there was a panic-stricken silence whilst he went thudding and bumping to the bottom of the flight. I did not greatly care if I killed him. But he was fortunate enough to get no worse hurt than a broken leg, which should keep him out of mischief for a season and teach him respect for me for all time.

His father scuttled down the steps to the assistance of that precious son, who lay moaning where he had fallen, the angle at which the half of one of his legs stood to the rest of it plainly announcing the nature of his punishment.

My mother swept me indoors, loading me with reproaches as we went. She despatched some to help Giojoso; others she sent in urgent quest of Fra Gervasio; me she hurried along to her private dining-room. I went very obediently, and even a little fearfully now that my passion had fallen from me.

There, in that cheerless room, which not even the splashes of sunlight falling from the high-placed windows upon the whitewashed wall could help to gladden, I stood a little sullenly what time she first upbraided me and then wept bitterly, sitting in her high-backed chair at the table's head.

At last Gervasio came, anxious and flurried, for already he had heard some rumour of what had chanced. His keen eyes went from me to my mother and then back again to me.

"What has happened?" he asked.

"What has not happened?" wailed my mother. "Agostino is possessed."

He knit his brows. "Possessed?" quoth he.

"Aye, possessed — possessed of devils. He has been violent. He has broken poor Rinolfo's leg."

"Ah!" said Gervasio, and turned to me frowning with full tutorial sternness. "And what have you to say, Agostino?"

"Why, that I am sorry," answered I, rebellious once more. "I had hoped to break his dirty neck."

"You hear him!" cried my mother. "It is the end of the world, Gervasio. The boy is possessed, I say."

"What was the cause of your quarrel?" quoth the friar, his manner still more stern.

"Quarrel?" quoth I, throwing back my head and lifting my voice in anger. "I do not quarrel with Rinolfos. I chastise them when they are insolent or displease me. This one did both."

He halted before me, erect and very stern — indeed, almost threatening. And I began to grow afraid; for, after all, I had a kindness for Gervasio, and I would not willingly engage in a quarrel with him. Yet here I was determined to carry through this thing as I had begun it.

It was my mother who saved the situation.

"Alas!" she moaned, "there is wicked blood in him. He has the abominable pride that was the ruin and downfall of his father."

Now, that was not the way to make an ally of Fra Gervasio. It did the very opposite. It set him instantly on my side, in antagonism to the abuser of my father's memory, a memory which he, poor man, still secretly revered.

The sternness fell away from him. He looked at her and sighed. Then, with bowed head, and hands clasped behind him, he moved away from me a little.

"Do not let us judge rashly," he said. "Perhaps Agostino received some provocation. Let us hear . . ."

"Oh, you shall hear," she promised tearfully, exultant to prove him wrong. "You shall hear a yet worse abomination that was the cause of it."

And out she poured the story that Rinolfo and his father had run to tell her — of how I had shown the fellow violence in the first instance because he had surprised me with Luisina in my arms.

The friar's face grew dark and grave as he listened. But ere she had quite done, unable longer to contain myself, I interrupted.

"In that he lied like the muckworm that he is," I exclaimed. "And it increases my regrets that I did not break his neck as I intended."

"He lied?" quoth she, her eyes wide open in amazement — not at the fact, but at the audacity of what she conceived my falsehood.

"It is not impossible," said Fra Gervasio. "What is your story, Agostino?"

I told it — how the child, out of a very gentle and Christian pity, had released the poor birds that were taken in Rinolfo's limed twigs, and how in a fury he had made to beat her, so that she had fled to me for shelter and protection; and how, thereupon, I had bidden him begone out of that garden, and never set foot in it again.

"And now," I ended, "you know all the violence that I showed him, and the reason for it. If you say that I did wrong, I warn you that I shall not believe you."

"Indeed . . ." began the friar with a faint smile of friendliness.

But my mother interrupted him, betwixt sorrow and anger.

"He lies, Gervasio. He lies shamelessly. Oh, into what a morass of sin has he not fallen, and every moment he goes deeper! Have I not said that he is possessed? We shall need the exorcist."

"We shall, indeed, madam mother, to clear your

mind of foolishness," I answered hotly, for it stung me to the soul to be branded thus a liar, to have my word discredited by that of a lout such as Rinolfo.

She rose a sombre pillar of indignation. "Agostino, I am your mother," she reminded me.

"Let us thank God that for that, at least, you cannot blame me," answered I, utterly reckless now.

The answer crushed her back into her chair. She looked appealingly at Fra Gervasio, who stood glum and frowning. "Is he . . . is he perchance bewitched?" she asked the friar, quite seriously. "Do you think that any spells might have . . ."

He interrupted her with a wave of the hand and an impatient snort.

"We are at cross-purposes here," he said. "Agostino does not lie. For that I will answer."

"But, Fra Gervasio, I tell you that I saw them — that I saw them with these two eyes — sitting together on the terrace steps, and he had his arm about her. Yet he denies it shamelessly to my face."

"Said I ever a word of that?" I appealed me to the friar. "Why, that was after Rinolfo left us. My tale never got so far. It is quite true. I did sit beside her. The child was troubled. I comforted her. Where was the harm?"

"The harm?" quoth he. "And you had your arm about her — and you to be a priest one day?'

"And why not, pray?" quoth I. "Is this some new sin that you have discovered — or that you have kept hidden from me until now? To console the afflicted is an ordination of Mother Church; to love our fellow-creatures an ordination of our Blessed Lord Himself. I was performing both. Am I to be abused for that?"

He looked at me very searchingly, seeking in my countenance — as I now know — some trace of irony or guile. Finding none, he turned to my mother. He was very solemn.

"Madonna," he said quietly, "I think that Agostino is nearer to being a saint than either you or I will ever get."

She looked at him, first in surprise, then very sadly. Slowly she shook her head. "Unhappily for him there is another arbiter of saintship, Who sees deeper than do you, Gervasio."

He bowed his head. "Better not to look deep enough than to do as you seem in danger of doing, Madonna, and by looking too deep imagine things which are not present."

"Ah, you will defend him against reason even," she complained. "His anger exists. His thirst to kill — to stamp himself with the brand of Cain — exists. He confesses that himself. His insubordination to me you have seen for yourself; and that again is sin, for it is ordained that we shall honour our parents.

"Oh!" she moaned. "My authority is all gone. He is beyond my control. He has shaken off the reins by which I sought to guide him."

"You had done well to have taken my advice a year ago, Madonna. Even now it is not too late. Let him go to Pavia, to the Sapienza, to study his humanities."

"Out into the world!" she cried in horror. "Oh, no, no! I have sheltered him here so carefully!"

"Yet you cannot shelter him forever," said he. "He must go out into the world some day."

"He need not," she faltered. "If the call were

strong enough within him, a convent . . ." She left her sentence unfinished, and looked at me.

"Go, Agostino," she bade me. "Fra Gervasio and I must talk."

I went reluctantly, since in the matter of their talk none could have had a greater interest than I, seeing that my fate stood in the balance of it. But I went, none the less, and her last words to me as I was departing were an injunction that I should spend the time, until I should take up my studies for the day with Fra Gervasio, in seeking forgiveness for the morning's sins and grace to do better in the future.

CHAPTER VI

FRA GERVASIO

I DID not again see my mother that day, nor did she sup with us that evening. I was told by Fra Gervasio that on my account was she in retreat, praying for light and guidance in the thing that must be determined concerning me.

I withdrew early to my little bedroom overlooking the gardens, a room that had more the air of a monastic cell than a bedchamber fitting the estate of the Lord of Mondolfo. The walls were whitewashed, and besides the crucifix that hung over my bed, their only decoration was a crude painting of Saint Augustine disputing with the little boy on the seashore.

For bed I had a plain hard pallet, and the room contained, in addition, a wooden chair, a stool upon which was set a steel basin with its ewer for my ablutions, and a cupboard for the few sombre black garments I possessed. The amiable vanity of raiment usual in young men of my years had never yet assailed me. I had none to emulate in that respect.

I got me to bed, blew out my taper, and composed myself to sleep. But sleep was playing truant from me. Long I lay there surveying the events of that day — the day in which I had embarked upon the discovery of myself; the most stirring day that I had yet lived; the day in which, although I scarcely realized it, if at all, I had at once tasted love and battle, the strongest meats that are in the dish of life.

For some hours, I think, had I lain there, reflecting and putting together pieces of the riddle of existence, when my door was softly opened, and I started up in bed to behold Fra Gervasio bearing a taper which he sheltered with one hand, so that the light of it was thrown upwards into his pale, gaunt face.

Seeing me astir he came forward and closed the door.

"What is it?" I asked.

"Sh!" he admonished me, a finger to his lips. He advanced to my side, set down the taper on the chair, and seated himself upon the edge of my bed.

"Lie down again, my son," he bade me. "I have something to say to you."

He paused a moment, whilst I settled down again and drew the coverlet to my chin, not without a certain premonition of important things to come.

"Madonna has decided," he informed me then. "She fears that, having once resisted her authority, you are now utterly beyond her control; and that to keep you here would be bad for yourself and for her. Therefore she has resolved that to-morrow you leave Mondolfo."

A faint excitement began to stir in me. To leave Mondolfo — to go out into that world of which I had read so much; to mingle with my fellow-man, with youths of my own age, perhaps with maidens like Luisina, to see cities and the ways of cities; here, indeed, was matter for excitement. Yet it was an excitement not altogether pleasurable; for with my very natural curiosity, and with my eagerness to have it gratified, were blended certain fears imbibed from the only quality of reading that had been mine.

The world was an evil place in which temptations seethed, and through which it was difficult to come unscathed. Therefore, I feared the world and the adventuring beyond the shelter of the walls of the castle of Mondolfo; and yet I desired to judge for myself the evil of which I read, the evil which in moments of doubt I even permitted myself to question.

My reasoning followed the syllogism that God being good and God having created the world, it was not possible that the creation should be evil. It was well enough to say that the Devil was loose in it. But that was not to say that the Devil had created it; and it would be necessary to prove this ere it could be established that it was evil in itself — as many theologians appeared to seek to show — and a place to be avoided.

Such was the question that very frequently arose in my mind, ultimately to be dismissed as a lure of Satan's to imperil my poor soul. It battled for existence now amid my fears; and it gained some little ascendancy.

"And whither am I to go?" I asked. "To Pavia, or to the University of Bologna?"

"Had my advice been heeded," said he, "one or the other would have been your goal. But your mother took counsel with Messer Arcolano."

He shrugged, and there was contempt in the lines of his mouth. He distrusted Arcolano, the regular cleric who was my mother's confessor and spiritual adviser, exerting over her a very considerable influence. She, herself, had admitted that it was this Arcolano who had induced her to that horrid traffic in my father's life and liberty which she was mercifully spared from putting into effect.

"Messer Arcolano," he resumed after a pause, "has a good friend in Piacenza, a pedagogue, a doctor of civil and canon law, a man who, he says, is very learned and very pious, named Astorre Fifanti. I have heard of this Fifanti, and I do not at all agree with Messer Arcolano. I have said so. But your mother . . ." He broke off. "It is decided that you go to him at once, to take up your study of the humanities under his tutelage, and that you abide with him until you are of an age for ordination, which your mother hopes will be very soon. Indeed, it is her wish that you should enter the subdeaconate in the autumn, and your novitiate next year, to fit you for the habit of Saint Augustine."

He fell silent, adding no comment of any sort, as if he waited to hear what of my own accord I might have to urge. But my mind was incapable of travelling beyond the fact that I was to go out into the world to-morrow.

The circumstance that I should become a monk was no departure from the idea to which I had been trained, although explicitly no more than my mere priesthood had been spoken of. So I lay there without thinking of any words in which to answer him.

Gervasio considered me steadily, and sighed a little. "Agostino," he said presently, "you are upon the eve of taking a great step, a step whose import you may never fully have considered. I have been your tutor, and your rearing has been my charge. That charge I have faithfully carried out as was ordained me, but not as I would have carried it out had I been free to follow my heart and my conscience in the matter.

"The idea of your ultimate priesthood has been so fostered in your mind that you may well have come to believe that to be a priest is your own inherent desire. I would have you consider it well now that the time approaches for a step which is irrevocable."

His words and his manner startled me alike.

"How?" I cried. "Do you say that it might be better if I did not seek ordination? What better can the world offer than the priesthood? Have you not, yourself, taught me that it is man's noblest calling?"

"To be a good priest, fulfilling all the teachings of the Master, becoming in your turn His mouthpiece, living a life of self-abnegation, of self-sacrifice and purity," he answered slowly, "that is the noblest thing a man can be. But to be a bad priest — there are other ways of being damned less hurtful to the Church."

"To be a bad priest?" quoth I. "Is it possible to be a bad priest?"

"It is not only possible, my son, but in these days it is very frequent. Many men, Agostino, enter the Church out of motives of self-seeking. Through such as these Rome has come to be spoken of as the Necropolis of the Living. Others, Agostino — and these are men most worthy of pity — enter the Church because they are driven to it in youth by ill-advised parents. I would not have you one of these, my son."

I stared at him, my amazement ever growing. "Do you . . . do you think I am in danger of it?" I asked.

"That is a question you must answer for yourself. No man can know what is in another's heart. I have trained you as I was bidden to train you. I have seen you devout, increasing in piety, and yet..." He paused, and looked at me again. "It may be that this is no more than the fruit of your training; it may be that your piety and devotion are purely intellectual. It is very often so. Men know the precepts of religion as a lawyer knows the law. It no more follows out of that that they are religious — though they conceive that it does — than it follows that a lawyer is law-abiding. It is in the acts of their lives that we must seek their real natures, and no single act of your life, Agostino, has yet given sign that the call is in your heart.

"To-day, for instance, at what is almost your first contact with the world, you indulge your human feelings to commit a violence; that you did not kill is as much an accident as that you broke Rinolfo's leg. I do not say that you did a very sinful thing. In a worldly youth of your years the provocation you received would have more than justified your action. But not in one who aims at a life of humility and self-forgetfulness such as the priesthood imposes."

"And yet," said I, "I heard you tell my mother below stairs that I was nearer sainthood than either of you."

He smiled sadly, and shook his head. "They were rash words, Agostino. I mistook ignorance for purity — a common error. I have pondered it since, and my reflection brings me to utter what in this household amounts to treason."

"I do not understand," I confessed.

"My duty to your mother I have discharged more faithfully, perhaps, than I had the right to do. My duty to my God I am discharging now, although to you I may rather appear as an advocatus diaboli. This duty is to warn you; to bid you consider well the step you are to take.

"Listen, Agostino. I am speaking to you out of the bitter experience of a very cruel life. I would not have you tread the path I have trodden. It seldom leads to happiness in this world or the next; it seldom leads anywhere but straight to Hell."

He paused, and I looked into his haggard face in utter stupefaction to hear such words from the lips of one whom I had ever looked upon as goodness incarnate.

"Had I not known that some day I must speak to you as I am speaking now, I had long since abandoned a task which I did not consider good. But I feared to leave you. I feared that if I were removed my place might be taken by some time-server who to earn a livelihood would tutor you as your mother would have you tutored, and thrust you forth without warning upon the life to which you have been vowed.

"Once, years ago, I was on the point of resisting your mother." He passed a hand wearily across his brow. "It was on the night that Gino Falcone left us, driven forth by her because she accounted it her duty. Do you remember, Agostino?"

"Oh, I remember!" I answered.

"That night," he pursued, "I was angered — righteously angered to see so wicked and unchristian an act performed in blasphemous self-righteousness. I was on the point of denouncing the deed as it deserved, of denouncing your mother for it to her face. And then I remembered you. I remembered the love I had borne your father, and my duty to him, to see

that no such wrong was done you in the end as that
which I feared. I reflected that if I spoke the words
that were burning my tongue for utterance, I should
go as Gino Falcone had gone.

"Not that the going mattered. I could better save
my soul elsewhere than here in this atmosphere of
Christianity misunderstood; and there are always
convents of my order to afford me shelter. But your
being abandoned mattered; and I felt that if I went,
abandoned you would be to the influences that drove
and moulded you without consideration for your
nature and your inborn inclinations. Therefore I remained, and left Falcone's cause unchampioned.
Later I was to learn that he had found a friend, and
that he was . . . that he was being cared for."

"By whom?" quoth I, more interested, perhaps, in
this than in anything that he had yet said.

"By one who was your father's friend," he said,
after a moment's hesitation, "a soldier of fortune by
name of Galeotto — a leader of free lances who goes
by the name of Il Gran Galeotto. But let that be. I
want to tell you of myself, that you may judge with
what authority I speak.

"I was destined, Agostino, for a soldier's life in the
following of my valiant foster-brother, your father.
Had I preserved the strength of my early youth, un-
doubtedly a soldier's harness would be strapped here
to-day in the place of this scapulary. But it happened
that an illness left me sickly and ailing, and unfitted
me utterly for such a life. Similarly it unfitted me for
the labour of the fields, so that I threatened to become
a useless burden upon my parents, who were peasant-
folk. To avoid this they determined to make a monk

of me; they offered me to God because they found me
unfitted for the service of man; and, poor, simple,
self-deluded folk, they accounted that in doing so
they did a good and pious thing.

"I showed aptitude in learning; I became interested
in the things I studied; I was absorbed by them in
fact, and never gave a thought to the future; I submitted without question to the wishes of my parents,
and before I awakened to a sense of what was done
and what I was, myself, I was in orders."

He sank his voice impressively as he concluded —
"For ten years thereafter, Agostino, I wore a hair-
shirt day and night, and for girdle a knotted length of
whipcord in which were embedded thorns that stung
and chafed me and tore my body. For ten years, then,
I never knew bodily ease or proper rest at night.
Only thus could I bring into subjection my rebellious
flesh, and save myself from the way of ordinary men
which to me must have been a path of sacrilege and
sin. I was devout. Had I not been devout and strong
in my devotion I could never have endured what I
was forced to endure as the alternative to damnation,
because without consideration for my nature I had
been ordained a priest.

"Consider this, Agostino; consider it well. I would
not have you go that way, nor feel the need to drive
yourself from temptation by such a spur. Because I
know — I say it in all humility, Agostino, I hope, and
thanking God for the exceptional grace He vouchsafed me to support me — that for one priest without
vocation who can quench temptation by such agonizing means, a hundred perish, which is bad; and by
the scandal of their example they drive many from

the Church and set a weapon in the hands of her enemies, which is a still heavier reckoning to meet hereafter."

A spell of silence followed. I was strangely moved by his tale, strangely impressed by the warning that I perceived in it. And yet my confidence, I think, was all unshaken.

And when presently he rose, took up his taper, and stood by my bedside to ask me once again did I believe myself to be called, I showed my confidence in my answer.

"It is my hope and prayer that I am called, indeed," I said. "The life that will best prepare me for the world to come is the life I would follow."

He looked at me long and sadly. "You must do as your heart bids you," he sighed. "And when you have seen the world, your heart will have learnt to speak to you more plainly." And upon that he left me.

Next day I set out.

My leave-takings were brief. My mother shed some tears and many prayers over me at parting. Not that she was moved to any grief at losing me. That were a grief I should respect and the memory of which I should treasure as a sacred thing. Her tears were tears of dread lest, surrounded by perils in the world, I should succumb and thus falsify her vows.

She, herself, confessed it in the valedictory words she addressed to me. Words that left the conviction clear upon my mind that the fulfilment of her vow was the only thing concerning me that mattered. To the price that later might be paid for it I cannot think that she ever gave a single thought.

Tears there were, too, in the eyes of Fra Gervasio. My mother had suffered me to do no more than kiss her hand — as was my custom. But the friar took me to his bosom, and held me tight a moment in his long arms.

"Remember!" he murmured huskily and impressively. And then, putting me from him, "God help and guide you, my son," were his last words.

I went down the steps into the courtyard where most of the servants were gathered to see their lord's departure, whilst Messer Arcolano, who was to go with me, paused to assure my mother of the care that he would have of me, and to receive her final commands concerning me.

Four men, mounted and armed, stood waiting to escort us, and with them were three mules, one for Arcolano, one for myself, and the third already laden with my baggage.

A servant held my stirrup, and I swung myself up into the saddle, with which I was but indifferently acquainted. Then Arcolano mounted too, puffing over the effort, for he was a corpulent, rubicund man with the fattest hands I have ever seen.

I touched my mule with the whip, and the beast began to move. Arcolano ambied beside me; and behind us, abreast, came the men-at-arms. Thus we rode down towards the gateway, and as we went the servants murmured their valedictory words.

"A safe journey, Madonnino!"

"A good return, Madonnino!"

I smiled back at them, and in the eyes of more than one I detected a look of commiseration.

Once I turned, when the end of the quadrangle was

reached, and I waved my cap to my mother and Fra
Gervasio, who stood upon the steps where I had left
them. The friar responded by waving back to me.
But my mother made no sign. Likely enough her eyes
were upon the ground again already.

Her unresponsiveness almost angered me. I felt
that a man had the right to some slight display of
tenderness from the woman who had borne him. Her
frigidity wounded me. It wounded me the more in
comparison with the affectionate clasp of old Gervasio's arms. With a knot in my throat I passed
from the sunlight of the courtyard into the gloom of
the gateway, and out again beyond, upon the drawbridge. Our hooves thudded briskly upon the timbers,
and then with a sharper note upon the cobbles beyond.

I was outside the walls of the castle for the first
time. Before me the long, rudely paved street of the
borgo sloped away to the market-place of the town of
Mondolfo. Beyond that lay the world, itself — all at
my feet, as I imagined.

The knot in my throat was dissolved. My pulses
quickened with anticipation. I dug my heels into the
mule's belly and pushed on, the portly cleric at my
side.

And thus I left my home and the gloomy, sorrowful
influence of my most dolorous mother.

BOOK II: GIULIANA

∴

CHAPTER I

THE HOUSE OF ASTORRE FIFANTI

LET me not follow in too close detail the incidents of that journey lest I be in danger of becoming tedious. In themselves they contained laughable matter enough, but in the mere relation they may seem dull.

Down the borgo, ahead of us, ran the rumour that here was the Madonnino of Mondolfo, and the excitement which the announcement caused was something at which I did not know whether to be flattered or offended.

The houses gave up their inhabitants, and all stood at gaze as we passed, to behold for the first time this lord of theirs of whom they had heard Heaven knows what stories — for where there are elements of mystery human invention is usually very active.

At first so many eyes confused me; so that I kept my own steadily upon the glossy neck of my mule. Very soon, however, growing accustomed to being stared at, I lost some of my shyness, and now it was that I became a trouble to Messer Arcolano. For as I looked about me there were a hundred things to hold my attention and to call for inquiry and nearer inspection.

We had come by this into the market-place, and it

chanced that it was a market-day and that the square
was thronged with peasants from the Val di Taro who
had come to sell their produce and to buy their
necessaries.

I was for halting at each booth and inspecting the
wares, and each time that I made as if to do so, the
obsequious peasantry fell away before me, making
way invitingly. But Messer Arcolano urged me along,
saying that we had far to go, and that in Piacenza
there were better shops and that I should have more
time to view them.

Then it was the fountain with its surmounting stat-
ues that caught my eye — Durfreno's group of the
Laocoön — and I must draw rein and cry out in my
amazement at so wonderful a piece of work, plaguing
Arcolano with a score of questions concerning the
identity of the central figure and how he came beset
by so monstrous a reptile, and whether he had
succeeded in the end in his attempt to strangle it.

Arcolano, out of patience by now, answered me
shortly that the reptile was the sculptor's pious
symbolization of sin, which Saint Hercules was over-
coming.

I am by no means sure that such was not, indeed,
his own conception of the matter, and that there did
not exist in his mind some confusion as to whether the
pagan demigod had a place in the Calendar or not.
For he was an uncultured, plebeian fellow, and what
my mother should have found in him to induce her to
prefer him for her confessor and spiritual counsellor
to the learned Fra Gervasio is one more of the many
mysteries which an attempt to understand her must
ever present to me.

Then there were the young peasant girls who thronged about and stood in groups, blushing furiously under my glance, which Arcolano vainly commanded me to lower. A score of times did it seem to me that one of these brown-legged, lithe, comely creatures was my little Luisina; and more than once I was on the point of addressing one or another, to discover my mistake and to be admonished for my astounding frivolity by Messer Arcolano.

And when once or twice I returned the friendly laughter of these girls, whilst the grinning servingmen behind me would nudge one another and wink to see me — as they thought — so very far off the road to priesthood, hot anathema poured from the fat cleric's lips, and he urged me roughly to go faster.

His tortures ended at last when we came into the open country. We rode in silence for a mile or two, I being full of thought of all that I had seen, and infected a little by the fever of life through which I had just passed. At last, I remember that I turned to Arcolano, who was riding with the ears of his mule in line with my saddle-bow, and asked him to point out to me where my dominions ended.

The meek question provoked an astonishingly churlish answer. I was shortly bidden to give my mind to other things than worldly vanities; and with that he began a homily, which lasted for many a weary mile, upon the vanities of the world and the glories of Paradise — a homily of the very tritest, upon subjects whereupon I, myself, could have dilated to better purpose than His Ignorance.

The distance from Mondolfo to Piacenza is a good eight leagues, and though we had set out very early, it was past noon before we caught our first glimpse of the city by the Po, lying low as it does in the vast Æmilian plain, and Arcolano set himself to name to me this church and that whose spires stood out against the cobalt background of the sky.

An hour or so after our first glimpse of the city, our weary beasts brought us up to the Gate of San Lazzaro. But we did not enter, as I had hoped. Messer Arcolano had had enough of me and my questions at Mondolfo, and he was not minded to expose himself to worse behaviour on my part in the more interesting thoroughfares of this great city.

So we passed it by, and rode under the very walls by way of an avenue of flowering chestnuts, round to the northern side, until we emerged suddenly upon the sands of the Po, and I had my first view at close quarters of that mighty river flowing gently about the islands, all thick with willows, that seemed to float upon its gleaming waters.

Fishermen were at work in a boat out in midstream, heaving their nets to the sound of the oddest cantilena, and I was all for pausing there to watch their operations. But Arcolano urged me onward with that impatience of his which took no account of my very natural curiosity. Presently I drew rein again with exclamations of delight and surprise to see the wonderful bridge of boats that spanned the river a little higher up.

But we had reached our destination. Arcolano called a halt at the gates of a villa that stood a little way back from the road on slightly rising ground near the Fodesta Gate. He bade one of the grooms get down and open, and presently we ambled up a short

avenue between tall banks of laurel, to the steps of
the villa itself.

It was a house of fair proportions, though to me at
the time, accustomed to the vast spaces of Mondolfo,
it seemed the merest hut. It was painted white, and it
had green Venetian shutters which gave it a cool and
pleasant air; and through one of the open windows
floated a sound of merry voices, in which a woman's
laugh was predominant.

The double doors stood open and through these
there emerged a moment after our halting a tall, thin
man whose restless eyes surveyed us swiftly, whose
thin-lipped mouth smiled a greeting to Messer Arcolano in the pause he made before hurrying down
the steps with a slip-slop of ill-fitting shoes.

This was Messer Astorre Fifanti, the pedant under
whom I was to study, and with whom I was to take up
my residence for some months to come.

Seeing in him one who was to be set in authority
over me, I surveyed him with the profoundest interest,
and from that instant I disliked him.

He was, as I have said, a tall, thin man; and he had
long hands that were very big and bony in the
knuckles. Indeed, they looked like monstrous skele-
ton hands with a glove of skin stretched over them.
He was quite bald, save for a curly grizzled fringe that
surrounded the back of his head, on a level with his
enormous ears, and his forehead ran up to the summit
of his egg-shaped head. His nose was pendulous and
his eyes were closely set, with too crafty a look for
honesty. He wore no beard, and his leathery cheeks
were blue from the razor. His age may have been
fifty; his air was mean and sycophantic. Finally he

was dressed in a black gaberdine that descended to his knees, and he ended in a pair of the leanest shanks and largest feet conceivable.

To greet us he fawned and washed his bony hands in the air.

"You have made a safe journey, then," he purred. "Benedicamus Dominum!"

"Deo gratias!" rumbled the fat priest, as he heaved his rotundity from the saddle with the assistance of one of the grooms.

They shook hands, and Fifanti turned to survey me for the second time.

"And this is my noble charge!" said he. "Salve! Be welcome to my house, Messer Agostino."

I got to earth, accepted his proffered hand, and thanked him.

Meanwhile the grooms were unpacking my baggage, and from the house came hurrying an elderly servant to receive it and convey it within doors.

I stood there a little awkwardly, shifting from leg to leg, what time Doctor Fifanti pressed Arcolano to come within and rest; he spoke, too, of some Vesuvian wine that had been sent him from the South and upon which he desired the priest's rare judgment.

Arcolano hesitated, and his gluttonous mouth quivered and twitched. But he excused himself, nevertheless. He must on. He had business to discharge in the town, and he must return at once and render an account of our safe journey to the Countess at Mondolfo. If he tarried now it would grow late ere he reached Mondolfo, and late travelling pleased him not at all. As it was his bones would be weary and his flesh tender from so much riding; but he would offer it up to Heaven for his sins.

And when the too-amiable Fifanti had protested how little there could be the need in the case of one so saintly as Messer Arcolano, the priest made his farewells. He gave me his blessing and enjoined upon me obedience to one who stood to me in loco parentis, heaved himself back on to his mule, and departed with the grooms at his heels.

Then Doctor Fifanti set a bony hand upon my shoulder, and opined that after my journey I must be in need of refreshment. With that he led me within doors, assuring me that in his house the needs of the body were as closely cared for as the needs of the mind.

"For an empty belly," he ended with his odious, sycophantic geniality, "makes an empty heart and an empty head."

We passed through a hall that was prettily paved in mosaics, into a chamber of good proportions, which seemed gay to me after the gloom by which I had ever been surrounded.

The ceiling was painted blue and flecked with golden stars, whilst the walls were hung with deep blue tapestries on which was figured in grey and brownish red a scene which, I was subsequently to learn, represented the metamorphosis of Actæon. At the moment I did not look too closely. The figures of Diana in her bath with her plump attendant nymphs caused me quickly to withdraw my bashful eyes.

A good-sized table stood in the middle of the floor, bearing, upon a broad strip of embroidered white napery, sparkling crystal and silver, vessels of wine and platters of early fruits. About it sat a very noble company of some half-dozen men and two very resplendent women. One of these was slight and little, very dark and vivacious, with eyes full of a malicious humour. The other, of very noble proportions, of a fine, willowy height, with coiled ropes of hair of a colour such as I had never dreamed could be found upon human being. It was ruddy and glowed like metal. Her face and neck — and of the latter there was a very considerable display — were of the warm pale tint of old ivory. She had large, low-lidded eyes, which lent her face a languid air. Her brow was low and broad, and her lips of a most startling red against the pallor of the rest.

She rose instantly upon my entrance, and came towards me with a slow smile, holding out her hand, and murmuring words of most courteous welcome.

"This, Ser Agostino," said Fifanti, "is my wife."

Had he announced her to be his daughter it would have been more credible on the score of their respective years, though equally incredible on the score of their respective personalities.

I gaped foolishly in my amazement, a little dazzled, too, by the effulgence of her eyes, which were now raised to the level of my own. I lowered my glance abashed, and answered her as courteously as I could. Then she led me to the table, and presented me to the company, naming each to me.

The first was a slim and very dainty young gentle-man in a scarlet walking-suit, over which he wore a long scarlet mantle. A gold cross was suspended from his neck by a massive chain of gold. He was delicately featured, with a little pointed beard, tiny mustachios, and long, fair hair that fell in waves about his effemi-nate face. He had the whitest of hands, very delicately veined in blue, and it was — as I soon observed — his habit to carry them raised, so that the blood might not flow into them to coarsen their beauty. Attached to his left wrist by a fine chain was a gold pomander-ball of the size of a small apple, very beautifully chiselled. Upon one of his fingers he wore the enormous sapphire ring of his rank.

That he was a prince of the Church I saw for myself; but I was far from being prepared for the revelation of his true eminence — never dreaming that a man of the humble position of Doctor Fifanti would entertain a guest so exalted.

He was no less a person than the Lord Egidio Oberto Gambara, Cardinal of Brescia, Governor of Piacenza and Papal Legate to Cisalpine Gaul.

The revelation of the identity of this elegant, effeminate, perfumed personage was a shock to me; for it was not thus by much that I had pictured the representative of our Holy Father the Pope.

He smiled upon me amiably and something wearily, the satiate smile of the man of the world, and he languidly held out to me the hand bearing his ring. I knelt to kiss it, overawed by his ecclesiastical rank, however little awed by the man within it.

As I rose again he looked up at me considering my inches.

"Why," said he, "here is a fine soldier lost to glory." And as he spoke, he half turned to a young man who sat beside him, a man at whom I was eager to take a fuller look, for his face was most strangely familiar to me.

He was tall and graceful, very beautifully dressed in purple and gold, and his blue-black hair was held in a net or coif of finest gold thread. His garments clung as tightly and smoothly as if he had been kneaded into them — as, indeed, he had. But it was his face that held my eyes. It was a sun-tanned, shaven hawk-face with black level brows, black eyes, and a strong jaw, handsome, save for something displeasing in the lines of the mouth, something sardonic, proud, and contemptuous.

The Cardinal addressed him. "You breed fine fellows in your family, Cosimo," were the words with which he startled me, and then I knew where I had seen that face before. In my mirror.

He was as like me — save that he was blacker and not so tall — as if he had been own brother to me instead of merely cousin as I knew at once he was. For he must be that Guelphic Anguissola renegade who served the Pope and was high in favour with Farnese, and Captain of Justice in Piacenza. In age he may have been some seven or eight years older than myself.

I stared at him now with interest, and I found attractions in him, the chief of which was his likeness to my father. So must my father have looked when he was this fellow's age. He returned my glance with a smile that did not improve his countenance, so contemptuously languid was it, so very supercilious.

"You may stare, cousin," said he, "for I think I do you the honour to be something like you."

"You will find him," lisped the Cardinal to me, "the most self-complacent dog in Italy. When he sees in you a likeness to himself he flatters himself grossly, which, as you know him better, you will discover to be his inveterate habit. He is his own most

assiduous courtier." And my Lord Gambara sank
back into his chair, languishing, the pomander to his
nostrils.

All laughed, and Messer Cosimo with them, still
considering me.

But Messer Fifanti's wife had yet to make me
known to three others who sat there beside the little
sloe-eyed lady. This last was a cousin of her own —
Donna Leocadia degli Allogati, whom I saw now for
the first and last time.

The three remaining men of the company are of
little interest save one, whose name was to be well
known — nay, was well known already, though not to
one who had lived in such seclusion as mine.

This was that fine poet Annibale Caro, whom I
have heard judged to be all but the equal of the great
Petrarca himself. A man who had less the air of a
poet it would not be easy to conceive. He was of
middle height and of a habit of body inclining to
portliness, and his age may have been forty. His face
was bearded, ruddy, and small-featured, and there
was about him an air of smug prosperity; he was
dressed with care, but he had none of the splendour of
the Cardinal or my cousin. Let me add that he was
secretary to the Duke Pier Luigi Farnese, and that he
was here in Piacenza on a mission to the Governor in
which his master's interests were concerned.

The other two who completed that company are of
no account, and indeed their names escape me, though
I seem to remember that one was named Pacini and
that he was said to be a philosopher of considerable
parts.

Bidden to table by Messer Fifanti, I took the chair

he offered me beside his lady, and presently came the
old servant whom already I had seen, bearing meat
for me. I was hungry, and I fell to with zest, what
time a pleasant ripple of talk ran round the board.
Facing me sat my cousin, and I never observed until
my hunger was become less clamorous with what an
insistence he regarded me. At last, however, our eyes
met across the board. He smiled that crooked, somewhat unpleasant smile of his.

"And so, Ser Agostino, they are to make a priest of
you?" said he.

"God pleasing," I answered soberly, and perhaps
shortly.

"And if his brains at all resemble his body," lisped
the Cardinal-Legate, "you may live to see an
Anguissola Pope, my Cosimo."

My stare must have betrayed my amazement at
such words. "Not so, Magnificent," I made answer.
"I am destined for the life monastic."

"Monastic!" quoth he, in a sort of horror, and
looking as if an evil smell had suddenly assailed his
nostrils. He shrugged and pouted and had fresh recourse to his pomander. "Oh, well! Friars have become popes before to-day."

"I am to enter the hermit order of Saint Augustine,"
I again corrected.

"Ah!" said Caro, in his big, full voice. "He aspires
not to Rome, but to Heaven, my lord."

"Then what the devil does he in your house,
Fifanti?" quoth the Cardinal. "Are you to teach him
sanctity?"

And the table shook with laughter at a jest I did
not understand any more than I understood my Lord
Cardinal.

Messer Fifanti, from his place at the head of the board, shot me a glance of anxious inquiry; he smiled foolishly, and washed his hands in the air again, his mind fumbling for an answer that should turn that barbed jest aside. But he was forestalled by my cousin Cosimo.

"The teaching might come more aptly from Monna Giuliana," said he, and smiled very boldly across at Fifanti's lady who sat beside me, whilst a frown grew upon the prodigious brow of the pedant.

"Indeed, indeed," the Cardinal murmured, considering her through half-closed eyes, "there is no man but may enter Paradise at her bidding." And he sighed furiously, whilst she chid him for his boldness; and for all that much of what they said was in a language that might have been unknown to me, yet was I lost in amazement to see a prelate made so free with. She turned to me, and the glory of her eyes fell about my soul like an effulgence.

"Do not heed them, Ser Agostino. They are profane and wicked men," she said, "and if you aspire to holiness, the less you see of them the better will it be for you."

I did not doubt it, yet I dared not make so bold as to confess it, and I wondered why they should laugh to hear her earnest censure of them.

"It is a thorny path, this path of holiness," said the Cardinal, sighing.

"Your excellency has been told so, we assume," quoth Caro, who had a very bitter tongue for one who looked so well-nourished and contented.

"I might have found it so for myself but that my lot has been cast among sinners," answered the

Cardinal, comprehending the company in his glance and gesture. "As it is, I do what I can to mend their lot. Non ignara mali, miseris succurrere disco."

"Now here is gallantry of a different sort!" cried the little Leocadia with a giggle.

"Oh, as to that," quoth Cosimo, showing his fine teeth in a smile, " there is a proverb as to the gallantry of priests. It is like the love of women, which again is like water in a basket — as soon in as out." And his eyes hung upon Giuliana.

"When you are the basket, sir captain, shall any one blame the women?" she countered with her lazy insolence.

"Body of God!" cried the Cardinal, and laughed whole-heartedly, whilst my cousin scowled. "There you have the truth, Cosimo, and the truth is better than proverbs."

"It is unlucky to speak of the dead at table," put in Caro.

"And who spoke of the dead, Messer Annibale?" quoth Leocadia.

"Did not my Lord Cardinal mention Truth?" answered the brutal poet.

"You are a derider — a gross sinner," said the Cardinal languidly. "Stick to your verses, man, and leave Truth alone."

"Agreed — if your excellency will stick to Truth and quit writing verses. I offer the compact in the interest of humanity."

The company shook with laughter at this direct and offensive hit. But my Lord Gambara seemed nowise incensed. Indeed, I was beginning to conclude that the man was of a singularly sweet and tolerant nature.

He sipped his wine thoughtfully, and held it up to the light so that the deep ruby of it sparkled in the Venetian crystal.

"You remind me that I have written a new song," said he.

"Then have I sinned, indeed," groaned Caro.

But Gambara, disregarding the interruption, his glass still raised, his mild eyes upon the wine, began to recite:

> "Bacchus sæpe visitans
> Mulierum genus
> Facit eas subditas
> Tibi, O tu Venus!"

Without completely understanding it, yet scandalized beyond measure at as much as I understood, to hear such sentiments upon his priestly lips, I stared at him in candid horror.

But he got no further. Caro smote the table with his fist.

"When wrote you that, my lord?" he cried.

"When?" quoth the Cardinal, frowning at the interruption. "Why, yestereve."

"Ha!" It was something between a bark and a laugh from Messer Caro. "In that case, my lord, memory usurped the place of invention. That song was sung at Pavia when I was a student — which is more years ago than I care to think of."

The Cardinal smiled upon him, unabashed. "And what, then, pray? Can we avoid these things? Why, the very Virgil whom you plagiarize so freely was himself a plagiarist."

Now this, as you may well conceive, provoked a

discussion about the board, in which all joined, not excepting Fifanti's lady and Donna Leocadia.

I listened in some amazement and deep interest to matters that were entirely strange to me, to the arguing of mysteries which seemed to me — even from what I heard of them — to be singularly attractive.

Anon Fifanti took part in the discussion, and I observed how as soon as he began to speak they all fell silent. All listened to him as to a master, what time he delivered himself of his opinions and criticisms of this Virgil, with a force, a lucidity, and an eloquence that revealed his learning even to one so ignorant as myself.

He was listened to with deference by all, if we except perhaps my Lord Gambara, who had no respect for anything and who preferred to whisper to Leocadia under cover of his hand, ogling her what time she simpered. Once or twice Monna Giuliana flashed him an unfriendly glance, and this I accounted natural, deeming that she resented this lack of attention to the erudite dissertation of her husband.

But as for the others, they were attentive, as I have said, and even Messer Caro, who at the time — as I gathered then — was engaged upon a translation of Virgil into Tuscan, and who, therefore, might be accounted something of an authority, held his peace and listened what time the Doctor reasoned and discoursed.

Fifanti's mean, sycophantic air fell away from him as by magic. Warmed by his subject and his enthusiasm he seemed suddenly ennobled, and I found him less antipathic; indeed, I began to see something admirable in the man, some of that divine quality that only deep culture and learning can impart. I conceived that now, at last, I held the explanation of how it came to pass that so distinguished a company frequented his house and gathered on such familiar terms about his board.

And I began to be less amazed at the circumstance that he should possess for wife so beautiful and superb a creature as Madonna Giuliana. I thought that I obtained glimpses of the charm which that elderly man might be able to exert upon a fine and cultured young nature with aspirations for things above the commonplace.

CHAPTER II

HUMANITIES

AS the days passed into weeks, and these, in their turn, accumulated into months, I grew rapidly learned in worldly matters at Doctor Fifanti's house.

The curriculum I now pursued was so vastly different from that which my mother had bidden Fra Gervasio to set me, and my acquaintance with the profane writers advanced so swiftly once it was engaged upon them, that I acquired knowledge as a weed grows.

Fifanti flung into strange passions when he discovered the extent of my ignorance and the amazing circumstance that, whilst Fra Gervasio had made of me a fluent Latin scholar, he had kept me in utter ignorance of the classic writers, and almost in as great an ignorance of history itself. This the pedant set himself at once to redress, and amongst the earliest works he gave me as preparation were Latin translations of Thucydides and Herodotus, which I devoured — especially the glowing pages of the latter — at a speed that alarmed my tutor.

But mere studiousness was not my spur, as he imagined. I was enthralled by the novelty of the matters that I read, so different from all those with which I had been allowed to become acquainted hitherto.

There followed Tacitus, and after him Cicero and Livy, which latter two I found less arresting; then

came Lucretius, and his "De Rerum Naturæ" proved
a succulent dish to my inquisitive appetite.

But the cream and glory of the ancient writers I had
yet to taste. My first acquaintance with the poets
came from the translation of Virgil upon which
Messer Caro was at the time engaged. He had
definitely taken up his residence in Piacenza, whither
it was said that Farnese, his master, who was to be
made our Duke, would shortly come. And in the
interval of labouring for Farnese, as Caro was doing,
he would toil at his translation, and from time to time
he would bring sheaves of his manuscript to the
Doctor's house, to read what he had accomplished.

He came, I remember, one languid afternoon in
August, when I had been with Messer Fifanti for close
upon three months, during which time my mind had
gradually, yet swiftly, been opening out like a bud
under the sunlight of much new learning. We sat in
the fine garden behind the house, on the lawn, in the
shade of mulberry trees laden with yellow translucent
fruit, by a pond that was all afloat with water-lilies.

There was a crescent-shaped seat of hewn marble,
over which Messer Gambara, who was with us, had
thrown his scarlet cardinal's cloak, the day being
oppressively hot. He was as usual in plain, walking
clothes, and save for the ring on his finger and the
cross on his breast, you had never conceived him an
ecclesiastic. He sat near his cloak, upon the marble
seat, and beside him sat Monna Giuliana, who was all
in white save for the gold girdle at her waist.

Caro, himself, stood to read, his bulky manuscript
in his hands. Against the sundial, facing the poet,
leaned the tall figure of Messer Fifanti, his bald head

uncovered and shining humidly, his eyes ever and anon stealing a look at his splendid wife where she sat so demurely at the prelate's side.

Myself, I lay on the grass near the pond, my hand trailing in the cool water, and at first I was not greatly interested. The heat of the day and the circumstance that we had dined, when added to the poet's booming and somewhat monotonous voice, had a lulling effect from which I was in danger of falling asleep. But anon, as the narrative warmed and quickened, the danger was well overpast. I was very wide-awake, my pulses throbbing, my imagination all on fire. I sat up and listened with an enthralled attention, unconscious of everything and everybody, unconscious even of the very voice of the reader, intent only upon the amazing, tragic matter that he read.

For it happened that this was the Fourth Book of the "Æneid," and the most lamentable, heartrending story of Dido's love for Æneas, of his desertion of her, of her grief and death upon the funeral pyre.

It held me spellbound. It was more real than anything that I had ever read or heard; and the fate of Dido moved me as if I had known and loved her; so that long ere Messer Caro came to an end I was weeping freely in a most exquisite misery.

Thereafter I was as one who has tasted strong wine and finds his thirst fired by it. Within a week I had read the "Æneid" through, and was reading it a second time. Then came the Comedies of Terence, the "Metamorphoses" of Ovid, Martial, and the Satires of Juvenal. And with those my transformation was complete. No longer could I find satisfaction in the writings of the fathers of the Church, or in

contemplating the lives of the saints, after the pag-
eantries which the eyes of my soul had looked upon
in the profane authors.

What instructions my mother supposed Fifanti to
have received concerning me from Arcolano, I cannot
think. But certain it is that she could never have
dreamed under what influences I was so soon to come,
no more than she could conceive what havoc they
played with all that hitherto I had learnt and with the
resolutions which I had formed — and which she had
formed for me — concerning the future.

All this reading perturbed me very oddly, as one
is perturbed who having long dwelt in darkness is
suddenly brought into the sunlight and dazzled by it,
so that, grown conscious of his sight, he is more effectively blinded than he was before. For the process that should have been a gradual one from tender
years was carried through in what amounted to little
more than a few weeks.

My Lord Gambara took an odd interest in me. He
was something of a philosopher in his trivial way;
something of a student of his fellow-man; and he
looked upon me as an odd human growth that was
being subjected to an unusual experiment. I think
he took a certain delight in helping that experiment
forward; and certain it is that he had more to do
with the debauching of my mind than any other, or
than any reading that I did.

It was not that he told me more than elsewhere I
could have learnt; it was the cynical manner in which
he conveyed his information. He had a way of telling
me of monstrous things as if they were purely normal
and natural to a properly focussed eye, and as if any

monstrousness they might present to me were due to some distortion imparted to them solely by the imperfection of my intellectual vision.

Thus it was from him that I learnt certain unsuspected things concerning Pier Luigi Farnese, who, it was said, was coming to be our Duke, and on whose behalf the Emperor was being importuned to invest him in the Duchy of Parma and Piacenza.

One day as we walked together in the garden — my Lord Gambara and I — I asked him plainly what was Messer Farnese's claim.

"His claim?" quoth he, checking, to give me a long, cool stare. He laughed shortly and resumed his pacing, I keeping step with him. "Why, is he not the Pope's son, and is not that claim enough?"

"The Pope's son!" I exclaimed. "But how is it possible that the Holy Father should have a son?"

"How is it possible?" he echoed mockingly. "Why, I will tell you, sir. When our present Holy Father went as Cardinal-Legate to the Mark of Ancona, he met there a certain lady whose name was Lola, who pleased him, and who was pleased with him. Alessandro Farnese was a handsome man, Ser Agostino. She bore him three children, of whom one is dead, another is Madonna Costanza, who is wed to Sforza of Santafiora, and the third — who really happens to have been the first-born — is Messer Pier Luigi, present Duke of Castro and future Duke of Piacenza."

It was some time ere I could speak.

"But his vows, then?" I exclaimed at last.

"Ah! His vows!" said the Cardinal-Legate. "True, there were his vows. I had forgotten that. No doubt he did the same." And he smiled sardonically, sniffing at his pomander-ball.

From that beginning in a fresh branch of knowledge much followed quickly. Under my questionings, Messer Gambara very readily made me acquainted through his unsparing eyes with that cesspool that was known as the Roman Curia. And my horror, my disillusionment increased at every word he said.

I learnt from him that Pope Paul III was no exception to the rule, no such scandal as I had imagined; that his own elevation to the purple was due in origin to the favour which his sister, the beautiful Giulia, had found in the eyes of the Borgia Pope, some fifty years ago. Through him I came to know the Sacred College as it really was; not the very home and fount of Christianity, as I had deemed it, controlled and guided by men of a sublime saintliness of ways, but a gathering of ambitious worldlings, who had become so brazen in their greed of temporal power that they did not even trouble to cloak the sin and evil in which they lived; men in whom the spirit that had actuated those saints, the study of whose lives had been my early delight, lived no more than it might live in the bosom of a harlot.

I said so to him one day in a wild, furious access of boldness, in one of those passionate outbursts that are begotten of illusions blighted.

He heard me through quite calmly, without the least trace of anger, smiling ever his quiet, mocking smile, and plucking at his little, auburn beard.

"You are wrong, I think," he said. "Say that the Church has fallen a prey to self-seekers who have entered it under the cloak of the priesthood. What

then? In their hands the Church has been enriched.
She has gained power, which she must retain. And
that is to the Church's good."

"And what of the scandal of it?" I stormed.

"Oh, as to that — why, boy, have you never read
Boccaccio?"

"Never," said I.

"Read him, then," he urged me. "He will teach
you much that you need to know. And read in
particular the story of Abraham, the Jew, who upon
visiting Rome was so scandalized by the licence and
luxury of the clergy that he straightway had himself
baptized and became a Christian, accounting that a
religion that could survive such wiles of Satan to
destroy it must, indeed, be the true religion, divinely
inspired." He laughed his little cynical laugh to see
my confusion increased by that bitter paradox.

It is little wonder that I was all bewildered, that I
was like some poor mariner upon unknown waters,
without stars or compass.

Thus that summer ebbed slowly, and the time of
my projected minor ordination approached. Messer
Gambara's visits to Fifanti's grew more and more
frequent, until they became a daily occurrence; and
now my cousin Cosimo came oftener too. But it was
their custom to come in the forenoon, when I was at
work with Fifanti. And often I observed the Doctor
to be oddly preoccupied, and to spend much time in
creeping to the window that was all wreathed in
clematis, and in peeping through that purple-decked
green curtain into the garden where his excellency and
Cosimo walked with Monna Giuliana.

When both visitors were there his anxiety seemed

less. But if only one were present he would give himself no peace. And once when Messer Gambara and
she went together within doors, he abruptly interrupted my studies, saying that it was enough for that
day; and he went below to join them.

Half a year earlier I should have had no solution for
his strange behaviour. But I had learnt enough of the
world by now to perceive what maggot was stirring in
that egg-shaped head. Yet I blushed for him, and for
his foul and unworthy suspicions. As soon would I
have suspected the painted Madonna from the brush
of Raffaele Santi that I had seen over the high altar of
the Church of San Sisto, as suspect the beautiful and
noble-souled Giuliana of giving that old pedant cause
for his uneasiness. Still, I conceived that this was the
penalty that such a withered growth of humanity
must pay for having presumed to marry a young wife.

We were much together in those days, Monna
Giuliana and I. Our intimacy had grown over a little
incident that it were well I should mention.

A young painter, Gianantonio Regillo, better
known to the world as "Il Pordenone," had come to
Piacenza that summer to decorate the Church of
Santa Maria della Campagna. He came furnished
with letters to the Governor, and Gambara had
brought him to Fifanti's villa. From Monna Giuliana
the young painter heard the curious story of my having been vowed prenatally to the cloister by my
mother, learnt her name and mien, and the hope that
was entertained that I should walk in the ways of
Saint Augustine after whom I had been christened.

It happened that he was about to paint a picture of
Saint Augustine, as a fresco for the chapel of the Magi

of the church I have named. And having seen me and heard that story of mine, he conceived the curious notion of using me as the model for the figure of the saint. I consented, and daily for a week he came to us in the afternoons to paint; and all the time Monna Giuliana would be with us, deeply interested in his work.

That picture he eventually transferred to his fresco, and there — oh, bitter irony! — you may see me to this day, as the saint in whose ways it was desired that I should follow.

Monna Giuliana and I would linger together in talk after the painter had gone; and this would be at about the time that I had my first lessons of Curial life from my Lord Gambara. You will remember that he mentioned Boccaccio to me, and I chanced to ask her was there in the library a copy of that author's tales.

"Has that wicked priest bidden you to read them?" she inquired, 'twixt seriousness and mockery, her dark eyes upon me in one of those glances that never left me easy.

I told her what had passed; and with a sigh and a comment that I would get an indigestion from so much mental nourishment as I was consuming, she led me to the little library to find the book.

Messer Fifanti's was a very choice collection of works, and every one in manuscript; for the Doctor was something of an idealist, and greatly averse to the printing-press and the wide dissemination of books to which it led. Out of his opposition to the machine grew a dislike for its productions, which he denounced as vulgar; and not even their comparative cheapness and the fact that, when all was said, he was a man of limited means, would induce him to harbour a single volume that was so produced.

Along the shelves she sought, and finally drew down four heavy tomes. Turning the pages of the first, she found there, with a readiness that argued a good acquaintance with the work, the story of Abraham the Jew, which I desired to read as it had been set down. She bade me read it aloud, which I did, she seated in the window, listening to me.

At first I read with some constraint and shyness, but presently warming to my task and growing interested, I became animated and vivacious in my manner, so that when I ceased I saw her sitting there, her hands clasped about one knee, her eyes upon my face, her lips parted a little, the very picture of interest.

And with that it happened that we established a custom, and very often, almost daily, after dinner, we would repair together to the library; and I — who hitherto had no acquaintance with any save Latin works — began to make and soon to widen my knowledge of our Tuscan writers. We varied our reading. We dipped into our poets. Dante we read, and Petrarca, and both we loved, though better than the works of either — and this for the sake of the swift movement and action that is in his narrative, though his melodies, I realized, were not so pure — the "Orlando" of Ariosto.

Sometimes we would be joined by Fifanti himself; but he never stayed very long. He had an old-fashioned contempt for writings in what he called the "dialettale," and he loved the solemn circumlocutions of the Latin tongue. Soon, as he listened, he would begin to yawn, and presently grunt and rise and depart, flinging a contemptuous word at the matter of my reading, and telling me at times that I might find more profitable amusement.

But I persisted in it, guided ever by Fifanti's lady. And whatever we read by way of divergence, ever and anon we would come back to the stilted, lucid, vivid pages of Boccaccio.

One day I chanced upon the tragical story of "Isabetta and the Pot of Basil," and whilst I read I was conscious that she had moved from where she had been sitting, and had come to stand behind my chair. And when I reached the point at which the heart-broken Isabetta takes the head of her murdered lover to her room, a tear fell suddenly upon my hand.

I stopped, and looked up at Giuliana. She smiled at me through unshed tears that magnified her matchless eyes.

"I will read no more," I said. "It is too sad."

"Ah, no!" she begged. "Read on, Agostino! I love its sadness."

So I read on to the story's cruel end, and when it was done I sat quite still, myself a little moved by the tragedy of it, whilst Giuliana continued to lean against my chair. I was moved, too, in another way; curiously and unaccountably; and I could scarcely have defined what it was that moved me.

I sought to break the spell of it, and turned the pages.

"Let me read something else," said I. "Something more gay, to dispel the sadness of this."

But her hand fell suddenly upon mine, enclasping and holding it. "Ah, no!" she begged me gently. "Give me the book. Let us read no more to-day."

I was trembling under her touch — trembling, my every nerve aquiver and my breath shortened — and suddenly there flashed through my mind a line of Dante's in the story of Paolo and Francesca:

"Quel giorno più non vi leggemo avanti."

Giuliana's words: "Let us read no more to-day" — had seemed an echo of that line, and the echo made me of a sudden conscious of an unsuspected parallel. All at once our position seemed to me strangely similar to that of the ill-starred lovers of Rimini.

But the next moment I was sane again. She had withdrawn her hand, and had taken the volume to restore it to its shelf.

Ah, no! At Rimini there had been two fools. Here there was but one. Let me make an end of him by persuading him of his folly.

Yet Giuliana did nothing to assist me in that task. She returned from the book-shelf, and in passing lightly swept her fingers over my hair.

"Come, Agostino; let us walk in the garden," said she.

We went, my mood now overpast. I was as sober and self-contained as was my habit. And soon thereafter came my Lord Gambara — a rare thing to happen in the afternoon.

Awhile the three of us were together in the garden, talking of trivial matters. Then she fell to wrangling with him concerning something that Caro had written and of which she had the manuscript. In the end she begged me would I go seek the writing in her chamber. I went, and hunted where she had bidden me and elsewhere, and spent a good ten minutes vainly in the task. Chagrined that I could not discover the thing, I went into the library, thinking that it might be there.

Doctor Fifanti was writing busily at the table when I intruded. He looked up, thrusting his horn-rimmed spectacles high upon his peaked forehead.

"What the devil!" quoth he very testily. "I thought you in the garden with Madonna Giuliana."

"My Lord Gambara is there," said I.

He crimsoned and banged the table with his bony hand.

"Do I not know that?" he roared, though I could see no reason for all this heat. "And why are you not with them?"

You are not to suppose that I was still the meek, sheepish lad who had come to Piacenza three months ago. I had not been learning my humanities and discovering Man to no purpose all this while.

"It has yet to be explained to me," said I, "under what obligation I am to be anywhere but where I please. That firstly. Secondly — but of infinitely lesser moment — Monna Giuliana has sent me for the manuscript of Messer Caro's 'Gigli d'Oro.'"

I know not whether it was my cool, firm tones that quieted him. But quiet he became.

"I . . . I was vexed by your interruption," he said lamely. "Here is the thing. I found it here when I came. Messer Caro might discover better employment for his leisure. But there, there" — he seemed in sudden haste again. "Take it to her in God's name. She will be impatient." I thought he sneered. "Oh, she will praise your diligence," he added, and this time I was sure that he sneered.

I took it, thanked him, and left the room intrigued.

And when I rejoined them, and handed her the manuscript, the odd thing was that the subject of their discourse having meanwhile shifted, it no longer interested her, and she never once opened the pages she had been in such haste to have me procure.

This, too, was puzzling, even to one who was beginning to know his world.

But I was not done with riddles. For presently out came Fifanti himself, looking, if possible, yellower and more sour and lean than usual. He was arrayed in his long, rusty gown, and there were the usual shabby slippers on his long, lean feet. He was ever a man of most indifferent personal habits.

"Ah, Astorre," his wife greeted him. "My Lord Cardinal brings you good tidings."

"Does he so?" quoth Fifanti, sourly as I thought; and he looked at the legate as though his excellency were anything but a happy harbinger.

"You will rejoice, I think, Doctor," said the smiling prelate, "to hear that I have letters from my Lord Pier Luigi appointing you one of the ducal secretaries. And this, I doubt not, will be followed, on his coming hither, by an appointment to his council. Meanwhile, the stipend is three hundred ducats, and the work is light."

There followed a long and baffling silence, during which the Doctor grew first red, then pale, then red again, and Messer Gambara stood with his scarlet cloak sweeping about his shapely limbs, sniffing his pomander and smiling almost insolently into the other's face; and some of the insolence of his look, I thought, was reflected upon the pale, placid countenance of Giuliana.

At last, Fifanti spoke, his little eyes narrowing.

"It is too much for my poor deserts," he said curtly.

"You are too humble," said the prelate. "Your loyalty to the House of Farnese, and the hospitality which I, its deputy, have received . . ."

"Hospitality!" barked Fifanti, and looked very oddly at Giuliana; so oddly that a faint colour began to creep into her cheeks. "You would pay for that?" he questioned, half mockingly. "Oh, but for that a stipend of three hundred ducats is too little."

And all the time his eyes were upon his wife, and I saw her stiffen as if she had been struck.

But the Cardinal laughed outright. "Come, now, you use me with an amiable frankness," he said. "The stipend shall be doubled when you join the council."

"Doubled?" he said. "Six hundred . . . ?" He checked. The sum was vast. I saw greed creep into his little eyes. What had troubled him hitherto, I could not fathom even yet. He washed his bony hands in the air, and looked at his wife again. "It . . . it is a fair price, no doubt, my lord," said he, his tone contemptuous.

"The Duke shall be informed of the value of your learning," lisped the Cardinal.

Fifanti knit his brows. "The value of my learning?" he echoed, as if slowly puzzled. "My learning? Oh! Is that in question?"

"Why else should we give you the appointment?" smiled the Cardinal, with a smile that was full of significance.

"It is what the town will be asking, no doubt," said

Messer Fifanti. "I hope you will be able to satisfy its curiosity, my lord."

And on that he turned, and stalked off again, very white and trembling, as I could perceive.

My Lord Gambara laughed carelessly again, and over the pale face of Monna Giuliana there stole a slow smile, the memory of which was to be hateful to me soon, but which at the moment went to increase my already profound mystification.

CHAPTER III

PREUX-CHEVALIER

IN the days that followed I found Messer Fifanti in
queerer moods than ever. Always impatient, he
would be easily moved to anger now, and not a day
passed but he stormed at me over the Greek with
which, under his guidance, I was wrestling.

And with Giuliana his manner was the oddest conceivable; at times he was mocking as an ape; at times
his manner had in it a suggestion of the serpent; more
rarely he was his usual, vulturine self. He watched
her curiously, ever between anger and derision, to all
of which she presented a calm front and a patience
almost saintly. He was as a man with some mighty
burden on his mind, undecided whether he shall bear
it or cast it off.

Her patience moved me most oddly to pity; and
pity for so beautiful a creature is Satan's most subtle
snare, especially when you consider what a power her
beauty had to move me as I had already discovered
to my erstwhile terror. She confided in me a little in
those days, but ever with a most saintly resignation.
She had been sold into wedlock, she admitted, with a
man who might have been her father, and she confessed to finding her lot a cruel one; but confessed it
with the air of one who intends none the less to bear
her cross with fortitude.

And then, one day, I did a very foolish thing. We
had been reading together, she and I, as was become

our custom. She had fetched me a volume of the lascivious verse of Panormitano, and we sat side by side on the marble seat in the garden what time I read to her, her shoulder touching mine, the fragrance of her all about me.

She wore, I remember, a clinging gown of russet silk, which did rare justice to the splendid beauty of her, and her heavy ruddy hair was confined in a golden net that was set with gems — a gift from my Lord Gambara. Concerning this same gift words had passed but yesterday between Giuliana and her husband; and I deemed the Doctor's anger to be the fruit of a base and unworthy mind.

I read, curiously enthralled — though whether by the beauty of the lines or the beauty of the woman there beside me I could not then have told you.

Presently she checked me. "Leave now Panormitano," she said. "Here is something else upon which you shall give me your judgment." And she set before me a sheet upon which there was a sonnet writ in her own hand, which was as beautiful as any copyist's that I have ever seen.

I read the poem. It was the tenderest and saddest little cry from a heart that ached and starved for an ideal love; and good as the manner seemed, the matter itself it was that chiefly moved me. At my admission of its moving quality her white hand closed over mine as it had done that day in the library when we had read of "Isabetta and the Pot of Basil." Her hand was warm, but not warm enough to burn me as it did.

"Ah, thanks, Agostino," she murmured. "Your praise is sweet to me. The verses are my own."

I was dumbfounded at this fresh and more intimate glimpse of her. The beauty of her body was there for all to see and worship; but here was my first glimpse of the rare beauties of her mind. In what words I should have answered her I do not know, for at that moment we suffered an interruption.

Sudden and harsh as the crackling of a twig came from behind us the voice of Messer Fifanti. "What do you read?"

We started apart, and turned.

Either he, of set purpose, had crept up behind us so softly that we should not suspect his approach, or else so engrossed were we that our ears had been deafened for the time. He stood there now in his untidy gown of black, and there was a leer of mockery on his long, white face. Slowly he put a lean arm between us, and took the sheet in his bony claw.

He peered at it very closely, being without glasses, and screwed his eyes up until they all but disappeared.

Thus he stood, and slowly read, whilst I looked on, a trifle uneasy, and Giuliana's face wore an odd look of fear, her bosom heaving unsteadily in its russet sheath.

He sniffed contemptuously when he had read, and looked at me.

"Have I not bidden you leave the vulgarities of dialect to the vulgar?" quoth he. "Is there not enough written for you in Latin, that you must be wasting your time and perverting your senses with such poor illiterate gibberish as this? And what is it that you have there?" He took the book. "Panormitano!" he roared. "Now, there's a fitting author for a saint in embryo! There's fine preparation for the cloister!"

He turned to Giuliana. He put forward his hand and touched her bare shoulder with his hideous forefinger. She cringed under the touch as if it were barbed.

"There is not the need that you should render yourself his preceptress," he said, with his deadly smile.

"I do not," she replied indignantly. "Agostino has a taste for letters, and . . ."

"Tcha! Tcha!" he interrupted, tapping her shoulder sharply. "I had no thought for letters. There is my Lord Gambara, and there is Messer Cosimo d'Anguissola, and there is Messer Caro. There is even Pordenone, the painter." His lips writhed over their names. "You have friends enough, I think. Leave, then, Ser Agostino here. Do not dispute him with God to whom he has been vowed."

She rose in a fine anger, and stood quivering there, magnificently tall, and Juno, I imagined, must have looked to the poets as she looked then to me.

"This is too much!" she cried.

"It is, madam," he snapped. "I agree with you."

She considered him with eyes that held a loathing and contempt unutterable. Then she looked at me, and shrugged her shoulders as who would say: "You see how I am used!" Lastly she turned, and took her way across the lawn towards the house.

There was a little silence between us after she had gone. I was on fire with indignation, and yet I could think of no words in which I might express it, realizing how utterly I lacked the right to be angry with a husband for the manner in which he chose to treat his wife.

At last, pondering me very gravely, he spoke.

"It were best you read no more with Madonna Giuliana," he said slowly. "Her tastes are not the tastes that become a man who is about to enter holy orders." He closed the book, which hitherto he had held open; closed it with an angry snap, and held it out to me.

"Restore it to its shelf," he bade me.

I took it, and quite submissively I went to do his bidding. But to gain the library I had to pass the door of Giuliana's room. It stood open, and Giuliana herself in the doorway. We looked at each other, and seeing her so sorrowful, with tears in her great dark eyes, I stepped forward to speak, to utter something of the deep sympathy that stirred me.

She stretched forth a hand to me. I took it and held it tight, looking up into her eyes.

"Dear Agostino!" she murmured in gratitude for my sympathy; and I, distraught, inflamed by tone and look, answered by uttering her name for the first time.

"Giuliana!"

Having uttered it I dared not look at her. But I stooped to kiss the hand which she had left in mine. And having kissed it I started upright and made to advance again; but she snatched her hand from my clasp and waved me away, at once so imperiously and beseechingly that I turned and went to shut myself in the library with my bewilderment.

For full two days thereafter, for no reason that I could clearly give, I avoided her, and save at table and in her husband's presence we were never once together.

The repasts were sullen things at which there was little said, Madonna sitting in a frozen dignity, and the Doctor, a silent man at all times, being now utterly and forbiddingly mute.

But once my Lord Gambara supped with us, and he was light and trivial as ever, an incarnation of frivolity and questionable jests, apparently entirely unconscious of Fifanti's chill reserve and frequent sneers. Indeed, I greatly marvelled that a man of my Lord Gambara's eminence and Governor of Piacenza should so very amiably endure the boorishness of that pedant.

Explanation was about to be afforded me.

On the third day, as we were dining, Giuliana announced that she was going afoot into the town, and solicited my escort. It was an honour that never before had been offered me. I reddened violently, but accepted it, and soon thereafter we set out, just she and I together.

We went by way of the Fodesta Gate, and passed the old Castle of Sant' Antonio, then in ruins — for Gambara was demolishing it and employing the material to construct a barrack for the Pontifical troops that garrisoned Piacenza. And presently we came upon the works of this new building, and stepped out into mid-street to avoid the scaffoldings, and so pursued our way into the city's main square — the Piazza del Commune, overshadowed by the red-and-white bulk of the Communal Palace. This was a noble building, rather in the Saracenic manner, borrowing a very warlike air from the pointed battlements that crowned it.

Near the Duomo we came upon a great concourse

of people who were staring up at the iron cage attached to the square tower of the belfry near its summit. In this cage there was what appeared at first to be a heap of rags, but which presently resolved itself into a human shape, crouching in that narrow, cruel space, exposed there to the pitiless beating of the sun, and suffering Heaven alone can say what agonies. The murmuring crowd looked up in mingled fear and sympathy.

He had been there since last night, a peasant girl informed us, and he had been confined there by order of my Lord the Cardinal-Legate for the odious sin of sacrilege.

"What!" I cried out, in such a tone of astonished indignation that Monna Giuliana seized my arm and pressed it to enjoin prudence.

It was not until she had made her purchases in a shop under the Duomo and we were returning home that I touched upon the matter. She chid me for the lack of caution that might have led me into some unpardonable indiscretions but for her warning.

"But the very thought of such a man as my Lord Gambara torturing a poor wretch for sacrilege!" I cried. "It is grotesque; it is ludicrous; it is infamous!"

"Not so loud," she laughed. "You are being stared at." And then she delivered herself of an amazing piece of casuistry. "If a man, being a sinner himself, shall on that account refrain from punishing sin in others, then is he twice a sinner."

"It was my Lord Gambara taught you that," said I, and involuntarily I sneered.

She considered me with a very searching look.

"Now, what precisely do you mean, Agostino?"

"Why, that it is by just such sophistries that the Cardinal-Legate seeks to cloak the disorders of his life. 'Video meliora proboque, deteriora sequor': that is his philosophy. If he would encage the most sacrilegious fellow in Piacenza, let him encage himself."

"You do not love him?" said she.

"Oh — as to that — as a man he is well enough. But as an ecclesiastic . . . Oh, but there!" I broke off shortly, and laughed. "The Devil take Messer Gambara!"

She smiled. "It is greatly to be feared that he will."

But my Lord Gambara was not so lightly to be dismissed that afternoon. As we were passing the Porta Fodesta, a little group of country-folk that had gathered there fell away before us, all eyes upon the dazzling beauty of Giuliana — as, indeed, had been the case ever since we had come into the town, so that I had been singularly and sweetly proud of being her escort. I had been conscious of the envious glances that many a tall fellow had sent after me, though, after all, theirs was but as the jealousy of Phœbus for Adonis.

Wherever we had passed and eyes had followed us, men and women had fallen to whispering and pointing after us. And so did they now, here at the Fodesta Gate, but with this difference, that, at last, I overheard for once what was said, for there was one who did not whisper.

"There goes the leman of my Lord Gambara," quoth a gruff, sneering voice, "the light of love of the saintly legate who is starving Domenico to death in a cage for the sin of sacrilege."

Not a doubt but that he would have added more, but that at that moment a woman's shrill voice drowned his utterance. "Silence, Giuffrè!" she admonished him fearfully. "Silence, on your life!"

I had halted in my stride, suddenly cold from head to foot, as on that day when I had flung Rinolfo from top to bottom of the terrace steps at Mondolfo. It happened that I wore a sword for the first time in my life — a matter from which I gathered great satisfaction — having been adjudged worthy of the honour by virtue that I was to be Madonna's escort. To the hilt I now set hand impetuously, and would have turned to strike that foul slanderer dead, but that Giuliana restrained me, a wild alarm in her eyes.

"Come!" she panted in a whisper. "Come away!"

So imperious was the command that it conveyed to my mind some notion of the folly I should commit did I not obey it. I saw at once that did I make an ensample of this scurrilous scandalmonger I should thereby render her the talk of that vile town. So I went on, but very white and stiff, and breathing somewhat hard; for pent-up passion is an evil thing to house.

Thus came we out of the town and to the shady banks of gleaming Po. And then, at last, when we were quite alone, and within two hundred yards of Fifanti's house, I broke at last the silence.

I had been thinking very busily, and the peasant's words had illumined for me a score of little obscure matters, had explained to me the queer behaviour and the odd speeches of Fifanti himself since that evening in the garden when the Cardinal-Legate had announced to him his appointment as ducal secretary.

I checked now in my stride, and turned to face her.

"Was it true?" I asked, rendered brutally direct by a queer pain I felt as a result of my thinking.

She looked up into my face so sadly and wistfully that my suspicions fell from me upon the instant, and I reddened from shame at having harboured them.

"Agostino!" she cried, such a poor little cry of pain that I set my teeth hard and bowed my head in self-contempt.

Then I looked at her again.

"Yet the foul suspicion of that lout is shared by your husband himself," said I.

"The foul suspicion — yes," she answered, her eyes downcast, her cheeks faintly tinted. And then, quite suddenly, she moved forward. "Come," she bade me. "You are being foolish."

"I shall be mad," said I, "ere I have done with this." And I fell into step again beside her. "If I could not avenge you there, I can avenge you here." And I pointed to the house. "I can smite this rumour at its foulest point."

Her hand fell on my arm. "What would you do?" she cried.

"Bid your husband retract and sue to you for pardon, or else tear out his lying throat," I answered, for I was in a great rage by now.

She stiffened suddenly. "You go too fast, Messer Agostino," said she. "And you are over-eager to enter into that which does not concern you. I do not know that I have given you the right to demand of my husband reason of the manner in which he deals with me. It is a thing that touches only my husband and myself."

I was abashed; I was humiliated; I was nigh to tears. I choked it all down, and I strode on beside her, my rage smouldering within me. But it was flaring up again by the time we reached the house with no more words spoken between us. She went to her room without another glance at me, and I repaired straight in quest of Fifanti.

I found him in the library. He had locked himself in, as was his frequent habit when at his studies, but he opened to my knock. I stalked in, unbuckled my sword, and set it in a corner. Then I turned to him.

"You are doing your wife a shameful wrong, Sir Doctor," said I, with all the directness of youth and indiscretion.

He stared at me as if I had struck him — as he might have stared, rather, at a child who had struck him, undecided whether to strike back for the child's good, or to be amused and smile.

"Ah!" he said at last. "She has been talking to you?" And he clasped his hands behind him and stood before me, his head thrust forward, his legs wide apart, his long gown, which was open, clinging to his ankles.

"No," said I. "I have been thinking."

"In that case nothing will surprise me," he said in his sour, contemptuous manner. "And you have concluded . . . ?"

"That you are harbouring an infamous suspicion."

"Your assurance that it is infamous would offend me did it not comfort me," he sneered. "And what, pray, is this suspicion?"

"You suspect that . . . that — O God! I can't utter the thing."

"Take courage," he mocked me. And he thrust his head farther forward. He looked singularly like a vulture in that moment.

"You suspect that Messer Gambara . . . that Messer Gambara and Madonna . . . that . . ." I clenched my hands together, and looked into his leering face. "You understand me well enough," I cried, almost angrily.

He looked at me seriously now, a cold glitter in his small eyes.

"I wonder do you understand yourself?" he asked. "I think not. I think not. Since God has made you a fool, it but remains for man to make you a priest, and thus complete God's work."

"You cannot move me by your taunts," I said. "You have a foul mind, Messer Fifanti."

He approached me slowly, his untidily shod feet slip-slopping on the wooden floor.

"Because," said he, "I suspect that Messer Gambara . . . that Messer Gambara and Madonna . . . that . . . You understand me," he mocked me, with a mimicry of my own confusion. "And what affair may it be of yours whom I suspect or of what I suspect them where my own are concerned?"

"It is my affair, as it is the affair of every man who would be accounted gentle, to defend the honour of a pure and saintly lady from the foul aspersions of slander."

"Knight-errantry, by the Host!" quoth he, and his brows shot up on his steep brow. Then they came down again to scowl. "No doubt, my preux-chevalier, you will have definite knowledge of the groundlessness of these same slanders," he said, moving backwards, away from me, towards the door; and as he moved now his feet made no sound, though I did not yet notice this nor, indeed, his movement at all.

"Knowledge?" I roared at him. "What knowledge can you need beyond what is afforded by her face? Look in it, Messer Fifanti, if you would see innocence and purity and chastity! Look in it!"

"Very well," said he. "Let us look in it."

And quite suddenly he pulled the door open to disclose Giuliana standing there, erect but in a listening attitude.

"Look in it!" he mocked me, and waved one of his bony hands towards that perfect countenance.

There was shame and confusion in her face, and some anger. But she turned without a word, and went quickly down the passage, followed by his evil, cackling laugh.

Then he looked at me quite solemnly. "I think," said he, "you had best get to your studies. You will find more than enough to engage you there. Leave my affairs to me, boy."

There was almost a menace in his voice, and after what had happened it was impossible to pursue the matter.

Sheepishly, overwhelmed with confusion, I went out — a knight-errant with a shorn crest.

CHAPTER IV

MY LORD GAMBARA CLEARS THE GROUND

I HAD angered her! Worse; I had exposed her to humiliation at the hands of that unworthy animal who defiled her in thought with the slime of his suspicions. Through me she had been put to the shameful need of listening at a door, and had been subjected to the ignominy of being so discovered. Through me she had been mocked and derided!

It was all anguish to me. For her there was no shame, no humiliation, no pain I would not suffer, and take joy in the suffering so that it be for her. But to have submitted that sweet, angelic woman to suffering — to have incurred her just anger! Woe me!

I came to the table that evening full of uneasiness, very unhappy, feeling it an effort to bring myself into her presence and endure be it her regard or her neglect. To my relief she sent word that she was not well and would keep her chamber; and Fifanti smiled oddly as he stroked his blue chin and gave me a sidelong glance. We ate in silence, and when the meal was done, I departed, still without a word to my preceptor, and went to shut myself up again in my room.

I slept ill that night, and very early next morning I was astir. I went down into the garden somewhere about the hour of sunrise, through the wet grass that was all scintillant with dew. On the marble bench by the pond, where the water-lilies were now rotting, I flung myself down, and there was I found a half-hour later by Giuliana herself.

She stole up gently behind me, and all absorbed and moody as I was, I had no knowledge of her presence until her crisp boyish voice startled me out of my musings.

"Of what do we brood here so early, Sir Saint?" quoth she.

I turned to meet her laughing eyes. "You . . . you can forgive me?" I faltered foolishly.

She pouted tenderly. "Should I not forgive one who has acted foolishly out of love for me?"

"It was, it was . . ." I cried; and there stopped, all confused, feeling myself growing red under her lazy glance.

"I know it was," she answered. She set her elbows on the seat's tall back until I could feel her sweet breath upon my brow. "And should I bear you a resentment, then? My poor Agostino, have I no heart to feel? Am I but a cold, reasoning intelligence like that thing my husband? O God! To have been mated to that withered pedant! To have been sacrificed, to have been sold into such bondage! Me miserable!"

"Giuliana!" I murmured soothingly, yet agonized myself.

"Could none have foretold me that you must come some day?"

"Hush!" I implored her. "What are you saying?"

But though I begged her to be silent, my soul was avid for more such words from her — from her, the most perfect and beautiful of women.

"Why should I not?" said she. "Is truth ever to be stifled? Ever?"

I was mad, I know — quite mad. Her words had made me so. And when, to ask me that insistent question, she brought her face still nearer, I flung down the reins of my unreason and let it ride amain upon its desperate, reckless course. In short, I too leaned forward. I leaned forward, and I kissed her full upon those scarlet, parted lips.

I kissed her, and fell back with a cry that was of anguish almost — so poignantly had the sweet, fierce pain of that kiss run through my every nerve. And as I cried out, so too did she, stepping back, her hands suddenly to her face. But the next moment she was peering up at the windows of the house — those inscrutable eyes that looked upon our deed; that looked and of which it was impossible to discern how much they might have seen.

"If he should have seen us!" was her cry; and it moved me unpleasantly that such should have been the first thought my kiss inspired in her. "If he should have seen us! Gesù! I have enough to bear already!"

"I care not," said I. "Let him see. I am not Messer Gambara. No man shall put an insult upon you on my account, and live."

I was become the very ranting, roaring, fire-breathing type of lover who will slaughter a whole world to do pleasure to his mistress or to spare her pain — I — I — I, Agostino d'Anguissola — who was to be ordained next month and walk in the ways of Saint Augustine!

Laugh as you read — for very pity, laugh!

"Nay, nay," she reassured herself. "He will be still abed. He was snoring when I left." And she dismissed her fears, and looked at me again, and returned to the matter of that kiss.

"What have you done to me, Agostino?"

I dropped my glance before her languid eyes. "What I have done to no other woman yet," I answered, a certain gloom creeping over the exultation that still thrilled me. "Oh, Giuliana, what have you done to me? You have bewitched me; you have made me mad!" And I set my elbows on my knees and took my head in my hands, and sat there, overwhelmed now by the full consciousness of the irrevocable thing that I had done, a thing that must brand my soul forever, so it seemed.

To have kissed a maid would have been ill enough for one whose aims were mine. But to kiss a wife, to become a cicisbeo! The thing assumed in my mind proportions foolishly, extravagantly beyond its evil reality.

"You are cruel, Agostino," she whispered behind me. She had come to lean again upon the back of the bench. "Am I alone to blame? Can the iron withstand the lodestone? Can the rain help falling upon the earth? Can the stream flow other than downhill?" She sighed. "Woe me! It is I who should be angered that you have made free of my lips. And yet I am here, wooing you to forgive me for the sin that is your own."

I cried out at that and turned to her again, and I was very white, I know.

"You tempted me!" was my coward's cry.

"So said Adam once. Yet God thought otherwise,

for Adam was as fully punished as was Eve." She smiled wistfully into my eyes, and my senses reeled again.

And then old Busio, the servant, came suddenly forth from the house upon some domestic errand to Giuliana, and thus was that situation mercifully brought to an end.

For the rest of the day I lived upon the memory of that morning, reciting to myself each word that she had uttered, conjuring up in memory the vision of her every look. And my absent-mindedness was visible to Fifanti when I came to my studies with him later. He grew more peevish with me than was habitual, dubbed me dunce and wooden-head, and commended the wisdom of those who had determined upon a claustral life for me, admitting that I knew enough Latin to enable me to celebrate as well as another without too clear a knowledge of the meaning of what I pattered. All of which was grossly untrue, for, as none knew better than himself, the fluency of my Latin was above the common wont of students. When I told him so, he delivered himself of his opin-ion upon the common wont of students with all the sourness of his crabbed nature.

"I'll write an ode for you upon any subject that you may set me," I challenged him.

"Then write one upon impudence," said he. "It is a subject you should understand." And upon that he got up and flung out of the room in a pet before I could think of an answer.

Left alone, I began an ode which should prove to him his lack of justice. But I got no further than two lines of it. Then for a spell I sat biting my quill, my mind and the eyes of my soul full of Giuliana.

Presently I began to write again. It was not an ode, but a prayer, oddly profane — and it was in Italian, in the "dialettale" that provoked Fifanti's sneers. How it ran I have forgotten these many years. But I recall that in it I likened myself to a sailor navigating shoals and besought the pharos of Giuliana's eyes to bring me safely through, besought her to anoint me with her glance and so hearten me to brave the dangers of that procellous sea.

I read it first with satisfaction, then with dismay as I realized to the full its amorous meaning. Lastly I tore it up and went below to dine.

We were still at table when my Lord Gambara arrived. He came on horseback attended by two grooms whom he left to await him. He was all in black velvet, I remember, even to his thigh-boots which were laced up the sides with gold, and on his breast gleamed a fine medallion of diamonds. Of the prelate there was about him, as usual, nothing but the scarlet cloak and the sapphire ring.

Fifanti rose and set a chair for him, smiling a crooked smile that held more hostility than welcome. None the less did his excellency pay Madonna Giuliana a thousand compliments as he took his seat, supremely calm and easy in his manner. I watched him closely, and I watched Giuliana, a queer fresh uneasiness pervading me.

The talk was trivial and chiefly concerned with the progress of the barracks the Legate was building and the fine new road from the middle of the city to the Church of Santa Chiara, which he intended should be called the Via Gambara, but which, despite his intentions, is known to-day as the Stradone Farnese.

Presently my cousin arrived, full-armed and very martial by contrast with the velvety Cardinal. He frowned to see Messer Gambara, then effaced the frown and smiled as, one by one, he greeted us. Last of all he turned to me.

"And how fares his saintliness?" quoth he.

"Indeed, none too saintly," said I, speaking my thoughts aloud.

He laughed. "Why, then, the sooner we are in orders, the sooner shall we be on the road to mending that. Is it not so, Messer Fifanti?"

"His ordination will profit you, I nothing doubt," said Fifanti, with his habitual discourtesy and acidity. "So you do well to urge it."

The answer put my cousin entirely out of countenance a moment. It was a blunt way of reminding me that in this Cosimo I saw one who followed after me in the heirship to Mondolfo, and in whose interests it was that I should don the conventual scapulary.

I looked at Cosimo's haughty face and cruel mouth, and conjectured in that hour whether I should have found him so very civil and pleasant a cousin had things been other than they were.

Oh, a very serpent was Messer Fifanti; and I have since wondered whether of intent he sought to sow in my heart hatred of my Guelphic cousin, that he might make of me a tool for his own service — as you shall come to understand.

Meanwhile, Cosimo, having recovered, waved aside the imputation, and smiled easily.

"Nay, there you wrong me. The Anguissola lose more than I shall gain by Agostino's renunciation of the world. And I am sorry for it. You believe me, cousin?"

I answered his courteous speech as it deserved, in very courteous terms. This set a pleasanter humour upon all. Yet some restraint abode. Each sat, it seemed, as a man upon his guard. My cousin watched Gambara's every look whenever the latter turned to speak to Giuliana; the Cardinal-Legate did the like by him; and Messer Fifanti watched them both.

And, meantime, Giuliana sat there, listening now to one, now to the other, her lazy smile parting those scarlet lips — those lips that I had kissed that morning — I, whom no one thought of watching!

And soon came Messer Annibale Caro, with lines from the last pages of his translation oozing from him. And when presently Giuliana smote her hands together in ecstatic pleasure at one of those same lines and bade him repeat it to her, he swore roundly by all the gods that are mentioned in Virgil that he would dedicate the work to her upon its completion.

At this the surliness became general once more and my Lord Gambara ventured the opinion — and there was a note of promise, almost of threat, in his sleek tones — that the Duke would shortly be needing Messer Caro's presence in Parma; whereupon Messer Caro cursed the Duke roundly and with all a poet's volubility of invective.

They stayed late, each intent, no doubt, upon outstaying the others. But since none would give way they were forced in the end to depart together.

And whilst Messer Fifanti, as became a host, was seeing them to their horses, I was left alone with Giuliana.

"Why do you suffer these men?" I asked her bluntly.

Her delicate brows were raised in surprise. "Why, what now? They are very pleasant gentlemen, Agostino."

"Too pleasant," said I, and rising I crossed to the window whence I could watch them getting to horse, all save Caro, who had come afoot. "Too pleasant by much. That prelate out of Hell, now . . ."

"Sh!" she hissed at me, smiling, her hand raised. "Should he hear you, he might send you to the cage for sacrilege. Oh, Agostino!" she cried, and the smiles all vanished from her face. "Will you grow cruel and suspicious, too?"

I was disarmed. I realized my meanness and unworthiness.

"Have patience with me," I implored her. "I . . . I am not myself to-day." I sighed ponderously, and fell silent as I watched them ride away. Yet I hated them all; and most of all I hated the dainty, perfumed, golden-headed Cardinal-Legate.

He came again upon the morrow, and we learnt from the news of which he was the bearer that he had carried out his threat concerning Messer Caro. The poet was on his way to Parma, to Duke Pier Luigi, despatched thither on a mission of importance by the Cardinal. He spoke, too, of sending my cousin to Perugia, where a strong hand was needed, as the town showed signs of mutiny against the authority of the Holy See.

When he had departed, Messer Fifanti permitted himself one of his bitter insinuations.

"He desires a clear field," he said, smiling his cold smile upon Giuliana. "It but remains for him to discover that his Duke has need of me as well."

He spoke of it as a possible contingency, but sarcastically, as men speak of things too remote to be seriously considered. He was to remember his words two days later when the very thing came to pass

We were at breakfast when the blow fell.

There came a clatter of hooves under our windows, which stood open to the tepid September morning, and soon there was old Busio ushering in an officer of the Pontificals with a parchment tied in scarlet silk and sealed with the arms of Piacenza.

Messer Fifanti took the package and weighed it in his hand, frowning. Perhaps already some foreboding of the nature of its contents was in his mind. Meanwhile, Giuliana poured wine for the officer, and Busio bore him the cup upon a salver.

Fifanti ripped away silk and seals, and set himself to read. I can see him now, standing near the window to which he had moved to gain a better light, the parchment under his very nose, his short-sighted eyes screwed up as he acquainted himself with the letter's contents. Then I saw him turn a sickly leaden hue. He stared at the officer a moment and then at Giuliana. But I do not think that he saw either of them. His look was the blank look of one whose thoughts are very distant.

He thrust his hands behind him, and with head forward, in that curious attitude so reminiscent of a bird of prey, he stepped slowly back to his place at the table-head. Slowly his cheeks resumed their normal tint.

"Very well, sir," he said, addressing the officer. "Inform his excellency that I shall obey the summons of the Duke's magnificence without delay."

The officer bowed to Giuliana, took his leave, and went, old Busio escorting him.

"A summons from the Duke?" cried Giuliana, and then the storm broke.

"Aye," he answered, grimly quiet, "a summons from the Duke." And he tossed it across the table to her.

I saw that fateful document float an instant in the air, and then, thrown out of poise by the blob of wax, swoop slanting to her lap.

"It will come, no doubt, as a surprise to you," he growled; and upon that his hard-held passion burst all bonds that he could impose upon it. His great bony fist crashed down upon the board and swept a precious Venetian beaker to the ground, where it burst into a thousand atoms, spreading red wine like a bloodstain upon the floor.

"Said I not that this rascal Cardinal would make a clear field for himself? Said I not so?" He laughed shrill and fiercely. "He would send your husband packing as he has sent his other rivals. Oh, there is a stipend waiting — a stipend of three hundred ducats yearly that shall be made into six hundred presently, and all for my complaisance, all that I may be a joyous and content cornuto!"

He strode to the window cursing horribly, whilst Giuliana sat white of face with lips compressed and heaving bosom, her eyes upon her plate.

"My Lord Cardinal and his Duke may take themselves together to Hell ere I obey the summons that the one has sent me at the desire of the other. Here I stay to guard what is my own."

"You are a fool," said Giuliana at length, "and a knave, too, for you insult me without cause."

"Without cause? Oh, without cause, eh? By the Host! Yet you would not have me stay?"

"I would not have you gaoled, which is what will happen if you disobey the Duke's magnificence," said she.

"Gaoled?" quoth he, of a sudden trembling in the increasing intensity of his passion. "Caged, perhaps — to die of hunger and thirst and exposure, like that poor wretch Domenico who perished yesterday, at last, because he dared to speak the truth. Gesù!" he groaned. "Oh, miserable me!" And he sank into a chair.

But the next instant he was up again, and his long arms were waving fiercely. "By the Eyes of God! They shall have cause to cage me. If I am to be horned like a bull, I'll use my horns. I'll gore their vitals. Oh, madam, since of your wantonness you inclined to harlotry, you should have wedded another than Astorre Fifanti."

It was too much. I leapt to my feet.

"Messer Fifanti," I blazed at him, "I'll not remain to hear such words addressed to this sweet lady."

"Ah, yes," he snarled, wheeling suddenly upon me as if he would strike me. "I had forgot the champion, the preux-chevalier, the saint in embryo! You will not remain to hear the truth, sir, eh?" And he strode, mouthing, to the door, and flung it wide so that it crashed against the wall. "This is your remedy. Get you hence! Go! What passes here concerns you not. Go!" he roared like a mad beast, his rage a thing terrific.

I looked at him and from him to Giuliana, and my eyes most clearly invited her to tell me how she would have me act.

"Indeed, you had best go, Agostino," she answered sadly. "I shall bear his insults easier if there be no witness. Yes, go."

"Since it is your wish, Madonna." I bowed to her, and very erect, very defiant of mien, I went slowly past the livid Fifanti, and so out. I heard the door slammed after me, and in the little hall I came upon Busio, who was wringing his hands and looking very white. He ran to me.

"He will murder her, Messer Agostino," moaned the old man. "He can be a devil in his anger."

"He is a devil always, in anger and out of it," said I. "He needs an exorcist. It is a task that I should relish. I'd beat the devils out of him, Busio, and she would let me. Meanwhile, stay we here, and if she needs our help, it shall be hers."

I dropped on to the carved settle that stood there, old Busio standing at my elbow, more tranquil now that there was help at hand for Madonna in case of need. And through the door came the sound of his storming, and presently the crash of more broken glassware, as once more he thumped the table. For well-nigh half an hour his fury lasted, and it was seldom that her voice was interposed. Once we heard her laugh, cold and cutting as a sword's edge, and I shivered at the sound, for it was not good to hear.

At last the door was opened and he came forth. His face was inflamed, his eyes wild and blood-injected. He paused for a moment on the threshold, but I do not think that he noticed us at first. He looked back at her over his shoulder, still sitting at table, the outline of her white-gowned body sharply defined against the deep blue tapestry of the wall behind her.

"You are warned," said he. "Do you heed the warning!" And he came forward.

Perceiving me at last where I sat, he bared his broken teeth in a snarling smile. But it was to Busio that he spoke. "Have my mule saddled for me in an hour," he said, and passed on and up the stairs to make his preparations. It seemed, therefore, that she had conquered his suspicions.

I went in to offer her comfort, for she was weeping and all shaken by that cruel encounter. But she waved me away.

"Not now, Agostino. Not now," she implored me. "Leave me to myself, my friend."

I had not been her friend had I not obeyed her without question.

CHAPTER V

PABULUM ACHERONTIS

IT was late that afternoon when Astorre Fifanti set out. He addressed a few brief words to me, informing me that he should return within four days, betide what might, setting me tasks upon which I was meanwhile to work, and bidding me keep the house and be circumspect during his absence.

From the window of my room I saw the Doctor get astride his mule. He was girt with a big sword, but he still wore his long, absurd, and shabby gown and his loose, ill-fitting shoes, so that it was very likely that the stirrup-irons would engage his thoughts ere he had ridden far.

I saw him dig his heels into the beast's sides and go ambling down the little avenue and out at the gate. In the road he drew rein, and stood in talk some moments with a lad who idled there, a lad whom he was wont to employ upon odd tasks about the garden and elsewhere.

This, Madonna also saw, for she was watching his departure from the window of a room below. That she attached more importance to that little circumstance than did I, I was to learn much later.

At last he pushed on, and I watched him as he dwindled down the long grey road that wound along the riverside until in the end he was lost to view — for all time, I hoped; and well had it been for me had my idle hope been realized.

I supped alone that night with no other company
than Busio's, who ministered to my needs.

Madonna sent word that she would keep her chamber.

When I had supped and after night had fallen, I
went upstairs to the library, and, shutting myself in,
I attempted to read, lighted by the three beaks of the
tall brass lamp that stood upon the table. Being
plagued by moths, I drew the curtains close across
the open window, and settled down to wrestle with
the opening lines of the "Prometheus" of Æschy-
lus.

But my thoughts wandered from the doings of the
son of Iapetus, until at last I flung down the book and
sat back in my chair all lost in thought, in doubt, and
in conjecture. I became seriously introspective. I
made an examination not only of conscience, but of
heart and mind, and I found that I had gone woefully
astray from the path that had been prepared for me.
Very late I sat there and sought to determine upon
what I should do.

Suddenly, like a manna to my starving soul, came
the memory of the last talk I had with Fra Gervasio
and the solemn warning he had given me. That
memory inspired me rightly. To-morrow — despite
Messer Fifanti's orders — I would take horse and
ride to Mondolfo, there to confess myself to Fra Gervasio and to be guided by his counsel. My mother's
vows concerning me I saw in their true light. They
were not binding upon me; indeed, I should be doing
a hideous wrong were I to follow them against my inclinations. I must not damn my soul for anything
that my mother had vowed or ever I was born, how-

ever much she might account that it would be no
more than filial piety so to do.

I was easier in mind after my resolve was taken,
and I allowed that mind of mine to stray thereafter
as it listed. It took to thoughts of Giuliana — Giuliana for whom I ached in every nerve, although I still
sought to conceal from myself the true cause of my
suffering. Better a thousand times had I envisaged
that sinful fact and wrestled with it boldly. Thus
should I have had a chance of conquering myself and
winning clear of all the horror that lay before me.

That I was weak and irresolute at such a time,
when I most needed strength, I still think to-day —
when I can take a calm survey of all — was the fault
of the outrageous rearing that was mine. At Mondolfo they had so nurtured me and so sheltered me
from the stinging blasts of the world that I was
grown into a very ripe and succulent fruit for the
Devil's mouth. The things to whose temptation us-
age would have rendered me in some degree immune
were irresistible to one who had been tutored as had I.

Let youth know wickedness, lest when wickedness
seeks a man out in his riper years he shall be fooled
and conquered by the beauteous garb in which the
Devil has the cunning to array it.

And yet to pretend that I was entirely innocent of
where I stood and in what perils were to play the hypocrite. Largely I knew; just as I knew that lacking
strength to resist, I must seek safety in flight. And
to-morrow I would go. That point was settled, and
the page, meanwhile, turned down. And for to-night
I delivered myself up to the savouring of this hunger
that was upon me.

And then, towards the third hour of night, as I still sat there, the door was very gently opened, and I beheld Giuliana standing before me. She detached from the black background of the passage, and the light of my three-beaked lamp set her ruddy hair aglow so that it seemed there was a luminous nimbus all about her head. For a moment this gave colour to my fancy that I beheld a vision evoked by the too great intentness of my thoughts. The pale face seemed so transparent, the white robe was almost diaphanous, and the great dark eyes looked so sad and wistful. Only in the vivid scarlet of her lips was there life and blood.

I stared at her. "Giuliana!" I murmured.

"Why do you sit so late?" she asked me, and closed the door as she spoke.

"I have been thinking, Giuliana," I answered wearily, and I passed a hand over my brow to find it moist and clammy. "To-morrow I go hence."

She started round and her eyes grew distended, her hand clutched her breast. "You go hence?" she cried, a note as of fear in her deep voice. "Hence? Whither?"

"Back to Mondolfo, to tell my mother that her dream is at an end."

She came slowly towards me. "And ... and then?" she asked.

"And then? I do not know. What God wills. But the scapulary is not for me. I am unworthy. I have no call. This I now know. And sooner than be such a priest as Messer Gambara — of whom there are too many in the Church to-day — I will find some other way of serving God."

"Since ... since when have you thought thus?"

"Since this morning, when I kissed you," I answered fiercely.

She sank into a chair beyond the table and stretched a hand across it to me, inviting the clasp of mine. "But if this is so, why leave us?"

"Because I am afraid," I answered. "Because . . . O God! Giuliana, do you not see?" And I sank my head into my hands.

Steps shuffled along the corridor. I looked up sharply. She set a finger to her lips. There fell a knock, and old Busio stood before us.

"Madonna," he announced, "my Lord the Cardinal-Legate is below and asks for you."

I started up as if I had been stung. So! At this hour! Then Messer Fifanti's suspicions did not entirely lack for grounds.

Giuliana flashed me a glance ere she made answer.

"You will tell my Lord Gambara that I have retired for the night and that . . . But stay!" She caught up a quill and dipped it in the ink-horn, drew paper to herself, and swiftly wrote three lines; then dusted it with sand, and proffered that brief epistle to the servant.

"Give this to my lord."

Busio took the note, bowed, and departed.

After the door had closed, a silence followed, in which I paced the room in long strides, aflame now with the all-consuming fire of jealousy. I do believe that Satan had set all the legions of Hell to achieve my overthrow that night. Naught more had been needed to undo me than this spur of jealousy. It brought me now to her side. I stood over her, looking down at her between tenderness and fierceness, she returning my glance with such a look as may haunt the eyes of sacrificial victims.

"Why dared he come?" I asked.

"Perhaps . . . perhaps some affair connected with Astorre . . ." she faltered.

I sneered. "That would be natural, seeing that he has sent Astorre to Parma."

"If there was aught else, I am no party to it," she assured me.

How could I do other than believe her? How could I gauge the turpitude of that beauty's mind — I, all unversed in the wiles that Satan teaches women? How could I have guessed that when she saw Fifanti speak to the lad at the gate that afternoon she had feared that he had set a spy upon the house, and that fearing this she had bidden the Cardinal begone? I knew it later. But not then.

"Will you swear that it is as you say?" I asked her, white with passion.

As I have said, I was standing over her and very close. Her answer now was suddenly to rise. Like a snake came she gliding upwards into my arms until she lay against my breast, her face upturned, her eyes languidly veiled, her lips a-pout.

"Can you do me so great a wrong, thinking you love me, knowing that I love you?" she asked me.

For an instant we swayed together in that sweetly hideous embrace. I was as a man sapped of all strength by some portentous struggle. I trembled from head to foot. I cried out once — a despairing prayer for help, I think it was — and then I seemed to plunge headlong down through an immensity of space until my lips found hers. The ecstasy, the living fire, the anguish, and the torture of it have left their indelible scars upon my memory. Even as I write the cruelly sweet poignancy of that moment is with me again — though very hateful now.

Thus I, blindly and recklessly, under the sway and thrall of that terrific and overpowering temptation. And then there leapt in my mind a glimmer of returning consciousness: a glimmer that grew rapidly to be a blazing light in which I saw revealed the vileness of the thing I did. I tore myself away from her in that second of revulsion and hurled her from me, fiercely and violently, so that, staggering to the seat from which she had risen, she fell into it rather than sat down.

And whilst, breathless with parted lips and galloping bosom, she observed me, something near akin to terror in her eyes, I stamped about that room and raved and heaped abuse and recriminations upon myself, ending by going down upon my knees to her, imploring her forgiveness for the thing I had done — believing like a fatuous fool that it was all my doing — and imploring her still more passionately to leave me and to go.

She set a trembling hand upon my head: she took my chin in the other, and raised my face until she could look into it.

"If it be your will — if it will bring you peace and happiness, I will leave you now and never see you more. But are you not deluded, my Agostino?"

And then, as if her self-control gave way, she fell to weeping.

"And what of me if you go? What of me wedded to that monster, to that cruel and inhuman pedant who tortures and insults me as you have seen?"

"Beloved, will another wrong cure the wrong of that?" I pleaded. "Oh, if you love me, go — go, leave me. It is too late — too late!"

I drew away from her touch, and crossed the room to fling myself upon the window-seat. For a space we sat apart thus, panting like wrestlers who have flung away from each other. At length —

"Listen, Giuliana," I said more calmly. "Were I to heed you, were I to obey my own desires, I should bid you come away with me from this to-morrow."

"If you but would!" she sighed. "You would be taking me out of Hell."

"Into another worse," I countered swiftly. "I should do you such a wrong as naught could ever right again."

She looked at me for a spell in silence. Her back was to the light and her face in shadow, so that I could not read what passed there. Then, very slowly, like one utterly weary, she got to her feet.

"I will do your will, beloved; but I do it not for the wrong that I should suffer — for that I should count no wrong — but for the wrong that I should be doing you."

She paused as if for an answer. I had none for her. I raised my arms, then let them fall again, and bowed my head. I heard the gentle rustle of her robe, and I looked up to see her staggering towards the door, her arms in front of her like one who is blind. She reached it, pulled it open, and from the threshold gave me one last ineffable look of her great eyes, heavy now with tears. Then the door closed again, and I was alone.

From my heart there rose a great surge of thankfulness. I fell upon my knees and prayed. For an hour

at least I must have knelt there, seeking grace and
strength; and comforted at last, my calm restored, I
rose, and went to the window. I drew back the curtains, and leaned out to breathe the physical calm of
that tepid September night.

And presently out of the gloom a great grey shape
came winging towards the window, the heavy pinions
moving ponderously with their uncanny sough. It
was an owl attracted by the light. Before that bird of
evil omen, that harbinger of death, I drew back and
crossed myself. I had a sight of its sphinx-like face
and round, impassive eyes ere it circled to melt again
into the darkness, startled by any sudden movement.
I closed the window and left the room.

Very softly I crept down the passage towards my
chamber, leaving the light burning in the library, for
it was not my habit to extinguish it, and I gave no
thought to the lateness of the hour.

Midway down the passage I halted. I was level
with Giuliana's door, and from under it there came a
slender blade of light. But it was not this that
checked me. She was singing. Such a pitiful little
heart-broken song it was:

> "Amor mi muojo; mi muojo amore mio!"

ran its last line.

I leaned against the wall, and a sob broke from me.
Then, in an instant, the passage was flooded with
light, and in the open doorway Giuliana stood all
white before me, her arms held out.

CHAPTER VI

THE IRON GIRDLE

FROM the distance, drawing rapidly nearer and ringing sharply in the stillness of the night, came the clatter of a mule's hooves.

But, though heard, it was scarcely heard consciously, and it certainly went unheeded until it was beneath the window and ceasing at the door.

Giuliana's fingers locked themselves upon my arm in a grip of fear.

"Who comes?" she asked, below her breath, fearfully.

I sprang from her side and crouched, listening, by the window, and so lost precious time.

Out of the darkness Giuliana's voice spoke again, hoarsely now and trembling.

"It will be Astorre," she said, with conviction. "At this hour it can be none else. I suspected when I saw him talking to that boy at the gate this afternoon that he was setting a spy upon me, to warn him wherever he was lurking, did the need arise."

"But how should the boy know . . . ?" I began, when she interrupted me almost impatiently.

"The boy saw Messer Gambara ride up. He waited for no more, but went at once to warn Astorre. He has been long in coming," she added in the tone of one who is still searching for the exact explanation of the thing that is happening. And then, suddenly and very urgently, "Go, go — go quickly!" she bade me.

As in the dark I was groping my way towards the door she spoke again:

"Why does he not knock? For what does he wait?"

Immediately, from the stairs, came a terrific answer to her question — the unmistakable, slip-slopping footstep of the Doctor.

I halted, and for an instant stood powerless to move. How he had entered I could not guess, nor did I ever discover. Sufficient was the awful fact that he was in.

I was ice-cold from head to foot. Then I was all on fire and groping forward once more whilst those footsteps, sinister and menacing as the very steps of Doom, came higher and nearer.

At last I found the door and wrenched it open. I stayed to close it after me, and already at the end of the passage beat the reflection of the light Fifanti carried. A second I stood there hesitating which way to turn. My first thought was to gain my own chamber. But to attempt it were assuredly to run into his arms. So I turned, and went as swiftly and stealthily as possible towards the library.

I was all but in when he turned the corner of the passage, and so caught sight of me before I had closed the door.

I stood in the library, where the lamp still burned, sweating, panting, and trembling. For even as he had had a glimpse of me, so had I had a glimpse of him, and the sight was terrifying to one in my situation.

I had seen his tall, gaunt figure bending forward in his eager, angry haste. In one hand he carried a lanthorn; a naked sword in the other. His face was malign and ghastly, and his bald, egg-like head shone yellow. The fleeting glimpse he had of me drew from him a sound between a roar and a snarl, and with quickened feet he came slip-slopping down the passage.

I had meant, I think, to play the fox: to seat myself at the table, a book before me, and feigning slumber, present the appearance of one who had been overcome by weariness at his labours. But now all thought of that was at an end. I had been seen, and that I fled was all too apparent. So that in every way I was betrayed.

The thing I did, I did upon instinct rather than reason; and this again was not well done. I slammed the door, and turned the key, placing at least that poor barrier between myself and the man I had so deeply wronged, the man whom I had given the right to slay me. A second later the door shook as if a hurricane had smitten it. He had seized the handle, and he was pulling at it frenziedly with a maniacal strength.

"Open!" he thundered, and fell to snarling and whimpering horribly. "Open!"

Then, quite abruptly he became oddly calm. It was as if his rage grew coldly purposeful; and the next words he uttered acted upon me as a dagger-prod, and reawakened my mind from its momentary stupefaction.

"Do you think these poor laths can save you from my vengeance, my Lord Gambara?" quoth he, with a chuckle horrible to hear.

My Lord Gambara! He mistook me for the Legate! In an instant I saw the reason of this. It was as

Giuliana had conceived. The boy had run to warn
him wherever he was — at Roncaglia, perhaps, a
league away upon the road to Parma. And the boy's
news was that my Lord the Governor had gone to
Fifanti's house. The boy had never waited to see the
Legate come forth again; but had obeyed his instructions to the letter, and it was Gambara whom Fifanti
came to take red-handed and to kill as he had the
right to do.

When he had espied my flying shape, the length of
the corridor had lain between us, Fifanti was short-
sighted, and since it was Gambara whom he expected
to find, Gambara at once he concluded it to be who
fled before him.

There was no villainy for which I was not ripe that
night, it seemed. For no sooner did I perceive this
error than I set myself to scheme how I might profit
by it. Let Gambara by all means suffer in my place
if the thing could be contrived. If not in fact, at least
in intent, the Cardinal-Legate had certainly sinned.
If he was not in my place now, it was through the
too great good fortune that attended him. Besides,
Gambara would be in better case to protect himself
from the consequences and from Fifanti's anger.

Thus cravenly I reasoned; and reasoning thus, I
reached the window. If I could climb down to the
garden, and then perhaps up again to my own chamber, I might get me to bed, what time Fifanti still
hammered at that door. Meanwhile his voice came
rasping through those slender timbers, as he mocked
the Lord Cardinal he supposed me.

"You would not be warned, my lord, and yet I
warned you enough. You would plant horns upon my

head. Well, well! Do not complain if you are gored
by them."

Then he laughed hideously. "This poor Astorre Fifanti is blind and a fool. He is to be sent packing on a
journey to the Duke, devised to suit my Lord Cardinal's convenience. But you should have bethought
you that suspicious husbands have a trick of pretend-
ing to depart whilst they remain."

Next his voice swelled up again in passion, and
again the door was shaken.

"Will you open, then, or must I break down the
door? There is no barrier in the world shall keep me
from you, there is no power can save you. I have the
right to kill you by every law of God and man. Shall
I forgo that right?" He laughed snarlingly.

"Three hundred ducats yearly to recompense the
hospitality I have given you — and six hundred later
upon the coming of the Duke!" he mocked. "That
was the price, my lord, of my hospitality — and my
wife's harlotry. Three hundred ducats! Ha! Ha!
Three hundred thousand million years in Hell! That
is the price, my lord — the price that you shall pay,
for I present the reckoning and enforce it. You shall
be shriven in iron — you and your wanton after you.

"Shall I be caged for having shed a prelate's sacred
blood? — for having sent a prelate's soul to Hell with
all its filth of sin upon it? Shall I? Speak, Magnificent; out of the fullness of your theological knowledge
inform me."

I had listened in a sort of fascination to that tirade
of venomous mockery. But now I stirred, and pulled
the casement open. I peered down into the darkness
and hesitated. The wall was creeper-clad to the win-

dow's height; but I feared the frail tendrils of the
clematis would never bear me. I hesitated. Then I
resolved to jump. It was but little more than some
twelve feet to the ground, and that was nothing to
daunt an active lad of my own build, with the soft
turf to land upon below. It should have been done
without hesitation; for that moment's hesitation was
my ruin.

Fifanti had heard the opening of the casement, and
fearing that, after all, his prey might yet escape him,
he suddenly charged the door like an infuriated bull,
and borrowing from his rage a strength far greater
than his usual he burst away the crazy fastenings.

Into the room hurtled the Doctor, to check and
stand there blinking at me, too much surprised for a
moment to grasp the situation.

When, at last, he understood, the returning flow of
rage was overwhelming.

"You!" he gasped; and then his voice mounting —
"You dog!" he screamed. "So it was you! You!"

He crouched and his little eyes, all blood-injected,
peered at me with horrid malice. He grew cold again
as he mastered his surprise. "You!" he repeated.
"Blind fool that I have been! You! The walker in
the ways of Saint Augustine — in his early ways, I
think. You saint in embryo, you postulant for holy
orders! You shall be ordained this night — with
this!" And he raised his sword so that little yellow
runnels of light sped down the livid blade.

"I will ordain you into Hell, you hound!" And
thereupon he leapt at me.

I sprang away from the window, urged by fear of
him into a very sudden activity. As I crossed the

room I had a glimpse of the white figure of Giuliana in the gloom of the passage, watching.

He came after me, snarling. I seized a stool and hurled it at him. He avoided it nimbly, and it went crashing through the half of the casement that was still closed.

And as he avoided it, grown suddenly cunning, he turned back towards the door to bar my exit should I attempt to lead him round the table.

We stood at gaze, the length of the little low-ceilinged chamber between us, both of us breathing hard.

Then I looked round for something with which to defend myself; for it was plain that he meant to have my life. By a great ill-chance it happened that the sword which I had worn upon that day when I went as Giuliana's escort into Piacenza was still standing in the very corner where I had set it down. Instinctively I sprang for it, and Fifanti, never suspecting my quest until he saw me with a naked iron in my hand, did nothing to prevent my reaching it.

Seeing me armed, he laughed. "Ho, ho! The saint-at-arms!" he mocked. "You'll be as skilled with weapons as with holiness!" And he advanced upon me in long, stealthy strides. The width of the table was between us, and he smote at me across it. I parried, and cut back at him, for being armed now, I no more feared him than I should have feared a child. Little he knew of the swordcraft I had learnt from old Falcone, a thing which once learnt is never forgotten, though lack of exercise may make us slow.

He cut at me again, and narrowly missed the lamp in his stroke. And now, I can most solemnly make oath that in the thing that followed there was no intent. It was over and done before I was conscious of the happening. I had acted purely upon instinct as men will in performing what they have been taught.

To ward his blow, I came almost unconsciously into that guard of Marozzo's which is known as the Iron Girdle. I parried and on the stroke I lunged, and so, taking the poor wretch entirely unawares, I sank the half of my iron into his vitals ere he or I had any thought that the thing was possible.

I saw his little eyes grow very wide, and the whole expression of his face become one of intense astonishment. He moved his lips as if to speak, and then the sword clattered from his one hand, the lanthorn from his other; he sank forward quietly, still looking at me with the same surprised glance, and so came further on to my rigidly held blade, until his breast brought up against the quillons. For a moment he remained supported thus, by just that rigid arm of mine and the table against which his weight was leaning. Then I withdrew the blade, and in the same movement flung the weapon from me. Before the sword had rattled to the floor, his body had sunk down into a heap beyond the table, so that I could see no more than the yellow, egg-like top of his bald head.

Awhile I stood watching it, filled with an extraordinary curiosity and a queer awe. Very slowly was it that I began to realize the thing I had done. It might be that I had killed Fifanti. It might be. And slowly, gradually I grew cold with the thought and the apprehension of its horrid meaning.

Then from the passage came a stifled scream, and Giuliana staggered forward, one hand holding flimsy draperies to her heaving bosom, the other at her mouth, which had grown hideously loose and uncontrolled. Her glowing copper hair, all unbound, fell about her shoulders like a mantle.

Behind her with ashen face and trembling limbs came old Busio. He was groaning and wringing his hands. Thus I saw the pair of them creep forward to approach Fifanti, who had made no sound since my sword had gone through him.

But Fifanti was no longer there to heed them — the faithful servant and the unfaithful wife. All that remained, huddled there at the foot of the table, was a heap of bleeding flesh and shabby garments.

It was Giuliana who gave me the information. With a courage that was almost stupendous she looked down into his face, then up into mine, which I doubt not was as livid.

"You have killed him," she whispered. "He is dead."

He was dead and I had killed him! My lips moved.

"He would have killed me," I answered in a strangled voice, and knew that what I said was a sort of lie to cloak the foulness of my deed.

Old Busio uttered a long, croaking wail, and went down on his knees beside the master he had served so long — the master who would never more need servant in this world.

It was upon the wings of that pitiful cry that the full understanding of the thing I had done was borne in upon my soul. I bowed my head, and took my face in my hands. I saw myself in that moment for what I was. I accounted myself wholly and irrevocably damned. Be God never so clement, surely here was something for which even His illimitable clemency could find no pardon.

I had come to Fifanti's house as a student of humanities and divinities; all that I had learnt there had been devilries culminating in this hour's work. And all through no fault of that poor, mean, ugly pedant, who, indeed, had been my victim — whom I had robbed of honour and of life.

Never man felt self-horror as I felt it then, self-loathing and self-contempt. And then, whilst the burden of it all, the horror of it all was full upon me, a soft hand touched my shoulder, and a soft, quivering voice murmured urgently in my ear:

"Agostino, we must go; we must go."

I plucked away my hands, and showed her a countenance before which she shrank in fear.

"We?" I snarled at her. "*We?*" I repeated still more fiercely, and drove her back before me as if I had done her a bodily hurt.

Oh, I should have imagined — had I had time in which to imagine anything — that already I had descended to the very bottom of the pit of infamy. But it seems that one more downward step remained me; and that step I took. Not by act, nor yet by speech, but just by thought.

For without the manliness to take the whole blame of this great crime upon myself, I must in my soul and mind fling the burden of it upon her. Like Adam of old, I blamed the woman, and charged her in my thoughts with having tempted me. Charging her thus, I loathed her as the cause of all this sin that had engulfed me; loathed her in that moment as a thing unclean and hideous; loathed her with a completeness of loathing such as I had never experienced before for any fellow-creature.

Instead of beholding in her one whom I had dragged with me into my pit of sin and whom it was incumbent upon my manhood thenceforth to shelter and protect from the consequences of my own iniquity, I attributed to her the blame of all that had befallen.

To-day I know that in so doing I did no more than justice. But it was not justly done. I had then no such knowledge as I have now by which to correct my judgment. The worst I had the right to think of her in that hour was that her guilt was something less than mine. In thinking otherwise was it that I took that last step to the very bottom of the hell that I had myself created for myself that night.

The rest was as nothing by comparison. I have said that it was not by act or speech that I added to the sum of my iniquities; and yet it was by both. First, in that fiercely echoed "We?" that I hurled at her to strike her from me; then in my precipitate flight alone.

How I stumbled from that room I scarcely know. The events of the time that followed immediately upon Fifanti's death are all blurred as the impressions of a sick man's dream.

I dimly remember that as she backed away from me until her shoulders touched the wall, that as she stood so, all white and lovely as any snare that Satan ever devised for man's ruin, staring at me with mutely pleading eyes, I staggered forward, avoiding the sight of that dreadful huddle on the floor, over which Busio was weeping foolishly.

As I stepped a sudden moisture struck my stock-inged feet. Its nature I knew by instinct upon the instant, and filled by it with a sudden unreasoning terror, I dashed with a loud cry from the room.

Along the passage and down the dark stairs I plunged until I reached the door of the house. It stood open and I went heedlessly forth. From overhead I heard Giuliana calling me in a voice that held a note of despair. But I never checked in my headlong career.

Fifanti's mule, I have since reflected, was tethered near the steps. I saw the beast, but it conveyed no meaning to my mind, which I think was numbed. I sped past it and on, through the gate, round the road by the Po, under the walls of the city, and so away into the open country.

Without cap, without doublet, without shoes, just in my trunks and shirt and hose, as I was, I ran, heading by instinct for home as heads the animal that has been overtaken by danger whilst abroad. Never since Phidippides, the Athenian courier, do I believe that any man had run as desperately and doggedly as I ran that night.

By dawn, having in some three hours put twenty miles or so between myself and Piacenza, I staggered exhausted and with cut and bleeding feet through the open door of a peasant's house.

The family sat at breakfast in the stone-flagged room into which I stumbled. I halted under their astonished eyes.

"I am the Lord of Mondolfo," I panted hoarsely, "and I need a beast to carry me home."

The head of that considerable family, a grizzled,

sun-tanned peasant, rose from his seat and pondered my condition with a glance that was laden with mistrust.

"The Lord of Mondolfo, you? Thus?" quoth he. "Now, by Bacchus, I am the Pope of Rome!"

But his wife, more tender-hearted, saw in my disorder cause for pity rather than irony.

"Poor lad!" she murmured, as I staggered and fell into a chair, unable longer to retain my feet. She rose immediately, and came hurrying towards me with a basin of goat's milk. The draught refreshed my body as her gentle words of comfort soothed my troubled soul. Seated there, her stout arm about my shoulders, my head pillowed upon her ample, motherly breast, I was very near to tears, loosened in my overwrought state by the sweet touch of sympathy, for which may God reward her.

I rested in that place awhile. Three hours I slept upon a litter of straw in an outhouse; whereupon, strengthened by my repose, I renewed my claim to be the Lord of Mondolfo and my demand for a horse to carry me to my fortress.

Still doubting me too much to trust me alone with any beast of his, the peasant nevertheless fetched out a couple of mules and set out with me for Mondolfo.

BOOK III: THE WILDERNESS

•.•

CHAPTER I

THE HOME-COMING

IT was still early morning when we came into the town of Mondolfo, my peasant escort and I.

The day being Sunday there was little stir in the streets at such an hour, and they presented a very different appearance from that which they had worn when last I had seen them. But the difference lay not only in the absence of bustle and the few folk abroad now as compared with that market-day on which, departing, I had ridden through. I viewed the place today with eyes that were able to draw comparisons, and after the wide streets and imposing buildings of Piacenza, I found my little township mean and rustic.

We passed the Duomo, consecrated to Our Lady of Mondolfo. Its portals stood wide, and in the opening swung a heavy crimson curtain, embroidered with a huge golden cross which was bellying outward like an enormous gonfalon. On the steps a few crippled beggars whined, and a few faithful took their way to early Mass.

On, up the steep, ill-paved street we climbed to the mighty grey citadel looming on the hill's crest, like a gigantic guardian brooding over the city of his trust. We crossed the drawbridge unchallenged, passed under the tunnel of the gateway, and so came into the vast, untenanted bailey of the fortress.

I looked about me, beat my hands together, and raised my voice to shout:

"Olà! Olà!"

In answer to my call the door of the guardhouse opened presently, and a man looked out. He frowned at first; then his brows went up and his mouth fell open.

"It is the Madonnino!" he shouted over his shoulder, and hurried forward to take my reins, uttering words of respectful welcome, which seemed to relieve the fears of my peasant, who had never quite believed me what I proclaimed myself.

There was a stir in the guardhouse, and two or three men of the absurd garrison my mother kept there shuffled in the doorway, whilst a burly fellow in leather with a sword girt on him thrust his way through and hurried forward, limping slightly. In the dark, lowering face I recognized my old friend Rinolfo, and I marvelled to see him thus accoutred.

He halted before me, and gave me a stiff and unfriendly salute; then he bade the man-at-arms to hold my stirrup.

"What is your authority here, Rinolfo?" I asked him shortly.

"I am the castellan," he informed me.

"The castellan? But what of Messer Giorgio?"

"He died a month ago."

"And who gave you this authority?"

"Madonna the Countess, in some recompense for the hurt you did me," he replied, thrusting forward his lame leg.

His tone was surly and hostile; but it provoked no resentment in me now. I deserved his unfriendliness. I had crippled him. At the moment I forgot the provocation I had received — forgot that since he had raised his hand to his lord, it would have been no great harshness to have hanged him. I saw in him but another instance of my wickedness, another sufferer at my hands; and I hung my head under the rebuke implicit in his surly tone and glance.

"I had not thought, Rinolfo, to do you an abiding hurt," said I, and here checked, bethinking me that I lied; for had I not expressed regret that I had not broken his neck?

I got down slowly and painfully, for my limbs were stiff and my feet very sore. He smiled darkly at my words and my sudden faltering; but I affected not to see.

"Where is Madonna?" I asked.

"She will have returned by now from chapel," he answered.

I turned to the man-at-arms. "You will announce me," I bade him. "And you, Rinolfo, see to these beasts and to this good fellow here. Let him have wine and food and what he needs. I will see him again ere he sets forth."

Rinolfo muttered that all should be done as I ordered, and I signed to the man-at-arms to lead the way.

We went up the steps and into the cool of the great hall. There the soldier, whose every feeling had been outraged no doubt by Rinolfo's attitude towards his lord, ventured to express his sympathy and indignation.

"Rinolfo is a black beast, Madonnino," he muttered.

"We are all black beasts, Eugenio," I answered heavily, and so startled him by words and tone that he ventured upon no further speech, but led me straight to my mother's private dining-room, opened the door and calmly announced me.

"Madonna, here is my Lord Agostino."

I heard the gasp she uttered before I caught sight of her. She was seated at the table's head in her great wooden chair, and Fra Gervasio was pacing the rush-strewn floor in talk with her, his hands behind his back, his head thrust forward.

At the announcement he straightened suddenly and wheeled round to face me, inquiry in his glance. My mother, too, half rose, and remained so, staring at me, her amazement at seeing me increased by the strange appearance I presented.

Eugenio closed the door and departed, leaving me standing there, just within it; and for a moment no word was spoken.

The cheerless, familiar room, looking more cheerless than it had done of old, with its high-set windows and ghastly Crucifix, affected me in a singular manner. In this room I had known a sort of peace — the peace that is peculiarly childhood's own, whatever the troubles that may haunt it. I came into it now with hell in my soul, sin-blackened before God and man, a fugitive in quest of sanctuary.

A knot rose in my throat and paralyzed awhile my speech. Then with a sudden sob, I sprang forward and hobbled to her upon my wounded feet. I flung myself down upon my knees, buried my head in her lap, and all that I could cry was:

"Mother! Mother!"

Whether perceiving my disorder, my distraught and suffering condition, what remained of the woman in her was moved to pity; whether my cry acting like a rod of Moses upon that rock of her heart which excess of piety had sterilized, touched into fresh life the springs that had so long been dry, and reminded her of the actual bond between us, her tone was more kindly and gentle than I had ever known it.

"Agostino, my child! Why are you here?" And her wax-like fingers very gently touched my head. "Why are you here — and thus? What has happened to you?"

"Me miserable!" I groaned.

"What is it?" she pressed me, an increasing anxiety in her voice.

At last I found courage to tell her sufficient to prepare her mind.

"Mother, I am a sinner," I faltered miserably.

I felt her recoiling from me as from the touch of something unclean and contagious, her mind conceiving already by some subtle premonition some shadow of the thing that I had done. And then Gervasio spoke, and his voice was soothing as oil upon troubled waters.

"Sinners are we all, Agostino. But repentance purges sin. Do not abandon yourself to despair, my son."

But the mother who bore me took no such charitable and Christian view.

"What is it? Wretched boy, what have you done?" And the cold repugnance in her voice froze anew the courage I was forming.

"O God, help me! God help me!" I groaned miserably.

Gervasio, seeing my condition, with that quick and saintly sympathy that was his, came softly towards me and set a hand upon my shoulder.

"Dear Agostino," he murmured, "would you find it easier to tell me first? Will you confess to me, my son? Will you let me lift this burden from your soul?"

Still on my knees I turned and looked up into that pale, kindly face. I caught his thin hand, and kissed it ere he could snatch it away. "If there were more priests like you," I cried, "there would be fewer sinners like me."

A shadow crossed his face; he smiled very wanly, a smile that was like a gleam of pale sunshine from an overclouded sky, and he spoke in gentle, soothing words of the Divine Mercy.

I staggered to my bruised feet. "I will confess to you, Fra Gervasio," I said, "and afterwards we will tell my mother."

She looked as she would make demur. But Fra Gervasio checked any such intent.

"It is best so, Madonna," he said gravely. "His most urgent need is the consolation that the Church alone can give."

He took me by the arm very gently, and led me forth. We went to his modest chamber, with its waxed floor, the hard, narrow pallet upon which he slept, the blue-and-gold image of the Virgin, and the little writing-pulpit upon which lay open a manuscript he was illuminating, for he was very skilled in that art which already was falling into desuetude.

At this pulpit, by the window, he took his seat, and signed to me to kneel. I recited the Confiteor. Thereafter, with my face buried in my hands, my soul writhing in an agony of penitence and shame, I poured out the hideous tale of the evil I had wrought.

Rarely did he speak while I was at that recitation. Save when I halted or hesitated he would interject a word of pity and of comfort that fell like a blessed balsam upon my spiritual wounds and gave me strength to pursue my awful story.

When I had done and he knew me to the full for the murderer and adulterer that I was, there fell a long pause, during which I waited as a felon awaits sentence. But it did not come. Instead, he set himself to examine more closely the thing I had told him. He probed it with a question here and a question there, and all of a shrewdness that revealed the extent of his knowledge of humanity, and the infinite compassion and gentleness that must be the inevitable fruits of such sad knowledge.

He caused me to go back to the very day of my arrival at Fifanti's; and thence, step by step, he led me again over the road that in the past four months I had trodden, until he had traced the evil to its very source, and could see the tiny spring that had formed the brook which, gathering volume as it went, had swollen at last into a raging torrent to lay waste its narrow confines.

"Who that knows all that goes to the making of a sin shall dare to condemn a sinner?" he cried at last, so that I looked up at him, startled, and penetrated by a ray of hope and comfort. He returned my glance with one of infinite pity.

"It is the woman here upon whom must fall the greater blame," said he.

But at that I cried out in hot remonstrance, adding that I had yet another vileness to confess — for it was now that for the first time I realized it. And I related to him how last night I had repudiated her, cast her off and fled, leaving her to bear the punishment alone.

Of my conduct in that he withheld his criticism. "The sin is hers," he repeated. "She was a wife, and the adultery is hers. More, she was the seducer. It was she who debauched your mind with lascivious readings, and tore away the foundations of virtue from your soul. If in the cataclysm that followed she was crushed and smothered, it is no more than she had incurred."

I still protested that this view was all too lenient to me, that it sprang of his love for me, that it was not just. Thereupon he began to make clear to me many things that may have been clear to you worldly ones who have read my scrupulous and exact confessions, but which at the time were still all wrapped in obscurity for me.

It was as if he held up a mirror — an intelligent and informing mirror — in which my deeds were reflected by the light of his own deep knowledge. He showed me the gradual seduction to which I had been subjected; he showed me Giuliana as she really was, as she must be from what I had told him; he reminded me that she was older by ten years than I, and greatly skilled in men and worldliness; that where I had gone blindly, never seeing what was the inevitable goal and end of the road I trod, she had con-

hose and shoes. And meanwhile munching my bread and salt and taking great draughts of the pure if somewhat sour wine, my mental peace was increased by the refreshment of my body.

At last I stood up more myself than I had been in these last twelve awful hours — for it was just noon, and into twelve hours had been packed the events that well might have filled a lifetime.

He put an arm about my shoulder, fondly as a father might have done, and so led me below again and into my mother's presence.

We found her kneeling before the Crucifix, telling her beads; and we stood waiting a few moments in silence until with a sigh and a rustle of her stiff black dress she rose gently, and turned to face us.

My heart thudded violently in that moment, as I looked into that pale face of sorrow. Then Fra Gervasio began to speak very gently and softly.

"Your son, Madonna, has been lured into sin by a wanton woman," he began, and there she interrupted him with a sudden and very piteous cry.

"Not that! Ah, not that!" she exclaimed, putting out hands gropingly before her.

"That and more, Madonna," he answered gravely. "Be brave to hear the rest. It is a very piteous story. But the founts of Divine Mercy are inexhaustible, and Agostino shall drink therefrom when by penitence he shall have cleansed his lips."

Very erect she stood there, silent and ghostly, her face looking diaphanous by contrast with the black draperies that enshrouded her, whilst her eyes were great pools of sorrow. Poor, poor mother! It is the last recollection I have of her; for after that day we never met again, and I would give ten years to Purgatory if I might recall the last words that passed between us.

As briefly as possible and ever thrusting into the foreground the immensity of the snare that had been spread for me and the temptation that had enmeshed me, Gervasio told her the story of my sin.

She heard him through in that immovable attitude, one hand pressed to her heart, her poor pale lips moving now and again, but no sound coming from them, her face a white mask of pain and horror.

When he had done, so wrought upon was I by the sorrow of that countenance that I went forward again to fling myself upon my knees before her.

"Mother, forgive!" I pleaded. And getting no answer I put up my hands to take hers. "Mother!" I cried, and the tears were streaming down my face.

But she recoiled before me.

"Are you my child?" she asked in a voice of horror. "Are you the thing that has grown out of that little child I vowed to chastity and to God? Then has my sin overtaken me — the sin of bearing a son to Giovanni d'Anguissola, that enemy of God!"

"Ah, mother, mother!" I cried again, thinking, perhaps, by that all-powerful word to move her yet to pity and to gentleness.

"Madonna," cried Gervasio, "be merciful if you would look for mercy."

"He has falsified my vows," she answered stonily. "He was my votive offering for the life of his impious father. I am punished for the unworthiness of my offering and the unworthiness of the cause in which I offered it. Accursed is the fruit of my womb!" She moaned, and sank her head upon her breast.

"I will atone!" I cried, overwhelmed to see her so distraught.

She wrung her pale hands.

"Atone!" she cried, and her voice trembled. "Go, then, and atone. But never let me see you more; never let me be reminded of the sinner to whom I have given life. Go! Begone!" And she raised a hand in tragical dismissal.

I shrank back, and came slowly to my feet. And then Gervasio spoke, and his voice boomed and thundered with righteous indignation.

"Madonna, this is inhuman!" he denounced. "Shall you dare to hope for mercy being yourself unmerciful?"

"I shall pray for strength to forgive him; but the sight of him might tempt me back with the memory of the thing that he has done," she answered, and she had returned to that cold and terrible reserve of hers.

And then things that Fra Gervasio had repressed for years welled up in a mighty flood. "He is your son, and he is as you have made him."

"As I have made him?" quoth she, and her glance challenged the friar.

"By what right did you make of him a votive offering? By what right did you seek to consecrate a child unborn to a claustral life without thought of his character, without reck of the desires that should be his? By what right did you make yourself the arbiter of the future of a man unborn?"

"By what right?" quoth she. "Are you a priest,

and do you ask me by what right I vowed him to the service of God?"

"And is there, think you, no way of serving God but in the sterility of the cloister?" he demanded. "Why, since no man is born to damnation, and since by your reasoning the world must mean damnation, then all men should be encloistered, and soon, thus, there would be an end to man. You are too arrogant, Madonna, when you presume to judge what pleases God. Beware lest you fall into the sin of the Pharisee, for often have I seen you stand in danger of it."

She swayed as if her strength were failing her, and again her pale lips moved.

"Enough, Fra Gervasio! I will go," I cried.

"Nay, it is not yet enough," he answered, and strode down the room until he stood between her and me. "He is what you have made him," he repeated in denunciation. "Had you studied his nature and his inclinations, had you left them free to develop along the way that God intended, you would have seen whether or not the cloister called him; and then would have been the time to have taken a resolve. But you thought to change his nature by repressing it; and you never saw that if he was not such as you would have him be, then most surely would you doom him to damnation by making an evil priest of him.

"In your Pharisaic arrogance, Madonna, you sought to superimpose your will upon God's will concerning him — you confounded God's will with your own. And so his sins recoil upon you as much as upon any. Therefore, Madonna, do I bid you beware. Take a humbler view if you would be acceptable in the Divine sight. Learn to forgive, for I say to you

to-day that you stand as greatly in need of forgiveness
for the thing that Agostino has done, as does Agostino
himself."

He paused at last, and stood trembling before her,
his eyes aflame, his high cheek-bones faintly tinted.
And she measured him very calmly and coldly with
her sombre eyes.

"Are you a priest?" she asked with steady scorn.
"Are you, indeed, a priest?" And then her invective
was loosened, and her voice shrilled and mounted as
her anger swayed her. "What a snake have I harboured here!" she cried. "Blasphemer! You show
me clearly whence came the impiety and ungodliness
of Giovanni d'Anguissola. It had the same source as
your own. It was suckled at your mother's breast."

A sob shook him. "My mother is dead, Madonna!"
he rebuked her.

"She is more blessed, then, than I; since she has
not lived to see what a power for sin she has brought
forth. Go, pitiful friar. Go, both of you. You are
very choicely mated. Begone from Mondolfo, and
never let me see either of you more."

She staggered to her great chair and sank into it,
whilst we stood there, mute, regarding her. For myself, it was with difficulty that I repressed the burning
things that rose to my lips. Had I given free rein to
my tongue, I had made of it a whip of scorpions.
And my anger sprang, not from the things she said to
me, but from what she said to that saintly man who
held out a hand to help me out of the morass of sin in
which I was being sunk. That he, that sweet and
charitable follower of his Master, should be abused by
her, should be dubbed blasphemer and have the cher-

ished memory of his mother defiled by her pietistic utterances, was something that inflamed me horribly.

But he set a hand upon my shoulder.

"Come, Agostino," he said, very gently. He was calm once more. "We will go, as we are bidden, you and I."

And then, out of the sweetness of his nature, he forged all unwittingly the very iron that should penetrate most surely into her soul.

"Forgive her, my son. Forgive her as you need forgiveness. She does not understand the thing she does. Come, we will pray for her, that God in His infinite mercy may teach her humility and true knowledge of Him."

I saw her start as if she had been stung.

"Blasphemer, begone!" she cried again; and her voice was hoarse with suppressed anger.

And then the door was suddenly flung open, and Rinolfo clanked in, very martial and important, his hand thrusting up his sword behind him.

"Madonna," he announced, "the Captain of Justice from Piacenza is here."

CHAPTER II

THE CAPTAIN OF JUSTICE

THERE was a moment's silence after Rinolfo had flung that announcement.

"The Captain of Justice?" quoth my mother at length, her voice startled. "What does he seek?"

"The person of my Lord Agostino d'Anguissola," said Rinolfo steadily.

She sighed very heavily. "A felon's end!" she murmured, and turned to me. "If thus you may expiate your sins," she said, speaking more gently, "let the will of Heaven be done. Admit the captain, Ser Rinolfo."

He bowed, and turned sharply to depart.

"Stay!" I cried, and rooted him there by the imperative note of my command.

Fra Gervasio was more than right when he said that mine was not a nature for the cloister. In that moment I might have realized it to the full by the readiness with which the thought of battle occurred to me, and more by the anticipatory glow that warmed me at the very thought of it. I was the very son of Giovanni d'Anguissola.

"What force attends the captain?" I inquired.

"He has six mounted men with him," replied Rinolfo.

"In that case," I answered, "you will bid him begone in my name."

"And if he should not go?" was Rinolfo's impudent question.

"You will tell him that I will drive him hence —
him and his braves. We keep a garrison of a score
of men, at least — sufficient to compel him to depart."

"He will return again with more," said Rinolfo.

"Does that concern you?" I snapped. "Let him
return with what he pleases. To-day I enrol more
forces from the countryside, take up the bridge and
mount our cannon. This is my lair and fortress, and
I'll defend it and myself as becomes my name and
blood. For I am the lord and master here, and the
Lord of Mondolfo is not to be dragged away thus at
the heels of a Captain of Justice. You have my orders. Obey them. About it, sir."

Circumstances had shown me the way that I must
take, and the folly of going forth a fugitive outcast at
my mother's bidding. I was Lord of Mondolfo, as I
had said, and they should know and feel it from this
hour — all of them, not excepting my mother.

But I reckoned without the hatred Rinolfo bore
me. Instead of the prompt obedience that I had
looked for, he had turned again to my mother.

"Is it your wish, Madonna?" he inquired.

"It is my wish that counts, you knave!" I thundered and advanced upon him.

But he fronted me intrepidly. "I hold my office
from my Lady the Countess. I obey none other
here."

"Body of God! Do you defy me?" I cried. "Am I
Lord of Mondolfo, or am I a lackey in my own house?
You'd best obey me ere I break you, Ser Rinolfo. We
shall see whether the men will take my orders," I
added confidently.

The faintest smile illumined his dark face. "The men will not stir a finger at the bidding of any but Madonna the Countess and myself," he answered hardily.

It was by an effort that I refrained from striking him. And then my mother spoke again.

"It is as Ser Rinolfo says," she informed me. "So cease this futile resistance, sir son, and accept the expiation that is offered you."

I looked at her, she avoiding my glance.

"Madonna, I cannot think that it is so," said I. "These men have known me since I was a little lad. Many of them have followed the fortunes of my father. They'll never turn their backs upon his son in the hour of his need. They are not all so inhuman as my mother."

"You mistake, sir," said Rinolfo. "Of the men you knew but one or two remain. Most of our present force has been enrolled by me in the past month."

This was defeat, utter and pitiful. His tone was too confident, he was too sure of his ground to leave me a doubt as to what would befall if I made appeal to his knavish followers. My arms fell to my sides, and I looked at Gervasio. His face was haggard, and his eyes were very full of sorrow as they rested on me.

"It is true, Agostino," he said.

And as he spoke, Rinolfo limped out of the room to fetch the Captain of Justice, as my mother had bidden him; and his lips smiled cruelly.

"Madam mother," I said bitterly, "you do a monstrous thing. You usurp the power that is mine, and you deliver me — me, your son — to the gallows. I hope that, hereafter, when you come to realize to the full your deed, you will be able to give your conscience peace."

"My first duty is to God," she answered; and to that pitiable answer there was nothing to be rejoined.

So I turned my shoulder to her and stood waiting, Fra Gervasio beside me, clenching his hands in his impotence and mute despair. And then an approaching clank of mail heralded the coming of the captain.

Rinolfo held the door, and Cosimo d'Anguissola entered with a firm, proud tread, two of his men following at his heels.

He wore a buff-coat, under which, no doubt, there would be a shirt of mail; his gorget and wristlets were of polished steel, and his headgear was a steel cap under a cover of peach-coloured velvet. Thigh-boots encased his legs; sword and dagger hung in the silver carriages at his belt; his handsome, aquiline face was very solemn.

He bowed profoundly to my mother, who rose to respond, and then he flashed me one swift glance of his piercing eyes.

"I deplore my business here," he announced shortly. "No doubt, it will be known to you already." And he looked at me again, allowing his eyes to linger on my face.

"I am ready, sir," I said.

"Then we had best be going, for I understand that none could be less welcome here than I. Yet in this, Madonna, let me assure you that there is nothing personal to myself. I am the slave of my office. I do but perform it."

"So much protesting where no doubt has been expressed," said Fra Gervasio, "in itself casts a doubt upon your good faith. Are you not Cosimo d'Anguissola — my lord's cousin and heir?"

"I am," said he, "yet that has no part in this, sir friar."

"Then let it have part. Let it have the part it should have. Will you bear one of your own name and blood to the gallows? What will men say of that when they perceive your profit in the deed?"

Cosimo looked him boldly between the eyes, his hawk-face very white.

"Sir priest, I know not by what right you address me so. But you do me wrong. I am the Podestà of Piacenza, bound by an oath that it would dishonour me to break; and break it I must or else fulfil my duty here. Enough!" he added, in his haughty, peremptory fashion. "Ser Agostino, I await your pleasure."

"I will appeal to Rome," cried Fra Gervasio, now beside himself with grief.

Cosimo smiled darkly, pityingly. "If you think that Rome will listen to appeals on behalf of the son of Giovanni d'Anguissola."

And with that he motioned me to precede him. Silently I pressed Fra Gervasio's hand, and on that departed without so much as another look at my mother, who sat there a silent witness of a scene which she approved.

The men-at-arms fell into step, one on either side of me, and so we passed out into the courtyard, where Cosimo's other men were waiting, and where was gathered the entire family of the castle — a gaping, rather frightened little crowd.

They brought forth a mule for me, and I mounted.

Then suddenly there was Fra Gervasio at my side again.

"I, too, am going hence," he said. "Be of good courage, Agostino. There is no effort I will not make on your behalf." In a broken voice he added his farewells ere he stood back at the captain's peremptory bidding. The little troop closed round me, and thus, within a couple of hours of my coming, I departed again from Mondolfo, surrendered to the hangman by the pious hands of my mother, who on her knees, no doubt, would be thanking God for having afforded her the grace to act in so righteous a manner.

Once only did my cousin address me, and that was soon after we had left the town behind us. He motioned the men away, and rode to my side. Then he looked at me with mocking, hating eyes.

"You had done better to have continued in your saint's trade than have become so very magnificent a sinner," said he.

I did not answer him, and he rode on beside me in silence some little way.

"Ah, well," he sighed at last. "Your course has been a brief one, but very eventful. And who would have suspected so very fierce a wolf under so sheepish an outside! Body of God! You fooled us all, you and that white-faced trull."

He said it through his teeth with such a concentration of rage in his tones that it was easy to guess where the sore rankled.

I looked at him gravely. "Does it become you, sir, do you think, to gird at one who is your prisoner?"

"And did you not gird at me when it was your turn?" he flashed back fiercely. "Did not you and she laugh together over that poor, fond fool Cosimo whose money she took so very freely, and yet who seems to have been the only one excluded from her favours?"

"You lie, you dog!" I blazed at him, so fiercely that the men turned in their saddles. He paled, and half raised the gauntleted hand in which he carried his whip. But he controlled himself, and barked an order to his followers:

"Ride on, there!"

When they had drawn off a little, and we were alone again, "I do not lie, sir," he said. "It is a practice which I leave to shavelings of all degrees."

"If you say that she took aught from you, then you lie," I repeated.

He considered me steadily. "Fool!" he said at last. "Whence else her jewels and fine clothes? From Fifanti, do you think — that impecunious pedant? Or perhaps you imagine that it was from Gambara? In time that grasping prelate might have made the Duke pay. But pay, himself? By the Blood of God! he was never known to pay for anything.

"Or, yet again, do you suppose her finery was afforded her by Caro? — Messer Annibale Caro — who is so much in debt that he is never like to return to Piacenza, unless some dolt of a patron rewards him for his poetaster's labours.

"No, no, my shaveling. It was I who paid — I who was the fool. God! I more than suspected the others. But you. You saint . . . You!"

He flung up his head, and laughed bitterly and unpleasantly.

"Ah, well!" he ended. "You are to pay, though in

different kind.   It is in the family, you see." And abruptly raising his voice he shouted to the men to wait.

Thereafter he rode ahead, alone and gloomy, whilst no less alone and gloomy rode I amid my guards. The thing he had revealed to me had torn away a veil from my silly eyes. It had made me understand a hundred little matters that hitherto had been puzzling me. And I saw how utterly and fatuously blind I had been to things which even Fra Gervasio had apprehended from just the relation he had drawn from me.

It was as we were entering Piacenza by the Gate of San Lazzaro that I again drew my cousin to my side.

"Sir Captain!" I called to him, for I could not bring myself to address him as cousin now. He came, inquiry in his eyes.

"Where is she now?" I asked.

He stared at me a moment, as if my effrontery astonished him. Then he shrugged and sneered. "I would I knew for certain," was his fierce answer. "I would I knew. Then I should have the pair of you." And I saw it in his face how unforgivingly he hated me out of his savage jealousy. "My Lord Gambara might tell you. I scarcely doubt it. Were I but certain, what a reckoning should I not present! He may be Governor of Piacenza, but were he Governor of Hell he should not escape me." And with that he rode ahead again, and left me.

The rumour of our coming sped through the streets ahead of us, and out of the houses poured the towns-folk to watch our passage and to point me out one to another with many whisperings and solemn head-waggings. And the farther we advanced, the greater was the concourse, until by the time we reached the square before the Communal Palace we found there what amounted to a mob awaiting us.

My guards closed round me as if to protect me from that crowd. But I was strangely without fear, and presently I was to see how little cause there was for any, and to realize that the action of my guards was sprung from a very different motive.

The people stood silent, and on every upturned face of which I caught a glimpse I saw something that was akin to pity. Presently, however, as we drew nearer to the Palace, a murmur began to rise. It swelled and grew fierce. Suddenly a cry rose vehement and clear.

"Rescue! Rescue!"

"He is the Lord of Mondolfo," shouted one tall fellow, "and the Cardinal-Legate makes a cat's-paw of him! He is to suffer for Messer Gambara's villainy!"

Again he was answered by the cry — "Rescue! Rescue!" whilst some added an angry — "Death to the Legate!"

Whilst I was deeply marvelling at all this, Cosimo looked at me over his shoulder, and though his lips were steady, his eyes seemed to smile, charged with a message of derision — and something more, something that I could not read. Then I heard his hard, metallic voice.

"Back there, you curs! To your kennels! Out of the way, or we ride you down."

He had drawn his sword, and his white hawk-face was so cruel and determined that they fell away before him and their cries perished.

We passed into the courtyard of the Communal Palace, and the great studded gates were slammed in the faces of the mob, and barred.

I got down from my mule, and was conducted at Cosimo's bidding to one of the dungeons under the Palace, where I was left with the announcement that I must present myself to-morrow before the Tribunal of the Ruota.

I flung myself down upon the dried rushes that had been heaped in a corner to do duty for a bed, and I abandoned myself to my bitter thoughts. In particular I pondered the meaning of the crowd's strange attitude. Nor was it a riddle difficult to resolve. It was evident that believing Gambara, as they did, to be Giuliana's lover, and informed, perhaps — invention swelling rumour as it will — that the Cardinal-Legate had ridden late last night to Fifanti's house, it had been put about that the foul murder done there was Messer Gambara's work.

Thus was the Legate reaping the harvest of all the hatred he had sown, of all the tyranny and extortion of his iron rule in Piacenza. And willing to believe any evil of the man they hated, they not only laid Fifanti's death at his door, but they went to further lengths and accounted that I was the cat's-paw; that I was to be sacrificed to save the Legate's face and reputation. They remembered, perhaps, the ill-odour in which we Anguissola of Mondolfo had been at Rome, for the Ghibelline leanings that ever had been ours and for the rebellion of my father against the Pontifical sway; and their conclusions gathered a sort of confirmation from that circumstance.

Long upon the very edge of mutiny and revolt

against Gambara's injustice, it had needed but what seemed a crowning one such as this to quicken their hatred into expression.

It was all very clear and obvious, and it seemed to me that to-morrow's trial should be very interesting. I had but to deny; I had but to make myself the mouthpiece of the rumour that was abroad, and Heaven alone could foretell what the consequences might be.

Then I smiled bitterly to myself. Deny? Oh, no! That was a last vileness I could not perpetrate. The Ruota should hear the truth, and Gambara should be left to shelter Giuliana, who — Cosimo was assured — had fled to him in her need as to a natural protector.

It was a bitter thought. The intensity of that bitterness made me realize with alarm how it still was with me. And pondering this, I fell asleep, utterly worn out in body and in mind by the awful turmoil of that day.

CHAPTER III

GAMBARA'S INTERESTS

I AWAKENED to find a man standing beside me. He was muffled in a black cloak and carried a lanthorn. Behind him the door gaped as he had left it.

Instantly I sat up, conscious of my circumstance and surroundings, and at my movement this visitor spoke.

"You sleep very soundly for a man in your case," said he, and the voice was that of my Lord Gambara, its tone quite coldly critical.

He set down the lanthorn on a stool, whence it shed a wheel of yellow light intersected with black beams. His cloak fell apart, and I saw that he was dressed for riding, very plainly, in sombre garments, and that he was armed.

He stood slightly to one side so that the light might fall upon my face, leaving his own in shadow; thus he considered me for some moments in silence. At last, very slowly, very bitterly, shaking his head as he spoke.

"You fool! You clumsy fool!" he said.

Having drawn, as you have seen, my own conclusions from the attitude of the mob, I was in a little doubt as to the precise bearing of his words.

I answered him sincerely. "If folly were all my guilt," said I, "it would be well."

He sniffed impatiently. "Still sanctimonious!" he sneered. "Tcha! Up, now, and play the man, at last.

You have shed your robe of sanctity, Messer Agostino; have done with pretence!"

"I do not pretend," I answered him. "And as for playing the man, I shall accept what punishment the law may have for me with fortitude, at least. If I can but expiate . . ."

"Expiate a fig!" he snapped, interrupting me. "Why do you suppose that I am here?"

"I wait to learn."

"I am here because through your folly you have undone us all. What need," he cried, the anger of expostulation quivering in his voice — "what need was there to kill that oaf Fifanti?"

"He would have killed me," said I. "I slew him in self-defence."

"Ha! And do you hope to save your neck with such a plea?"

"Nay. I have no thought of urging it. I but tell it you."

"There is not the need to tell me anything," he answered, his anger plain. "I am very well informed of all. Rather, let me tell you something. Do you realize, sir, that you have made it impossible for me to abide another day in Piacenza?"

"I am sorry . . ." I began lamely.

"Present your regrets to Satan," he snapped. "Me they avail nothing. I am put to the necessity of abandoning my governorship and fleeing by night like a hunted thief. And I have you to thank for it. You see me on the point of departure. My horses wait above. So you may add my ruin to the other fine things you accomplished yesternight. For a saint you are busy, sir." And he turned away and strode the length of my cell and back, so that, at last, I had a glimpse of his face, which was drawn and scowling. Gone now was the last vestige of his habitual silkiness; the pomander-ball hung neglected, and his delicate fingers tugged viciously at his little pointed beard, his great sapphire ring flashing sombrely.

"Look you, Ser Agostino, I could kill you and take joy in it. I could, by God!"

His eyes upon me, he drew from his breast a folded paper. "Instead, I bring you liberty. I open your doors for you, and bid you escape. Here, man, take this paper. Present it to the officer at the Fodesta Gate. He will let you pass. And then away with you, out of the territory of Piacenza."

For an instant my heart-beats seemed suspended by astonishment. I swung my legs round, and half rose, excited. Then I sank back again. My mind was made up. I was tired of the world; sick of life the first draught of which had turned so bitter in my throat. If by my death I might expiate my sins and win pardon by my submission and humility, it was all I could desire. I should be glad to be released from all the misery and sorrow into which I had been born.

I told him so in some few words. "You mean me well, my lord," I ended, "and I thank you. But . . ."

"By God and the Saints!" he blazed, "I do not mean you well at all. I mean you anything but well. Have I not said that I could kill you with satisfaction? Whatever be the sins of Egidio Gambara, he is no hypocrite, and he lets his enemies see his face unmasked."

"But, then," I cried, amazed, "why do you offer me my freedom?"

"Because this cursed populace is in such a temper that if you are brought to trial, I know not what may happen. As likely as not we shall have an insurrection, open revolt against the Pontifical authority, and red war in the streets. And this is not the time for it.

"The Holy Father requires the submission of these people. We are upon the eve of Duke Pier Luigi's coming to occupy his new States, and it imports that he should be well received, that he should be given a loving welcome by his subjects. If, instead, they meet him with revolt and defiance, the reasons will be sought, and the blame of the affair will recoil upon me. Your cousin Cosimo will see to that. He is a very subtle gentleman, this cousin of yours, and he has a way of working to his own profit. So now you understand. I have no mind to be crushed in this business. Enough have I suffered already through you, enough am I suffering in resigning my governorship. So there is but one way out. There must be no trial to-morrow. It must be known that you have escaped. Thus they will be quieted, and the matter will blow over. So now, Ser Agostino, we understand each other. You must go."

"And whither am I to go?" I cried, remembering my mother and that Mondolfo — the only place of safety — was closed to me by her cruelly pious hands.

"Whither?" he echoed. "What do I care? To Hell — anywhere, so that you get out of this."

"I'd sooner hang," said I, quite seriously.

"You'd hang and welcome, for all the love I bear you," he answered, his impatience growing. "But if you hang, blood will be shed, innocent lives will be lost, and I myself may come to suffer."

"For you, sir, I care nothing," I answered him, taking his own tone, and returning him the same brutal frankness that he used with me. "That you deserve to suffer I do not doubt. But since other blood than yours might be shed as you say, since innocent lives might be lost . . . Give me the paper."

He was frowning upon me, and smiling viperishly at the same time. "I like your frankness better than your piety," said he. "So now we understand each other, and know that neither is in the other's debt. Hereafter beware of Egidio Gambara. I give you this last loyal warning. See that you do not come into my way again."

I rose and looked at him — looked down from my greater height. I knew well the source of this last, parting show of hatred. Like Cosimo's it sprang from jealousy. And a growth more potential of evil does not exist.

He bore my glance a moment, then turned and took up the lanthorn. "Come," he said, and obediently I followed him up the winding, stone staircase, and so to the very gates of the Palace.

We met no one. What had become of the guards, I cannot think; but I am satisfied that Gambara himself had removed them. He opened the wicket for me, and as I stepped out he gave me the paper and whistled softly. Almost at once I heard a sound of muffled hooves under the colonnade, and presently loomed the figures of a man and a mule, both dim and ghostly in the pearly light of dawn — for that was the hour.

Gambara followed me out, and pulled the wicket after him.

"That beast is for you," he said curtly. "It will the better enable you to get away."

As curtly I acknowledged the gift, and mounted whilst the groom held the stirrup for me.

Oh, it was the oddest of transactions! My Lord Gambara with death in his heart very reluctantly giving me a life I did not want.

I dug my heels into the mule's sides and started across the silent, empty square, then plunged into a narrow street where the gloom was almost as of midnight, and so pushed on.

I came out into the open space before the Porta Fodesta, and so to the gate itself. From one of the windows of the gatehouse, a light shone yellow, and, presently, in answer to my call, out came an officer followed by two men, one of whom carried a lanthorn swinging from his pike. He held this light aloft, whilst the officer surveyed me.

"What now?" he challenged. "None passes out to-night."

For answer I thrust the paper under his nose. "Orders from my Lord Gambara," said I.

But he never looked at it. "None passes out to-night," he repeated imperturbably. "So run my orders."

"Orders from whom?" quoth I, surprised by his tone and manner.

"From the Captain of Justice, if you must know. So you may get you back whence you came, and wait till daylight."

"Ah, but stay," I said. "I do not think you can have heard me. I carry orders from my Lord the Governor. The Captain of Justice cannot overbear these." And I shook the paper insistently.

"My orders are that none is to pass — not even the Governor himself," he answered firmly.

It was very daring of Cosimo, and I saw his aim. He was, as Gambara had said, a very subtle gentleman. He, too, had set his finger upon the pulse of the populace, and perceived what might be expected of it. He was athirst for vengeance, as he had shown me, and determined that neither I nor Gambara should escape. First, I must be tried, condemned, and hanged, and then he trusted, no doubt, that Gambara would be torn in pieces; and it was quite possible that Messer Cosimo himself would secretly find means to fan the mob's indignation against the Legate into fierce activity. And it seemed that the game was in his hands, for this officer's resoluteness showed how implicitly my cousin was obeyed.

Of that same resoluteness of the lieutenant's I was to have a yet more signal proof. For presently, whilst still I stood there vainly remonstrating, down the street behind me rode Gambara himself on a tall horse followed by a mule-litter and an escort of half a score of armed grooms.

He uttered an exclamation when he saw me still there, the gate shut and the officer in talk with me. He spurred quickly forward.

"How is this?" he demanded haughtily and angrily. "This man rides upon the business of the State. Why this delay to open for him?"

"My orders," said the lieutenant, civilly but firmly, "are that none passes out to-night."

"Do you know me?" demanded Gambara.

"Yes, my lord."

"And you dare talk to me of your orders? There

are no orders here in Piacenza but my orders. Set me wide the wicket of that gate. I myself must pass."

"My lord, I dare not."

"You are insubordinate," said the Legate, of a sudden very cold.

He had no need to ask whose orders were these. At once he saw the trammel spread for him. But if Messer Cosimo was subtle, so, too, was Messer Gambara. By not so much as a word did he set his authority in question with the officer.

"You are insubordinate," was all he answered him, and then to the two men-at-arms behind the lieutenant — "Ho, there!" he called. "Bring out the guard. I am Egidio Gambara, your Governor."

So calm and firm and full of assurance was his tone, so unquestionable his right to command them, that the men sprang instantly to obey him.

"What would you do, my lord?" quoth the officer, and he seemed daunted.

"Buffoon!" said Gambara between his teeth. "You shall see."

Six men came hurrying from the gatehouse, and the Cardinal called to them.

"Let the corporal stand forth," he said.

A man advanced a pace from the rank they had hastily formed, and saluted.

"Place me your officer under arrest," said the Legate coldly, advancing no reason for the order. "Let him be locked in the gatehouse until my return; and do you, sir corporal, take command here meanwhile."

The startled fellow saluted again, and advanced upon his officer. The lieutenant looked up with sudden

uneasiness in his eyes. He had gone too far. He had
not reckoned upon being dealt with in this summary
fashion. He had been bold so long as he conceived
himself no more than Cosimo's mouthpiece, obeying
orders for the issuing of which Cosimo must answer.
Instead, it seemed, the Governor intended that he
should answer for them himself. Whatever he, himself, now dared, he knew — as Gambara knew — that
his men would never dare to disobey the Governor,
who was the supreme authority there under the Pope.

"My lord," he exclaimed, "I had my orders from
the Captain of Justice."

"And dare you to say that your orders included my
messengers and my own self?" thundered the dainty
prelate.

"Explicitly, my lord," answered the lieutenant.

"It shall be dealt with on my return, and if what
you say is proved true, the Captain of Justice shall
suffer with yourself for this treason — for that is the
offence. Take him away, and some one open me that
gate."

There was an end to disobedience, and a moment or
two later we stood outside the town, on the bank of
the river, which gurgled and flowed away smoothly
and mistily in the growing light, between the rows of
stalwart poplars that stood like sentinels to guard it.

"And, now, begone," said Gambara curtly to me;
and wheeling my mule I rode for the bridge of boats,
crossed it, and set myself to breast the slopes beyond.

Midway up I checked and looked back across the
wide water. The light had grown quite strong by now,
and in the east there was a faint pink flush to herald
the approaching sun. Away beyond the river, moving

southward, I could just make out the Legate's little cavalcade. And then, for the first time, a question leapt in my mind concerning the litter whose leathern curtains had remained so closely drawn. Whom did it contain? Could it be Giuliana? Had Cosimo spoken the truth when he said that she had gone to Gambara for shelter?

A little while ago I had sighed for death and exulted in the chance of expiation and of purging myself of the foulness of sin. And now, at the sudden thought that occurred to me, I fell a prey to an insensate jealousy touching the woman whom I had lately loathed as the cause of my downfall. Oh, the inconstancy of the human heart, and the eternal battles in such poor natures as mine between the knowledge of right and the desire for wrong!

It was in vain that I sought to turn my thoughts to other things; in vain that I cast them back upon my recent condition and my recent resolves; in vain that I remembered the penitence of yestermorn, the confession at Fra Gervasio's knee, and the strong resolve to do penance and make amends by the purity of all my after-life. Vain was it all.

I turned my mule about, and still wrestling with my conscience, choking it, I rode down the hill again, and back across the bridge, and then away to the south, to follow Messer Gambara and set an end to doubt.

I must know. I must! It was no matter that conscience told me that here was no affair of mine; that Giuliana belonged to the past from which I was divorced, the past for which I must atone and seek forgiveness. I must know. And so I rode along the dusty highway in pursuit of Messer Gambara, who was proceeding, I imagined, to join the Duke at Parma.

I had no difficulty in following them. A question here, and a question there, accompanied by a description of the party, was all that was necessary to keep me on their track. And ever, it seemed to me from the answers that I got, was I lessening the distance that separated us.

I was weak for want of food, for the last time that I had eaten was yesterday at noon, at Mondolfo; and then but little. Yet all I had this day were some bunches of grapes that I stole in passing from a vineyard and ate as I trotted on along that eternal Via Æmilia.

It was towards noon, at last, that a taverner at Castel Guelfo informed me that my party had passed through the town but half an hour ahead of me. At the news I urged my already weary beast along, for unless I made good haste now it might well happen that Parma should swallow up Gambara and his party ere I overtook them. And then, some ten minutes later, I caught a flutter of garments half a mile or so ahead of me, amid the elms. I quitted the road and entered the woodland. A little way I still rode; then, dismounting, I tethered my mule, and went forward cautiously on foot.

I found them in a little sunken dell by a tiny rivulet. Lying on my belly in the long grass above, I looked down upon them with a black hatred of jealousy in my heart.

They were reclining there, in that cool, fragrant spot in the shadow of a great beech-tree. A cloth had been spread upon the ground, and upon this were platters of roast meats, white bread and fruits, and a flagon of wine, a second flagon standing in the brook to cool.

My Lord Gambara was talking and she was regarding him with eyes that were half veiled, a slow, insolent smile upon her matchless face. Presently at something that he said she laughed outright, a laugh so tuneful and light-hearted that I thought I must be dreaming all this. It was the gay, frank, innocent laughter of a child; and I never heard in all my life a sound that caused me so much horror. He leaned across to her, and stroked her velvet cheek with his delicate hand, whilst she suffered it in that lazy fashion that was so peculiarly her own.

I stayed for no more. I wriggled back a little way to where a clump of hazel permitted me to rise without being seen. Thence I fled the spot. And as I went, my heart seemed as it must burst, and my lips could frame but one word which I kept hurling out of me like an imprecation, and that word was "Trull!"

Two nights ago had happened enough to stamp her soul forever with sorrow and despair. Yet she could sit there, laughing and feasting and trulling it lightly with the Legate!

The little that remained me of my illusions was shivered in that hour. There was, I swore, no good in all the world; for even where goodness sought to find a way, it grew distorted, as in my mother's case. And yet through all her pietism surely she had been right! There was no peace, no happiness save in the cloister. And at last the full bitterness of penitence and regret overtook me when I reflected that by my own act I had rendered myself forever unworthy of the cloister's benign shelter.

16th to 31st

16th to 17th, cold over the Northern States. On the 18th a storm will form over the East Gulf States. 19th to 20th, a storm over the South Atlantic States. 21st to 22nd, snowstorm. 23rd to 24th, very cold. Snow over Northern States. 25th, snow and blizzards over the Northern States. 26th to 27th, clearing, windy. 28th to 29th, cold and clear. 31st, clear

CHAPTER IV

THE ANCHORITE OF MONTE ORSARO

I WENT blindly through the tangle of undergrowth, stumbling at every step and scarce noticing that I stumbled; and in this fashion I came presently back to my mule.

I mounted and rode amain, not by the way that I had come, but westward; not by road, but by bridle-paths, through meadow-land and forest, up hill and down, like a man entranced, not knowing whither I went nor caring.

Besides, whither was I to go? Like my father before me I was an outcast, a fugitive outlaw. But this troubled me not yet. My mind, my wounded, tortured mind, was all upon the past. It was of Giuliana that I thought as I rode in the noontide warmth of that September day. And never can human brain have held a sorer conflict of reflection than was mine.

No shadow now remained of the humour that had possessed me in the hour in which I had repudiated her after the murder of Fifanti. I had heard Fra Gervasio deliver judgment upon her, and I had doubted his justice, felt that he used her mercilessly. My own sight had now confirmed to me the truth of what he had said; but in doing so — in allowing me to see her in another man's possession — a very rage of jealousy had been stirred in me and a greater rage of longing.

There was the mule; that should yield a ducat or two. But when this was spent, what then? To go a suppliant to that pious icicle my mother were worse than useless.

Whither was I to turn — I, Lord of Mondolfo and Carmina, one of the wealthiest and most puissant tyrants of this Val di Taro? It provoked me almost to laughter, of a fierce and bitter sort. Perhaps some peasant of the contado would take pity on his lord and give him shelter and nourishment in exchange for such labour as that in which his lord might employ his stout limbs on that peasant's land, which was my own.

I might perhaps essay it. Certainly it was the only thing that was left me. For against my mother and to support my rights I might not invoke a law which had placed me under a ban, a law that would deal me out its rigours did I reveal myself.

Then I had thoughts of seeking sanctuary in some monastery, of offering myself as a lay-brother, to do menial work, and in this way, perhaps, I might find peace, and, in a lesser degree than was originally intended, the consolations of the religion to which I had been so grossly unfaithful. The thought grew and developed into a resolve. It brought me some comfort. It became a desire.

I pushed on, following the river along ground that grew swiftly steeper, conscious that perforce my journey must end soon, for my mule was showing signs of weariness.

Some three miles farther, having by then penetrated the green rampart of the foothills, I came upon the little village of Pojetta. It is a village composed of a

single street throwing out as its branches a few narrow
alleys, possessing a dingy church and a dingier tavern;
this last had for only sign a bunch of withered rosemary that hung above its grimy doors.

I drew rein there as utterly weary as my mule,
hungry and thirsty and weak. I got down and invited
the suspicious scrutiny of the lantern-jawed taverner,
who, for all that my appearance was humble enough
in such garments as I wore, must have accounted me
none the less of too fine an air for such a house as
his.

"Care for my beast," I bade him. "I shall stay
here an hour or two."

He nodded surlily, and led the mule away, whilst I
entered the tavern's single room. Coming into it from
the sunlight I could scarcely see anything at first, so
dark did the place seem. What light there was came
through the open door; for the chamber's single
window had long since been rendered opaque by a
screen of accumulated dust and cobwebs. It was a
roomy place, low-ceilinged with blackened rafters
running parallel across its dirty yellow wash.

The floor was strewn with foul rushes that must
have lain unchanged for months, slippery with grease
and littered with bones that had been flung there by
the polite guests the place was wont to entertain.
And it stank most vilely of rancid oil and burnt meats
and other things indefinable in all but their acrid,
nauseating, unclean pungency.

A fire was burning low at the room's far end, and
over this a girl was stooping, tending something in a
stew-pot. She looked round at my advent, and revealed herself for a tall, black-haired, sloe-eyed wench,

comely in a rude, brown way, and strong, to judge by
the muscular arms which were bared to the elbow.

Interest quickened her face at sight of so unusual a
patron. She slouched forward, wiping her hands upon
her hips as she came, and pulled out a stool for me at
the long trestle-table that ran down the middle of the
floor.

Grouped about the upper end of this table sat four
men of the peasant type, sun-tanned, bearded, and
rudely garbed in loose jerkins and cross-gartered leg-
cloths.

A silence had fallen upon them as I entered, and
they, too, were now inspecting me with a frank interest which in their simple way they made no attempt to conceal.

I sank wearily to the stool, paying little heed to
them, and in answer to the girl's invitation to command her, I begged for meat and bread and wine.
Whilst she was preparing these, one of the men addressed me civilly; and I answered him as civilly but
absently, for I had enough of other matters to engage
my thoughts. Then another of them questioned me in
a friendly tone as to whence I came. Instinctively I
concealed the truth, answering vaguely that I was
from Castel Guelfo — which was the neighbourhood in which I had overtaken my Lord Gambara
and Giuliana.

"And what do they say at Castel Guelfo of the
things that are happening in Piacenza?" asked another.

"In Piacenza?" quoth I. "Why, what is happening
in Piacenza?"

Eagerly, with an ardour to show themselves inti-

mate with the affairs of towns, as is the way of rustics,
they related to me what already I had gathered to be
the vulgar version of Fifanti's death. Each spoke in
turn, cutting in the moment another paused to
breathe, and sometimes they spoke together, each
anxious to have the extent of his information revealed
and appreciated.

And their tale, of course, was that Gambara, being
the lover of Fifanti's wife, had despatched the Doctor
on a trumped-up mission, and had gone to visit her by
night. But that the suspicious Fifanti lying near by in
wait, and having seen the Cardinal enter, followed
him soon after and attacked him, whereupon the Lord
Gambara had slain him. And then that wily, fiendish
prelate had sought to impose the blame upon the
young Lord of Mondolfo, who was a student in the
pedant's house, and he had caused the young man's
arrest. But this the Piacentini would not endure.
They had risen, and threatened the Governor's life;
and he was fled to Rome or Parma, whilst the au-
thorities to avoid a scandal had connived at the escape of Messer d'Anguissola, who was also gone, no
man knew whither.

The news had travelled speedily into that mountain
fastness, it seemed. But it had been garbled at its
source. The Piacentini conceived that they held some
evidence of what they believed — the evidence of the
lad whom Fifanti had left to spy and who had borne
him the tale that the Cardinal was within. This evidence they accounted well confirmed by the Legate's
flight.

Thus is history written. Not a doubt but that
some industrious scribe in Piacenza with a grudge

against Gambara, would set down what was the talk of the town; and hereafter, it is not to be doubted, the murder of Astorre Fifanti for the vilest of all motives will be added to the many crimes of Egidio Gambara, that posterity may execrate his name even beyond its already rich enough deserts.

I heard them in silence and but little moved, yet with a question now and then to probe how far this silly story went in detail. And whilst they were still heaping abuse upon the Legate — of whom they spoke as Jews may speak of pork — came the lantern-jawed host with a dish of broiled goat, some bread, and a jug of wine. This he set before me, then joined them in their vituperation of Messer Gambara.

I ate ravenously, and for all that I do not doubt the meat was tough and burnt, yet at the time those pieces of broiled goat upon that dirty table seemed the sweetest food that ever had been set before me.

Finding that I was but indifferently communicative and had little news to give them, the peasants fell to gossiping among themselves, and they were presently joined by the girl, whose name, it seemed, was Giovannozza. She came to startle them with the rumour of a fresh miracle attributed to the hermit of Monte Orsaro.

I looked up with more interest than I had hitherto shown in anything that had been said, and I inquired who might be this anchorite.

"Sainted Virgin!" cried the girl, setting her hands upon her generous hips, and turning her bold sloe-eyes upon me in a stare of incredulity. "Whence are you, sir, that you seem to know nothing of the world? You had not heard the news of Piacenza, which must be known to every one by now; and you have never heard of the anchorite of Monte Orsaro!" She appealed by a gesture to Heaven against the Stygian darkness of my mind.

"He is a very holy man," said one of the peasants.

"And he dwells alone in a hut midway up the mountain," added a second.

"In a hut which he built for himself with his own hands," a third explained.

"And he lives on nuts and herbs and such scraps of food as are left him by the charitable," put in the fourth, to show himself as full of knowledge as his fellows.

But now it was Giovannozza who took up the story, firmly and resolutely; and being a woman she easily kept her tongue going and overbore the peasants so that they had no further share in the tale until it was entirely told. From her I learnt that the anchorite, one Fra Sebastiano, possessed a miraculous image of the blessed martyr Saint Sebastian, whose wounds miraculously bled during Passion Week, and that there were no ills in the world that this blood would not cure, provided that those to whom it was applied were clean of mortal sin and imbued with the spirit of grace and faith.

No pious wayfarer going over the Pass of Cisa into Tuscany but would turn aside to kiss the image and ask a blessing at the hands of the anchorite; and yearly in the season of the miraculous manifestation, great pilgrimages were made to the hermitage by folk from the valleys of the Taro and Bagnanza, and even from beyond the Apennines. So that Fra Sebastiano gathered great store of alms, part of which he redistributed amongst the poor, part of which he was saving to build a bridge over the Bagnanza torrent, in crossing which so many poor folk had lost their lives.

I listened intently to the tale of wonders that followed, and now the peasants joined in again, each with a story of some marvellous cure of which he had direct knowledge. And many and amazing were the details they gave me of the saint — for they spoke of him as a saint already — so that no doubt lingered in my mind of the holiness of this anchorite.

Giovannozza related how a goatherd coming one night over the pass had heard from the neighbourhood of the hut the sounds of singing, and the music was the strangest and sweetest ever heard on earth, so that it threw the poor fellow into a strange ecstasy, and it was beyond doubt that what he had heard was an angel choir. And then one of the peasants, the tallest and blackest of the four, swore with a great oath that one night when he himself had been in the hills he had seen the hermit's hut all aglow with heavenly light against the black mass of the mountain.

All this left me presently very thoughtful, filled with wonder and amazement. Then their talk shifted again, and it was of the vintage they discoursed, the fine yield of grapes about Fontana Fredda, and the heavy crop of oil that there would be that year. And then with the hum of their voices gradually receding, it ceased altogether for me, and I was asleep with my head pillowed upon my arms.

It would be an hour later when I awakened, a little stiff and cramped from the uncomfortable position in which I had rested. The peasants had departed and the surly-faced host was standing at my side.

"You should be resuming your journey," said he, seeing me awake. "It wants but a couple of hours to sunset, and if you are going over the pass, it were well not to let the night overtake you."

"My journey?" said I aloud, and looked askance at him.

Whither, in Heaven's name, was I journeying?

Then I bethought me of my earlier resolve to seek shelter in some convent, and his mention of the pass caused me to think now that it would be wiser to cross the mountains into Tuscany. There I should be beyond the reach of the talons of the Farnese law, which might close upon me again at any time so long as I was upon Pontifical territory.

I rose heavily, and suddenly bethought me of my utter lack of money. It dismayed me for a moment. Then I remembered the mule, and determined that I must go afoot.

"I have a mule to sell," said I, "the beast in your stables."

He scratched his ear, reflecting, no doubt, upon the drift of my announcement. "Yes?" he said dubiously. "And to what market are you taking it?"

"I am offering it to you," said I.

"To me?" he cried, and instantly suspicion entered his crafty eye and darkened his brow. "Where got you the mule?" he asked, and snapped his lips together.

The girl entering at that moment stood at gaze, listening.

"Where did I get it?" I echoed. "What is that to you?"

He smiled unpleasantly. "It is this to me: that if the bargelli were to come up here and discover a stolen mule in my stables, it would be an ill thing for me."

I flushed angrily. "Do you imply that I stole the mule?" said I, so fiercely that he changed his air.

"Nay, now, nay, now," he soothed me. "And, after all, it happens that I do not want a mule. I have one mule already, and I am a poor man, and ..."

"A fig for your whines," said I. "Here is the case. I have no money — not a grosso. So the mule must pay for my dinner. Name your price, and let us have done."

"Ha!" he fumed at me. "I am to buy your stolen beast, am I? I am to be frightened by your violence into buying it? Be off, you rogue, or I'll raise the village and make short work of you. Be off, I say!"

He backed away as he spoke, towards the fireplace, and from the corner took a stout oaken staff. He was a villain, a thieving rogue. That much was plain. And it was no less plain that I must submit, and leave my beast to him, or else perhaps suffer a worse alternative.

Had those four honest peasants still been there, he would not have dared to have so borne himself. But as it was, without witnesses to say how the thing had truly happened, if he raised the village against me how should they believe a man who confessed that he had eaten a dinner for which he could not pay? It must go very ill with me.

If I tried conclusions with him, I could break him in two notwithstanding his staff. But there would remain the girl to give the alarm, and when to dishonesty I should have added violence, my case would be that of any common bandit.

"Very well," I said. "You are a dirty, thieving rascal, and a vile one to take advantage of one in my position. I shall return for the mule another day. Meanwhile, consider it in pledge for what I owe you. But see that you are ready for the reckoning when I present it."

With that, I swung on my heel, strode past the big-eyed girl, out of that foul kennel into God's sweet air, followed by the ordures of speech which that knave flung after me.

I turned up the street, setting my face towards the mountains, and trudged amain.

Soon I was out of the village and ascending the steep road towards the Pass of Cisa that leads over the Apennines to Pontremoli. This way had Hannibal come when he penetrated into Etruria some two thousand years ago. I quitted the road and took to bridle-paths under the shoulder of the mighty Mount Prinzera. Thus I pushed on and upward through grey-green of olive and deep enamelled green of fig-trees, and came at last into a narrow gorge between two great mountains, a place of ferns and moisture where all was shadow and the air felt chill.

Above me the mountains towered to the blue heavens, their flanks of a green that was in places turned to golden, where Autumn's fingers had already touched those heights, in places gashed with grey and purple wounds, where the bare rock thrust through.

I went on aimlessly, and came presently upon a little fir thicket, through which I pushed towards a sound of tumbling waters. I stood at last upon the rocks above a torrent that went thundering down the mighty gorge which it had cloven itself between the hills. Thence I looked down a long, wavering valley over which the rays of the evening sun were slanting, and hazily in the distance I could see the russet city of Fornovo which I had passed earlier that day. This torrent was the Bagnanza, and it effectively barred all passage. So I went up, along its bed, scrambling over lichened rocks or sinking my feet into carpets of soft, yielding moss.

At length, grown weary and uncertain of my way, I sank down to rest and think. And my thoughts were chiefly of that hermit somewhere above me in these hills, and of the blessedness of such a life, remote from the world that man had made so evil. And then, with thinking of the world, came thoughts of Giuliana. Two nights ago I had held her in my arms. Two nights ago! And already it seemed a century remote — as remote as all the rest of that life of which it seemed a part. For there had been a break in my existence with the murder of Fifanti, and in the past two days I had done more living and I had aged more than in all the eighteen years before.

Thinking of Giuliana, I evoked her image, the glowing, ruddy copper of her hair, the dark mystery of her eyes, so heavy-lidded and languorous in their smile. My spirit conjured her to stand before me all white and seductive as I had known her, and my longings were again upon me like a searing torture.

I fought them hard. I sought to shut that image out. But it abode to mock me. And then faintly from the valley, borne upon the breeze that came sighing through the fir-trees, rose the tinkle of an Angelus bell.

I fell upon my knees and prayed to the Mother of Purity for strength, and thus I came once more to peace. That done I crept under the shelter of a projecting rock, wrapped my cloak tightly about me, and lay down upon the hard ground to rest, for I was very weary.

Lying there I watched the colour fading from the sky. I saw the purple lights in the east turn to an orange that paled into faintest yellow, and this again into turquoise. The shadows crept up those heights. A star came out overhead, then another, then a score of stars to sparkle silvery in the blue-black heavens.

I turned on my side, and closed my eyes, seeking to sleep; and then quite suddenly I heard a sound of unutterable sweetness — a melody so faint and subtle that it had none of the form and rhythm of earthly music. I sat up, my breath almost arrested, and listened more intently. I could still hear it, but very faint and distant. It was as a sound of silver bells, and yet it was not quite that. I remembered the stories I had heard that day in the tavern at Pojetta, and the talk of the mystic melodies by which travellers had been drawn to the anchorite's abode. I noted the direction of the sound, and I determined to be guided by it, and to cast myself at the feet of that holy man, to implore of him who could heal bodies the miracle of my soul's healing and my mind's purging from its torment.

I pushed on, then, through the luminous night, keeping as much as possible to the open, for under trees lesser obstacles were not to be discerned. The melody grew louder as I advanced, ever following the Bagnanza towards its source; and the stream, too, being much less turbulent now, did not overbear that other sound.

It was a melody on long humming notes, chiefly, it seemed to me, upon two notes with the occasional interjection of a third and fourth, and, at long and rare intervals, of a fifth. It was harmonious beyond all description, just as it was weird and unearthly; but now that I heard it more distinctly it had much more the sound of bells — very sweet and silvery.

And then, quite suddenly, I was startled by a human cry — a piteous, wailing cry that told of helplessness and pain. I went forward more quickly in the direction whence it came, rounded a stout hazel coppice, and stood suddenly before a rude hut of pine logs built against the side of the rock. Through a small unglazed window came a feeble shaft of light.

I halted there, breathless and a little afraid. This must be the dwelling of the anchorite. I stood upon holy ground.

And then the cry was repeated. It proceeded from the hut. I advanced to the window, took courage and peered in. By the light of a little brass oil lamp with a single wick I could faintly make out the interior.

The rock itself formed the far wall of it, and in this a niche was carved — a deep, capacious niche in the shadows of which I could faintly discern a figure some two feet in height, which I doubted not would be the miraculous image of Saint Sebastian. In front of this was a rude wooden pulpit set very low, and upon it a great book with iron clasps and a yellow, grinning skull.

All this I beheld at a single glance. There was no other furniture in that little place, neither chair nor table; and the brass lamp was set upon the floor, near a heaped-up bed of rushes and dried leaves upon which I beheld the anchorite himself. He was lying upon his back, and seemed a vigorous, able-bodied man of a good length.

He wore a loose brown habit roughly tied about his middle by a piece of rope from which was suspended an enormous string of beads. His beard and hair were black, but his face was livid as a corpse's, and as I looked at him he emitted a fresh groan, and writhed as if in mortal suffering.

"O my God! My God!" I heard him crying. "Am I to die alone? Mercy! I repent me!" And he writhed, moaning, and rolled over on his side so that he faced me, and I saw that his livid countenance was glistening with sweat.

I stepped aside and lifted the latch of the rude door.

"Are you suffering, father?" I asked, almost fearfully.

At the sound of my voice, he suddenly sat up, and there was a great fear in his eyes. Then he fell back again with a cry.

"I thank Thee, my God! I thank Thee!"

I entered, and, crossing to his side, I went down on my knees beside him.

Without giving me time to speak, he clutched my arm with one of his clammy hands, and raised himself painfully upon his elbow, his eyes burning with the fever that was in him.

"A priest!" he gasped. "Get me a priest! Oh, if you would be saved from the flames of everlasting Hell, get me a priest to shrive me. I am dying, and I would not go hence with the burden of all this sin upon my soul."

I could feel the heat of his hand through the sleeve of my coat. His condition was plain. A raging fever was burning out his life.

"Be comforted," I said. "I will go at once." And I rose, whilst he poured forth his blessings upon me.

At the door I checked to ask what was the nearest place.

"Casi," he said hoarsely. "To your right, you will see the path down the hillside. You cannot miss it. In half an hour you should be there. And return at once, for I have not long. I feel it."

With a last word of reassurance and comfort I closed the door, and plunged away into the darkness.

CHAPTER V

THE RENUNCIATION

I FOUND the path the hermit spoke of, and followed its sinuous downhill course, now running when the ground was open, now moving more cautiously, yet always swiftly, when it led me through places darkened by trees.

At the end of a half-hour I espied below me the twinkling lights of a village on the hillside, and a few minutes later I was among the houses of Casi. To find the priest in his little cottage by the church was an easy matter; to tell him my errand and to induce him to come with me, to tend the holy man who lay dying alone in the mountain, was as easy. To return, however, was the most difficult part of the undertaking; for the upward path was steep, and the priest was old and needed such assistance as my own very weary limbs could scarcely render him. We had the advantage of a lanthorn which he insisted upon bringing, and we made as good progress as could be expected. But it was best part of two hours after my setting out before we stood once more upon the little platform where the hermit had his hut.

We found the place in utter darkness. Through lack of oil his little lamp had burned itself out; and when we entered, the man on the bed of wattles lay singing a lewd tavern-song, which, coming from such holy lips, filled me with horror and amazement. But the old priest, with that vast and doleful ex-

perience of death-beds which belongs to men of his
class, was quick to perceive the cause of this. The
fever was flickering up before life's final extinction,
and the poor moribund was delirious and knew not
what he said.

For an hour we watched beside him, waiting. The
priest was confident that there would be a return of
consciousness and a spell of lucidity before the end.

Through that lugubrious hour I squatted there,
watching the awful process of human dissolution for
the first time.

Save in the case of Fifanti I had never yet seen
death; nor could it be said that I had really seen it
then. With the pedant, death had been a sudden
sharp severing of the thread of life, and I had been
conscious that he was dead without any appreciation
of death itself, blinded in part by my own exalted
condition at the time.

But in this death of Fra Sebastiano I was heated by
no participation. I was an unwilling and detached
spectator, brought there by force of circumstance;
and my mind received from the spectacle an impression not easily to be effaced, an impression which
may have been answerable in part for that which
followed.

Towards dawn at last the sick man's babblings —
and they were mostly as profane and lewd as his
occasional bursts of song — were quieted. The un-
seeing glitter of his eyes that had ever and anon been
turned upon us was changed to a dull and heavy
consciousness, and he struggled to rise, but his limbs
refused their office.

The priest leaned over him with a whispered word

of comfort, then turned and signed to me to leave the hut. I rose, and went towards the door. But I had scarcely reached it when there was a hoarse cry behind me followed by a gasping sob from the priest. I started round to see the hermit lying on his back, his face rigid, his mouth open and idiotic, his eyes more leaden than they had been a moment since.

"What is it?" I cried, despite myself.

"He has gone, my son," answered the old priest sorrowfully. "But he was contrite, and he had lived a saint." And drawing from his breast a little silver box, he proceeded to perform the last rites upon the body from which the soul was already fled.

I came slowly back and knelt beside him, and long we remained there in silent prayer for the repose of that blessed spirit. And whilst we prayed the wind rose outside, and a storm grew in the bosom of the night that had been so fair and tranquil. The lightning flashed and illumined the interior of that hut with a vividness as of broad daylight, throwing into livid relief the arrow-pierced Saint Sebastian in the niche and the ghastly, grinning skull upon the hermit's pulpit.

The thunder crashed and crackled, and the echoes of its artillery went booming and rolling round the hills, whilst the rain fell in a terrific lashing downpour. Some of it finding a weakness in the roof, trickled and dripped and formed a puddle in the middle of the hut.

For upwards of an hour the storm raged, and all the while we remained upon our knees beside the dead anchorite. Then the thunder receded and gradually died away in the distance; the rain ceased;

and the dawn crept pale as a moonstone adown the valley.

We went out to breathe the freshened air just as the first touches of the sun quickened to an opal splendour the pallor of that daybreak. All the earth was steaming, and the Bagnanza, suddenly swollen, went thundering down the gorge.

At sunrise we dug a grave just below the platform with a spade which I found in the hut. There we buried the hermit, and over the spot I made a great cross with the largest stones that I could find. The priest would have given him burial in the hut itself; but I suggested that perhaps there might be some other who would be willing to take the hermit's place, and consecrate his life to carrying on the man's pious work of guarding that shrine and collecting alms for the poor and for the building of the bridge.

My tone caused the priest to look at me with sharp, kindly eyes.

"Have you such thoughts for yourself, perchance?" he asked me.

"Unless you should adjudge me too unworthy for the office," I answered humbly.

"But you are very young, my son," he said, and laid a kindly hand upon my shoulder. "Have you suffered, then, so sorely at the hands of the world that you should wish to renounce it and to take up this lonely life?"

"I was intended for the priesthood, father," I replied. "I aspired to holy orders. But through the sins of the flesh I have rendered myself unworthy. Here, perhaps, I can expiate and cleanse my heart of all the foulness it gathered in the world."

He left me an hour or so later, to make his way back
to Casi, having heard enough of my past and having
judged sufficiently of my attitude of mind to approve
me in my determination to do penance and seek peace
in that isolation. Before going he bade me seek him
out at Casi at any time should any doubts assail me,
or should I find that the burden I had taken up was
too heavy for my shoulders.

I watched him go down the winding, mountain
path, watched the bent old figure in his long black
gaberdine, until a turn in the path and a clump of
chestnuts hid him from my sight.

Then I first tasted the loneliness to which on that
fair morning I had vowed myself. The desolation of
it touched me and awoke self-pity in my heart, to
extinguish utterly the faint flame of ecstasy that had
warmed me when first I thought of taking the dead
anchorite's place.

I was not yet twenty; I was lord of great possessions;
and of life I had tasted no more than one poisonous,
reckless draught; yet I was done with the world —
driven out of it by penitence. It was just; but it was
bitter. And then I felt again that touch of ecstasy to
reflect that it was the bitterness of the resolve that
made it worthy; that through its very harshness was
it that this path should lead to grace.

Later on I busied myself with an inspection of the
hut, and my first attentions were for the miraculous
image. I looked upon it with awe, and I knelt to it in
prayer for forgiveness for the unworthiness I brought
to the service of the shrine.

The image itself was very crude of workmanship
and singularly ghastly. It reminded me poignantly of

the Crucifix that had hung upon the whitewashed wall
of my mother's private dining-room and had been so
repellent to my young eyes.

From two arrow wounds in the breast descended
two brown streaks, relics of the last miraculous
manifestation. The face of the young Roman
centurion who had suffered martyrdom for his conversion to Christianity was smiling very sweetly and
looking upwards, and in that part of his work the
sculptor had been very happy. But the rest of the
carving was gruesome and the anatomy was gross and
bad, the figure being so disproportionately broad as to
convey the impression of a stunted dwarf.

The big book standing upon the pulpit of plain deal
proved, as I had expected, to be a missal; and it became my custom to recite from it each morning thereafter the office for the day.

In a rude cupboard I found a jar of baked earth
that was half full of oil, and another larger jar containing some cakes of maize bread and a handful of
chestnuts. There was also a brown bundle which resolved itself into a monkish habit within which was
rolled a hair-shirt.

I took pleasure in this discovery, and I set myself at
once to strip off my secular garments and to don this
coarse brown habit, which, by reason of my great
height, descended but midway down my calves. For
lack of sandals I went barefoot, and having made a
bundle of the clothes I had removed I thrust them into
the cupboard in the place of those which I had taken
thence.

Thus did I, who had been vowed to the anchorite
order of Saint Augustine, enter upon my life as an un-

ordained anchorite. I dragged out the wattles upon which my blessed predecessor had breathed his last, and having swept the place clean with a bundle of hazel-switches which I cut for the purpose, I went to gather fresh boughs and rushes by the swollen torrent, and with these I made myself a bed.

My existence became not only one of loneliness, but of grim privation. People rarely came my way, save for a few faithful women from Casi or Fiori who solicited my prayers in return for the oil and maize-cakes which they left me, and sometimes whole days would pass without the sight of a single human being. These maize-cakes formed my chief nourishment, together with a store of nuts from the hazel coppice that grew before my door and some chestnuts which I went farther afield to gather in the woods. Occasionally, as a gift, there would be a jar of olives, which was the greatest delicacy that I savoured in those days. No flesh-food or fish did I ever taste, so that I grew very lean and often suffered hunger.

My days were spent partly in prayer and partly in meditation, and I pondered much upon what I could remember of the "Confessions" of Saint Augustine, deriving great consolation from the thought that if that great father of the Church had been able to win to grace out of so much sin as had befouled his youth, I had no reason to despair. And as yet I had received no absolution for the mortal offences I had committed at Piacenza. I had confessed to Fra Gervasio, and he had bidden me do penance first, but the penance had never been imposed. I was imposing it now. All my life should I impose it thus.

Yet, ere it was consummated I might come to die;

and the thought appalled me, for I must not die in sin. So I resolved that when I should have spent a year in that fastness I would send word to the priest at Casi by some of those who visited my hermitage, and desire him to come to me that I might seek absolution at his hands.

CHAPTER VI

HYPNEROTOMACHIA

AT first I seemed to make good progress in my quest after grace, and a certain solatium of peace descended upon me, beneficent as the dew of a summer night upon the parched and thirsty earth. But anon this changed and I would catch the mind that should have been bent upon pious meditation glancing backward with regretful longings at that life out of which I had departed.

I would start up in a pious rage and cast out such thoughts by more strenuous prayer and still more strenuous fasting. But as my body grew accustomed to the discomforts to which it was subjected, my mind assumed a rebellious freedom that clogged the work of purification upon which I strove to engage it. My stomach out of its very emptiness conjured up evil visions to torment me in the night, and with these I vainly wrestled until I remembered the measures which Fra Gervasio told me that he had taken in like case. I had then the happy inspiration to have recourse to the hair-shirt, which hitherto I had dreaded.

It would be towards the end of October, as the days were growing colder, that I first put on that armour against the shafts of Satan. It galled me horribly and fretted my tender flesh at almost every movement; but so, at least, at the expense of the body, I won back to some peace of mind, and the flesh, being quelled and subdued, no longer interposed its evil humours to the purity I desired for my meditations.

For upwards of a month, then, the mild torture of the goat's-hair cilice did the office I required of it. But towards December, my skin having grown tough and callous from the perpetual irritation, and inured to the fretting of the sharp hair, my mind once more began to wander mutinously. To check it again I put off the cilice, and with it all other under-garments, retaining no more clothing than just the rough brown monkish habit. Thus I exposed myself to the rigours of the weather, for it had grown very cold in those heights where I dwelt, and the snows were creeping nearer adown the mountain-side.

I had seen the green of the valley turn to gold and then to flaming brown. I had seen the fire perish out of those autumnal tints, and with the falling of the leaves, a slow, grey, bald decrepitude covering the world. And to this had now succeeded chill wintry gales that howled and whistled through the logs of my wretched hut, whilst the western wind coming down over the frozen zone above cut into me like a knife's edge.

And famished as I was I felt this coldness the more, and daily I grew leaner until there was little left of my erstwhile lusty vigour, and I was reduced to a parcel of bones held together in a bag of skin, so that it almost seemed that I must rattle as I walked.

I suffered, and yet I was glad to suffer, and took a joy in my pain, thanking God for the grace of permitting me to endure it, since the greater the discomforts of my body, the more numbed became the pain of my mind, the more removed from me were the lures of longing with which Satan still did battle for my soul.

In pain itself I seemed to find the nepenthes that
others seek from pain; in suffering was my Lethean
draught that brought the only oblivion that I craved.

I think that in those months my reason wandered a
little under all this strain; and I think to-day that the
long ecstasies into which I fell were largely the result
of a feverishness that burned in me as a consequence
of a chill that I had taken.

I would spend long hours upon my knees in prayer
and meditation. And remembering how others in such
case as mine had known the great boon and blessing
of heavenly visions, I prayed and hoped for some such
sign of grace, confident in its power to sustain me
thereafter against all possible temptation.

And then, one night, as the year was touching its
end, it seemed to me that my prayer was answered. I
do not think that my vision was a dream; leastways, I
do not think that I was asleep when it visited me. I
was on my knees at the time, beside my bed of wattles,
and it was very late at night. Suddenly the far end of
my hut grew palely lucent, as if a phosphorescent va-
pour were rising from the ground; it waved and rolled
as it ascended in billows of incandescence, and then
out of the heart of it there gradually grew a figure all
in white over which there was a cloak of deepest blue
all flecked with golden stars, and in the folded hands a
sheaf of silver lilies.

I knew no fear. My pulses throbbed and my heart
beat ponderously but rapturously as I watched the
vision growing more and more distinct until I could
make out the pale face of ineffable sweetness and the
veiled eyes.

It was the Blessed Madonna, as Messer Pordenone

had painted her in the Church of Santa Chiara at Piacenza; the dress, the lilies, the sweet pale visage, all were known to me, even the billowing cloud upon which one little naked foot was resting.

I cried out in longing and in rapture, and I held out my arms to that sweet vision. But even as I did so its aspect gradually changed. Under the upper part of the blue mantle, which formed a veil, was spread a mass of ruddy, gleaming hair; the snowy pallor of the face was warmed to the tint of ivory, and the lips deepened to scarlet and writhed in a worldly smile; the dark eyes glowed languidly; the lilies faded away, and the pale hands were held out to me.

"Giuliana!" I cried, and my pure and piously joyous ecstasy was changed upon the instant to fierce, carnal longings.

"Giuliana!" I held out my arms, and slowly she floated towards me, over the rough earthen floor of my cell.

A frenzy of craving seized me. I sought to rise, to go to meet her slow approach, to lessen by a second this agony of waiting. But my limbs were powerless. I was as if cast in lead, whilst more and more slowly she approached me, so languorously mocking.

And then revulsion took me, suddenly and without any cause or warning. I put my hands to my face to shut out a vision whose true significance I realized as in a flash.

"Retro me, Sathanas!" I thundered. "Jesus! Maria!"

I rose at last numbed and stiff. I looked again. The vision had departed. I was alone in my cell, and the rain was falling steadily outside. I groaned despairingly. Then I swayed, reeled sideways and lost all consciousness.

When I awoke it was broad day, and the pale wintry sun shone silvery from a winter sky. I was very weak and very cold, and when I attempted to rise all things swam round me, and the floor of my cell appeared to heave like the deck of a ship upon a rolling sea.

For days thereafter I was as a man entranced, alternately frozen with cold and burning with fever; and but that a shepherd who had turned aside to ask the hermit's blessing discovered me in that condition, and remained, out of his charity, for some three days to tend me, it is more than likely I should have died.

He nourished me with the milk of goats, a luxury upon which my strength grew swiftly, and even after he had quitted my hut he still came daily for a week to visit me, and daily he insisted that I should consume the milk he brought me, overruling my protests that my need being overpast there was no longer the excuse to pamper me.

Thereafter I knew a season of peace.

It was, I then reasoned, as if the Devil having tried me with a master stroke of temptation, and having suffered defeat, had abandoned the contest. Yet I was careful not to harbour that thought unduly, nor glory in my power, lest such presumption should lead to worse. I thanked Heaven for the strength it had lent me, and implored a continuance of its protection for a vessel so weak.

And now the hillside and valley began to put on the raiment of a new year. February, like a benignant nymph, tripped down by meadow and stream, and

touched the slumbering earth with gentler breezes.
And soon, where she had passed, the crocus reared its
yellow head, anemones, scarlet, blue, and purple,
tossed from her lap, sang the glories of spring in their
tender harmonies of hue, coy violet and sweet-smell-
ing nardosmia waved their incense on her altars, and
the hellebore sprouted by the streams.

Then as birch and beech and oak and chestnut put
forth a garb of tender pallid green, March advanced
and Easter came on apace.

But the approach of Easter filled me with a staggering dread. It was in Passion Week that the miracle of
the image that I guarded was wont to manifest itself.
What if through my unworthiness it should fail? The
fear appalled me, and I redoubled my prayers. There
was need; for spring which touched the earth so
benignly had not passed me by. And at moments
certain longings for the world would stir in me again,
and again would come those agonizing thoughts of
Giuliana which I had conceived were forever laid to
rest, so that I sought refuge once more in the hair-
shirt; and when this had again lost its efficacy, I took
long whip-like branches of tender eglantine to fashion
a scourge with which I flagellated my naked body so
that the thorns tore my flesh and set my rebellious
blood to flow.

One evening, at last, as I sat outside my hut, gazing
over the rolling emerald uplands, I had my reward. I
almost fainted when first I realized it in the extremity
of my joy and thankfulness. Very faintly, just as I had
heard it that night when first I came to the hermitage,
I heard now the mystic, bell-like music that had
guided my footsteps thither. Never since that night

had the sound of it reached me, though often I had listened for it.

It came now wafted down to me, it seemed, upon the evening breeze, a sound of angelic chimes infinitely ravishing to my senses, and stirring my heart to such an ecstasy of faith and happiness as I had never yet known since my coming thither.

It was a sign — a sign of pardon, a sign of grace. It could be naught else. I fell upon my knees and rendered my deep and joyous thanks.

And in all the week that followed that unearthly silver music was with me, infinitely soothing and solacing. I could wander afield, yet it never left me, unless I chanced to go so near the tumbling waters of the Bagnanza that their thunder drowned that other blessed sound. I took courage and confidence. Passion Week drew nigh; but it no longer had any terrors for me. I was adjudged worthy of the guardianship of the shrine. Yet I prayed, and made Saint Sebastian the special object of my devotions, that he should not fail me.

April came, as I learnt of the stray visitors who, of their charity, brought me the alms of bread, and the second day of it was the first of Holy Week.

CHAPTER VII

INTRUDERS

IT was on Holy Thursday that the image usually began to bleed, and it would continue so to do until the dawn of Easter Sunday.

Each day now, as the time drew nearer, I watched the image closely, and on the Wednesday I watched it with a dread anxiety I could not repress, for as yet there was no faintest sign. The brown streaks that marked the course of the last bleeding continued dry. All that night I prayed intently, in a torture of doubt, yet soothed a little by the gentle music that was never absent now.

With the first glint of dawn I heard steps outside the hut; but I did not stir. By sunrise there was a murmur of voices like the muttering of a sea upon its shore. I rose and peered more closely at the saint. He was just wood, inanimate and insensible, and there was still no sign. Outside, I knew, a crowd of pilgrims was already gathered. They were waiting, poor souls. But what was their waiting when compared with mine?

Another hour I knelt there, still beseeching Heaven to take mercy upon me. But Heaven remained unresponsive and the wounds of the image continued dry.

I rose, at last, in a sort of despair, and going to the door of the hut, I flung it wide.

The platform was filled with a great crowd of

peasantry, and an overflow poured down the sides of it and surged up the hill on the right and the left. At sight of me, so gaunt and worn, my eyes wild with despair and feverish from sleeplessness, a tangled growth of beard upon my hollow cheeks, they uttered as with one voice a great cry of awe. The multitude swayed and rippled, and then with a curious sound as that of a great wind, all went down upon their knees before me — all save the array of cripples huddled in the foreground, brought thither, poor wretches, in the hope of a miraculous healing.

As I was looking round upon that assembly, my eyes were caught by a flash and glitter on the road above us leading to the Cisa Pass. A little troop of men-at-arms was descending that way. A score of them there would be, and from their lance-heads fluttered scarlet bannerols bearing a white device which at that distance I could not make out.

The troop had halted, and one upon a great black horse, a man whose armour shone like the sun itself, was pointing down with his mail-clad hand. Then they began to move again, and the brightness of their armour, the fluttering pennons on their lances stirred me strangely in that fleeting moment, ere I turned again to the faithful who knelt there waiting for my words. Dolefully, with hanging head and downcast eyes, I made the dread announcement.

"My children, there is yet no miracle."

A deathly stillness followed the words. Then came an uproar, a clamour, a wailing. One bold mountaineer thrust forward to the foremost ranks, though without rising from his knees.

"Father," he cried, "how can that be? The saint

has never failed to bleed by dawn on Holy Thursday, these five years past."

"Alas!" I groaned, "I do not know. I but tell you what is. All night have I held vigil. But all has been vain. I will go pray again, and do you, too, pray."

I dared not tell them of my growing suspicion and fear that the fault was in myself; that here was a sign of Heaven's displeasure at the impurity of the guardian of that holy place.

"But the music!" cried one of the cripples raucously. "I hear the blessed music!"

I halted, and the crowd fell very still to listen. We all heard it pealing softly, soothingly, as from the womb of the mountain, and a great cry went up once more from that vast assembly, a hopeful cry that where one miracle was happening another must happen, that where the angelic choirs were singing all must be well.

And then with a thunder of hooves and clank of metal the troop that I had seen came over the pasturelands, heading straight for my hermitage, having turned aside from the road. At the foot of the hillock upon which my hut was perched they halted at a word from their leader.

I stood at gaze, and most of the people too craned their necks to see what unusual pilgrim was this who came to the shrine of Saint Sebastian.

The leader swung himself unaided from the saddle, full-armed as he was; then going to a litter in the rear, he assisted a woman to alight from it.

All this I watched, and I observed too that the device upon the bannerols was the head of a white horse. By that device I knew them. They were of the

House of Cavalcanti — a house that had, as I had heard, been in alliance and great friendship with my father. But that their coming hither should have anything to do with me or with that friendship I was assured was impossible. Not a single soul could know of my whereabouts or the identity of the present hermit of Monte Orsaro.

The pair advanced, leaving the troop below to await their return, and as they came I considered them, as did, too, the multitude.

The man was of middle height, very broad and active, with long arms, to one of which the little lady clung for help up the steep path. He had a proud, stern, aquiline face that was shaven, so that the straight lines of his strong mouth and powerful length of jaw looked as if chiselled out of stone. It was only at closer quarters that I observed how the general hardness of that countenance was softened by the kindliness of his deep brown eyes. In age I judged him to be forty, though in reality he was nearer fifty.

The little lady at his side was the daintiest maid that I had ever seen. The skin, white as a water-lily, was very gently flushed upon her cheeks; the face was delicately oval; the little mouth, the tenderest in all the world; the forehead low and broad, and the slightly slanting eyes — when she raised the lashes that hung over them like long shadows — were of the deep blue of sapphires. Her dark brown hair was coifed in a jewelled net of thread of gold, and on her white neck a chain of emeralds sparkled sombrely. Her close-fitting robe and her mantle were of the hue of bronze, and the light shifted along the silken fabric as she moved, so that it gleamed like metal. About her waist there was a girdle of hammered gold, and pearls were sewn upon the back of her brown velvet gloves.

One glance of her deep blue eyes she gave me as she approached; then she lowered them instantly, and so weak — so full of worldly vanities was I still that in that moment I took shame at the thought that she should see me thus, in this rough hermit's habit, my face a tangle of unshorn beard, my hair long and unkempt. And the shame of it dyed my gaunt cheeks. And then I turned pale again, for it seemed to me that out of nowhere a voice had asked me:

"Do you still marvel that the image will not bleed?"

So sharp and clear did those words arise from the lips of Conscience that it seemed to me as if they had been uttered aloud, and I looked almost in alarm to see if any other had overheard them.

The cavalier was standing before me, and his brows were knit, a deep amazement in his eyes. Thus awhile in utter silence. Then quite suddenly, his voice a ringing challenge:

"What is your name?" he said.

"My name?" quoth I, astonished by such a question, and remarking now the intentness and surprise of his own glance. "It is Sebastian," I answered, and truthfully, for that was the name of my adoption, the name I had taken when I entered upon my hermitage.

"Sebastian of what and where?" quoth he.

He stood before me, his back to the peasant crowd, ignoring them as completely as if they had no existence, supremely master of himself. And meanwhile, the little lady on his arm stole furtive upward glances at me.

"Sebastian of nowhere," I answered. "Sebastian the hermit, the guardian of this shrine. If you are come to . . ."

"What was your name in the world?" he interrupted impatiently, and all the time his eyes were devouring my gaunt face.

"The name of a sinner," answered I. "I have stripped it off and cast it from me."

An expression of impatience rippled across the white face.

"But the name of your father?" he insisted.

"I have none," answered I. "I have no kin or ties of any sort. I am Sebastian the hermit."

His lips smacked testily. "Were you baptized Sebastian?" he inquired.

"No," I answered him. "I took the name when I became the guardian of this shrine."

"And when was that?"

"In September of last year, when the holy man who was here before me died."

I saw a sudden light leap to his eyes and a faint smile to his lips. He leaned towards me. "Heard you ever of the name of Anguissola?" he inquired, and watched me closely, his face within a foot of mine.

But I did not betray myself, for the question no longer took me by surprise. I was accounted to be very like my father, and that a member of the House of Cavalcanti, with which Giovanni d'Anguissola had been so intimate, should detect the likeness was not unnatural. I was convinced, moreover, that his presence was fortuitous; that he had been guided thither by merest curiosity at the sight of that crowd of pilgrims.

"Sir," I said, "I know not your intentions; but in all humility let me say that I am not here to answer questions of worldly import. The world has done with me, and I with the world. So that unless you are come hither out of piety for this shrine, I beg that you will depart with God and molest me no further. You come at a singularly inauspicious moment, when I need all my strength to forget the world and my sinful past, that through me the will of Heaven may be done here."

I saw the maid's tender eyes raised to my face with a look of great compassion and sweetness whilst I spoke. I observed the pressure which she put upon his arm. Whether he gave way to that, or whether it was the sad firmness of my tone that prevailed upon him I cannot say. But he nodded shortly.

"Well, well!" he said, and with a final searching look, he turned, the little lady with him, and went clanking off through the lane which the crowd opened out for him.

That they resented his presence, since it was not due to motives of piety, they very plainly signified. They feared that the intrusion at such a time of a personality so worldly must raise fresh difficulties against the performance of the expected miracle.

Nor were matters improved when at the crowd's edge he halted and questioned one of them as to the meaning of this pilgrimage. I did not hear the peasant's answer; but I saw the white, haughty face suddenly thrown up, and I caught his next question:

"When did it last bleed?"

Again an inaudible reply, and again his ringing voice — "That would be before this young hermit came? And to-day it will not bleed, you say?"

He flashed me a last keen glance of his eyes, which had grown narrow and seemed laden with mockery. The little lady whispered something to him, in answer to which he laughed contemptuously.

"Fool's mummery," he snapped, and drew her on, she going, it seemed to me, reluctantly.

But the crowd had heard him and the insult offered to the shrine. A deep-throated bay rose up in menace, and some leapt to their feet as if they would attack him.

He checked, and wheeled at the sound. "How now?" he cried, his voice a trumpet-call, his eyes flashing terribly upon them; and as dogs crouch to heel at the angry bidding of their master, the multitude grew silent and afraid under the eyes of that single steel-clad man.

He laughed a deep-throated laugh, and strode down the hill with his little lady on his arm.

But when he had mounted and was riding off, the crowd, recovering courage from his remoteness, hurled its curses after him and shrilly branded him, "Derider!" and "Blasphemer!"

He rode contemptuously amain, however, looking back but once, and then to laugh at them.

Soon he had dipped out of sight, and of his company nothing was visible but the fluttering red pennons with the device of the white horse-head. Gradually these also sank and vanished, and once more I was alone with the crowd of pilgrims.

Enjoining prayer upon them again, I turned and re-entered the hut.

all that murk of sinful desire in which I had lain despite myself; for my desire of her was the blessed, noble desire to serve, to guard, to cherish.

Pure was she as the pale narcissus by the streams, and serving her what could I be but pure?

And then, quite suddenly, upon the heels of such thoughts came the reaction. Horror and revulsion were upon me. This was but a fresh snare of Satan's baiting to lure me to destruction. Where the memory of Giuliana had failed to move me to aught but penance and increasing rigours, the foul fiend sought to engage me with a seeming purity to my ultimate destruction. Thus had Anthony, the Egyptian monk, been tempted; and under one guise or another it was ever the same Circean lure.

I would make an end. I swore it in a mighty frenzy of repentance, in a very lust to do battle with Satan and with my own flesh and a phrenetic joy to engage in the awful combat.

I stripped off my ragged habit, and standing naked I took up my scourge of eglantine and beat myself until the blood flowed freely. But that was not enough. All naked as I was, I went forth into the blue night, and ran to a pool of the Bagnanza, going of intent through thickets of bramble and briar-rose that gripped and tore my flesh and lacerated me so that at times I screamed aloud in pain, to laugh ecstatically the next moment and joyfully taunt Satan with his defeat.

Thus I tore on, my very body ragged and bleeding from head to foot, and thus I came to the pool in the torrent's course. Into this I plunged, and stood with the icy waters almost to my neck, to purge the unholy fevers out of me. The snows above were melting at the time, and the pool was little more than liquid ice. The chill of it struck through me to the very marrow, and I felt my flesh creep and contract until it seemed like the rough hide of some fabled monster, and my wounds stung as if fire were being poured into them.

Thus awhile; then all feeling passed, and a complete insensibility to the cold of the water or the fire of the wounds succeeded. All was numbed, and every nerve asleep. At last I had conquered. I laughed aloud, and in a great voice of triumph I shouted so that the shout went echoing round the hills in the stillness of the night:

"Satan, thou art defeated!"

And upon that I crawled up the mossy bank, the water gliding from my long limbs. I attempted to stand. But the earth rocked under my feet; the blueness of the night deepened into black, and consciousness was extinguished like a candle that is blown out.

She appeared above me in a great effulgence that emanated from herself as if she were grown luminous. Her robe was of cloth of silver and of a dazzling sheen, and it hung closely to her lissom, virginal form; and by the chaste beauty of her I was moved to purest ecstasy of awe and worship.

The pale, oval face was infinitely sweet, the slanting eyes of heavenly blue were infinitely tender, the brown hair was plaited into two long tresses that hung forward upon either breast and were entwined with threads of gold and shimmering jewels. On the pale brow a brilliant glowed with pure white fires, and her hands were held out to me in welcome.

Her lips parted to breathe my name.

"Agostino d'Anguissola!" There were whole tomes of tender meaning in those syllables, so that hearing her utter them I seemed to learn all that was in her heart.

And then her shining whiteness suggested to me the name that must be hers.

"Bianca!" I cried, and in my turn held out my arms, and made as if to advance towards her. But I was held back in icy, clinging bonds, whose relentlessness drew from me a groan of misery.

"Agostino, I am waiting for you at Pagliano," she said, and the words dragged from the dark recesses of my memory the recollection that Pagliano was the Lombard stronghold of the Cavalcanti. "Come to me soon."

"I may not come," I answered miserably. "I am an anchorite, the guardian of a shrine; and my life that has been full of sin must be given henceforth to expiation. It is the will of Heaven."

She smiled all undismayed, smiled confidently and tenderly.

"Presumptuous!" she gently chid me. "What know you of the will of Heaven? The will of Heaven is inscrutable. If you have sinned in the world, in the world must you atone by deeds that shall serve the world — God's world. In your hermitage you are become barren soil that will yield naught to yourself or any. Come, then, from the wilderness. Come soon! I am waiting!"

And on that the splendid vision faded, and utter darkness once more encompassed me, a darkness through which still boomed repeatedly the fading echo of the words:

"Come soon! I am waiting!"

I lay upon my bed of wattles in the hut, and through the little unglazed windows the sun was pouring, but the dripping eaves told of rain that had lately ceased.

Over me was bending a kindly faced old man in whom I recognized the good priest of Casi.

I lay quite still for a long while, just gazing up at him. Soon my memory got to work of its own accord, and I bethought me of the pilgrims who must by now have come and who must be impatiently awaiting news.

How came I to have slept so long? Vaguely I remembered my last night's penance, and then came a black gulf in my memory, a gap I could not bridge. But uppermost leapt the anxieties concerning the image of Saint Sebastian.

I struggled up to discover that I was very weak; so weak that I was glad to sink back again.

"Does it bleed? Does it bleed yet?" I asked, and my voice was so small and feeble that the sound of it startled me.

The old priest shook his head, and his eyes were very full of compassion.

"Poor youth, poor youth!" he sighed.

Without all was silent; there was no such rustle of a multitude as I listened for. And then I observed in my cell a little shepherd-lad who had been wont to come that way for my blessing upon occasions. He was half naked, as lithe as a snake and almost as brown. What did he there? And then some one else stirred — an elderly peasant-woman with a wrinkled kindly face and soft dark eyes, whom I did not know at all.

Somehow, as my mind grew clearer, last night seemed ages remote. I looked at the priest again.

"Father," I murmured, "what has happened?"

His answer amazed me. He started violently. Looked more closely, and suddenly cried out:

"He knows me! He knows me! Deo gratias!" And he fell upon his knees.

Now here it seemed to me was a sort of madness. "Why should I not know you?" quoth I.

The old woman peered at me. "Aye, blessed be Heaven! He is awake at last, and himself again." She turned to the lad, who was staring at me, grinning. "Go tell them, Beppo! Haste!"

"Tell them?" I cried. "The pilgrims? Ah, no, no — not unless the miracle has come to pass!"

"There are no pilgrims here, my son," said the priest.

"Not?" I cried, and cold horror descended upon me. "But they should have come. This is Holy Friday, father."

"Nay, my son, Holy Friday was a fortnight ago."

I stared askance at him, in utter silence. Then I smiled half tolerantly. "But, father, yesterday they were all here. Yesterday was . . ."

"Your yesterday, my son, is sped these fifteen days," he answered. "All that long while, since the night you wrestled with the Devil, you have lain exhausted by that awful combat, lying there betwixt life and death. All that time we have watched by you, Leocadia here and I and the lad Beppo."

Now here was news that left me speechless for some

little while. My amazement and slow understanding were spurred on by a sight of my hands lying on the rude coverlet which had been flung over me. Emaciated they had been for some months now. But at present they were as white as snow and almost as translucent in their extraordinary frailty. I became increasingly conscious, too, of the great weakness of my body and the great lassitude that filled me.

"Have I had the fever?" I asked him presently.

"Aye, my son. And who would not? Blessed Virgin, who would not after what you underwent?"

And now he poured into my astonished ears the amazing story that had overrun the countryside. It would seem that my cry in the night, my exultant cry to Satan that I had defeated him, had been overheard by a goatherd who guarded his flock in the hills. In the stillness he distinctly heard the words that I had uttered, and he came trembling down, drawn by a sort of pious curiosity to the spot whence it had seemed to him that the cry had proceeded.

And there by a pool of the Bagnanza he had found me lying prone, my white body glistening like marble and almost as cold. Recognizing in me the anchorite of Monte Orsaro, he had taken me up in his strong arms and had carried me back to my hut. There he had set about reviving me by friction and by forcing between my teeth some of the grape-spirit that he carried in a gourd.

Finding that I lived, but that he could not arouse me and that my icy coldness was succeeded by the fire of fever, he had covered me with my habit and his own cloak, and had gone down to Casi to relate his story and fetch the priest.

This story was no less than that the hermit of Monte Orsaro had been fighting with the Devil, who had dragged him naked from his hut and had sought to hurl him into the torrent; but that on the very edge of the river the anchorite had found strength, by the grace of God, to overthrow the tormentor and to render him powerless; and in proof of it there was my body all covered with Satan's claw-marks by which I had been torn most cruelly.

The priest had come at once, bringing with him such restoratives as he needed, and it is a thousand mercies that he did not bring a leech, or else I might have been bled of the last drops remaining in my shrunken veins.

And meanwhile the goatherd's story had gone abroad. By morning it was on the lips of all the countryside, so that explanations were not lacking to account for Saint Sebastian's refusal to perform the usual miracle, and no miracle was expected — nor had the image yielded any.

The priest was mistaken. A miracle there had been. But for what had chanced, the multitude must have come again confidently expecting the bleeding of the image which had never failed in five years, and had the image not bled it must have fared ill with the guardian of the shrine. In punishment for his sacrilegious ministry which would be held responsible for the absence of the miracle they so eagerly awaited, well might the crowd have torn me limb from limb.

Next the old man went on to tell me how three days ago there had come to the hermitage a little troop of men-at-arms, led by a tall, bearded man whose device was a sable band upon an argent field, and accompanied by a friar of the order of Saint Francis, a tall, gaunt fellow who had wept at sight of me.

"That would be Fra Gervasio!" I exclaimed. "How came he to discover me?"

"Yes — Fra Gervasio is his name," replied the priest.

"Where is he now?" I asked.

"I think he is here."

In that moment I caught the sound of approaching steps. The door opened, and before me stood the tall figure of my best friend, his eyes all eagerness, his pale face flushed with joyous excitement.

I smiled my welcome.

"Agostino! Agostino!" he cried, and ran to kneel beside me and take my hand in his. "Oh, blessed be God!"

In the doorway stood now another man, who had followed him — one whose face I had seen somewhere, yet could not at first remember where. He was very tall, so that he was forced to stoop to avoid the lintel of the low door — as tall as Gervasio or myself — and the tanned face was bearded by a heavy brown beard in which a few strands of grey were showing. Across his face there ran the hideous livid scar of a blow that must have crushed the bridge of his nose. It began just under the left eye, and crossed the face downwards until it was lost in the beard on the right side almost in line with the mouth. Yet, notwithstanding that disfigurement, he still possessed a certain beauty, and the deep-set, clear, grey-blue eyes were the eyes of a brave and kindly man.

He wore a leather jerkin and great thigh-boots of grey leather, and from his girdle of hammered steel hung a dagger and the empty carriages of a sword. His cropped black head was bare, and in his hand he carried a cap of black velvet.

We looked at each other awhile, and his eyes were sad and wistful, laden with pity, as I thought, for my condition. Then he moved forward with a creak of leather and jingle of spurs that made pleasant music.

He set a hand upon the shoulder of the kneeling Gervasio.

"He will live now, Gervasio?" he asked.

"Oh, he will live," answered the friar with an almost fierce satisfaction in his positive assurance. "He will live and in a week we can move him hence. Meanwhile he must be nourished." He rose. "My good Leocadia, have you the broth? Come, then, let us build up this strength of his. There is haste, good soul; great haste!"

She bustled at his bidding, and soon outside the door there was a crackling of twigs to announce the lighting of a fire. And then Gervasio made known to me the stranger.

"This is Galeotto," he said. "He was your father's friend, and would be yours."

"Sir," said I, "I could not desire otherwise with any who was my father's friend. You are not, perchance, the Gran Galeotto?" I inquired, remembering the sable device on argent of which the priest had told me.

"I am that same," he answered, and I looked with interest upon one whose name had been ringing through Italy these last few years. And then, I suddenly realized why his face was familiar to me. This was the man who in a monkish robe had stared so insistently at me that day at Mondolfo five years ago.

He was a sort of outlaw, a remnant of the days of chivalry and free-lances, whose sword was at the disposal of any purchaser. He rode at the head of a last fragment of the famous company that Giovanni de' Medici had raised and captained until his death. The sable band which they adopted in mourning for that warrior, earned for their founder the posthumous title of Giovanni delle Bande Nere.

He was called Il Gran Galeotto (as another was called Il Gran Diavolo) in play upon the name he bore and the life he followed. He had been in bad odour with the Pope for his sometime association with my father, and he was not well viewed in the Pontifical domains until, as I was soon to learn, he had patched up a sort of peace with Pier Luigi Farnese, who thought that the day might come when he should need the support of Galeotto's free-lances.

"I was," he said, "your father's closest friend. I took this at Perugia, where he fell," he added, and pointed to his terrific scar. Then he laughed. "I wear it gladly in memory of him."

He turned to Gervasio, smiling. "I hope that Giovanni d'Anguissola's son will hold me in some affection for his father's sake, when he shall come to know me better."

"Sir," I said, "from my heart I thank you for that pious, kindly wish; and I would that I might fully correspond to it. But Agostino d'Anguissola, who has been so near to death in the body, is, indeed, dead to the world already. Here you see but a poor hermit named Sebastian, who is the guardian of this shrine."

Gervasio rose suddenly. "This shrine . . ." he began in a fierce voice, his face inflamed as with sudden wrath. And there he stopped short. The priest was staring at him, and through the open door came Leocadia with a bowl of steaming broth. "We'll talk of this again," he said, and there was a sort of thunder rumbling in the promise.

CHAPTER IX

THE ICONOCLAST

IT was a week later before we returned to the subject.

Meanwhile, the good priest of Casi and Leocadia had departed, bearing with them a princely reward from the silent, kindly eyed Galeotto.

To tend me there remained only the boy Beppo; and after my long six months of lenten fare there followed now a period of feasting that began to trouble me as my strength returned. When, finally, on the seventh day, I was able to stand, and, by leaning on Gervasio's arm, to reach the door of the hut and to look out upon the sweet spring landscape and the green tents that Galeotto's followers had pitched for themselves in the dell below my platform, I vowed that I would make an end of broths and capons' breasts and trout and white bread and red wine and all such succulences.

But when I spoke so to Gervasio, he grew very grave.

"There has been enough of this, Agostino," said he. "You have gone near your death; and had you died, you had died a suicide and had been damned — deserving it for your folly if for naught else."

I looked at him with surprise and reproach. "How, Fra Gervasio?" I said.

"How?" he answered. "Do you conceive that I am to be fooled by tales of fights with Satan in the night and the marks of the Fiend's claws upon your body? Is this your sense of piety, to add to the other foul impostures of this place by allowing such a story to run the breadth of the countryside?"

"Foul impostures?" I echoed, aghast. "Fra Gervasio, your words are sacrilege."

"Sacrilege?" he cried, and laughed bitterly. "Sacrilege? And what of that?" And he flung out a stern, rigid, accusing arm at the image of Saint Sebastian in its niche.

"You think because it did not bleed . . ." I began.

"It did not bleed," he cut in, "because you are not a knave. That is the only reason. This man who was here before you was an impious rogue. He was no priest. He was a follower of Simon Mage, trafficking in holy things, battening upon the superstition of poor humble folk. A black villain who is dead — dead and damned, for he was not allowed time when the end took him to confess his ghastly sin of sacrilege and the money that he had extorted by his simonies."

"My God! Fra Gervasio, what do you say? How dare you say so much?"

"Where is the money that he took to build his precious bridge?" he asked me sharply. "Did you find any when you came hither? No. I'll take oath that you did not. A little longer, and this brigand had grown rich and had vanished in the night — carried off by the Devil, or borne away to realms of bliss by the angels, the poor rustics would have said."

Amazed at his vehemence, I sank to a tree-bole that stood near the door to do the office of a stool.

"But he gave alms!" I cried, my senses all bewildered.

"Dust in the eyes of fools. No more than that. That image" — his scorn became tremendous — "is an impious fraud, Agostino."

Could the monstrous thing that he suggested be possible? Could any man be so lost to all sense of God as to perpetrate such a deed as that without fear that the lightnings of Heaven would blast him?

I asked the question. Gervasio smiled.

"Your notions of God are heathen notions," he said, more quietly. "You confound Him with Jupiter the Thunderer. He does not use His lightnings quite in the manner of the father of Olympus. And yet . . . Consider how that brigand met his death."

"But . . . but . . ." I stammered. And then, quite suddenly, I stopped short, and listened. "Hark, Fra Gervasio! Do you not hear it?"

"Hear it? Hear what?"

"The music — the angelic melodies! And you can say that this place is a foul imposture; this holy image an impious fraud! And you a priest! Listen! It is a sign to warn you against stubborn unbelief."

He listened, with frowning brows, a moment; then he smiled.

"Angelic melodies!" he echoed with gentlest scorn. "By what snarcs does the Devil delude men, using even suggested holiness for his purpose! That, boy — that is no more than the dripping of water into little wells of different depths, producing different notes. It is in there, in some cave in the mountain where the Bagnanza springs from the earth."

I listened, already half disillusioned, yet fearing that my senses were too slavishly obeying his suggestion. "The proof of that? The proof!" I cried.

"The proof is that you have never heard it after heavy rain, or while the river was swollen."

I looked back upon the time I had spent there, upon the despair that had beset me when the music ceased, upon the joy that had been mine when again I heard it, accepting it always as a sign of grace. And it was as he said. Not my unworthiness, but the rain, had ever silenced it. In memory I ran over the occasions, and so clearly did I perceive the truth of this, that I marvelled the coincidence should not earlier have discovered it to me.

Moreover, now that my illusions concerning it were gone, the sound was clearly no more than he had said. I recognized its nature. It might have intrigued a sane man for a day or a night. But it could never longer have deceived any whose mind was not fevered with fanatic ecstasy.

Then I looked again at the image in the niche, and the pendulum of my faith was suddenly checked in its counter-swing. About that image there could be no delusions. The whole countryside had witnessed the miracle of the bleeding, and it had wrought cures, wondrous cures, among the faithful. They could not all have been deceived. Besides, from the wounds in the breast there were still the brown signs of the last manifestation.

But when I had given some utterance to these thoughts, Gervasio for only answer stooped and picked up a woodman's axe that stood against the wall. With this he went straight towards the image.

"Fra Gervasio!" I cried, leaping to my feet, a premonition of what he was about turning me cold with horror. "Stay!" I almost screamed.

But too late. My answer was a crashing blow. The next instant, as I sank back to my seat and covered my face, the two halves of the image fell at my feet, flung there by the friar.

"Look!" he bade me in a roar.

Fearfully I looked. I saw. And yet I could not believe.

He came quickly back, and picked up the two halves. "The oracle of Delphi was not more impudently worked," he said. "Observe this sponge, these plates of metal that close down upon it and exert the pressure necessary to send the liquid with which it is laden oozing forth." As he spoke he tore out the fiendish mechanism. "And see now how ingeniously it was made to work — by pressure upon this arrow in the flank."

There was a laugh from the door. I looked up, startled, to find Galeotto standing at my elbow. So engrossed had I been that I had never heard his soft approach over the turf.

"Body of Bacchus!" said he. "Here is Gervasio become an image-breaker to some purpose. What now of your miraculous saint, Agostino?"

My answer was first a groan over my shattered illusion, and then a deep-throated curse at the folly that had made a mock of me.

The friar set a hand upon my shoulder. "You see, Agostino, that your excursions into holy things do not promise well. Away with you, boy! Off with this hypocrite robe, and get you out into the world to do useful work for God and man. Had your heart truly called you to the priesthood, I had been the first to have guided your steps thither. But your

mind upon such matters has been warped, and your
views are all false; you confound mysticism with
true religion, and mouldering in a hermitage with the
service of God. How can you serve God here? Is
not the world God's world that you must shun it as
if Satan had created it? Go, I say — and I say it
with the authority of the orders that I bear — go and
serve man, and thus shall you best serve God. All
else are but snares to such a nature as yours."

I looked at him helplessly, and from him to
Galeotto, who stood there, his black brows knit,
watching me with intentness as if great issues hung
upon my answer. And Gervasio's words touched in
my mind some chord of memory. They were words
that I had heard before — or something very like
them, something whose import was the same.

Then I groaned miserably and took my head in my
hands. "Whither am I to go?" I cried. "What place
is there in all the world for me? I am an outcast.
My very home is held against me. Whither, then,
shall I go?"

"If that is all that troubles you," said Galeotto,
his tone unctuously humorous, "why, we will ride to
Pagliano."

I leapt at the word — literally leapt to my feet,
and stared at him with blazing eyes.

"Why, what ails him now?" quoth he.

Well might he ask. That name — Pagliano — had
stirred my memory so violently, that of a sudden as
in a flash I had seen again the strange vision that visited my delirium; I had seen again the inviting eyes,
the beckoning hands, and heard again the gentle
voice saying, "Come to Pagliano! Come soon!"

And now I knew, too, where I had heard words urging my return to the world that were of the same import as those which Gervasio used.

What magic was there here? What wizardry was at play? I knew — for they had told me — that it had been that cavalier who had visited me, that man whose name was Ettore de' Cavalcanti, who had borne news to them of one who was strangely like what Giovanni d'Anguissola had been.

"You are faint, Agostino," cried Gervasio, with a sudden solicitude, and put an arm about my shoulders as I staggered.

"No, no," said I. "It is nothing. Tell me —" And I paused almost afraid to put the question, lest the answer should dash my sudden hope. For it seemed to me that in this place of false miracles, one true miracle at least had been wrought; if it should be proved so indeed, then would I accept it as a sign that my salvation lay indeed in the world. If not . . .

"Tell me," I began again; "this Cavalcanti has a daughter. She was with him upon that day when he came here. What is her name?"

Galeotto looked at me out of narrowing eyes.

"Why, what has that to do with anything?" quoth Gervasio.

"More than you think. Answer me, then. What is her name?"

"Her name is Bianca," said Galeotto.

Something within me seemed to give way, so that I fell to laughing foolishly as women laugh who are on the verge of tears. By an effort I regained my self-control.

"It is very well," I said. "I will ride with you to Pagliano."

Both stared, amazed by the suddenness of my consent following upon information that, in their minds, could have no possible bearing upon the matter at issue.

"Is he quite sane, do you think?" quoth Galeotto gruffly.

"I think he is becoming so," said Fra Gervasio after a pause.

"God give me patience, then," grumbled the soldier, and left me puzzled by the words.

BOOK IV: THE WORLD

∴

CHAPTER I

PAGLIANO

THE lilac was in bloom when we came to the grey walls of Pagliano in that May of '45, and its scent, arousing the memory of my return to the world, has ever since been to me symbolical of the world itself.

Mine was no half-hearted, backward-glancing return. Having determined upon the step, I took it resolutely and completely at a single stride. Since Galeotto placed his resources at my disposal, to be repaid him later when I should have entered upon the enjoyment of my heritage of Mondolfo, I did not scruple to draw upon them for my needs.

I accepted the fine linen and noble raiment that he offered, and I took pleasure in the brave appearance that I made in them, my face shorn now of its beard and my hair trimmed to a proper length. Similarly I accepted weapons, money, and a horse; and thus equipped, looking for the first time in my life like a patrician of my own lofty station, I rode forth from Monte Orsaro with Galeotto and Gervasio, attended by the former's troop of twenty lances.

And from the moment of our setting out there came upon me a curious peace, a happiness and a great sense of expectancy. No longer was I oppressed by the fear of proving unworthy of the life which I had chosen — as had been the case when that life had been monastic.

Galeotto was in high spirits to see me so blithe, and he surveyed with pride the figure that I made, vowing that I should prove a worthy son of my father ere all was done.

The first act of my new life was performed as we were passing through the village of Pojetta.

I called a halt before the doors of that mean hostelry, over which hung what, no doubt, would still be the same withered bunch of rosemary that had been there in autumn when last I went that way.

To the sloe-eyed, deep-bosomed girl who lounged against the doorpost to see so fine a company ride by, I gave an order to fetch the taverner. He came with a slouch, a bent back, and humble, timid eyes — a very different attitude from that which he had last adopted towards me.

"Where is my mule, you rogue?" quoth I.

He looked at me askance. "Your mule, Magnificent?" said he.

"You have forgotten me, I think — forgotten the lad in rusty black who rode this way last autumn and whom you robbed."

At the words he turned a sickly yellow, and fell to trembling and babbling protestations and excuses.

"Have done," I broke in. "You would not buy the mule then. You shall buy it now, and pay for it with interest."

"What is this, Agostino?" quoth Galeotto at my elbow.

"An act of justice, sir," I answered shortly, whereupon he questioned me no further, but looked on with a grim smile. Then to the taverner: "Your manners to-day are not quite the same as on the last occasion when we met. I spare you the gallows that you may live to profit by the lesson of your present near escape. And now, rogue, ten ducats for that mule." And I held out my hand.

"Ten ducats!" he cried, and gathering courage, perhaps, since he was not to hang. "It is twice the value of the beast," he protested.

"I know," I said. "It will be five ducats for the mule, and five for your life. I am merciful to rate the latter as cheaply as it deserves. Come, thief, the ten ducats without more ado, or I'll burn your nest of infamy and hang you above the ruins."

He cowered and shrivelled. Then he scuttled within doors to fetch the money, whilst Galeotto laughed deep in his throat.

"You are well advised," said I, when the rogue returned and handed me the ducats. "I told you I should come back to present my reckoning. Be warned by this."

As we rode on Galeotto laughed again. "Body of Satan! There is a thoroughness about you, Agostino. As a hermit you did not spare yourself; and now as a tyrant you do not seem likely to spare others."

"It is the Anguissola way," said Gervasio quietly.

"You mistake," said I. "I conceive myself in the world for some good purpose, and the act you have witnessed is a part of it. It was not a revengeful deed. Vengeance would have taken a harsher course. It was justice, and justice is righteous."

"Particularly a justice that puts ten ducats in your pocket," laughed Galeotto.

"There, again, you mistake me," said I. "My aim is that thieves be mulcted to the end that the poor shall profit." And I drew rein again.

A little crowd had gathered about us, mostly of very ragged, half-clad people, for this village of Pojetta was a very poverty-stricken place. Into that little crowd I flung the ten ducats — with the consequence that on the instant it became a seething, howling, snarling, quarrelling mass. In the twinkling of an eye a couple of heads were cracked and blood was flowing, so that to quell the riot my charity had provoked, I was forced to spur my horse forward and bid them with threats disperse.

"And I think now," said Galeotto when it was done, "that you are just as reckless in the manner of doing charity. For the future, Agostino, you would do well to appoint an almoner."

I bit my lip in vexation; but soon I smiled again. Were such little things to fret me? Did we not ride to Pagliano and to Bianca de' Cavalcanti? At the very thought my pulses would quicken, and a sweetness of anticipation would invade my soul, to be clouded at moments by an indefinable dread.

And thus we came to Pagliano in that month of May, when the lilac was in bloom, as I have said, and after Fra Gervasio had left us, to return to his convent at Piacenza.

We were received in the courtyard of that mighty fortress by that sturdy, hawk-faced man who had recognized me in the hermitage on Monte Orsaro. But he was no longer in armour. He wore a surcoat of yellow velvet, and his eyes were very kindly and affectionate when they rested on Galeotto and from Galeotto passed on to take survey of me.

"So this is our hermit!" quoth he, a note of some surprise in his crisp tones. "Somewhat changed!"

"By a change that goes deeper than his pretty doublet," said Galeotto.

We dismounted, and grooms, in the Cavalcanti livery of scarlet with the horse-head in white upon their breasts, led away our horses. The seneschal acted as quartermaster to our lances, whilst Cavalcanti himself led us up the great stone staircase with its carved balustrade of marble, from which rose a file of pillars to support the groined ceiling. This last was frescoed in dull red with the white horse-head at intervals. On our right, on every third step, stood orange-trees in tubs, all flowering and shedding the most fragrant perfume.

Thus we ascended to a spacious gallery, and through a succession of magnificent rooms we came to the noble apartments that had been made ready for us.

A couple of pages came to tend me, bringing perfumed water and macerated herbs for my ablutions. These performed, they helped me into fresh garments that awaited me — black hose of finest silk and velvet trunks of the same sable hue, and for my body a fine close-fitting doublet of cloth of gold, caught at the waist by a jewelled girdle from which hung a dagger that was the merest toy.

When I was ready they went before me, to lead the way to what they called the private dining-room, where supper awaited us. At the very mention of a private dining-room I had a vision of whitewashed walls and high-set windows and a floor strewn with rushes. Instead we came into the most beautiful chamber that I had ever seen. From floor to ceiling it was hung with arras of purple brocade alternating with cloth of gold; thus on three sides. On the fourth there was an opening for the embayed window which glowed like a gigantic sapphire in the deepening twilight.

The floor was spread with a carpet of the ruddy purple of porphyry, very soft and silent to the feet. From the frescoed ceiling, where a joyous Phœbus drove a team of spirited white stallions, hung a chain that was carved in the semblance of interlocked Titans to support a great candelabrum, each branch of which was in the image of a Titan holding a stout candle of scented wax. It was all in gilded bronze and the workmanship — as I was presently to learn — of that great artist and rogue Benvenuto Cellini. From this candelabrum there fell upon the board a soft golden radiance that struck bright gleams from crystal and plate of gold and silver.

By a buffet laden with meats stood the master of the household in black velvet, his chain of office richly carved, his badge a horse's head in silver, and he was flanked on either hand by a nimble-looking page.

Of all this my first glance gathered but the most fleeting of impressions. For my eyes were instantly arrested by her who stood between Cavalcanti and Galeotto, awaiting my arrival. And, miracle of miracles, she was arrayed exactly as I had seen her in my vision.

Her supple maiden body was sheathed in a gown of

cloth of silver; her brown hair was dressed into two plaits interlaced with gold threads and set with tiny gems, and these plaits hung one on either breast. Upon the low, white brow a single jewel gleamed — a brilliant of the very whitest fire.

Her long blue eyes were raised to look at me as I entered, and their glance grew startled when it encountered mine, the delicate colour faded gradually from her cheeks, and her eyes fell at last as she moved forward to bid me welcome to Pagliano in her own name.

They must have perceived her emotion as they perceived mine. But they gave no sign. We got to the round table — myself upon Cavalcanti's left, Galeotto in the place of honour, and Bianca facing her father so that I was on her right.

The seneschal bestirred himself, and the silken ministering pages fluttered round us. My Lord of Pagliano was one who kept a table as luxurious as all else in his splendid palace. First came a broth of veal in silver basins, then a stew of cocks' combs and capons' breasts, then the ham of a roasted boar, the flesh very lusciously saturated with the flavour of rosemary; and there was venison that was as soft as velvet, and other things that I no longer call to mind. And to drink there was a fragrant, well-sunned wine of Lombardy that had been cooled in snow.

Galeotto ate enormously, Cavalcanti daintily, I but little, and Bianca nothing. Her presence had set up such emotions in me that I had no thought for food. But I drank deeply, and so came presently to a spurious ease which enabled me to take my share in the talk that was toward, though when all is said it was but a slight share, since Cavalcanti and Galeotto discoursed of matters wherein my knowledge was not sufficient to enable me to bear a conspicuous part.

More than once I was on the point of addressing Bianca herself, but always courage failed me. I had ever in mind the memory she must have of me as she had last seen me, to increase the painful diffidence which her presence itself imposed. Nor did I hear her voice more than once or twice when she demurely answered such questions as her father set her. And though now and again I found her stealing a look at me, she would instantly avert her eyes when our glances crossed.

Thus was our first meeting, and for a little time it was to be our last, because I lacked the courage to seek her out. She had her own apartments at Pagliano with her own maids of honour, like a princess; and the castle garden was entirely her domain into which even her father seldom intruded. He gave me the freedom of it; but it was a freedom of which I never took advantage in the week that we abode there. Several times was I on the point of doing so. But I was ever restrained by my unconquerable diffidence.

And there was something else to impose restraint upon me. Hitherto the memory of Giuliana had come to haunt me in my hermitage, by arousing in me yearnings which I had to combat with fasting and prayer, with scourge and cilice. Now the memory of her haunted me again; but in a vastly different way. It haunted me with the reminder of all the sin in which through her I had steeped myself; and just as the memory of that sin had made me in purer moments deem myself all unworthy to be the guardian of the shrine on Monte Orsaro, so now did it cause me to deem myself all unworthy to enter the garden that enshrined Madonna Bianca de' Cavalcanti.

Before the purity that shone from her I recoiled in an awe whose nature was as the feelings of a religion. I felt that to seek her presence would be almost to defile her. And so I abstained, my mind very full of her the while, for all that the time was beguiled for me in daily exercise with horse and arms under the guidance of Galeotto.

I was not so tutored merely for the sake of repairing a grave omission in my education. It had a definite scope, as Galeotto frankly told me, informing me that the time approached in which to avenge my father and strike a blow for my own rights.

And then at the end of a week a man rode into the courtyard of Pagliano one day, and flung down from his horse shouting to be led to Messer Galeotto. There was something about this courier's mien and person that awoke a poignant memory. I was walking in the gallery when the clatter of his advent drew my attention, and his voice sent a strange thrill through me.

One glance I gave to make quite sure, and then I leapt down the broad steps four at a time, and a moment later, to the amazement of all present, I had caught the dusty rider in my arms, and I was kissing the wrinkled, scarred, and leathery old cheeks.

"Falcone!" I cried. "Falcone, do you not know me?"

He was startled by the passion of my onslaught. Indeed, he was almost borne to the ground; for his old legs were stiff now from riding.

And then — how he stared! What oaths he swore! "Madonnino!" he babbled. "Madonnino!" And he shook himself free of my embrace, and stood back that he might view me. "Body of Satan! But you are finely grown, and how like to what your father was when he was no older than are you! And they have not made a shaveling of you, after all. Now, blessed be God for that!" Then he stopped short, and his eyes went past me, and he seemed to hesitate.

I turned, and there, leaning on the balustrade of the staircase, looking on with smiling eyes stood Galeotto with Messer Cavalcanti at his elbow.

I heard Galeotto's words to the Lord of Pagliano. "His heart is sound — which is a miracle. That unhappy woman, it seems, could not quite dehumanize him." And he came down heavily, to ask Falcone what news he bore.

The old equerry drew a letter from under his leathern jacket.

"From Ferrante?" quoth the Lord of Pagliano eagerly, peering over Galeotto's shoulder.

"Aye," said Galeotto, and he broke the seal. He stood to read, with knitted brows. "It is well," he said, at last, and passed the sheet to Cavalcanti. "Farnese is in Piacenza already, and the Pope will sway the College to give his bastard the ducal crown. It is time we stirred."

He turned to Falcone, whilst Cavalcanti read the letter. "Take food and rest, good Gino. For tomorrow you ride again with me. And so shall you, Agostino."

"I ride again?" I echoed, my heart sinking

and some of my dismay showing upon my face. "Whither?"

"To right the wrongs of Mondolfo," he answered shortly, and turned away.

CHAPTER II

THE GOVERNOR OF MILAN

WE rode again upon the morrow as he had said, and with us went Falcone and the same goodly company of twenty lances that had escorted me from Monte Orsaro. But I took little thought for them or pride in such an escort now. My heart was leaden. I had not seen Bianca again ere I departed, and Heaven knew when we should return to Pagliano. Thus at least was I answered by Galeotto when I made bold to ask the question.

Two days we rode, going by easy stages, and came at last upon that wondrously fair and imposing city of Milan, in the very heart of the vast plain of Lombardy with the distant Alps for background and northern rampart.

Our destination was the castle; and in a splendid ante-chamber, packed with rustling, silken courtiers and clanking captains in steel, a sprinkling of prelates and handsome, insolent-eyed women, more than one of whom reminded me of Giuliana, and every one of whom I disparaged by comparing her with Bianca, Galeotto and I stood waiting.

To many there he seemed known, and several came to greet him and some to whisper in his ear. At last a pert boy in a satin suit that was striped in the Imperial livery of black and yellow, pushed his way through the throng.

"Messer Galeotto," his shrill voice announced, "His Excellency awaits you."

Galeotto took my arm, and drew me forward with him. Thus we went through a lane that opened out before us in that courtly throng, and came to a curtained door. An usher raised the curtain for us at a sign from the page, who, opening, announced us to the personage within.

We stood in a small closet, whose tall, slender windows overlooked the courtyard, and from the table, on which there was a wealth of parchments, rose a very courtly gentleman to receive us out of a gilded chair, the arms of which were curiously carved into the shape of serpents' heads.

He was a well-nourished, florid man of middle height, with a resolute mouth, high cheek-bones, and crafty, prominent eyes that reminded me vaguely of the eyes of the taverner of Pojetta. He was splendidly dressed in a long gown of crimson damask edged with lynx fur, and the fingers of his fat hands and one of his thumbs were burdened with jewels.

This was Ferrante Gonzaga, Prince of Molfetta, Duke of Ariano, the Emperor's Lieutenant and Governor of the State of Milan.

The smile with which he had been ready to greet Galeotto froze slightly at sight of me. But before he could voice the question obviously in his mind my companion had presented me.

"Here, my lord, is one upon whom I trust that we may count when the time comes. This is Agostino d'Anguissola, of Mondolfo and Carmina."

Surprise overspread Gonzaga's face. He seemed about to speak, and checked, and his eyes were very searchingly bent upon Galeotto's face, which remained inscrutable as stone. Then the Governor looked at me, and from me back again at Galeotto. At last he smiled, whilst I bowed before him, but very vaguely conscious of what might impend.

"The time," he said, "seems to be none too distant. The Duke of Castro — this Pier Luigi Farnese — is so confident of ultimate success that already he has taken up his residence in Piacenza, and already, I am informed, is being spoken of as Duke of Parma and Piacenza."

"He has cause," said Galeotto. "Who is to withstand his election since the Emperor, like Pilate, has washed his hands of the affair?"

A smile overspread Gonzaga's crafty face. "Do not assume too much concerning the Emperor's wishes in the matter. His answer to the Pope was that if Parma and Piacenza are Imperial fiefs — integral parts of the State of Milan — it would ill become the Emperor to alienate them from an empire which he holds merely in trust; whereas if they can be shown rightly to belong to the Holy See, why, then the matter concerns him not, and the Holy See may settle it."

Galeotto shrugged and his face grew dark. "It amounts to an assent," he said.

"Not so," purred Gonzaga, seating himself once more. "It amounts to nothing. It is a Sibylline answer which nowise prejudices what he may do in future. We still hope," he added, "that the Sacred College may refuse the investiture. Pier Luigi Farnese is not in good odour in the Curia."

"The Sacred College cannot withstand the Pope's wishes. He has bribed it with the undertaking to restore Nepi and Camerino to the States of the Church in exchange for Parma and Piacenza, which are to form a State for his son. How long, my lord, do you think the College will resist him?"

"The Spanish Cardinals all have the Emperor's desires at heart."

"The Spanish Cardinals may oppose the measure until they choke themselves with their vehemence," was the ready answer. "There are enough of the Pope's creatures to carry the election, and if there were not it would be his to create more until there should be sufficient for his purpose. It is an old subterfuge."

"Well, then," said Gonzaga, smiling, "since you are so assured, it is for you and the nobles of Piacenza to be up and doing. The Emperor depends upon you; and you may depend upon him."

Galeotto looked at the Governor out of his scarred face, and his eyes were very grave.

"I had hoped otherwise," he said. "That is why I have been slow to move. That is why I have waited, why I have even committed the treachery of permitting Pier Luigi to suppose me ready at need to engage in his service."

"Ah, there you play a dangerous game," said Gonzaga frankly.

"I'll play a more dangerous still ere I have done," he answered stoutly. "Neither Pope nor Devil shall dismay me. I have great wrongs to right, as none knows better than Your Excellency, and if my life should go in the course of it, why" — he shrugged and sneered — "it is all that is left me; and life is a little thing when a man has lost all else."

"I know, I know," said the sly Governor, wagging his big head, "else I had not warned you. For we need you, Messer Galeotto."

"Aye, you need me; you'll make a tool of me — you and your Emperor. You'll use me as a cat's-paw to pull down this inconvenient duke."

Gonzaga rose, frowning. "You go a little far, Messer Galeotto," he said.

"I go no further than you urge me."

"But patience, patience!" the Lieutenant soothed him, growing sleek again in tone and manner. "Consider now the position. What the Emperor has answered the Pope is no more than the bare and precise truth. It is not clear whether the States of Parma and Piacenza belong to the Empire or the Holy See. But once they shall have been bestowed as a dukedom upon Farnese, they will belong to the Holy See no more, even if they so belong now. Once that has happened, let the people rise and show themselves ill-governed, let them revolt against Farnese, and then you may count upon the Emperor to step in as your liberator and to buttress up your revolt."

"Do you promise us so much?" asked Galeotto.

"Explicitly," was the ready answer, "upon my honour. Send me word that you are in arms, that the first blow has been struck, and I shall be with you with all the force that I can raise in the Emperor's name."

"Your Excellency has warrant for this?" demanded Galeotto.

"Should I promise it else? About it, sir. You may work with confidence."

"With confidence, yes," replied Galeotto gloomily, "but with no great hope. The Pontifical Government has ground the spirit out of half the nobles of the Val di Taro. They have suffered so much and so repeatedly — in property, in liberty, in life itself — that they are grown rabbit-hearted, and would sooner cling to the little liberty that is still theirs than strike a blow to gain what belongs to them by every right. Oh, I know them of old! What man can do, I shall do; but . . ." He shrugged, and shook his head sorrowfully.

"Can you count on none?" asked Gonzaga, very serious, stroking his smooth, fat chin.

"I can count upon one," answered Galeotto. "The Lord of Pagliano; he is Ghibelline to the very marrow, and he belongs to me. At my bidding there is nothing he will not do. There is an old debt between us, and he is a noble soul who will not leave his debts unpaid. Upon him I can count; and he is rich and powerful. But, then, he is not really a Piacentino himself. He holds his fief directly from the Emperor. Pagliano is part of the State of Milan, and Cavalcanti is no subject of Farnese. His case, therefore, is exceptional and he has less than the usual cause for timidity. But the others . . ." Again he shrugged. "What man can do to stir them, that will I do. You shall hear from me soon again, my lord."

Gonzaga looked at me. "Did you not say that here was another?"

Galeotto smiled sadly. "Aye — just one arm and one sword. That is all. Unless this emprise succeeds he is never like to rule in Mondolfo. He may be counted upon; but he brings no lances with him."

"I see," said Gonzaga, his lip between thumb and forefinger. "But his name . . ."

"That and his wrongs shall be used, depend upon it, my lord — the wrongs which are his by inheritance."

I said no word. A certain resentment filled me to hear myself so disposed of without being consulted; and yet it was tempered by a certain trust in Galeotto, a faith that he would lead me into nothing unworthy.

Gonzaga conducted us to the door of the closet. "I shall look to hear from you, Ser Galeotto," he said. "And if at first the nobles of the Val di Taro are not to be moved, perhaps after they have had a taste of Messer Pier Luigi's ways they will gather courage out of despair. I think we may be hopeful if patient. Meanwhile, my master the Emperor shall be informed."

Another moment and we were out of that florid, crafty, well-nourished presence. The curtains had dropped behind us, and we were thrusting our way through the press in the ante-chamber, Galeotto muttering to himself things which as we gained the open air I gathered to be curses directed against the Emperor and his Milanese Lieutenant.

In the inn of the sign of the Sun, by the gigantic Duomo of Visconti's building, he opened the gates to his anger and let it freely forth.

"It is a world of cravens," he said, "a world of slothful, self-seeking, supine cowards, Agostino. In the Emperor, at least, I conceived that we should have found a man who would not hesitate to act boldly where his interests must be served. More I had not expected of him; but that, at least. And even in that

he fails me. Oh, this Charles V!" he cried. "This
prince upon whose dominions the sun never sets!
Fortune has bestowed upon him all the favours in her
gift, yet for himself he can do nothing.

"He is crafty, cruel, irresolute, and mistrustful of
all. He is without greatness of any sort, and he is all
but Emperor of the World! Others must do his work
for him; others must compass the conquests which he
is to enjoy.

"Ah, well!" he ended, with a sneer, "perhaps as
the world views these things there is a certain greatness in that — the greatness of the fox."

Naturally there was much in this upon which I
needed explanation, and I made bold to intrude upon
his anger to crave it. And it was then that I learnt the
true position of affairs.

Between France and the Empire, the State of Milan
had been in contention until quite lately, when Henri
II had abandoned it to Charles V. And in the State of
Milan were the States of Parma and Piacenza, which
Pope Julius II had wrested from it and incorporated
in the domain of the Church. The act, however, was
unlawful, and although these States had ever since
been under Pontifical rule, it was to Milan that they
belonged, though Milan never yet had had the power
to enforce her rights. She had that power at last, now
that the Emperor's rule there was a thing determined,
and it was in this moment that papal nepotism was to
make a further alienation of them by constituting
them into a duchy for the Farnese bastard, Pier Luigi,
who was already Duke of Castro.

Under papal rule the nobles — more particularly
the Ghibellines — and the lesser tyrants of the Val di

Taro had suffered rudely, plundered by Pontifical brigandage, enduring confiscations and extortions until they were reduced to a miserable condition. It was against the beginnings of this that my father had raised his standard, to be crushed through the supineness of his peers, who would not support him to save themselves from being consumed in the capacious maw of Rome.

But what they had suffered hitherto would be as nothing to what they must suffer if the Pope now had his way and if Pier Luigi Farnese were to become their duke — an independent prince. He would break the nobles utterly, to remain undisputed master of the territory. That was a conclusion forgone. And yet our princelings saw the evil approaching them, and cowered irresolute to await and suffer it.

They had depended, perhaps, upon the Emperor, who, it was known, did not favour the investiture, nor would confirm it. It was remembered that Ottavio Farnese — Pier Luigi's son — was married to Margaret of Austria, the Emperor's daughter, and that if a Farnese dominion there was to be in Parma and Piacenza, the Emperor would prefer that it should be that of his own son-in-law, who would hold the duchy as a fief of the Empire. Further was it known that Ottavio was intriguing with Pope and Emperor to gain the investiture in his own father's stead.

"The unnatural son!" I exclaimed upon learning that.

Galeotto looked at me, and smiled darkly, stroking his great beard.

"Say, rather, the unnatural father," he replied. "More honour to Ottavio Farnese in that he has chosen to forget that he is Pier Luigi's son. It is not a parentage in which any man — be he the most abandoned — could take pride."

"How so?" quoth I.

"You have, indeed, lived out of the world if you know nothing of Pier Luigi Farnese. I should have imagined that some echo of his turpitudes must have penetrated even to a hermitage — that they would be written upon the very face of Nature, which he outrages at every step of his infamous life. He is a monster, a sort of antichrist; the most ruthless, bloody, vicious man that ever drew the breath of life. Indeed, there are not wanting those who call him a warlock, a dealer in black magic who has sold his soul to the Devil. Though for that matter, they say the same of the Pope his father, and I doubt not that his magic is just the magic of a wickedness that is scarcely human.

"There is a fellow named Paolo Giovio, Bishop of Nocera, a charlatan and a wretched dabbler in necromancy and something of an alchemist, who has lately written the life of another Pope's son — Cesare Borgia, who lived nigh upon half a century ago, and who did more than any man to consolidate the States of the Church, though his true aim, like Pier Luigi's, was to found a State for himself. I am given to think that for his model of a Pope's bastard this Giovio has taken the wretched Farnese rogue, and attributed to the son of Alexander VI the vices and infamies of this son of Paul III.

"Even to attempt to draw a parallel is to insult the memory of the Borgia; for he, at least, was a great captain and a great ruler, and he knew how to endear to himself the folk that he governed; so that when I was a lad — thirty years ago — there were still those in the Romagna who awaited the Borgia's return, and prayed for it as earnestly as pray the faithful for the second coming of the Messiah, refusing to believe that he was dead. But this Pier Luigi!" He thrust out a lip contemptuously. "He is a thief, a murderer, a defiler, a bestial, lecherous dog!"

And with that he began to relate some of the deeds of this man; and his life, it seemed, was written in blood and filth — a tale of murders and rapes and worse. And when as a climax he told me of the horrible, inhuman outrage done to Cosimo Gheri, the young Bishop of Fano, I begged him to cease, for my horror turned me almost physically sick.[1]

"That bishop was a holy man, of very saintly life," Galeotto insisted, "and the deed permitted the German Lutherans to say that here was a new form of martyrdom for saints invented by the Pope's son. And his father pardoned him the deed and others as bad, by a secret bull, absolving him from all pains and penalties that he might have incurred through youthful frailty or human incontinence!"

It was the relation of those horrors, I think, which, stirring my indignation, spurred me even more than the thought of redressing the wrongs which the Pontifical or Farnesian Government would permit my mother to do me.

I held out my hand to Galeotto. "To the utmost of my little might," said I, "you may depend upon me in this good cause in which you have engaged."

"There speaks the son of the House of Anguissola,"

[1] The incident to which Agostino here alludes is fully set forth by Benedetto Varchi at the end of Book XVI of his *Storia Fiorentina*.

said he, a light of affection in his steel-coloured eyes.
"And there are your father's wrongs to right as well
as the wrongs of humanity, remember. By this Pier
Luigi was he crushed; whilst those who bore arms with
him at Perugia and were taken alive . . ." He paused
and turned livid, great beads of perspiration standing
upon his brow. "I cannot," he faltered, "I cannot
even now, after all these years, bear to think upon
those horrors perpetrated by that monster."

I was strangely moved at the sight of emotion in one
who seemed emotionless as iron.

"I left the hermitage," said I, "in the hope that I
might the better be able to serve God in the world. I
think you are showing me the way, Ser Galeotto."

CHAPTER III

PIER LUIGI FARNESE

WE left Milan that same day, and there followed for some months a season of wandering through Lombardy, going from castle to castle, from tyranny to tyranny, just the three of us — Galeotto and myself with Falcone for our equerry and attendant.

Surely something of the fanatic's temperament there must have been in me; for now that I had embraced a cause, I served it with all the fanaticism with which on Monte Orsaro I sought to be worthy of the course I had taken then.

I was become as an apostle, preaching a crusade of holy war against the Devil's lieutenant on earth, Messer Pier Luigi Farnese, sometime Duke of Castro, now Duke of Parma and Piacenza — for the investiture duly followed in the August of that year, and soon his iron hand began to be felt throughout the State of which the Pope had constituted him a prince.

And to the zest that was begotten of pure righteousness, Galeotto cunningly added yet another and more worldly spur. We were riding one day in late September of that year from Cortemaggiore, where we had spent a month in seeking to stir the Pallavicini to some spirit of resistance, and we were making our way towards Romagnese, the stronghold of that great Lombard family of dal Verme.

As we were ambling by a forest path, Galeotto

abruptly turned to me, Falcone at the time being some little way in advance of us, and startled me by his words.

"Cavalcanti's daughter seemed to move you strangely, Agostino," he said, and watched me turn pale under his keen glance.

In my confusion — more or less at random — "What should Cavalcanti's daughter be to me?" I asked.

"Why, what you will, I think," he answered, taking my question literally. "Cavalcanti would consider the Lord of Mondolfo and Carmina a suitable mate for his daughter, however he might hesitate to marry her to the landless Agostino d'Anguissola. He loved your father better than any man that ever lived, and such an alliance was mutually desired."

"Do you think I need this added spur?" quoth I.

"Nay, I know that you do not. But it is well to know what reward may wait upon our labour. It makes that labour lighter and increases courage."

I hung my head, without answering him, and we rode silently amain.

He had touched me where the flesh was raw and tender. Bianca de' Cavalcanti! It was a name I uttered like a prayer, like a holy invocation. Just so had I been in a measure content to carry that name and the memory of her sweet face. To consider her as the possible Lady of Mondolfo when I should once more have come into my own, was to consider things that filled me almost with despair.

Again I experienced such hesitations as had kept me from ever seeking her at Pagliano, though I had been given the freedom of her garden. Giuliana had

left her brand upon me. And though Bianca had by
now achieved for me what neither prayers nor fasting
could accomplish, and had exorcised the unholy visions of Giuliana from my mind, yet when I came to
consider Bianca as a possible companion — as something more or something less than a saint enthroned
in the heaven created by my worship of her — there
rose between us ever that barrier of murder and
adultery, a barrier which not even in imagination did
I dare to overstep.

I strove to put such thoughts from my mind that I
might leave it free to do the work to which I had now
vowed myself.

All through that winter we pursued our mission.
With the dal Verme we had but indifferent success,
for they accounted themselves safe, being, like Cavalcanti, feudatories of the Emperor himself, and nowise
included in the territories of Parma and Piacenza.
From Romagnese we made our way to the stronghold
of the Anguissola of Albarola, my cousins, who gave
me a very friendly welcome, and who, though with us
in spirit and particularly urged by their hatred of our
Guelphic cousin Cosimo who was now Pier Luigi's
favourite, yet hesitated as the others had done. And
we met with little better success with Sforza of Santafiora, to whose castle we next repaired, or yet with the
Landi, the Scotti, or Confalonieri. Everywhere the
same spirit of awe was abroad, and the same pusil-
lanimity, content to hug the little that remained
rather than rear its head to demand that which by
right belonged.

So that when the spring came round again, and our
mission done, our crusade preached to hearts that

would not be inflamed, we turned our steps once more towards Pagliano, we were utterly dispirited men — although, for myself, my despondency was tempered a little by the thought that I was to see Bianca once more.

Yet before I come to speak of her again, let me have done with these historical matters in so far as they touched ourselves.

We had left the nobles unresponsive, as you have seen. But soon the prognostications of the crafty Gonzaga were realized. Soon Farnese, through his excessive tyranny, stung them out of their apathy. The first to feel his iron hand were the Pallavicini, whom he stripped of their lands of Cortemaggiore, taking as hostages Girolamo Pallavicini's wife and mother. Next he hurled his troops against the dal Verme, forcing Romagnese to capitulate, and then seeking similarly to reduce their other fief of Bobbio. Thence upon his all-conquering way, he marched upon Castel San Giovanni, whence he sought to oust the Sforza, and at the same time he committed the mistake of attempting to drive the Gonzaga out of Soragna.

This last rashness brought down upon his head the direct personal resentment of Ferrante Gonzaga. With the Imperial troops at his heels the Governor of Milan not only intervened to save Soragna for his family, but forced Pier Luigi to disgorge Bobbio and Romagnese, restoring them to the dal Verme, and compelled him to raise the siege of San Giovanni upon which he was at the time engaged — claiming that both these noble houses were feudatories of the Empire.

Intimidated by that rude lesson, Pier Luigi was

forced to draw in his steely claws. To console himself, he turned his attention to the Val di Taro, and issued an edict commanding all nobles there to disarm, disband their troops, quit their fortresses, and go to reside in the principal cities of their districts. Those who resisted or demurred, he crushed at once with exile and confiscation; and even those who meekly did his will, he stripped of all privileges as feudal lords.

Even my mother, we heard, was forced to dismiss her trivial garrison, having been ordered to close the Citadel of Mondolfo, and take up her residence in our palace in the city itself. But she went further than she was bidden — she took the veil in the Convent of Santa Chiara, and so retired from the world.

The State began to ferment in secret at so much and such harsh tyranny. Farnese was acting in Piacenza as Tarquin of old had acted in his garden, slicing the tallest poppies from their stems. And soon to swell his treasury, which not even his plunder, brigandage, and extortionate confiscations could fill sufficiently to satisfy his greed, he set himself to look into the past lives of the nobles, and to promulgate laws that were retroactive, so that he was enabled to levy fresh fines and perpetrate fresh sequestrations in punishment of deeds that had been done long years ago.

Amongst these, we heard that he had Giovanni d'Anguissola decapitated in effigy for his rebellion against the authority of the Holy See, and that my tyrannies of Mondolfo and Carmina were confiscated from me because of my offence in being Giovanni d'Anguissola's son. And presently we heard that Mondolfo had been conferred by Farnese upon his good and loyal servant and captain, the Lord Cosimo d'Anguissola, subject to a tax of a thousand ducats yearly!

Galeotto ground his teeth in passion when the news was brought us from Piacenza, whilst I felt my heart sink and the last hope of Bianca — the hope secretly entertained almost against hope itself — withering in my soul.

But soon came consolation. Pier Luigi had gone too far. Even rats when cornered will turn at bay and bare their teeth for combat. So now the nobles of the Valnure and the Val di Taro.

The Scotti, the Pallavicini, the Landi, and the Anguissola of Albarola, came one after the other in secret to Pagliano to interview the gloomy Galeotto. And at one gathering that was secretly held in a chamber of the castle, he lashed them with his furious scorns.

"You are come now," he jeered at them, "now that you are maimed; now that you have been bled of half your strength; now that most of your teeth are drawn. Had you but had the spirit and good sense to rise six months ago when I summoned you so to do, the struggle had been brief and the victory certain. Now the fight will be all fraught with risk, dangerous to engage, and uncertain of issue."

But it was they — these men who themselves had been so pusillanimous at first — who now urged him to take the lead, swearing to follow him to the death, to save for their children what little was still left them.

"In that spirit I will not lead you a step," he answered them. "If we raise our standard, we fight for all our ancient rights, for all our privileges, and for the restoration of all that has been confiscated; in short, for the expulsion of the Farnese from these lands. If that is your spirit, then I will consider what is to be done — for, believe me, open warfare will no longer avail us here. What we have to do must be done by guile. You have waited too long to resolve yourselves. And whilst you have grown weak, Farnese has been growing strong. He has fawned upon and flattered the populace; he has set the people against the nobles; he has pretended that in crushing the nobles he was serving the people, and they — poor fools! — have so far believed him that they will run to his banner in any struggle that may ensue."

He dismissed them at last with the promise that they should hear from him, and on the morrow, attended by Falcone only, he rode forth again from Pagliano, to seek out the dal Verme and the Sforza of Santafiora and endeavour to engage their interest against the man who had outraged them.

And that was early in August of the year '46.

I remained at Pagliano by Galeotto's request. He would have no need of me upon his mission. But he might desire me to seek out some of the others of the Val di Taro with such messages as he should send me.

And in all this time I had seen but little of Monna Bianca. We met under her father's eye in that gold-and-purple dining-room; and there I would devoutly, though surreptitiously, feast my eyes upon the exquisite beauty of her. But I seldom spoke to her, and then it was upon the most trivial matters; whilst although the summer was now full fragrantly unfolded, yet I never dared to intrude into that garden of hers to which I had been bidden, ever restrained by the overwhelming memory of the past.

So poignant was this memory that at times I

caught myself wondering whether, after all, I had not
been mistaken in lending an ear so readily to the arguments of Fra Gervasio, whether Fra Gervasio himself
had not been mistaken in assuming that my place
was in the world, and whether I had not done best to
have carried out my original intention of seeking refuge in some monastery in the lowly position of a lay-
brother.

Meanwhile the Lord of Pagliano used me in the
most affectionate and fatherly manner. But not even
this sufficed to encourage me where his daughter was
concerned, and I seemed to observe also that Bianca
herself, if she did not actually avoid my society, was
certainly at no pains to seek it.

What the end would have been but for the terrible
intervention there was in our affairs, I have often sur-
mised without result.

It happened that one day, about a week after
Galeotto had left us there rode up to the gates of
Pagliano a very magnificent company, and there was
great braying of horns, stamping of horses and rattle
of arms.

My Lord Pier Luigi Farnese had been on a visit to
his city of Parma, and on his return journey had
thought well to turn aside into the lands of ultra-Po,
and pay a visit to the Lord of Pagliano, whom he did
not love, yet whom, perhaps, it may have been his
intention to conciliate, since hurt him he could not.

Sufficiently severe had been the lesson he had received for meddling with Imperial fiefs; and he must
have been mad had he thought of provoking further
the resentment of the Emperor. To Farnese, Charles
V was a sleeping dog it was as well to leave asleep.

He rode, then, upon his friendly visit into the Castle of Pagliano, attended by a vast retinue of courtiers and ladies, pages, lackeys, and a score of men-at-arms. A messenger had ridden on in advance to warn Cavalcanti of the honour that the Duke proposed to do him, and Cavalcanti, relishing the honour no whit, yet submitting out of prudence, stood to receive His Excellency at the foot of the marble staircase with Bianca on one side and myself upon the other.

Under the archway they rode, Farnese at the head of the cavalcade. He bestrode a splendid white palfrey, whose mane and tail were henna-dyed, whose crimson velvet trappings trailed almost to the ground. He was dressed in white velvet, even to his thighboots which were laced with gold and armed with heavy gold spurs. A scarlet plume was clasped by a great diamond in his velvet cap, and on his right wrist was perched a hooded falcon.

He was a tall and gracefully shaped man of something over forty years of age, black-haired and olive-skinned, wearing a small pointed beard that added length to his face. His nose was aquiline, and he had fine eyes, but under them there were heavy brown shadows, and as he came nearer it was seen that his countenance was marred by an unpleasant eruption of sores.

After him came his gentlemen, a round dozen of them, with half that number of splendid ladies, all a very dazzling company. Behind these, in blazing liveries, there was a cloud of pages upon mules, and lackeys leading sumpter-beasts; and then to afford them an effective background, a grey, steel phalanx of men-at-arms.

I describe his entrance as it appeared at a glance, for I did not study it or absorb any of its details. My horrified gaze was held by a figure that rode on his right hand, a queenly woman with a beautiful pale countenance and a lazy, insolent smile.

It was Giuliana.

How she came there I did not at the moment trouble to reflect. She was there. That was the hideous fact that made me doubt the sight of my own eyes, made me conceive almost that I was at my disordered visions again, the fruit of too much brooding. I felt as if all the blood were being exhausted from my heart, as if my limbs would refuse their office, and I leaned for support against the terminal of the balustrade by which I stood.

She saw me. And after the first slight start of astonishment, her lazy smile grew broader and more insolent. I was but indifferently conscious of the hustle about me, of the fact that Cavalcanti himself was holding the Duke's stirrup, whilst the latter got slowly to the ground and relinquished his falcon to a groom who wore a perch suspended from his neck, bearing three other hooded birds. Similarly I was no more than conscious of being forced to face the Duke by words that Cavalcanti was uttering. He was presenting me.

"This, my lord, is Agostino d'Anguissola."

I saw, as through a haze, the swarthy, pustuled visage frown down upon me. I heard a voice which was at once harsh and effeminate and quite detestable, saying in unfriendly tones:

"The son of Giovanni d'Anguissola of Mondolfo, eh?"

"The same, my lord," said Cavalcanti, adding generously — "Giovanni d'Anguissola was my friend."

"It is a friendship that does you little credit, sir," was the harsh answer. "It is not well to befriend the enemies of God."

Was it possible that I had heard aright? Had this human foulness dared to speak of God?

"That is a matter upon which I will not dispute with a guest," said Cavalcanti with an urbanity of tone belied by the anger that flashed from his brown eyes.

At the time I thought him greatly daring, little dreaming that, forewarned of the Duke's coming, his measures were taken, and that one blast of the silver whistle that hung upon his breast would have produced a tide of men-at-arms that would have engulfed and overwhelmed Messer Pier Luigi and his suite.

Farnese dismissed the matter with a casual laugh. And then a lazy, drawling voice — a voice that once had been sweetest music to my ears, but now was loathsome as the croaking of Stygian frogs — addressed me.

"Why, here is a great change, sir saint! We had heard you had turned anchorite; and behold you in cloth of gold, shining as you would out-dazzle Phœbus."

I stood palely before her, striving to keep the loathing from my face, and I was conscious that Bianca had suddenly turned and was regarding us with eyes of grave concern.

"I like you better for the change," pursued Giuliana. "And I vow that you have grown at least another inch. Have you no word for me, Agostino?"

I was forced to answer her. "I trust that all is well with you, Madonna," I said.

Her lazy smile grew broader, displaying the dazzling whiteness of her strong teeth. "Why, all is very well with me," said she, and her sidelong glance at the Duke, half mocking, half kindly with an odious kindliness, seemed to give added explanations.

That he should have dared bring here this woman whom no doubt he had wrested from his creature Gambara — here into the shrine of my pure and saintly Bianca! — was something for which I could have killed him then, for which I hated him far more bitterly than for any of those dark turpitudes that I had heard associated with his odious name.

And meanwhile there he stood, that Pope's bastard, leaning over my Bianca, speaking to her, and in his eyes the glow of a dark and unholy fire what time they fed upon her beauty like a slug feeding upon a lily. He seemed to have no thought for any other, nor for the circumstance that he kept us all standing there.

"You must come to our Court at Piacenza, Madonna," I heard him murmuring. "We knew not that so fair a flower was blossoming unseen in this garden of Pagliano. It is not well that such a jewel should be hidden in this grey casket. You were made to queen it in a court, Madonna; and at Piacenza you shall be hailed and honoured as its queen." And so he rambled on with his rough and trivial flattery, his foully pimpled face within a foot of hers, and she shrinking before him, very white and mute and frightened. Her father looked on with darkling brows, and Giuliana began to gnaw her lip and look less lazy, whilst in the courtly background there was a respectful murmuring babble, supplying a sycophantic chorus to the Duke's detestable adulation.

It was Cavalcanti, at last, who came to his daughter's rescue by a peremptory offer to escort the Duke and his retinue within.

CHAPTER IV

MADONNA BIANCA

PIER LUIGI'S original intent had been to spend no more than a night at Pagliano. But when the morrow came, he showed no sign of departing, nor upon the next day, nor yet upon the next.

A week passed, and still he lingered, seeming to settle more and more in the stronghold of the Cavalcanti, leaving the business of his Duchy to his secretary Filarete and to his Council, at the head of which, as I learnt, was my old friend Annibale Caro.

And meanwhile, Cavalcanti, using great prudence, suffered the Duke's presence, and gave him and his following most noble entertainment.

His position was perilous and precarious in the extreme, and it needed all his strength of character to hold in curb the resentment that boiled within him to see himself thus preyed upon; and that was not the worst. The worst was Pier Luigi's ceaseless attentions to Bianca, the attentions of the satyr for the nymph, a matter in which I think Cavalcanti suffered little less than did I.

He hoped for the best, content to wait until cause for action should be forced upon him. And meanwhile that courtly throng took its ease at Pagliano. The garden that hitherto had been Bianca's own sacred domain, the garden into which I had never yet dared set foot, was overrun now by the Duke's gay suite —

a cloud of poisonous butterflies. There in the green,
shaded alleys they disported themselves; in the
lemon-grove, in the perfumed rose-garden, by hedges
of box and screens of purple clematis they fluttered.

Bianca sought to keep her chamber in those days,
and kept it for as long on each day as was possible to
her. But the Duke, hobbling on the terrace — for as
a consequence of his journey on horseback he had developed a slight lameness, being all rotten with disease — would grow irritable at her absence, and insistent upon her presence, hinting that her retreat
was a discourtesy; so that she was forced to come
forth again, and suffer his ponderous attentions and
gross flatteries.

And three days later there came another to Pagliano, bidden thither by the Duke, and this other was
none else than my cousin Cosimo, who now called
himself Lord of Mondolfo, having been invested in
that tyranny, as I have said.

On the morning after his arrival, we met upon the
terrace.

"My saintly cousin!" was his derisive greeting.
"And yet another change in you — out of sackcloth
into velvet! The calendar shall know you as Saint
Weathercock, I think — or, perhaps, Saint Mountebank."

What followed was equally bitter and sardonic on
his part, fiercely and openly hostile on mine. At my
hostility he had smiled cruelly.

"Be content with what is, my strolling saint," he
said, in the tone of one who gives a warning, "unless
you would be back in your hermitage, or within the
walls of some cloister, or even worse. Already have

you found trouble enough in meddling with the affairs of the world. You were destined for sanctity." He came closer, and grew very fierce. "Do not put it upon me to make a saint of you by sending you to Heaven."

"It might end in your own despatch to Hell," said I. "Shall we essay it?"

"Body of God!" he snarled, laughter still lingering on his white face. "Is this the mood of your holiness at present? What a bloodthirsty brave are you become! Consider, pray, sir, that if you trouble me I have no need to do my own office of hangman. There is sufficient against you to make the Tribunal of the Ruota very busy; there is — can you have forgotten it? — that little affair at the house of Messer Fifanti."

I dropped my glance, browbeaten for an instant. Then I looked at him again, and smiled.

"You are but a poor coward, Ser Cosimo," said I, "to use a shadow as a screen. You know that nothing can be proved against me unless Giuliana speaks, and that she dare not for her own sake. There are witnesses who will swear that Gambara went to Fifanti's house that night. There is not one to swear that Gambara did not kill Fifanti ere he came forth again; and it is the popular belief, for his traffic with Giuliana is well known, as it is well known that she fled with him after the murder — which, in itself, is evidence of a sort. Your Duke has too great a respect for the feelings of the populace," I sneered, "to venture to outrage them in such a matter. Besides," I ended, "it is impossible to incriminate me without incriminating Giuliana, and Messer Pier Luigi seems,

I should say, unwilling to relinquish the lady to the brutalities of a tribunal."

"You are greatly daring," said he, and he was pale now, for in that last mention of Giuliana, it seemed that I had touched him where he was still sensitive.

"Daring?" I rejoined. "It is more than I can say for you, Ser Cosimo. Yours is the coward's fault of caution."

I thought to spur him. If this failed, I was prepared to strike him, for my temper was beyond control. That he, standing towards me as he did, should dare to mock me, was more than I could brook. But at that moment there spoke a harsh voice just behind me.

"How, sir? What words are these?"

There, very magnificent in his suit of ivory velvet, stood the Duke. He was leaning heavily upon his cane, and his face was more blotched than ever, the sunken eyes more sunken.

"Are you seeking to quarrel with the Lord of Mondolfo?" quoth he, and I saw by his smile that he used my cousin's title as a taunt.

Behind him was Cavalcanti with Bianca leaning upon his arm just as I had seen her that day when she came with him to Monte Orsaro, save that now there was a look as of fear in the blue depths of her eyes. A little on one side there was a group composed of three of the Duke's gentlemen with Giuliana and another of the ladies, and Giuliana was watching us with half-veiled eyes.

"My lord," I answered, very stiff and erect, and giving him back look for look, something, perhaps, of the loathing with which he inspired me imprinted on my face, "my lord, you give yourself idle alarms. Ser Cosimo is too cautious to embroil himself."

He limped towards me; leaning heavily upon his stick, and it pleased me that of a good height though he was, he was forced to look up into my face.

"There is too much bad Anguissola blood in you," he said. "Be careful lest, out of our solicitude for you, we should find it well to let our leech attend you."

I laughed, looking into his blotched face, considering his lame leg and all the evil humours in him.

"By my faith, I think it is Your Excellency needs the attentions of a leech," said I, and flung all present into consternation by that answer.

I saw his face turn livid, and I saw the hand shake upon the golden head of his cane. He was very sensitive upon the score of his foul infirmities. His eyes grew baleful as he controlled himself. Then he smiled, displaying a ruin of blackened teeth.

"You had best take care," he said. "It were a pity to cripple such fine limbs as yours. But there is a certain matter upon which the Holy Office might desire to set you some questions. Best be careful, sir, and avoid disagreements with my captains."

He turned away. He had had the last word, and had left me cold with apprehension, yet warmed by the consciousness that in the brief encounter it was he who had taken the deeper wound.

He bowed before Bianca. "Oh, pardon me," he said. "I did not dream you stood so near. Else no such harsh sounds should have offended your fair ears. As for Messer d'Anguissola . . ." He shrugged as who would say, "Have pity on such a boor!"

But her answer, crisp and sudden as come words that are spoken on impulse or inspiration, dashed his confidence.

"Nothing that he said offended me," she told him boldly, almost scornfully.

He flashed me a glance that was full of venom, and I saw Cosimo smile, whilst Cavalcanti started slightly at such boldness from his meek child. But the Duke was sufficiently master of himself to bow again.

"Then am I less aggrieved," said he, and changed the subject. "Shall we to the bowling lawn?" And his invitation was direct to Bianca, whilst his eyes passed over her father. Without waiting for their answer, his question, indeed, amounting to a command, he turned sharply to my cousin. "Your arm, Cosimo," said he, and leaning heavily upon his captain he went down the broad granite steps, followed by the little knot of courtiers, and, lastly, by Bianca and her father.

As for me, I turned and went indoors, and there was little of the saint left in me in that hour. All was turmoil in my soul, turmoil and hatred and anger. Anon to soothe me came the memory of those sweet words that Bianca had spoken in my defence, and those words emboldened me at last to seek her out as I had never yet dared in all the time that I had spent at Pagliano.

I found her that evening, by chance, in the gallery over the courtyard. She was pacing slowly, having fled thither to avoid that hateful throng of courtiers. Seeing me she smiled timidly, and her smile gave me what little further encouragement I needed. I approached, and very earnestly rendered her my thanks for having championed my cause and supported me with the express sign of her approval.

She lowered her eyes; her bosom quickened slightly, and the colour ebbed and flowed in her cheeks.

"You should not thank me," said she. "What I did was done for justice' sake."

"I have been presumptuous, in conceiving that it might have been for the sake of me."

"But it was that also," she answered quickly, fearing, perhaps, that she had pained me. "It offended me that the Duke should attempt to browbeat you. I took pride in you to see you bear yourself so well and return thrust for thrust."

"I think your presence must have heartened me," said I. "No pain could be so cruel as to seem base or craven in your eyes."

Again the telltale colour showed upon her lovely cheek. She began to pace slowly down the gallery, and I beside her. Presently she spoke again.

"And yet," she said, "I would have you cautious. Do not wantonly affront the Duke, for he is very powerful."

"I have little left to lose," said I.

"You have your life," said she.

"A life which I have so much misused that it must ever cry out to me in reproach."

She gave me a little fluttering, timid glance, and looked away again. Thus we came in silence to the gallery's end, where a marble seat was placed, with gay cushions of painted and gilded leather. She sank to it with a little sigh, and I leaned on the balustrade beside her and slightly over her. And now I grew strangely bold.

"Set me some penance," I cried, "that shall make me worthy."

Again came that little fluttering, frightened glance. "A penance?" quoth she. "I do not understand."

"All my life," I explained, "has been a vain striving after something that eluded me. Once I deemed myself devout; and because I had sinned and rendered myself unworthy, you found me a hermit on Monte Orsaro, seeking by penance to restore myself to the estate from which I had succumbed. That shrine was proved a blasphemy; and so the penance I had done, the signs I believed I had received, were turned to mockery. It was not there that I should save myself. One night I was told so in a vision."

She gave an audible gasp, and looked at me so fearfully that I fell silent, staring back at her.

"You knew!" I cried.

Long did her blue, slanting eyes meet my glance without wavering, as never yet they had met it. She seemed to hesitate, and at the same time openly to consider me.

"I know now," she breathed.

"What do you know?" My voice was tense with excitement.

"What was your vision?" she rejoined.

"Have I not told you? There appeared to me one who called me back to the world; who assured me that there I should best serve God; who filled me with the conviction that she needed me. She addressed me by name, and spoke of a place of which I had scarcely heard until that hour, but which to-day I know."

"And you? And you?" she asked. "What answer did you make?"

"I called her by name, although until that hour I did not know it."

She bowed her head. Emotion set her all atremble.

"It is what I have so often wondered," she confessed, scarce above a whisper. "And it is true — as true as it is strange!"

"True?" I echoed. "It was the only true miracle in that place of false ones, and it was so clear a call of destiny that it decided me to return to the world which I had abandoned. And yet I have since wondered why. Here there seems to be no place for me any more than there was yonder. I am devout again with a worldly devotion now, yet with a devotion that must be Heaven-inspired, so pure and sweet it is. It has shut out from me all the foulness of that past; and yet I am unworthy. And that is why I cry to you to set me some penance ere I can make my prayer."

She could not understand me, nor did she. We were not as ordinary lovers. We were not as man and maid who, meeting and being drawn each to the other, fence and trifle in a pretty game of dalliance until the maid opines that the appearances are safe, and that, her resistance having been of a seemly length, she may now make the ardently desired surrender with all war's honours. Nothing of that was in our wooing, a wooing which seemed to us, now that we spoke of it, to have been done when we had scarcely met, done in the vision that I had of her, and the vision that she had of me.

With averted eyes she set me now a question.

"Madonna Giuliana used you with a certain freedom on her arrival, and I have since heard your name coupled with her own by the Duke's ladies. But I have asked no questions of them. I know how false can be the tongues of courtly folk. I ask it now of you. What is or was this Madonna Giuliana to you?"

"She was," I answered bitterly — "and God pity me that I must say it to you — she was to me what Circe was to the followers of Ulysses."

She made a little moan, and I saw her clasp her hands in her lap; and the sound and sight filled me with sorrow and despair. She must know. Better that the knowledge should stand between us as a barrier which both could see than that it should remain visible only to the eyes of my own soul, to daunt me.

"Oh, Bianca! Forgive me!" I cried. "I did not know! I did not know! I was a poor fool reared in seclusion and ripened thus for the first temptation that should touch me. That is what on Monte Orsaro I sought to expiate, that I might be worthy of the shrine I guarded then. That is what I would expiate now, that I might be worthy of the shrine whose guardian I would become, the shrine at which I worship now."

I was bending very low above her little brown head, in which the threads of the gold coif-net gleamed in the fading light.

"If I had but had my vision sooner," I murmured, "how easy it would have been! Can you find mercy for me in your gentle heart? Can you forgive me, Bianca?"

"Oh, Agostino," she answered very sadly, and the sound of my name from her lips, coming so naturally and easily, thrilled me like the sound of the mystic music of Monte Orsaro. "What shall I answer you?

I cannot now. Give me leisure to think. You have hurt me so!"

"Me miserable!" I cried.

"I had believed you one who erred through excess of holiness."

"Whereas I am one who attempted holiness through excess of error."

"I had believed you so, so . . . Oh, Agostino!" It was a little wail of pain.

"Set me a penance," I implored her.

"What penance can I set you? Will any penance restore to me my shattered faith?"

I groaned miserably and covered my face with my hands. It seemed that I was, indeed, come to the end of all my hopes; that the world was as much a mockery to me as had been the hermitage; that the one was to end for me upon the discovery of a fraud, as had the other ended — with the difference that in this case the fraud was in myself.

It seemed, indeed, that our first communion must be our last. Ever since she had seen me step into that gold-and-purple dining-room at Pagliano, the incarnation of her vision, as she was the incarnation of mine, Bianca must have waited confidently for this hour, knowing that it was foreordained to come. Bitterness and disillusion were all that it had brought her.

And then, ere more could be said, a thin, flute-like voice hissed down the vaulted gallery:

"Madonna Bianca! To hide your beauty from our hungry eyes. To quench the light by which we guide our footsteps. To banish from us the happiness and joy of your presence! Unkind, unkind!"

It was the Duke. In his white velvet suit he looked almost ghostly in the deepening twilight. He hobbled towards us, his stick tapping the black-and-white squares of the marble floor. He halted before her, and she put aside her emotion, donned a worldly mask, and rose to meet him.

Then he looked at me, and his brooding eyes seemed to scan my face.

"Why! It is Ser Agostino, Lord of Nothing," he sneered, and down the gallery rang the laugh of my cousin Cosimo, and there came, too, a ripple of other voices.

Whether to save me from friction with those steely gentlemen who aimed at grinding me to powder, whether from other motives, Bianca set her finger-tips upon the Duke's white sleeve and moved away with him.

I leaned against the balustrade all numb, watching them depart. I saw Cosimo come upon her other side and lean over her as he moved, so slim and graceful, beside her own slight, graceful figure. Then I sank to the cushions of the seat she had vacated, and stayed there with my misery until the night had closed about the place, and the white marble pillars looked ghostly and unreal.

CHAPTER V

THE WARNING

I PRAYED that evening more fervently than I had prayed since quitting Monte Orsaro. It was as if all the influences of my youth, which lately had been shaken off in the stir of intrigue and of rides that had seemed the prelude to battle, were closing round me again.

Even as a woman had lured me once from the ways to which I seemed predestined, only to drive me back once more the more frenziedly, so now it almost seemed as if again a woman should have lured me to the world but to drive me from it again and more resolutely than ever. For I was anew upon the edge of a resolve to have done with all human interests and to seek the peace and seclusion of the cloister.

And then I bethought me of Gervasio. I would go to him for guidance, as I had done aforetime. I would ride on the morrow to seek him out in the convent near Piacenza to which he had withdrawn.

I was disturbed at last by the coming of a page to my chamber with the announcement that my lord was already at supper.

I had thoughts of excusing myself, but in the end I went.

The repast was spread, as usual, in the banqueting-hall of the castle; and about the splendid table was Pier Luigi's company, amounting to nigh upon a score in all. The Duke himself sat on Monna Bianca's right, whilst on her left was Cosimo.

Heeding little whether I was observed or not, I sank to a vacant place, midway down the board, between one of the Duke's pretty young gentlemen and one of the ladies of that curious train — a bold-eyed Roman woman, whose name, I remember, was Valeria Cesarini, but who matters nothing in these pages. Almost facing me sat Giuliana, but I was hardly conscious of her, or conscious, indeed, of any save Monna Bianca.

Once or twice Bianca's glance met mine, but it fell away again upon the instant. She was very pale, and there were wistful lines about her lips; yet her mood was singular. Her eyes had an unnatural sparkle, and ever and anon she would smile at what was said to her in half-whispers, now by the Duke, now by Cosimo, whilst once or twice she laughed outright. Gone was the usual chill reserve with which she hedged herself about to distance the hateful advances of Pier Luigi. There were moments now when she seemed almost flattered by his vile ogling and adulatory speeches, as if she had been one of those brazen ladies of his Court.

It wounded me sorely. I could not understand it, lacking the wit to see that this queer mood sprang from the blow I had dealt her, and was the outward manifestation of her own pain at the shattering of the illusions she had harboured concerning myself.

And so I sat there moodily, gnawing my lip and scowling darkly upon Pier Luigi and upon my cousin, who was as assiduous in his attentions as his master, and who seemed to be receiving an even greater

proportion of her favours. One little thing there was
to hearten me. Looking at the Lord of Pagliano, who
sat at the table's head, I observed that his glance was
dark as it kept watch upon his daughter — that
chaste white lily that seemed of a sudden to have
assumed such wanton airs.

It was a matter that stirred me to battle, and
forgotten again were my resolves to seek Gervasio,
forgotten all notion of abandoning the world for the
second time. Here was work to be done. Bianca was
to be guarded. Perhaps it was in this that she would
come to have need of me.

Once Cosimo caught my gloomy looks, and he
leaned over to speak to the Duke, who glanced my
way with languid, sneering eyes. He had a score to
settle with me for the discomfiture he had that
morning suffered at my hands thanks to Bianca's
collaboration. He was a clumsy fool, when all is said,
and confident now of her support — from the sudden
and extreme friendliness of her mood — he ventured
to let loose a shaft at me in a tone that all the table
might overhear.

"That cousin of yours wears a very conventual
hang-dog look," said he to Cosimo. And then to the
lady on my right — "Forgive, Valeria," he begged,
"the scurvy chance that should have sat a shaveling
next to you."

Lastly he turned to me to complete this gross work
of offensiveness.

"When do you look, sir, to enter the life monastic
for which Heaven has so clearly designed you?"

There were some sycophants who tittered at his
stupid pleasantry; then the table fell silent to hear

what answer I should make, and a frown sat like a thunder-cloud upon the brow of Cavalcanti.

I toyed with my goblet, momentarily tempted to fling its contents in his pustuled face, and risk the consequences. But I bethought me of something else that would make a deadlier missile.

"Alas!" I sighed. "I have abandoned the notion — constrained to it."

He took my bait. "Constrained?" quoth he. "Now, what fool did so constrain you?"

"No fool, but circumstance," I answered. "It has occurred to me," I explained, and I boldly held his glance with my own, "that as a simple monk my life would be fraught with perils, seeing that in these times even a bishop is not safe."

Saving Bianca (who in her sweet innocence did not so much as dream of the existence of such vileness as that to which I was referring and by which a saintly man had met his death) I do not imagine that there was a single person present who did not understand to what foul crime I alluded.

The silence that followed my words was as oppressive as the silence which in nature preludes thunder.

A vivid flame of scarlet had overspread the Duke's countenance. It receded, leaving his cheeks a greenish white, even to the mottling pimples. Abashed, his smouldering eyes fell away before my bold, defiant glance. The fingers of his trembling hand tightened about the slender stem of his Venetian goblet, so that it snapped, and there was a gush of crimson wine upon the snowy napery. His lips were drawn back — like a dog's in the act of snarling —

and showed the black stumps of his broken teeth. But he made no sound, uttered no word.

It was Cosimo who spoke, half rising as he did so.

"This insolence, my Lord Duke, must be punished; this insult wiped out. Suffer me . . ."

But Pier Luigi reached forward across Bianca, set a hand upon my cousin's sleeve, and pressed him back into his seat, silencing him.

"Let be," he said. And looked up the board at Cavalcanti. "It is for my Lord of Pagliano to say if a guest shall be thus affronted at his board."

Cavalcanti's face was set and rigid. "You place a heavy burden on my shoulders," said he, "when Your Excellency, my guest, appeals to me against another guest of mine — against one who is all but friendless and the son of my own best friend."

"And my worst enemy," cried Pier Luigi hotly.

"That is Your Excellency's own concern, not mine," said Cavalcanti coldly. "But since you appeal to me I will say that Messer d'Anguissola's words were ill-judged in such a season. Yet in justice I must add that it is not the way of youth to weigh its words too carefully; and you gave him provocation. When a man — be he never so high — permits himself to taunt another, he would do well to see that he is not himself vulnerable to taunts."

Farnese rose with a horrible oath, and every one of his gentlemen with him.

"My lord," he said, "this is to take sides against me; to endorse the affront."

"Then you mistake my intention," rejoined Cavalcanti, with an icy dignity. "You appeal to me for judgment. And between guests I must hold the scales dead-level, with no thought for the rank of either. Of your chivalry, my Lord Duke, you must perceive that I could not do else."

It was the simplest way in which he could have told Farnese that he cared nothing for the rank of either, and of reminding His Excellency that Pagliano, being an Imperial fief, was not a place where the Duke of Parma might ruffle it unchecked.

Messer Pier Luigi hesitated, entirely out of countenance. Then his eyes turned to Bianca, and his expression softened.

"What says Madonna Bianca?" he inquired, his manner reassuming some measure of its courtliness. "Is her judgment as unmercifully level?"

She looked up, startled, and laughed a little excitedly, touched by the tenseness of a situation which she did not understand.

"What say I?" quoth she. "Why, that here is a deal of pother about some foolish words."

"And there," cried Pier Luigi, "spoke, I think, not only beauty but wisdom — Minerva's utterances from the lips of Diana!"

In glad relief the company echoed his forced laugh, and all sat down again, the incident at an end, and my contempt of the Duke increased to see him permit such a matter to be so lightly ended.

But that night, when I had retired to my chamber, I was visited by Cavalcanti. He was very grave.

"Agostino," he said, "let me implore you to be circumspect, to keep a curb upon your bitter tongue. Be patient, boy, as I am — and I have more to endure."

"I marvel, sir, that you endure it," answered I, for my mood was petulant.

"You will marvel less when you are come to my years — if, indeed, you come to them. For if you pursue this course and strike back when such men as Pier Luigi tap you, you will not be likely to see old age. Body of Satan! I would that Galeotto were here! If aught should happen to you . . ." He checked, and set a hand upon my shoulder. "For your father's sake I love you, Agostino, and I speak as one who loves you."

"I know, I know!" I cried, seizing his hand in a sudden penitence. "I am an ingrate and a fool. And you upheld me nobly at table. Sir, I swear that I will not submit you to so much concern again."

He patted my shoulder in a very friendly fashion, and his kindly eyes smiled upon me. "If you but promise that — for your own sake, Agostino — we need say no more. God send this papal by-blow takes his departure soon, for he is as unwelcome here as he is unbidden."

"The foul toad!" said I. "To see him daily, hourly bending over Monna Bianca, whispering and ogling — ugh!"

"It offends you, eh? And for that I love you! There. Be circumspect and patient, and all will be well. Put your faith in Galeotto, and endure insults which you may depend upon him to avenge when the hour strikes."

Upon that he left me, and he left me with a certain comfort. And in the days that followed, I acted upon his injunction, though, truth to tell, there was little provocation to do otherwise. The Duke ignored me, and all the gentlemen of his following did the like, including Cosimo. And meanwhile they revelled at Pagliano and made free with the hospitality to which they had not been bidden.

Thus sped another week in which I had not the courage again to approach Bianca after what had passed between us at our single interview. Nor for that matter was I afforded the opportunity. The Duke and Cosimo were ever at her side, and yet it almost seemed as if the Duke had given place to his captain, for Cosimo's was the greater assiduity now.

The days were spent at bowls or pallone within the castle, or upon hawking-parties or hunting-parties when presently the Duke's health was sufficiently improved to enable him to sit his horse; and at night there was feasting which Cavalcanti must provide, and on some evenings we danced, though that was a diversion in which I took no part, having neither the will nor the art.

One night as I sat in the gallery above the great hall, watching them footing it upon the mosaic floor below, Giuliana's deep, slow voice behind me stirred me out of my musings. She had espied me up there and had come to join me, although hitherto I had most sedulously avoided her, neither addressing her nor giving her the opportunity to address me since the first brazen speech on her arrival.

"That white-faced lily, Madonna Bianca de' Cavalcanti, seems to have caught the Duke in her net of innocence," said she.

I started round as if I had been stung, and at sight of my empurpling face she slowly smiled, the same hateful smile that I had seen upon her face that day in the garden when Gambara had bargained for her with Fifanti.

"You are greatly daring," said I.

"To take in vain the name of her white innocence?" she answered, smiling superciliously. And then she grew more serious. "Look, Agostino, we were friends once. I would be your friend now."

"It is a friendship, Madonna, best not given expression."

"Ha! We are very scrupulous — are we not? — since we have abandoned the ways of holiness, and returned to this world of wickedness, and raised our eyes to the pale purity of the daughter of Cavalcanti!" She spoke sneeringly.

"What is that to you?" I asked.

"Nothing," she answered frankly. "But that another may have raised his eyes to her is something. I am honest with you. If this child is aught to you, and you would not lose her, you would do well to guard her more closely than you are wont. A word in season. That is all my message."

"Stay!" I begged her now, for already she was gliding away through the shadows of the gallery.

She laughed over her shoulder at me — the very incarnation of effrontery and insolence.

"Have I moved you into sensibility?" quoth she. "Will you condescend to questions with one whom you despise? — as, indeed," she added with a stinging scorn, "you have every right to do."

"Tell me more precisely what you mean," I begged her, for her words had moved me fearfully.

"Gesù!" she exclaimed. "Can I be more precise? Must I add counsels? Why, then, I counsel that a change of air might benefit Madonna Bianca's health, and that, if my Lord of Pagliano is wise, he will send her into retreat in some convent until the Duke's visit here is at an end. And I can promise you that in that case it will be the sooner ended. Now, I think that even a saint should understand me."

With that last gibe she moved resolutely on and left me.

Of the gibe I took little heed. What imported was her warning. And I did not doubt that she had good cause to warn me. I remembered with a shudder her old-time habit of listening at doors. It was very probable that in like manner had she now gathered information that entitled her to give me such advice.

It was incredible. And yet I knew that it was true, and I cursed my blindness and Cavalcanti's. What precisely Farnese's designs might be I could not conceive. It was hard to think that he should dare so much as Giuliana more than hinted. It may be that, after all, there was no more than just the danger of it, and that her own base interests urged her to do what she could to avert it.

In any case, her advice was sound; and perhaps, as she said, the removal of Bianca quietly might be the means of helping Pier Luigi's unwelcome visit to an end.

Indeed, it was so. It was Bianca who held him at Pagliano, as the blindest idiot should have perceived.

That very night I would seek out Cavalcanti ere I retired to sleep.

CHAPTER VI

THE TALONS OF THE HOLY OFFICE

ACTING upon my resolve, I went to wait for Cavalcanti in the little anteroom that communicated with his bedroom. My patience was tried, for he was singularly late in coming; fully an hour passed after all the sounds had died down in the castle and it was known that all had retired, and still there was no sign of him.

I asked one of the pages who lounged there waiting for their master, did he think my lord would be in the library, and the boy was conjecturing upon this unusual tardiness of Cavalcanti's in seeking his bed, when the door opened, and at last he appeared.

When he found me awaiting him, a certain eagerness seemed to light his face; a second's glance showed me that he was in the grip of some unusual agitation. He was pale, with a dull flush under the eyes, and the hand with which he waved away the pages shook, as did his voice when he bade them depart, saying that he desired to be alone with me awhile.

When the two slim lads had gone, he let himself fall wearily into a tall, carved chair that was placed near an ebony table with silver feet in the middle of the room.

But instead of unburdening himself as I fully expected, he looked at me, and —

"What is it, Agostino?" he inquired.

scarce above a whisper, overawed as men are when
they perceive precisely what their folly and wickedness have cost them.

He halted before me, and set one hand of his upon
my shoulder, looking up into my face. "It has been
my fondest dream, Agostino," he said.

I groaned. "It is a dream that never can be realized
now," said I miserably.

"Never, indeed, if Cosimo d'Anguissola continues
to be Lord of Mondolfo," he answered, his keen,
friendly eyes considering me.

I reddened and paled under his glance.

"Nor otherwise," said I. "For Monna Bianca
holds me in the contempt which I deserve. Better a
thousand times that I should have remained out of
this world to which you caused me to return —
unless, indeed, my present torment is the expiation
that is required of me; unless, indeed, I was but
brought back that I might pay with suffering for all
the evil that I have wrought."

He smiled a little. "Is it so with you? Why, then,
you afflict yourself too soon, boy. You are over-
hasty to judge. I am her father, and my little
Bianca is a book in which I have studied deeply. I
read her better than do you, Agostino. But we will
talk of this again."

He turned away to resume his pacing in the very
moment in which he had fired me with such exalted
hopes. "Meanwhile, there is this Farnese dog with
his parcel of minions and harlots making a sty of my
house. He threatens to remain until I come to what
he terms a reasonable mind — until I consent to do
his will and allow my daughter to marry his hench-

man; and he parted from me enjoining me to give the matter thought, and impudently assuring me that in Cosimo d'Anguissola — in that Guelphic jackal — I had a husband worthy of Bianca de' Cavalcanti."

He spoke it between his teeth, his eyes kindling angrily again.

"The remedy, my lord, is to send Bianca hence," I said. "Let her seek shelter in a convent until Messer Pier Luigi shall have taken his departure. And if she is no longer here, Cosimo will have little inclination to linger."

He flung back his head, and there was defiance in every line of his clear-cut face.

"Never!" he snapped. "The thing could have been done two weeks ago, when they first came. It would have seemed that the step was determined before his coming, and that in my independence I would not alter my plans. But to do it now were to show fear of him; and that is not my way.

"Go, Agostino. Let me have the night to think. I know not how to act. But we will talk again to-morrow."

It was best so; best leave it to the night to bring counsel, for we were face to face with grave issues which might need determining sword in hand.

That I slept little will be readily conceived. I plagued my mind with this matter of Cosimo's suit, thinking that I saw the ultimate intent — to bring Pagliano under the ducal sway by rendering master of it one who was devoted to Farnese.

And then, too, I would think of that other thing that Cavalcanti had said: that I had been hasty in my judgment of his daughter's mind. My hopes rose and tortured me with the suspense they held. Then came to me the awful thought that here there might be a measure of retribution, and that it might be intended as my punishment that Cosimo, whom I had unconsciously bested in my sinful passion, should best me now in this pure and holy love.

I was astir betimes, and out in the gardens before any, hoping, I think, that Bianca, too, might seek the early morning peace of that place, and that so we might have speech.

Instead, it was Giuliana who came to me. I had been pacing the terrace some ten minutes, inhaling the matutinal fragrance, drawing my hands through the cool dew that glistened upon the boxwood hedges, when I saw her issue from the loggia that opened to the gardens.

Upon her coming I turned to go within, and I would have passed her without a word, but that she put forth a hand to detain me.

"I was seeking you, Agostino," she said in greeting.

"Having found me, Madonna, you will give me leave to go," said I.

But she was resolutely barring my way. A slow smile parted her scarlet lips and broke over that ivory countenance that once I had deemed so lovely and now I loathed.

"I mind me another occasion in a garden betimes one morning when you were in no such haste to shun me."

I crimsoned under her insolent regard. "Have you the courage to remember?" I exclaimed.

"Half the art of life is to harbour happy memories," said she.

"Happy?" quoth I.

"Do you deny that we were happy on that morning? — it would be just about this time of year, two years ago. And what a change in you since then! Heigho! And yet men say that woman is inconstant!"

"I did not know you then," I answered harshly.

"And do you know me now? Has womanhood no mysteries for you since you gathered wisdom in the wilderness?"

I looked at her with detestation in my eyes. The effrontery, the ease and insolence of her bearing, all confirmed my conviction of her utter shamelessness and heartlessness.

"The day after . . . after your husband died," I said, "I saw you in a dell near Castel Guelfo with my Lord Gambara. In that hour I knew you."

She bit her lip, then smiled again. "What would you?" answered she. "Through your folly and crime I was become an outcast. I went in danger of my life. You had basely deserted me. My Lord Gambara, more generous, offered me shelter and protection. I was not born for martyrdom and dungeons," she added, and sighed with smiling plaintiveness. "Are you, of all men, the one to blame me?"

"I have not the right, I know," I answered. "Nor do I blame you more than I blame myself. But since I blame myself most bitterly — since I despise and hate myself for what is past, you may judge what my feelings are for you. And judging them, I think it were well you gave me leave to go."

"I came to speak of other than ourselves, Ser Agostino," she answered, all unmoved still by my scorn, or leastways showing nothing of what emotions might be hers. "It is of that simpering daughter of my Lord of Pagliano."

"There is nothing I could less desire to hear you talk upon," said I.

"It is so very like a man to scorn the thing I could tell him after he has already heard it from me."

"The thing you told me was false," said I. "It was begotten of fear to see your own base interests thwarted. It is proven so by the circumstance that the Duke has sought the hand of Madonna Bianca for Cosimo d'Anguissola."

"For Cosimo?" she cried, and I never saw her so serious and thoughtful. "For Cosimo? You are sure of this?" The urgency of her tone was such that it held me there and compelled my answer.

"I have it from my lord himself."

She knit her brows, her eyes upon the ground; then slowly she raised them, and looked at me again, the same unusual seriousness and alertness in every line of her face.

"Why, by what dark ways does he burrow to his ends?" she mused.

And then her eyes grew lively, her expression cunning and vengeful.

"I see it!" she exclaimed. "Oh, it is as clear as crystal. This is the Roman manner of using complaisant husbands."

"Madonna!" I rebuked her angrily — angry to think that any one should conceive that Bianca could be so abused.

"Gesù!" she returned with a shrug. "The thing is plain enough if you will but look at it. Here His Excellency dares nothing, lest he should provoke the resentment of that uncompromising Lord of Pagliano. But once she is safely away — as Cosimo's wife . . ."

"Stop!" I cried, putting out a hand as if I would cover her mouth. Then, collecting myself: "Do you suggest that Cosimo could lend himself to so infamous a compact?"

"Lend himself? That greedy pander? You do not know your cousin. There is nothing he will not do for profit. If you have any interest in this Madonna Bianca, you will get her hence without delay, and see that Pier Luigi has no knowledge of the convent to which she is consigned. He enjoys the privileges of a papal offspring, and there is no sanctuary he will respect. So let the thing be done speedily and in secret."

I looked at her between doubt and horror.

"Why should you mistrust me?" she asked, answering my look. "I have been frank with you. It is not you nor that white-faced ninny I would serve. You may both go hang for me, though I loved you once, Agostino." And the sudden tenderness of tone and smile were infinitely mocking. "No, no, beloved, if I meddle in this at all, it is because my own interests are in peril."

I shuddered at the cold, matter-of-fact tone in which she alluded to such interests as those which she could have in Pier Luigi.

"Aye, shrink and cringe, sir saint," she sneered. "Having cast me off and taken up holiness, you have the right, of course." And with that she moved past me, and down the terrace-steps without ever turning her head to look at me again. And that was the last I ever saw of her, as you shall find, though little was it to have been supposed so then.

I stood hesitating, half minded to go after her and question her more closely as to what she knew and what she did no more than surmise. But then I reflected that it mattered little. What really mattered was that her good advice should be acted upon without delay.

I went towards the house and in the loggia came face to face with Cosimo.

"Still pursuing the old love," he greeted me, smiling and jerking his head in the direction of Giuliana. "We ever return to it in the end, they say; yet you had best have a care. It is not well to cross my Lord Pier Luigi in such matters; he can be a very jealous tyrant."

I wondered was there some double meaning in the words. I made shift to pass on, leaving his taunt unanswered, when suddenly he stepped up to me and tapped my shoulder.

"One other thing, sweet cousin. You little deserve a warning at my hands. Yet you shall have it. Make haste to shake the dust of Pagliano from your feet. An evil is hanging over you here."

I looked into his wickedly handsome face, and smiled coldly.

"It is a warning which in my turn I will give to you, you jackal," said I, and watched the expression of his countenance grow set and frozen, the colour recede from it.

"What do you mean?" he growled, touched to suspicion of my knowledge by the term I had employed. "What things has that trull dared to . . ."

I cut in. "I mean, sir, to warn you. Do not drive me to do more."

We were quite alone. Behind us stretched the long, empty room, before us the empty gardens. He was without weapons as was I. But my manner was so fierce that he recoiled before me, in positive fear of my hands, I think.

I swung on my heel and pursued my way.

I went above to seek Cavalcanti, and found him newly risen. Wrapped in a gown of miniver, he received me with the news that, having given the matter thought, he had determined to sacrifice his pride and remove Bianca not later than the morrow, as soon as he could arrange it. And to arrange it he would ride forth at once.

I offered to go with him, and that offer he accepted, whereafter I lounged in his ante-chamber waiting until he should be dressed, and considering whether to impart to him the further information I had that morning gleaned. In the end I decided not to do so, unable to bring myself to tell him that so much turpitude might possibly be plotting against Bianca. It was a statement that soiled her, so it seemed to me. Indeed, I could scarcely bear to think of it.

Presently he came forth full-dressed, booted, and armed, and we went along the corridor and out upon the gallery. As side by side we were descending the steps, we caught sight of a singular group in the courtyard.

Six mounted men in black were drawn up there, and a little in the foreground a seventh, in a corselet of blackened steel and with a steel cap upon his head, stood by his horse in conversation with Farnese. In attendance upon the Duke were Cosimo and some three of his gentlemen.

We halted upon the steps, and I felt Cavalcanti's hand suddenly tighten upon my arm.

"What is it?" I asked innocently, entirely unalarmed.

"These are familiars of the Holy Office," he answered me, his tone very grave.

In that moment the Duke, turning, espied us. He came towards the staircase to meet us, and his face, too, was very solemn.

We went down, I filled by a strange uneasiness, which I am sure was entirely shared by Cavalcanti.

"Evil tidings, my Lord of Pagliano," said Farnese. "The Holy Office has sent to arrest the person of Agostino d'Anguissola, for whom it has been seeking for over a year."

"For me?" I cried, stepping forward ahead of Cavalcanti. "What has the Holy Office to do with me?"

The leading familiar advanced. "If you are Agostino d'Anguissola, there is a charge of sacrilege against you, for which you are required to answer before the courts of the Holy Office in Rome."

"Sacrilege?" I echoed, entirely bewildered — for my first thought had been that here might be something concerning the death of Fifanti, and that the dread tribunal of the Inquisition dealing with the matter secretly, there would be no disclosures to be feared by those who had evoked its power.

The thought was, after all, a foolish one; for the death of Fifanti was a matter that concerned the Ruota and the open courts, and those, as I well knew,

did not dare to move against me, on Messer Gambara's account.

"Of what sacrilege can I be guilty?" I asked.

"The tribunal will inform you," replied the familiar — a tall, sallow, elderly man.

"The tribunal will need, then, to await some other
opportunity," said Cavalcanti suddenly. "Messer
d'Anguissola is my guest; and my guests are not so
rudely plucked forth from Pagliano."

The Duke drew away, and leaned upon the arm of
Cosimo, watching. Behind me in the gallery I heard
a rustle of feminine gowns; but I did not turn to look.
My eyes were upon the stern sable figure of the familiar.

"You will not be so ill-advised, my lord," he was
saying, "as to compel us to use force."

"You will not, I trust, be so ill-advised as to at-
tempt it," laughed Cavalcanti, tossing his great head.
"I have five score men-at-arms within these walls,
Messer Black-Clothes."

The familiar bowed. "That being so, the force for
to-day is yours, as you say. But I would solemnly
warn you not to employ it contumaciously against the
officers of the Holy Office, nor to hinder them in the
duty which they are here to perform, lest you render
yourself the object of their just resentment."

Cavalcanti took a step forward, his face purple
with anger that this tipstaff ruffian should take such
a tone with him. But in that instant I seized his arm.

"It is a trap!" I muttered in his ear. "Beware!"

I was no more than in time. I had surprised upon
Farnese's mottled face a sly smile — the smile of the
cat which sees the mouse come venturing from its lair.

And I saw the smile perish — to confirm my suspicions — when at my whispered words Cavalcanti checked in his rashness.

Still holding him by the arm, I turned to the familiar.

"I shall surrender to you in a moment, sir," said I. "Meanwhile, and you, gentlemen — give us leave apart." And I drew the bewildered Cavalcanti aside and down the courtyard under the colonnade of the gallery.

"My lord, be wise for Bianca's sake," I implored him. "I am sure that here is nothing but a trap baited for you. Do not gorge their bait as your valour urges you. Defeat them, my lord, by circumspection. Do you not see that if you resist the Holy Office, they can issue a ban against you, and that against such a ban not even the Emperor can defend you? Indeed, if they told him that his feudatory, the Lord of Pagliano, had been guilty of contumaciously thwarting the ends of the Holy Inquisition, that bigot Charles V would be the first to deliver you over to that tribunal. It should not need, my lord, that I should tell you this."

"My God!" he groaned in utter misery. "But you, Agostino?"

"There is nothing against me," I answered impatiently. "What sacrilege have I ever committed? The thing is a trumped-up business, conceived with a foul purpose by Messer Pier Luigi there. Courage, then, and self-restraint; and thus we shall foil their aims. Come, my lord, I will ride to Rome with them. And do not doubt that I shall return very soon."

He looked at me with eyes that were full of trouble,

indecision in every line of a face that was wont to look so resolute. He knew himself between the sword and the wall.

"I would that Galeotto were here!" cried that man, usually so self-reliant. "What will he say to me when he comes? You were a sacred charge, boy."

"Say to him that I will be returning shortly — which must be true. Come, then. You may serve me this way. The other way you will but have to endure ultimate arrest, and so leave Bianca at their mercy, which is precisely what they seek."

He braced himself at the thought of Bianca. We turned, and in silence we paced back, quite leisurely as if entirely at our ease, for all that Cavalcanti's face had grown very haggard.

"I yield me, sir," I said to the familiar.

"A wise decision," sneered the Duke.

"I trust you'll find it so, my lord," I answered, sneering too.

They led forward a horse for me, and when I had embraced Cavalcanti, I mounted and my funereal escort closed about me. We rode across the courtyard under the startled eyes of the folk of Pagliano, for the familiars of the Holy Office were dread and fearful objects even to the stoutest-hearted man. As we neared the gateway, a shrill cry rang out on the morning air:

"Agostino!"

Fear and tenderness and pain were all blent in that cry.

I swung round in the saddle to behold the white form of Bianca, standing in the gallery with parted lips and startled eyes that were gazing after me, her arms outheld. And then, even as I looked, she crumpled and sank with a little moan into the arms of the ladies who were with her.

I looked at Pier Luigi and from the depths of my heart I cursed him, and I prayed that the day might not be far distant when he should be made to pay for all the sins of his recreant life.

And then, as we rode out into the open country, my thoughts were turned to tenderer matters, and it came to me that, when all was done, that cry of Bianca's made it worth while to have been seized by the talons of the Holy Office.

CHAPTER VII

THE PAPAL BULL

AND now, that you may understand to the full the thing that happened, it is necessary that I should relate it here in its proper sequence, although that must entail my own withdrawal for a time from pages upon which too long I have intruded my own doings and thoughts and feelings.

I set it down as it was told to me later by those who bore their share in it, and particularly by Falcone, who, as you shall learn, came to be a witness of all, and retailed to me the affair with the greatest detail of what this one said and how that one looked.

I reached Rome on the fourth day after my setting out with my grim escort, and on that same day, at much the same hour as that in which the door of my dungeon in Sant' Angelo closed upon me, Galeotto rode into the courtyard of Pagliano on his return from his treasonable journey.

He was attended only by Falcone, and it so chanced that his arrival was witnessed by Farnese, who with various members of his suite was lounging in the gallery at the time.

Surprise was mutual at the encounter; for Galeotto had known nothing of the Duke's sojourn at Pagliano, believing him to be still at Parma, whilst the Duke as little suspected that of the fivescore men-at-arms garrisoned in Pagliano, threescore lances were of Galeotto's free company.

But at sight of this condottiero, whose true aims he was far from suspecting, and whose services he was eager to enlist, the Duke heaved himself up from his seat and went down the staircase shouting greetings to the soldier, and playfully calling him Galeotto in its double sense, and craving to know where he had been hiding himself this while.

The condottiero swung down from his saddle unaided — a thing which he could do even when full-armed — and stood before Farnese, a grim, dust-stained figure, with a curious smile twisting his scarred face.

"Why," said he, in answer, "I have been upon business that concerns Your Magnificence somewhat closely."

And with Falcone at his heels he advanced, the horses relinquished to the grooms who had hastened forward.

"Upon business that concerns me?" quoth the Duke, intrigued.

"Why, yes," said Galeotto, who stood now face to face with Farnese at the foot of the steps up which the Duke's attendants were straggling. "I have been re-cruiting forces, and since one of these days Your Magnificence is to give me occupation, you will see that the matter concerns you."

Above leaned Cavalcanti, his face grey and haggard, without the heart to relish the wicked humour of Galeotto that could make jests for his own entertainment. True, there was also Falcone to overhear, appreciate, and grin under cover of his great brown hand.

"Does this mean that you are come to your senses

on the score of a stipend, Ser Galeotto?" quoth the Duke.

"I am not a trader out of the Giudecca to haggle over my wares," replied the burly condottiero. "But I nothing doubt that Your Magnificence and I will come to an understanding at the last."

"Five thousand ducats yearly is my offer," said Farnese, "provided that you bring three hundred lances."

"Ah, well!" said Galeotto softly, "you may come to regret one of these days, Highness, that you did not think well to pay me the price I ask."

"Regret?" quoth the Duke, with a frown of displeasure at so much frankness.

"When you see me engaged in the service of some other," Galeotto explained. "You need a condottiero, my lord; and you may come to need one even more than you do now."

"I have the Lord of Mondolfo," said the Duke.

Galeotto stared at him with round eyes. "The Lord of Mondolfo?" quoth he, intentionally uncomprehending.

"You have not heard? Why, here he stands." And he waved a jewelled hand towards Cosimo, a handsome figure in green and blue, standing nearest to Farnese.

Galeotto looked at this Anguissola, and his brow grew very black.

"So," he said slowly, "you are the Lord of Mondolfo, eh? I think you are very brave."

"I trust my valour will not be lacking when the proof of it is needed," answered Cosimo haughtily, feeling the other's unfriendly mood and responding to it.

"It cannot," said Galeotto, "since you have the courage to assume that title, for the lordship of Mondolfo is an unlucky one to bear, Ser Cosimo. Giovanni d'Anguissola was unhappy in all things, and his was a truly miserable end. His father before him was poisoned by his best friend, and as for the last who legitimately bore that title — why, none can say that the poor lad was fortunate."

"The last who *legitimately* bore that title?" cried Cosimo, very ruffled. "I think, sir, it is your aim to affront me."

"And what is more," continued the condottiero, as if Cosimo had not spoken, "not only are the lords of Mondolfo unlucky in themselves, but they are a source of ill-luck to those they serve. Giovanni's father had but taken service with Cesare Borgia when the latter's ruin came at the hands of Pope Julius II. What Giovanni's own friendship cost his friends none knows better than Your Highness. So that, when all is said, I think you had better look about you for another condottiero, Magnificent."

The Magnificent stood gnawing his beard and brooding darkly, for he was a grossly superstitious fellow who studied omens and dabbled in horoscopes, divinations, and the like. And he was struck by the thing that Galeotto said. He looked at Cosimo darkly. But Cosimo laughed.

"Who believes such old wives' tales? Not I, for one."

"The more fool you!" snapped the Duke.

"Indeed, indeed," Galeotto applauded. "A disbelief in omens can but spring from ignorance. You should study them, Messer Cosimo. I have done so, and I tell you that the lordship of Mondolfo is unlucky to all dark-complexioned men. And when such a man has a mole under the left ear as you have — in itself a sign of death by hanging — it is well to avoid all risks."

"Now, that is very strange!" muttered the Duke, much struck by this whittling-down of Cosimo's chances, whilst Cosimo shrugged and smiled contemptuously. "You seem to be greatly versed in these matters, Ser Galeotto," added Farnese.

"He who would succeed in whatever he may undertake should qualify to read all signs," said Galeotto sententiously. "I have sought this knowledge."

"Do you see aught in me that you can read?" inquired the Duke in all seriousness.

Galeotto considered him a moment without any trace in his eyes of the wicked mockery that filled his soul. "Why," he answered slowly, "not in your own person, Magnificent — leastways, not upon so brief a glance. But since you ask me, I have lately been considering the new coinage of Your Highness."

"Yes, yes!" exclaimed the Duke, all eagerness, whilst several of his followers came crowding nearer — for all the world is interested in omens. "What do you read there?"

"Your fate, I think."

"My fate?"

"Have you a coin upon you?"

Farnese produced a gold ducat, fire-new from the mint. The condottiero took it and placed his finger upon the four letters P L A C — the abbreviation of "Placentia" in the inscription.

"P — L — A — C," he spelled. "That contains

your fate, Magnificent, and you may read it for yourself." And he returned the coin to the Duke, who stared at the letters foolishly and then at this reader of omens.

"But what is the meaning of PLAC?" he asked, and he had paled a little with excitement.

"I have a feeling that it is a sign. I cannot say more. I can but point it out to you, my lord, and leave the deciphering of it to yourself, who are more skilled than most men in such matters. Have I Your Excellency's leave to go doff this dusty garb?" he concluded.

"Aye, go, sir," answered the Duke abstractedly, puzzling now with knitted brows over the coin that bore his image.

"Come, Falcone," said Galeotto, and with his equerry at his heels he set his foot on the first step.

Cosimo leaned forward, a sneer on his white hawk-face. "I trust, Ser Galeotto, that you are a better condottiero than a charlatan."

"And you, sir," said Galeotto, smiling his sweetest in return, "are, I trust, a better charlatan than a condottiero."

He went up the stairs, the gaudy throng making way before him, and he came at last to the top, where stood the Lord of Pagliano awaiting him, a great trouble in his eyes. They clasped hands in silence, and Cavalcanti went in person to lead his guest to his apartments.

"You have not a happy air," said Galeotto as they went. "And, Body of God! it is no matter for marvel considering the company you keep. How long has the Farnese beast been here?"

"His visit is now in its third week," said Cavalcanti, answering mechanically.

Galeotto swore in sheer surprise. "By the Host! And what keeps him?"

Cavalcanti shrugged and let his arms fall to his sides. To Galeotto this proud, stern baron seemed most oddly dispirited.

"I see that we must talk," he said. "Things are speeding well and swiftly now," he added, dropping his voice. "But more of that presently. I have much to tell you."

When they had reached the chamber that was Galeotto's, and the doors were closed and Falcone was unbuckling his master's spurs —

"Now for my news," said the condottiero. "But first, to spare me repetitions, let us have Agostino here. Where is he?"

The look on Cavalcanti's face caused Galeotto to throw up his head like a spirited animal that scents danger.

"Where is he?" he repeated, and old Falcone's fingers fell idle upon the buckle on which they had been engaged.

Cavalcanti's answer was a groan. He flung his long arms to the ceiling, as if invoking Heaven's aid; then he let them fall again heavily, all strength gone out of them.

Galeotto stood an instant looking at him and turning very white. Suddenly he stepped forward, leaving Falcone upon his knees.

"What is this?" he said, his voice a rumble of thunder. "Where is the boy? I say."

The Lord of Pagliano could not meet the gaze of those steel-coloured eyes.

"O God!" he groaned. "How shall I tell you?"

"Is he dead?" asked Galeotto, his voice hard.

"No, no — not dead. But ... But ..." The plight of one usually so strong, so full of mastery and arrogance, was pitiful.

"But what?" demanded the condottiero. "Gesù! Am I a woman, or a man without sorrows, that you need to stand hesitating? Whatever it may be, speak, then, and tell me."

"He is in the clutches of the Holy Office," answered Cavalcanti miserably.

Galeotto looked at him, his pallor increasing. Then he sat down suddenly, and, elbows on knees, he took his head in his hands and spoke no word for a spell, during which time Falcone, still kneeling, looked from one to the other in an agony of apprehension and impatience to hear more.

Neither noticed the presence of the equerry; nor would it have mattered if they had, for he was trusty as steel, and they had no secrets from him.

At last, having gained some measure of self-control, Galeotto begged to know what had happened, and Cavalcanti related the event.

"What could I do? What could I do?" he cried when he had finished.

"You let them take him?" said Galeotto, like a man who repeats the thing he has been told, because he cannot credit it. "You let them take him?"

"What alternative had I?" groaned Cavalcanti, his face ashen and seared with pain.

"There is that between us, Ettore, that ... that will not let me credit this, even though you tell it me."

And now the wretched Lord of Pagliano began to

use the very arguments that I had used to him. He spoke of Cosimo's suit of his daughter, and how the Duke sought to constrain him to consent to the alliance. He urged that in this matter of the Holy Office was a trap set for him to place him in Farnese's power.

"A trap?" roared the condottiero, leaping up. "What trap? Where is this trap? You had fivescore men-at-arms under your orders here — threescore of them my own men, each one of whom would have laid down his life for me, and you allowed the boy to be taken hence by six rascals from the Holy Office, intimidated by a paltry score of troopers that rode with this filthy Duke!"

"Nay, nay — not that," the other protested. "Had I dared to raise a finger I should have brought myself within the reach of the Inquisition without benefiting Agostino. That was the trap, as Agostino himself perceived. It was he himself who urged me not to intervene, but to let them take him hence, since there was no possible charge which the Holy Office could prefer against him."

"No charge!" cried Galeotto, with a withering scorn. "Did villainy ever want for invention? And this trap? Body of God, Ettore, am I to account you a fool after all these years? What trap was there that could be sprung upon you as things stood? Why, man, the game was in your hands entirely. Here was this Farnese in your power. What better hostage than that could you have held? You had but to whistle your war-dogs to heel and seize his person, demanding of the Pope his father a plenary absolution and indemnity for yourself and for Agostino from any prosecutions of the Holy Office ere you surrendered him. And had they attempted to employ force against you, you could have held them in check by threatening to hang the Duke unless the parchments you demanded were signed and delivered to you. My God, Ettore! Must I tell you this?"

Cavalcanti sank to a seat and took his head in his hands.

"You are right," he said. "I deserve all your reproaches. I have been a fool. Worse — I have wanted for courage." And then, suddenly, he reared his head again, and his glance kindled. "But it is not yet too late," he cried, and started up. "It is still time!"

"Time!" sneered Galeotto. "Why, the boy is in their hands. It is hostage for hostage now, a very different matter. He is lost — irretrievably lost!" he ended, groaning. "We can but avenge him. To save him is beyond our power."

"No," said Cavalcanti. "It is not. I am a dolt, a dotard; and I have been the cause of it. Then I shall pay the price."

"What price?" quoth the condottiero, pondering the other with an eye that held no faintest gleam of hope.

"Within an hour you shall have in your hands the necessary papers to set Agostino at liberty; and you shall carry them yourself to Rome. It is the amend I owe you. It shall be made."

"But how is it possible?"

"It is possible, and it shall be done. And when it is done you may count upon me to the last breath to help you to pull down this pestilential Duke in ruin."

He strode to the door, his step firm once more and his face set, though it was very grey. "I will leave you now. But you may count upon the fulfilment of my promise."

He went out, leaving Galeotto and Falcone alone, and the condottiero flung himself into a chair and sat there moodily, deep in thought, still in his dusty garments and with no thought for changing them. Falcone stood by the window, looking out upon the gardens and not daring to intrude upon his master's mood.

Thus Cavalcanti found them an hour later when he returned. He brought a parchment, to which was appended a great seal bearing the Pontifical arms. He thrust it into Galeotto's hand.

"There," he said, "is the discharge of the debt which through my weakness and folly I have incurred."

Galeotto looked at the parchment, then at Cavalcanti, and then at the parchment once more. It was a papal bull of plenary pardon and indemnity to me.

"How came you by this?" he asked, astonished.

"Is not Farnese the Pope's son?" quoth Cavalcanti scornfully.

"But upon what terms was it conceded? If it involves your honour, your life, or your liberty, here's to make an end of it." And he held it across in his hands as if to tear it, looking up at the Lord of Pagliano.

"It involves none of these," the latter answered steadily. "You had best set out at once. The Holy Office can be swift to act."

CHAPTER VIII

THE THIRD DEGREE

I WAS haled from my dungeon by my gaoler accompanied by two figures that looked immensely tall in their black monkish gowns, their heads and faces covered by visored cowls in which two holes were cut for their eyes. Seen by the ruddy glare of the torch which the gaoler carried to that subterranean place of darkness, those black, silent figures, their very hands tucked away into the wide-mouthed sleeves of their habits, looked spectral and lurid — horrific messengers of death.

By chill, dark passages of stone, through which our steps reverberated, they brought me to a pillared, vaulted underground chamber, lighted by torches in iron brackets on the walls.

On a dais stood an oaken writing-table bearing two massive wax tapers and a Crucifix. At this table sat a portly, swarthy-visaged man in the black robes of the order of Saint Dominic. Immediately below and flanking him on either hand sat two mute cowled figures to do the office of amanuenses.

Away on the right, where the shadows were but faintly penetrated by the rays of the torches, stood an engine of wood somewhat of the size and appearance of the framework of a couch, but with stout straps of leather to pinion the patient, and enormous wooden screws upon which the frame could be made to lengthen or contract. From the ceiling grey ropes dangled from pulleys, like the tentacles of some dread monster of cruelty.

One glance into that gloomy part of the chamber was enough for me.

Repressing a shudder, I faced the inquisitor, and thereafter kept my eyes upon him to avoid the sight of those other horrors. And he was horror enough for any man in my circumstances to envisage.

He was very fat, with a shaven, swarthy face and the dewlap of an ox. In that round fleshliness his eyes were sunken like two black buttons, malicious through their very want of expression. His mouth was loose-lipped and gluttonous and cruel.

When he spoke, the deep rumbling quality of his voice was increased by the echoes of that vaulted place.

"What is your name?" he said.

"I am Agostino d'Anguissola, Lord of Mondolfo and . . ."

"Pass over your titles," he boomed. "The Holy Office takes no account of worldly rank. What is your age?"

"I am in my twenty-first year."

"Benedicamus Dominum," he commented, though I could not grasp the appositeness of the comment. "You stand accused, Agostino d'Anguissola, of sacrilege and of defiling holy things. What have you to say? Do you confess your guilt?"

"I am so far from confessing it," I answered, "that I have yet to learn what is the nature of the sacrilege with which I am charged. I am conscious of no such sin. Far from it, indeed . . ."

"You shall be informed," he interrupted, imposing

silence upon me by a wave of his fat hand; and heaving his vast bulk sideways — "Read him the indictment," he bade one of the amanuenses.

From the depths of a visored cowl came a thin, shrill voice:

"The Holy Office has knowledge that Agostino d'Anguissola did for a space of some six months, during the winter of the year of Our Blessed Lord 1544, and the spring of the year of Our Blessed Lord 1545, pursue a fraudulent and sacrilegious traffic, adulterating, for moneys which he extorted from the poor and the faithful, things which are holy, and adapting them to his own base purposes. It is charged against him that in a hermitage on Monte Orsaro he did claim for an image of Saint Sebastian that it was miraculous, that it had power to heal suffering, and that miraculously it bled from its wounds each year during Passion Week, whence it resulted that pilgrimages were made to this false shrine and great store of alms was collected by the said Agostino d'Anguissola, which moneys he appropriated to his own purposes. It is further known that ultimately he fled the place, fearing discovery, and that after his flight the image was discovered broken and the cunning engine by which this diabolical sacrilege was perpetrated was revealed."

Throughout the reading, the fleshy eyes of the inquisitor had been steadily, inscrutably regarding me. He passed a hand over his pendulous chin, as the thin voice faded into silence.

"You have heard," said he.

"I have heard a tangle of falsehood," answered I. "Never was truth more untruly told than this."

The beady eyes vanished behind narrowing creases of fat; and yet I knew that they were still regarding me. Presently they appeared again.

"Do you deny that the image contained this hideous engine of fraud?"

"I do not," I answered.

"Set it down," he eagerly bade one of the amanuenses. "He confesses thus much." And then to me — "Do you deny that you occupied the hermitage during the season named?"

"I do not."

"Set it down," he said again. "What, then, remains?" he asked me.

"It remains that I knew nothing of the fraud. The trickster was a pretended monk who dwelt there before me and at whose death I was present. I took his place thereafter, implicitly believing in the miraculous image, refusing, when its fraud was ultimately suggested to me, to credit that any man could have dared so vile and sacrilegious a thing. In the end, when it was broken and its fraud discovered, I quitted that ghastly shrine of Satan's in horror and disgust."

There was no emotion on the huge, yellow face. "That is the obvious defence," he said slowly. "But it does not explain the appropriation of the moneys."

"I appropriated none," I cried angrily. "That is the foulest lie of all."

"Do you deny that alms were made?"

"Certainly they were made; though to what extent I am unaware. A vessel of baked earth stood at the door to receive the offerings of the faithful.

It had been my predecessor's practice to distribute a part of these alms among the poor; a part, it was said, he kept to build a bridge over the Bagnanza torrent, which was greatly needed."

"Well, well?" quoth he. "And when you left you took with you the moneys that had been collected?"

"I did not," I answered. "I gave the matter no thought. When I left I took nothing with me — not so much as the habit I had worn in that hermitage."

There was a pause. Then he spoke slowly. "Such is not the evidence before the Holy Office."

"What evidence?" I cried, breaking in upon his speech. "Where is my accuser? Set me face to face with him."

Slowly he shook his huge head with its absurd fringe of greasy locks about the tonsured scalp — that symbol of the Crown of Thorns.

"You must surely know that such is not the way of the Holy Office. In its wisdom this tribunal holds that to produce delators would be to subject them, perhaps, to molestation, and thus dry up the springs of knowledge and information which it now enjoys. So that your request is idle; as idle as is the attempt at defence that you have made, the falsehoods with which you have sought to clog the wheels of justice."

"Falsehood, sir monk?" quoth I, so fiercely that one of my attendants set a restraining hand upon my arm.

The beady eyes vanished and reappeared, and they considered me impassively.

"Your sin, Agostino d'Anguissola," said he in his booming, level voice, "is the most hideous that the wickedness of man could conceive or diabolical greed put into execution. It is the sin that more than any other closes the door to mercy. It is the offence of Simon Mage, and it is to be expiated only through the gates of death. You shall return hence to your cell, and when the door closes upon you, it closes upon you for all time in life, nor shall you ever see your fellow-man again. There hunger and thirst shall be your executioners, slowly to deprive you of a life of which you have not known how to make a better use. Without light or food or drink shall you remain there until you die. This is the punishment for such sacrilege as yours."

I could not believe it. I stood before him what time he mouthed out those horrible and emotionless words. He paused a moment, and again came that broad gesture of his that stroked mouth and chin. Then he resumed:

"So much for your body. There remains your soul. In its infinite mercy, the Holy Office desires that your expiation be fulfilled in this life, and that you may be rescued from the fires of everlasting Hell. Therefore it urges you to cleanse yourself by a full and contrite avowal ere you go hence. Confess, then, my son, and save your soul."

"Confess?" I echoed. "Confess to a falsehood? I have told you the truth of this matter. I tell you that in all the world there is none less prone to sacrilege than I; that I am by nature and rearing devout and faithful. These are lies which have been uttered to my hurt. In dooming me you doom an innocent man. Be it so. I do not know that I have found the world so delectable a place as to quit it with any great regret. My blood be upon your own heads and upon this iniquitous and monstrous tribunal. But spare yourselves at least the greater offence of asking my confession of a falsehood."

The little eyes considered me long, their gaze inscrutable. At last, very slowly, the Dominican spoke, an odd, almost sorrowful solemnity in his tone.

"The merciful laws of this tribunal accord you twenty-four hours for reflection and meditation. It is my prayer that in that time, my son, Divine Grace may move you from your impenitence, may soften a heart which sin has hardened, and dispose you freely to confess your offence. Otherwise our duty is clear, and we command the means to constrain confession from you.

"Reflect on that, my son, and spare yourself unnecessary suffering.

"Take him away."

I made him no answer, and in silence suffered the familiars to reconduct me by the same dark, chill passages, back to the dungeon in which it was decreed that I should perish.

Yet ere that should come to pass there were horrors to be faced, torments other than those of hunger and of thirst, unless by falsehood I should purchase redemption from them. I was aghast at this frenzy to save my soul, which proceeded by the very means that must ensure its damnation, which out of eagerness to have me surge one sacrilege was driving me headlong into another.

What course I should have found myself pursuing at the end of that four-and-twenty hours I dare not say. Thankful am I that I was spared the test. For within three hours of my return to that dungeon, I was again aroused from my dejection by the gaoler, who came this time accompanied not only by the familiars, but by the inquisitor, himself.

He rolled forward into the half-light of that place to which the sunshine never penetrated, bearing in his hand a parchment that was heavily sealed.

He beckoned me towards him.

"See," he said, "how inscrutable are the Divine ways, and how truth must in the end prevail. Your innocence is established, after all, since the Holy Father himself has seen cause to intervene to save you. You are at liberty. You are free to depart and to go wheresoever you will. This bull concerns you." And he held it out to me.

My mind was groping as a man gropes his way through a dense fog, faltering and hesitating at every step. I took the parchment and considered it. Satisfied as to its nature, however mystified as to how the Pope had come to intervene, I folded the document and thrust it into my belt.

Then the inquisitor waved a huge hand doorwards. "Ite!" he said, and added, whilst his raised hand seemed to perform a benedictory gesture — "Pax Domini sit tecum."

"Et cum spiritu tuo," I replied mechanically, as, turning, I stumbled out of that dread place in the wake of the familiars who went ahead to guide me.

CHAPTER IX

THE RETURN

ABOVE in the blessed sunlight, which hurt my eyes — for I had not seen it for a full week — I found Galeotto awaiting me in a bare room; and scarcely was I aware of his presence than his great arms went round me and enclasped me so fervently that his corselet almost hurt my breast, and brought back as in a flash a poignant memory of another man fully as tall, who had held me to him one night many years ago, and whose armour, too, had hurt me as he embraced me.

Then he held me at arms' length and considered me, and his steely eyes were blurred and moist. He muttered something to the familiars, linked his arm through mine and drew me away, down passages, through doors, and so at last into the busy Roman street.

We went in silence by ways that were well known to him, but in which I should assuredly have lost myself, and so we came at last to a fair tavern — the Osteria del Sole — near the Tower of Nona.

His horse was stalled here, and a servant led us abovestairs to the room that he had hired.

How wrong had I not been, I reflected, to announce before the Inquisition that I should have no regrets in leaving this world. How ungrateful was that speech, considering this faithful one who loved me for my father's sake! And was there not Bianca, who, surely — if her last cry, wrung from her by anguish, contained the truth — must love me for my own?

How sweet the revulsion that now came upon me as I sank into a chair by the window, and gave myself up to the enjoyment of that truly happy moment in which the grey shadow of death had been lifted from me.

Servants bustled in, to spread the board with the choice meats that Galeotto had ordered, and great baskets of luscious fruits and flagons of red Puglia wine; and soon we seated ourselves to the feast.

But ere I began to eat, I asked Galeotto how this miracle had been wrought; what magic powers he wielded that even the Holy Office must open its doors at his bidding. With a glance at the servants who attended us, he bade me eat, saying that we should talk anon. And as my reaction had brought a sharp hunger in its train, I fell to with the best will in all the world, and from broth to figs there were few words between us.

At last, our goblets charged and the servants withdrawn, I repeated my inquiry.

"The magic is not mine," said Galeotto. "It is Cavalcanti's. It was he who obtained this bull."

And with that he set himself briefly to relate the matters that already are contained here concerning that transaction, but the minuter details of which I was later to extract from Falcone. And as he proceeded with his narrative I felt myself growing cold again with apprehension, just as I had grown cold that morning in the hands of the executioners. Until at last, seeing me dead-white, Galeotto checked to inquire what ailed me.

"What — what was the price that Cavalcanti paid for this?" I inquired in answer.

"I could not glean it, nor did I stay to insist, for there was haste. He assured me that the thing had been accomplished without hurt to his honour, life, or liberty; and with that I was content, and spurred for Rome."

"And you have never since thought what the price was that Cavalcanti might have paid?"

He looked at me with troubled eyes. "I confess that in this matter the satisfaction of coming to your salvation has made me selfish. I have had thoughts for nothing else."

I groaned, and flung out my arms across the table. "He has paid such a price," I said, "that a thousand times sooner would I that you had left me where I was."

He leaned forward, frowning darkly. "What do you mean?" he cried.

And then I told him what I feared; told him how Farnese had sued for Bianca's hand for Cosimo; how proudly and finally Cavalcanti had refused; how the Duke had insisted that he would remain at Pagliano until my lord changed his mind; how I had learned from Giuliana the horrible motive that urged the Duke to press for that marriage.

Lastly — "And that is the price he consented to pay," I cried wildly. "His daughter — that sweet virgin — was the price! And at this hour, maybe, the price is paid and that detestable bargain consummated. Oh, Galeotto! Galeotto! Why was I not left to rot in that dungeon of the Inquisition — since I could have died happily, knowing naught of this?"

"By the Blood of God, boy! Do you imply that I
had knowledge? Do you suggest that I would have
bought any life at such a price?"

"No, no!" I answered. "I know that you did not
— that you could not . . ." And then I leaped to my
feet. "And we sit talking here, whilst this . . . whilst
this . . . O God!" I sobbed. "We may yet be in time.
To horse, then! Let us away!"

He, too, came to his feet. "Aye, you are right. It
but remains to remedy the evil. Come, then. Anger
shall mend my spent strength. It can be done in
three days. We will ride as none ever rode yet since
the world began."

And we did — so desperately that by the morning
of the third day, which was a Sunday, we were in
Forli (having crossed the Apennines at Arcangelo)
and by that same evening in Bologna. We had not
slept and we had scarcely rested since leaving Rome.
We were almost dead from weariness.

Since such was my own case, what must have been
Galeotto's? He was of iron, it is true. But consider
that he had ridden this way at as desperate a pace
already, to save me from the clutches of the Inquisition; and that, scarce rested, he was riding north
again. Consider this, and you will not marvel that
his weariness conquered him at last.

At the inn at Bologna where we dismounted, we
found old Falcone awaiting us. He had set out with
his master to ride to Rome. But being himself saddle-
worn at the time, he had been unable to proceed
farther than this, and here Galeotto in his fierce impatience had left him, pursuing his way alone.

Here, then, we found the equerry again, consumed

by anxiety. He leapt forward to greet me, addressing me by the old title of Madonnino which I loved to hear from him, however much that title might otherwise arouse harsh and gloomy memories.

Here at Bologna Galeotto announced that he would be forced to rest, and we slept for three hours — until night had closed in. We were shaken out of our slumbers by the host as he had been ordered; but even then I lay entranced, my limbs refusing their office, until the memory of what was at issue acted like a spur upon me, and caused me to fling my weariness aside as if it had been a cloak.

Galeotto, however, was in a deplorable case. He could not move a limb. He was exhausted — utterly and hopelessly exhausted with fatigue and want of sleep. Falcone and I pulled him to his feet between us; but he collapsed again, unable to stand.

"I am spent," he muttered. "Give me twelve hours — twelve hours' sleep, Agostino, and I'll ride with you to the Devil."

I groaned and cursed in one. "Twelve hours!" I cried. "And she . . . I can't wait, Galeotto. I must ride on alone."

He lay on his back and stared up at me, and his eyes had a glassy stare. Then he roused himself by an effort, and raised himself upon his elbow.

"That is it, boy — ride on alone. Take Falcone. Listen, there are threescore men of mine at Pagliano who will follow you to Hell at a word that Falcone shall speak to them from me. About it, then, and save her. But . . . wait, boy! Do no violence to Farnese, if you can help it."

"But if I can't?" I asked.

"If you can't — no matter. But endeavour not to offer him any hurt! Leave that to me — anon when all is ripe for it. To-day it would be premature, and . . . and we . . . we should be . . . crushed by the . . ." His speech trailed off into incoherent mutterings; his eyelids dropped, and he was fast asleep once more.

Ten minutes later we were riding north again, and all that night we rode, along the endless Æmilian Way, pausing for no more than a draught of wine from time to time, and munching a loaf as we rode. We crossed the Po, and kept steadily on, taking fresh horses when we could, until towards sunset a turn in the road brought Pagliano into our view — grey and lichened on the crest of its smooth emerald hill.

The dusk was falling and lights began to gleam from some of the castle windows when we brought up in the shadow of the gateway.

A man-at-arms lounged out of the guardhouse to inquire our business.

"Is Madonna Bianca wed yet?" was the breathless greeting I gave him.

He peered at me, and then at Falcone, and he swore in some surprise.

"Well returned, my lord! Madonna Bianca? The nuptials were celebrated to-day. The bride has gone."

"Gone?" I roared. "Gone whither, man?"

"Why, to Piacenza — to my Lord Cosimo's palace there. They set out some three hours since."

"Where is your lord?" I asked him, flinging myself from the saddle.

"Within doors, most noble."

How I found him, or by what ways I went to do so,

are things that are effaced completely from my memory. But I know that I came upon him in the library. He was sitting hunched in a great chair, his face ashen, his eyes fevered. At sight of me — the cause, however innocent, of all this evil — his brows grew dark, and his eyes angry. If he had reproaches for me, I gave him no time to utter them, but hurled him mine.

"What have you done, sir?" I demanded. "By what right did you do this thing? By what right did you make a sacrifice of that sweet dove? Did you conceive me so vile as to think that I should ever owe you gratitude — that I should ever do aught but abhor the deed, abhor all who had a hand in it, abhor the very life itself purchased for me at such a cost?"

He cowered before my furious wrath; for I must have seemed terrific as I stood thundering there, my face wild, my eyes bloodshot, half mad from pain and rage and sleeplessness.

"And do you know what you have done?" I went on. "Do you know to what you have sold her? Must I tell you?"

And I told him, in a dozen brutal words that brought him to his feet, the lion in him roused at last, his eyes ablaze.

"We must after them," I urged. "We must wrest her from these beasts, and make a widow of her for the purpose. Galeotto's lances are below and they will follow me, You may bring what more you please. Come, sir — to horse!"

He sprang forward with no answer beyond a muttered prayer that we might come in time.

"We must," I answered fiercely, and ran madly

from the room, along the gallery and down the stairs, shouting and raging like a maniac, Cavalcanti following me.

Within ten minutes, Galeotto's threescore men and another score of those who garrisoned Pagliano for Cavalcanti were in the saddle and galloping hell-for-leather to Piacenza. Ahead on fresh horses went Falcone and I, the Lord of Pagliano spurring beside me and pestering me with questions as to the source of my knowledge.

Our great fear was lest we should find the gates of Piacenza closed on our arrival. But we covered the ten miles in something under an hour, and the head of our little column was already through the Fodesta Gate when the first hour of night rang out from the Duomo, giving the signal for the closing of the gates.

The officer in charge turned out to view so numerous a company, and challenged us to stand. But I flung him the answer that we were the Black Bands of Ser Galeotto and that we rode by order of the Duke, with which perforce he had to be content; for we did not stay for more and were too numerous to be detained by such meagre force as he commanded.

Up the dark street we swept — the same street down which I had last ridden on that night when Gambara had opened the gates of the prison for me — and so we came to the square and to Cosimo's palace.

All was in darkness, and the great doors were closed. A strange appearance this for a house to which a bride had so newly come.

I dismounted as lightly as if I had not ridden lately more than just the ten miles from Pagliano. Indeed,

I had become unconscious of all fatigue, entirely
oblivious of the fact that for three nights now I had
not slept — save for the three hours at Bologna.

I knocked briskly on the iron-studded gates. We
stood there waiting, Cavalcanti and Falcone afoot
with me, the men on horseback still, a silent phalanx.

I issued an order to Falcone. "Ten of them to
secure our egress, the rest to remain here and allow
none to leave the house."

The equerry stepped back to convey the command
in his turn to the men, and the ten he summoned
slipped instantly from their saddles and ranged themselves in the shadow of the wall.

I knocked again, more imperatively, and at last
the postern in the door was opened by an elderly
serving-man.

"What's this?" he asked, and thrust a lanthorn
into my face.

"We seek Messer Cosimo d'Anguissola," I answered.

He looked beyond me at the troop that lined the
street, and his face became troubled. "Why, what is
amiss?" quoth he.

"Fool, I shall tell that to your master. Conduct
me to him. The matter presses."

"Nay, then — but have you not heard? My lord
was wed to-day. You would not have my lord disturbed at such a time?" He seemed to leer.

I put my foot into his stomach and bore him
backward, flinging him full length upon the ground.
He went over and rolled away into a corner, where
he lay bellowing.

"Silence him!" I bade the men who followed us in.

"Then, half of you remain here to guard the stairs; the rest attend us."

The house was vast, and it remained silent, so that it did not seem that the clown's scream when he went over had been heard by any.

Up the broad staircase we sped, guided by the light of the lanthorn, which Falcone had picked up — for the place was ominously in darkness. Cavalcanti kept pace with me, panting with rage and anxiety.

At the head of the stairs we came upon a man whom I recognized for one of the Duke's gentlemen-in-waiting. He had been attracted, no doubt, by the sound of our approach; but at sight of us he turned to escape. Cavalcanti reached forward in time to take him by the ankle, so that he came down heavily upon his face.

In an instant I was sitting upon him, my dagger at his throat.

"A sound," said I, "and you shall finish it in Hell!"

Eyes bulging with fear stared at me out of his white face.

He was an effeminate cur, of the sort that the Duke was wont to keep about him, and at once I saw that we should have no trouble with him.

"Where is Cosimo?" I asked him shortly. "Come, man, conduct us to the room that holds him if you would buy your dirty life."

"He is not here," wailed the fellow.

"You lie, you hound," said Cavalcanti, and turning to me — "Finish him, Agostino," he bade me.

The man under me writhed, filled now by the terror that Cavalcanti had so cunningly known how to inspire in him. "I swear to God that he is not here," he answered, and but that fear had robbed him of his voice, he would have screamed it. "Gesù! I swear it — it is true!"

I looked up at Cavalcanti, baffled, and sick with sudden dismay. I saw Cavalcanti's eye, which had grown dull, kindle anew. He stooped over the prostrate man.

"Is the bride here — is my daughter in this house?"

The fellow whimpered and did not answer until my dagger's edge was at his throat again. Then he suddenly screeched — "Yes!"

In an instant I had dragged him to his feet again, his pretty clothes and daintily curled hair all crumpled, so that he looked the most pitiful thing in all the world.

"Lead us to her chamber," I bade him.

And he obeyed as men obey when the fear of death is upon them.

CHAPTER X

THE NUPTIALS OF BIANCA

AN awful thought was in my mind as we went, evoked by the presence in such a place of one of the Duke's gentlemen; an awful question rose again and again to my lips, and yet I could not bring myself to utter it.

So we went on in utter silence now, my hand upon his shoulder, clutching velvet doublet and flesh and bone beneath it, my dagger bare in my other hand.

We crossed an ante-chamber whose heavy carpet muffled our footsteps, and we halted before tapestry curtains that masked a door. Here, curbing my fierce impatience, I paused. I signed to the five attendant soldiers to come no farther; then I consigned the courtier who had guided us to the care of Falcone, and I restrained Cavalcanti, who was shaking from head to foot.

I raised the heavy, muffling curtain, and standing there an instant by the door, I heard my Bianca's voice, and her words seem to freeze the very marrow in my bones.

"Oh, my lord," she was imploring in a choking voice, "oh, my lord, have pity on me!"

"Sweet," came the answer, "it is I who beseech pity at your hands. Do you not see how I suffer? Do you not see how fiercely love of you is torturing me — how I burn — that you can so cruelly deny me?"

It was Farnese's voice. Cosimo, that dastard, had,

indeed, carried out the horrible compact of which Giuliana had warned me, carried it out in a more horrible and inhuman manner than even she had suggested or suspected.

Cavalcanti would have hurled himself against the door but that I set a hand upon his arm to restrain him, and a finger of my other hand — the one that held the dagger — to my lips.

Softly I tried the latch. I was amazed to find the door yield. And yet, where was the need to lock it? What interruption could the Duke have feared in a house that evidently had been delivered over to him by the bridegroom, a house that was in the hands of his own people?

Very quietly I thrust the door open, and we stood there upon the threshold — Cavalcanti and I — father and lover of that sweet maid who was the prey of this foul Duke. We stood whilst a man might count a dozen, silent witnesses of that loathsome scene.

The bridal chamber was all hung in golden arras, save the great carved bed which was draped in dead-white velvet and ivory damask — symbolizing the purity of the sweet victim to be offered up.

And to that dread sacrifice she had come — for my sake, as I was to learn — with the fearful willingness of Iphigenia. For that sacrifice she had been prepared; but not for this horror that was thrust upon her now.

She crouched upon a tall-backed praying-stool, her gown not more white than her face, her little hands convulsively clasped to make her prayer to that monster who stood over her, his mottled face all flushed, his eyes glowing as they considered her help-lessness and terror with horrible, pitiless greed.

Thus we observed them, ourselves unperceived for some moments, for the praying-stool on which she crouched was placed to the left, by the cowled fire-place, in which a fire of scented wood was crackling, the scene lighted by two golden candle-branches that stood upon the table near the curtained window.

"Oh, my lord!" she cried in her despair, "of your mercy leave me, and no man shall ever know that you sought me thus. I will be silent, my lord. Oh, if you have no pity for me, have, at least, pity for yourself. Do not cover yourself with infamy — an infamy that will make you hateful to all men."

As the hawk that has been long poised closes its wings and drops at last upon its prey, so swooped he of a sudden down upon her, caught and dragged her up from the praying stool to crush her to him.

She screamed in that embrace, and sought to battle, swinging round so that her back was fully towards us, and Farnese, swinging round also in that struggle, faced and beheld us.

It was as if a mask had been abruptly plucked from his face, so sudden and stupendous was its alteration. From flushed that it had been, it grew livid and sickly; the unholy fires were spent in his eyes, and they grew dull and dead as a snake's; his jaw was loosened, and the sensual mouth looked unutterably foolish.

For a moment I think I smiled upon him, and then Cavalcanti and I sprang forward, both together. As we moved, his arms loosened their hold, and Bianca would have fallen but that I caught her.

Her terror still upon her, she glanced upwards to

see what fresh enemy was this, and then, at sight of my face, as my arms closed about her, and held her safe —

"Agostino!" she cried, and closed her eyes to lie panting on my breast.

The Duke, fleeing like a scared rat before the anger of Cavalcanti, scuttled down the room to a small door in the wall that held the fireplace. He tore it open and sprang through, Cavalcanti following recklessly.

There was a snarl and a cry, and the Lord of Pagliano staggered back, clutching one hand to his breast, and through his fingers came an ooze of blood. Falcone ran to him. But Cavalcanti swore like a man possessed.

"It is nothing!" he snapped. "By the horns of Satan! it is nothing. A flesh wound, and like a fool I gave back before it. After him! In there! Kill! Kill!"

Out came Falcone's sword with a swish, and into the dark closet beyond went the equerry with a roar, Cavalcanti after him.

It seemed that scarce had Farnese got within that closet than, flattening himself against the wall, he had struck at Cavalcanti as the latter followed, thus driving him back and gaining all the respite he needed. For now they found the closet empty. There was a door beyond, that opened to a corridor, and this was locked. Not a doubt but that Farnese had gone that way. They broke that door down. I heard them at it what time I comforted Bianca, and soothed her, stroking her head, her cheek, and murmuring fondly to her until presently she was weeping softly.

Thus Cavalcanti and Falcone found us presently when they returned. Farnese had escaped with one of his gentlemen who had reached him in time to warn him that the street was full of soldiers and the palace itself invaded. Thereupon the Duke had dropped from one of the windows to the garden, his gentleman with him, and Cavalcanti had been no more than in time to see them disappearing through the garden gate.

The Lord of Pagliano's buff-coat was covered with blood where Pier Luigi had stabbed him. But he would give the matter no thought. He was a tiger now. He ran out into the ante-chamber, and I heard him bellowing orders. Some one screamed horribly, and then followed a fierce din as if the very place were coming down about our ears.

"What is it?" cried Bianca, quivering in my arms. "Are . . . are they fighting?"

"I do not think so, sweet," I answered her. "We are in great strength. Have no fear."

And then Falcone came in again.

"The Lord of Pagliano is raging like a madman," he said. "We had best be getting away or we shall have a brush with the Captain of Justice."

Supporting Bianca, I led her from that chamber.

"Where are we going?" she asked me.

"Home to Pagliano," I answered her, and with that answer comforted that sorely tried maid.

We found the ante-chamber in wreckage. The great chandelier had been dragged from the ceiling, pictures were slashed and cut to ribbons, the arras had been torn from the walls, and the costly furniture was reduced to firewood; the double-windows opening to the balcony stood wide, and not a pane of glass left whole, the fragments lying all about the place.

Thus, it seemed, childishly almost, had Cavalcanti vented his terrible rage, and I could well conceive what would have befallen any of the Duke's people upon whom in that hour he had chanced. I did not know then that the poor pimp who had acted as our guide was hanging from the balcony dead, nor that his had been the horrible scream I had heard.

On the stairs we met the raging Cavalcanti re-ascending, the stump of his shivered sword in his hand.

"Hasten!" he cried. "I was coming for you. Let us begone!"

Below, just within the main doors we found a pile of furniture set on a heap of straw.

"What is this?" I asked.

"You shall see," he roared. "Get to horse."

I hesitated a moment, then obeyed him, and took Bianca on the withers in front of me, my arm about her to support her.

Then he called to one of the men-at-arms who stood by with a flaring torch. He snatched the brand from his hand, and stabbed the straw with it in a dozen places, from each of which there leapt at once a tongue of flame. When, at last, he flung the torch into the heart of the pile, it was all a roaring, hissing, crackling blaze.

He stood back and laughed. "If there are any more of his brothel-mates in the house, they can escape as he did. They will be more fortunate than that one." And he pointed up to the limp figure hanging from the balcony, so that I now learnt what already I have told you.

With my hand I screened Bianca's eyes. "Do not look," I bade her.

I shuddered at the sight of that limply hanging body. And yet I reflected that it was just. Any man who could have lent his aid to the foul crime that was attempted there that night deserved his fate and worse.

Cavalcanti got to horse, and we rode down the street, bringing folk to their windows in alarm. Behind us the flames began to lick out from the ground floor of Cosimo's palace.

We reached the Porta Fodesta, and peremptorily bade the guard to open for us. He answered, as became his duty, with the very words that had been addressed to me at that place on a night two years ago:

"None passes out to-night."

In an instant a group of our men surrounded him, others made a living barrier before the guard-house, whilst two or three dismounted, drew the bolts, and dragged the great gates open.

We rode on, crossing the river, and heading straight for Pagliano.

For a while it was the sweetest ride that ever I rode, with my Bianca nestling against my breast, and responding faintly to all the foolishness that poured from me in that ambrosial hour.

And then it seemed to me that we rode, not by night, but in the blazing light of day, along a dusty road, flanking an arid, sun-drenched stretch of the Campagna; and despite the aridity there must be water somewhere, for I heard it thundering as the Bagnanza had thundered after rain, and yet I knew that could not be the Bagnanza, for the Bagnanza was nowhere in the neighbourhood of Rome.

Suddenly a great voice, and I knew it for the voice of Bianca, called me by name.

"Agostino!"

The vision was dissipated. It was night again and we were riding for Pagliano through the fertile lands of ultra-Po; and there was Bianca clutching at my breast and uttering my name in accents of fear, whilst the company about me was halting.

"What is it?" cried Cavalcanti. "Are you hurt?"

I understood. I had been dozing in the saddle, and I must have rolled out of it but that Bianca awakened me with her cry. I said so.

"Body of Satan!" he swore. "To doze at such a time!"

"I have scarce been out of the saddle for three days and three nights — this is the fourth," I informed him. "I have had but three hours' sleep since we left Rome. I am done," I admitted. "You, sir, had best take your daughter. She is no longer safe with me."

It was so. The fierce tension which had banished sleep from me whilst these things were doing, being now relaxed, left me exhausted as Galeotto had been at Bologna. And Galeotto had urged me to halt and rest there! He had begged for twelve hours! I could now thank Heaven from a full heart for having given me the strength and resolution to ride on, for those twelve hours would have made all the difference between Heaven and Hell.

Cavalcanti himself would not take her, confessing to some weakness. For all that he insisted that his wound was not serious, yet he had lost much blood through having neglected in his rage to stanch it. So it was to Falcone that fell the charge of that sweet burden.

The last thing I remember was Cavalcanti's laugh,

as, from the high ground we had mounted, he stopped to survey a ruddy glare above the city of Piacenza, where, in a vomit of sparks, Cosimo's fine palace was being consumed.

Then we rode down into the valley again; and as we went the thud of hooves grew more and more distant, and I slept in the saddle as I rode, a man-at-arms on either side of me, so that I remember no more of the doings of that strenuous night.

CHAPTER XI

THE PENANCE

I AWAKENED in the chamber that had been mine at Pagliano before my arrest by order of the Holy Office, and I was told upon awakening that I had slept a night and a day and that it was eventide once more.

I rose, bathed, and put on a robe of furs, and then Galeotto came to visit me.

He had arrived at dawn, and he, too, had slept for some ten hours since his arrival, yet despite of it his air was haggard, his glance overcast and heavy.

I greeted him joyously, conscious that we had done well. But he remained gloomy and unresponsive.

"There is ill news," he said at last. "Cavalcanti is in a raging fever, and he is sapped of strength, his body almost drained of blood. I even fear that he is poisoned, that Farnese's dagger was laden with some venom."

"Oh, surely . . . it will be well with him!" I faltered.

He shook his head sombrely, his brows furrowed.

"He must have been stark mad last night. To have raged as he did with such a wound upon him, and to have ridden ten miles afterwards! Oh, it was midsummer frenzy that sustained him. Here in the courtyard he reeled unconscious from the saddle; they found him drenched with blood from head to foot; and he has been unconscious ever since. I am afraid . . ." He shrugged despondently.

"Do you mean that . . . that he may die?" I asked, scarce above a whisper.

"It will be a miracle if he does not. And that is one more crime to the score of Pier Luigi." He said it in a tone of indescribable passion, shaking his clenched fist at the ceiling.

The miracle did not come to pass. Two days later, in the presence of Galeotto, Bianca, Fra Gervasio, who had been summoned from his Piacenza convent to shrive the unfortunate baron, and myself, Ettore Cavalcanti sank quietly to rest.

Whether he was dealt an envenomed wound, as Galeotto swore, or whether he died as a result of the awful draining of his veins, I do not know.

At the end he had a moment of lucidity.

"You will guard my Bianca, Agostino," he said to me, and I swore it fervently, as he bade me, whilst upon her knees beyond the bed, clasping one of his hands that had grown white as marble, Bianca was sobbing broken-heartedly.

Then the dying man turned his head to Galeotto. "You will see justice done upon that monster ere you die," he said. "It is God's holy work."

And then his mind became clouded again by the mists of approaching dissolution, and he sank into a sleep from which he never awakened.

We buried him on the morrow in the Chapel of Pagliano, and on the next day Galeotto drew up a memorial wherein he set forth all the circumstances of the affair in which that gallant gentleman had met his end. It was a terrible indictment of Pier Luigi Farnese. Of this memorial he prepared two copies, and to these — as witnesses of all the facts therein related —

Bianca, Falcone, and I appended our signatures, and Fra Gervasio added his own. One of these copies Galeotto despatched to the Pope, the other to Ferrante Gonzaga in Milan, with a request that it should be submitted to the Emperor.

When the memorial was signed, he rose, and, taking Bianca's hand in his own, he swore by his every hope of salvation that ere another year was sped her father should be avenged together with all the other of Pier Luigi's victims.

That same day he set out again upon his conspirator's work, whose aim was not only the life of Pier Luigi, but the entire shattering of the Pontifical sway in Parma and Piacenza. Some days later he sent me another score of lances — for he kept his forces scattered about the country whilst gradually he increased their numbers.

Thereafter we waited for events at Pagliano, the drawbridge raised, and none entering save after due challenge.

We expected an attack which never came; for Pier Luigi did not dare to lead an army against an Imperial fief upon such hopeless grounds as were his own. Possibly, too, Galeotto's memorial may have caused the Pope to impose restraint upon his dissolute son.

Cosimo d'Anguissola, however, had the effrontery to send a messenger a week later to Pagliano, to demand the surrender of his wife, saying that she was his by God's law and man's, and threatening to enforce his rights by an appeal to the Vatican.

That we sent the messenger empty-handed away, it is scarce necessary to chronicle. I was in command at Pagliano, holding it in Bianca's name, as Bianca's lieutenant and castellan, and I made oath that I would never lower the bridge to admit an enemy.

But Cosimo's message aroused in us a memory that had lain dormant these days. She was no longer for my wooing. She was the wife of another.

It came to us almost as a flash of lightning in the night; and it startled us by all that it revealed.

"The fault of it is all mine," said she, as we sat that evening in the gold-and-purple dining-room where we had supped.

It was with those words that she broke the silence that had endured throughout the repast, until the departure of the pages and the seneschal who had ministered to us precisely as in the days when Cavalcanti had been alive.

"Ah, not that, sweet!" I implored her, reaching a hand to her across the table.

"But it is true, my dear," she answered, covering my hand with her own. "If I had shown you more mercy when so contritely you confessed your sin, mercy would have been shown to me. I should have known from the sign I had that we were destined for each other; that nothing that you had done could alter that. I did know it, and yet . . ." She halted there, her lip tremulous.

"And yet you did the only thing that you could do when your sweet purity was outraged by the knowledge of what I really had been."

"But you were so no more," she said with a something of pleading in her voice.

"It was you — the blessed sight of you that cleansed me," I cried. "When love for you awoke in me, I knew love for the first time, for that other thing which I deemed love had none of love's holiness. Your image drove out all the sin from my soul. The peace which half a year of penance, of fasting and flagellation could not bring me, was brought me by my love for you when it awoke. It was as a purifying fire that turned to ashes all the evil of desires that my heart had held."

Her hand pressed mine. She was weeping softly.

"I was an outcast," I continued. "I was a mariner without compass, far from the sight of land, striving to find my way by the light of sentiments implanted in me from early youth. I sought salvation desperately — sought it in a hermitage, as I would have sought it in a cloister but that I had come to regard myself as unworthy of the cloistered life. I found it at last, in you, in the blessed contemplation of you. It was you who taught me the lesson that the world is God's world and that God is in the world as much as in the cloister. Such was the burden of your message that night when you appeared to me on Monte Orsaro."

"Oh, Agostino!" she cried, "and all this being so how can you not blame me for what has come to pass? If I had but had faith in you — the faith in the sign which we both received — I should have known all this; known that if you had sinned you had been tempted and that you had atoned."

"I think the atonement lies here and now, in this," I answered, very gravely. "She was the wife of another who dragged me down. You are the wife of another who have lifted me up. She through sin was attainable. That you can never, never be, else should I have done with life in earnest. But do not blame yourself, sweet saint. You did as your pure spirit

bade you; soon all would have been well but that
already Messer Pier Luigi had seen you."

She shuddered.

"You know, dear, that if I submitted to wed your
cousin, it was to save you — that such was the price
imposed?"

"Dear saint!" I cried.

"I mention it only so that you may have no doubt
of my motives."

"How could I doubt?" I protested.

I rose, and moved down the room towards the
window, behind which the night gleamed deepest
blue. I looked out upon the gardens from which the
black shadows of stark poplars thrust upward against
the sky, and I thought out this thing. Then I turned
to her, having as I imagined found the only and rather
obvious solution.

"There is but one thing to do, Bianca."

"And that?" her eyes were very anxious, and
looked perhaps even more so in consequence of the
pallor of her face and the lines of pain that had come
into it in these weeks of such sore trial.

"I must remove the barrier that stands between us.
I must seek out Cosimo and kill him."

I said it without anger, without heat of any sort: a
calm, cold statement of a step that it was necessary to
take. It was a just measure, the only measure that
could mend an unjust situation. And so, I think, she
too viewed it. For she did not start, or cry out in
horror, or manifest the slightest surprise at my
proposal. But she shook her head, and smiled very
wistfully.

"What a folly would not that be!" she said. "How

would it amend what is? You would be taken, and justice would be done upon you summarily. Would that make it any easier or any better for me? I should be alone in the world and entirely undefended."

"Ah, but you go too fast," I cried. "By justice I could not suffer. I need but to state the case, the motive of my quarrel, the iniquitous wrong that was attempted against you, the odious traffic of this marriage, and all men would applaud my act. None would dare do me a hurt."

"You are too generous in your faith in man," she said. "Who would believe your claims?"

"The courts," I said.

"The courts of a State in which Pier Luigi governs?

"But I have witnesses of the facts."

"Those witnesses would never be allowed to testify. Your protests would be smothered. And how would your case really look?" she cried. "The world would conceive that the lover of Bianca de' Cavalcanti had killed her husband that he might take her for his own. What could you hope for in the face of that? Men might even remember that other affair, of Fifanti's; and even the populace, which may be said to have saved you erstwhile, might veer round and change from the opinion which it has ever held. They would say that who has done such a thing once may do it twice; that . . ."

"Oh, for pity's sake, stop! Have mercy!" I cried, flinging out my arms towards her. And mercifully she ceased, perceiving that she had said enough.

I turned to the window again, and pressed my brow against the cool glass. She was right. That keen mind of hers had pierced straight to the very core of this matter. To do the thing that had been in my mind would be not only to destroy myself, but to defile her; for upon her would recoil a portion of the odium that must be flung at me. And — as she said — what then must be her position? They would even have a case upon which to drag her from these walls of Pagliano. She would be a victim of the civil courts; she might, at Pier Luigi's instigation, be proceeded against as my accomplice in what would be accounted a dastardly murder for the basest of motives.

I turned to her again.

"You are right," I said. "I see that you are right. Just as I was right when I said that my atonement lies here and now. The penance for which I have cried out so long is imposed at last. It is as just as it is cruelly apt."

I came slowly back to the table, and stood facing her across it. She looking up at me with very piteous eyes.

"Bianca, I must go hence," I said. "That, too, is clear."

Her lips parted; her eyes dilated; her face, if anything, grew paler.

"Oh, no, no!" she cried piteously.

"It must be," I said. "How can I remain? Cosimo may appeal for justice against me — claiming that I hold his wife in duress — and justice will be done."

"But you can resist. Pagliano is strong and well-manned. The Black Bands are very faithful men, and they will stand by you to the end."

"And the world?" I cried. "What will the world say of you? It is yourself have made me see it. Shall

your name be dragged in the foul mire of scandal?
The wife of Cosimo d'Anguissola a runagate with her
husband's cousin? Shall the world say that?"

She moaned, and covered her face with her hands.
Then she controlled herself again, and looked at me
almost fiercely.

"Do you care so much for what men say?"

"I am thinking of you."

"Then think of me to better purpose, my Agostino.
Consider that we are confronted by two evils, and
that the choice of the lesser is forced upon us. If you
go, I am all unprotected, and . . . and . . . the harm is
done already."

Long I looked at her with such a yearning to take
her in my arms and comfort her! And I had the
knowledge that if I remained, daily must I experience
this yearning which must daily grow crueller and
more fierce from the very restraint I must impose
upon it. And then that rearing of mine, all drenched
in sanctity misunderstood, came to my help, and
made me see in this an added burden to my penance,
a burden which I must accept if I would win to ultimate grace.

And so I consented to remain, and I parted from her
with no more than a kiss bestowed upon her finger-
tips, and went to pray for patience and strength to
bear my heavy cross and so win to my ultimate reward, be it in this world or the next.

In the morning came news by a messenger from
Galeotto — news of one more foul crime that the
Duke had committed on that awful night when we
had rescued Bianca from his evil claws. The unfortunate Giuliana had been found dead in her bed

upon the following morning, and the popular voice said that the Duke had strangled her.

Of that rumour I subsequently had confirmation. It would appear that, maddened with rage at the loss of his prey, that ravening wolf had looked about to discover who might have betrayed his purpose and procured that intervention. He bethought him of Giuliana. Had not Cosimo seen her in intimate talk with me on the morning of my arrest, and would he not have reported it to his master?

So to the handsome mansion in which he housed her, and to which at all hours he had access, the Duke went instantly. He must have taxed her with it; and, knowing her nature, I can imagine that she not only admitted that his thwarting was due to her, but admitted it mockingly, exultingly, jeering as only a jealous woman can jeer, until in his rage he seized her by the throat.

How bitterly must she not have repented that she had not kept a better guard upon her tongue, during those moments of her agony, brief in themselves, yet horribly long to her, until her poor wanton spirit went forth from the weak clay that she had loved too well.

When I heard of the end of that unfortunate, all my bitterness against her went out of me, and in my heart I set myself to find excuses for her. Witty and cultured in much; in much else she had been as stupid as the dumb beast. She was irreligious as were many because what she saw of religion did not inspire respect in her. and whilst one of her lovers had been a prince of the Church another had been the son of the Pope. She was by nature sensuous, and her sensuousness stifled in her all perception of right or wrong.

I like to think that her death was brought about as the result of a good deed — so easily might it have been the consequence of an evil one. And I trust that this deed — good in itself, whatever the sources from which it sprang — may have counted in her favour and weighed in the balance against the sins that were largely of her nature.

I bethought me of Fra Gervasio's words to me: "Who that knows all that goes to the making of a sin shall ever dare to blame a sinner?" He had applied those words to my own case where Giuliana was concerned. But do they not apply equally to Giuliana? Do they not apply to every sinner, when all is said?

CHAPTER XII

BLOOD

THE words that passed between Bianca and me that evening in the dining-room express all that can be said of our attitude to each other during the months that followed. Daily we met, and the things which our lips no longer dared to utter, our eyes expressed.

Days passed and grew to weeks, and these accumulated into months. The autumn faded from gold to grey, and the winter came and laid the earth to sleep, and then followed spring to awaken it once more.

None troubled us at Pagliano, and we began with some justice to consider ourselves secure. Galeotto's memorial, not a doubt, had stirred up matters; and Pier Luigi would be under orders from his father not to add one more scandal to the many of his life by venturing to disturb Madonna Bianca in her stronghold at Pagliano.

From time to time we were visited by Galeotto. It was well for him that fatigue had overwhelmed him that day at Bologna, and so hindered him from taking a hand with us in the doings of that hideous night, else he might no longer have freedom to roam the State unchallenged as he did.

He told us of the new citadel the Duke was building in Piacenza, and how for the purpose he was pulling down houses relentlessly to obtain material and to

clear himself a space, and how, further, he was widen-
ing and strengthening the walls of the city.

"But I doubt," he said one morning in that spring,
"if he will live to see the work completed. For we are
resolved at last. There is no need for an armed rising.
Fivescore of my lances will be all that is necessary.
We are planning a surprise, and Ferrante Gonzaga is
to be at hand to support us with Imperial troops and
to receive the State as the Emperor's vicegerent
when the hour strikes. It will strike soon," he added,
"and this too, shall be paid for with the rest." And
he touched the black mourning gown that Bianca
wore.

He rode away again that day, and he went north
for a last interview with the Emperor's Lieutenant,
but promising to return before the blow was struck to
give me the opportunity to bear my share in it.

Spring turned to summer, and we waited, wandering in the gardens together; reading together, playing
at bowls or tennis, though the latter game was not
considered one for women, and sometimes exercising
the men-at-arms in the great inner bailey where they
lodged. Twice we rode out a-hawking, accompanied
by a strong escort, and returned without mishap,
though I would not consent to a third excursion, lest a
rumour having gone abroad, our enemies should lie in
wait to trap us. I grew strangely fearful of losing her
who did not and who never might belong to me.

And all this time my penance, as I regarded it, grew
daily heavier to bear. Long since I had ceased so
much as to kiss her finger-tips. But to kiss the very
air she breathed was fraught with danger to my peace
of mind. And then one evening, as we paced the

garden together, I had a moment's madness, a moment in which my yearnings would no longer be repressed. Without warning I swung about, caught her in my arms, and crushed her to me.

I saw the sudden flicker of her eyelids, the one swift upward glance of her blue eyes, and I beheld in them a yearning akin to my own, but also a something of fear that gave me pause.

I put her from me. I knelt and kissed the hem of her mourning gown.

"Forgive me, sweet!" I besought her very humbly.

"My poor Agostino," was all she answered me, what time her fingers fluttered gently over my sable hair.

Thereafter I shunned her for a whole week, and was never in her company save at meals under the eyes of our attendants.

At last, one day in the early part of September, on the very anniversary of her father's death — the eighth of that month it was, and a Thursday — came Galeotto with a considerable company of men-at-arms; and that night he was gay and blithe as I had never seen him in these twelve months past.

When we were alone, the cause of it, which already I suspected, at last transpired.

"It is the hour," he said very pregnantly. "His sands are swiftly running out. To-morrow, Agostino, you ride with me to Piacenza. Falcone shall remain here to captain the men in case any attempt should be made upon Pagliano, which is not likely."

And now he told us of the gay doings there had been in Piacenza for the occasion of the visit of the Duke's son Ottavio — that same son-in-law of the

Emperor whom the latter befriended, yet not to the extent of giving him the duchy in his father's place when that father should have gone to answer for his sins.

Daily there had been jousts and tournaments and all manner of gaieties, for which the Piacentini had been sweated until they could sweat no more. Having fawned upon the people that they might help him to crush the barons, Farnese was now crushing the people whose service he no longer needed. Extortion had reduced them to poverty and despair, and their very houses were being pulled down to supply material for the new citadel, the Duke recking little who might thus be left without a roof over his head.

"He has gone mad," said Galeotto, and laughed. "Pier Luigi could not more effectively have played his part so as to serve our ends. The nobles he alienated long ago, and now the very populace is incensed against him and weary of his rapine. It is so bad with him that of late he has remained shut in the citadel, and seldom ventures abroad, so as to avoid the sight of the starving faces of the poor and the general ruin that he is making of that fair city. He has given out that he is ill. A little blood-letting will cure all his ills forever."

Upon the morrow Galeotto picked thirty of his men, and gave them their orders. They were to depose their black liveries, and clad as country-folk, but armed as country-folk would be for a long journey, they were severally to repair afoot to Piacenza, and assemble there upon the morning of Saturday at the time and place he indicated. They went, and that afternoon we followed.

"You will come back to me, Agostino?" Bianca said to me at parting.

"I will come back," I answered, and bowing I left her, my heart very heavy.

But as we rode the prospect of the thing to do warmed me a little, and I shook off my melancholy. Optimism coloured the world for me all of the rosy hue of promise.

We slept in Piacenza that night, in a big house in the street that leads to the Church of San Lazzaro, and there was a company of perhaps a dozen assembled there, the principals being the brothers Pallavicini of Cortemaggiore, who had been among the first to feel the iron hand of Pier Luigi; there were also present Agostino Landi, and the head of the house of Confalonieri.

We sat after supper about a long table of smooth brown oak, which reflected as in a pool the beakers and flagons with which it was charged, when suddenly Galeotto span a coin upon the middle of it. It fell flat presently, showing the ducal arms and the inscription of which the abbreviation P L A C was a part.

Galeotto set his finger to it. "A year ago I warned him," said he, "that his fate was written there in that shortened word. To-morrow I shall read the riddle for him."

I did not understand the allusion, and said so.

"Why," he explained, not only to me, but to others whose brows had also been knit, "first 'Plac' stands for Placentia where he will meet his doom; and then it contains the initials of the four chief movers in this undertaking — Pallavicini, Landi, Anguissola, and Confalonieri."

"You force the omen to come true when you give me a leader's rank in this affair," said I.

He smiled, but did not answer, and returned the coin to his pocket.

And now the happening that is to be related is to be found elsewhere, for it is a matter of which many men have written in different ways, according to their feelings or to the hand that hired them to the writing.

Soon after dawn Galeotto quitted us, each of us instructed how to act.

Later in the morning, as I was on my way to the castle, where we were to assemble at noon, I saw Galeotto riding through the streets at the Duke's side. He had been beyond the gates with Pier Luigi on an inspection of the new fortress that was building. It appeared that once more there was talk between the Duke and Galeotto of the latter's taking service under him, and Galeotto made use of this circumstance to forward his plans. He was, I think, the most self-contained and patient man that it would have been possible to find for such an undertaking.

In addition to the condottiero, a couple of gentlemen on horseback attended the Duke, and half a score of his Swiss lanzknechte in gleaming corselets and steel morions, shouldering their formidable pikes, went afoot to hedge His Excellency.

The people fell back before that little company; the citizens doffed their caps with the respect that is begotten of fear, but their air was sullen and in the main they were silent, though here and there some knave, with the craven adulation of those born to serve at all costs, raised a feeble shout of "Duca!"

The Duke moved slowly at little more than a walking pace, for he was all crippled again by the disease that ravaged him, and his face, handsome in itself, was now repulsive to behold; it was a livid background for the fiery pustules that mottled it, and under the sunken eyes there were great brown stains of suffering.

I flattened myself against a wall in the shadow of a doorway lest he should see me, for my height made me an easy mark in that crowd. But he looked neither to right nor to left as he rode. Indeed, it was said that he could no longer bear to meet the glances of the people he had so grossly abused and outraged with deeds that are elsewhere abundantly related, and with which I need not turn your stomachs here.

When they had gone by, I followed slowly in their wake towards the castle. As I turned out of the fine road that Gambara had built, I was joined by the brothers Pallavicini, a pair of resolute, grizzled gentlemen, the elder of whom, as you will remember, was slightly lame. With an odd sense of fitness they had dressed themselves in black. They were accompanied by half a dozen of Galeotto's men, but these bore no device by which they could be identified. We exchanged greetings, and stepped out together across the open space of the Piazza della Citadella towards the fortress.

We crossed the drawbridge, and entered unchallenged by the guard. People were wont to come and go, and to approach the Duke it was necessary to pass the guard in the ante-chamber above, whose business it was to question all comers.

Moreover, the only guard set consisted of a couple of Swiss who lounged in the gateway, the garrison being all at dinner, a circumstance upon which Galeotto had calculated in appointing noon as the hour for the striking of the blow.

We crossed the quadrangle, and passing under a second archway came into the inner bailey as we had been bidden. Here we were met by Confalonieri, who also had half a dozen men with him. He greeted us, and issued his orders sharply.

"You, Ser Agostino, are to come with us, whilst you others are to remain here until Messer Landi arrives with the remainder of our forces. He should have a score of men with him, and they will cut down the guard when they enter. The moment that is done let a pistol-shot be discharged as the signal to us above, and proceed immediately to take up the bridge and overpower the Swiss who should still be at table. Landi has his orders and knows how to act."

The Pallavicini briefly spoke their assents, and Confalonieri, taking me by the arm, led me quickly above-stairs, his half-dozen men following close upon our heels. Upon none was there any sign of armour. But every man wore a shirt of mail under his doublet or jerkin.

We entered the ante-chamber — a fine, lofty apartment, richly hung and richly furnished. It was empty of courtiers, for all were gone to dine with the captain of the guard, who had been married upon that very morning and was giving a banquet in honour of the event, as Galeotto had informed himself when he appointed the day.

Over by a window sat four of the Swiss — the entire guard — about a table playing at dice, their lances deposited in an angle of the wall.

Watching their game — for which he had lingered
after accompanying the Duke thus far — stood the
tall, broad-shouldered figure of Galeotto. He turned
as we entered, and gave us an indifferent glance as if
we were of no interest to him, then returned his attention to the dicers.

One or two of the Swiss looked up at us casually.
The dice rattled merrily, and there came from the
players little splutters of laughter and deep guttural,
German oaths.

At the room's far end, by the curtains that masked
the door of the chamber where Farnese sat at dinner,
stood an usher in black velvet, staff in hand, who took
no more interest in us than did the Swiss.

We sauntered over to the dicers' table, and in placing ourselves the better to watch their game, we so
contrived that we entirely hemmed them into the em-
brasure, whilst Confalonieri himself stood with his
back to the pikes, an effective barrier between the
men and their weapons.

We remained thus for some moments whilst the
game went on, and we laughed with the winners and
swore with the losers, as if our hearts were entirely in
the dicing and we had not another thought in the
world.

Suddenly a pistol-shot crackled below, and startled
the Swiss, who looked at one another. One burly fellow whom they named Hübli held the dice-box poised
for a throw that was never made.

Across the courtyard below men were running with
drawn swords, shouting as they ran, and hurled themselves through the doorway leading to the quarters
where the Swiss were at table. This the guards saw

through the open window, and they stared, muttering German oaths to express their deep bewilderment.

And then there came a creak of winches and a grinding of chains to inform us that the bridge was being taken up. At last those four lanzknechte looked at us.

"Beim blute Gottes!" swore Hübli. "Was giebt es?"

Our set faces, showing no faintest trace of surprise, quickened their alarm, and this became flavoured by suspicion when they perceived at last how closely we pressed about them.

"Continue your game," said Confalonieri quietly, "it will be best for you."

The great blond fellow Hübli flung down the dice-box and heaved himself up truculently to face the speaker who stood between him and the lances. Instantly Confalonieri stabbed him, and he sank back into his chair with a cry, intensest surprise in his blue eyes, so sudden and unlooked-for had the action been.

Galeotto had already left the group about the table, and with a blow of his great hand he felled the usher who sought to bar his passage to the Duke's chamber. He tore down the curtains, and he was wrapping and entangling the fellow in the folds of them when I came to his aid followed by Confalonieri, whose six men remained to hold the three sound and the one wounded Swiss in check.

And now from below there rose such a din of steel on steel, of shouts and screams and curses, that it behoved us to make haste.

Bidding us follow him, Galeotto flung open the door. At table sat Farnese with two of his gentlemen, one of whom was the Marquis Sforza-Fogliani, the other a doctor of canon law named Copallati.

Alarm was already written on their faces. At sight of Galeotto —

"Ah! You are still here!" cried Farnese. "What is taking place below? Have the Swiss fallen to fighting among themselves?"

Galeotto returned no answer, but advanced slowly into the room; and now Farnese's eyes went past him and fastened upon me, and I saw them suddenly dilate; beyond me they went and met the cold glance of Confalonieri, that other gentleman he had so grievously wronged and whom he had stripped of the last rag of his possessions and his rights. The sun coming through the window caught the steel that Confalonieri still carried in his hands; its glint drew the eyes of the Duke, and he must have seen that the baron's sleeve was bloody.

He rose, leaning heavily upon the table.

"What does this mean?" he demanded in a quavering voice, and his face had turned grey with apprehension.

"It means," Galeotto answered him, firmly and coldly, "that your rule in Piacenza is at an end, that the Pontifical sway is broken in these States, and that beyond the Po Ferrante Gonzaga waits with an army to take possession here in the Emperor's name. Finally, my Lord Duke, it means that the Devil's patience shall be tried no further, and that he is at last to have you who have so faithfully served him upon earth."

Farnese made a gurgling sound and put a jewelled hand to his throat as if he choked. He was all in green

velvet, and every button of his doublet was a brilliant
of price; and that gay raiment by its incongruity
seemed to heighten the tragedy of the moment.

Of his gentlemen the doctor sat frozen with terror
in his high-backed seat, clutching the arms of it so
that his knuckles showed white as marble. In like
case were the two attendant servants, who hung mo-
tionless by the buffet. But Sforza-Fogliani, a man
of some spirit for all his effeminate appearance, leapt
to his feet and set a hand to his weapons.

Instantly Confalonieri's sword flashed from its
sheath. He had passed his dagger into his left hand.

"On your life, my Lord Marquis, do not meddle
here," he warned him in a voice that was like a
trumpet-call.

And before that ferocious aspect and those naked
weapons, Sforza-Fogliani stood checked and intimidated.

I, too, had drawn my poniard, determined that
Farnese should fall to my steel in settlement of the
score that lay between us. He saw the act, and if
possible his fears were increased, for he knew that the
wrongs he had done me were personal matters between us for which it was not likely I should prove
forgiving.

"Mercy!" he gasped, and held out supplicating
hands to Galeotto.

"Mercy?" I echoed, and laughed fiercely. "What
mercy would you have shown me against whom you
set the Holy Office, but that you could sell my life at
a price that was merciless? What mercy would you
have shown to the daughter of Cavalcanti when she
lay in your foul power? What mercy did you show

her father who died by your hand? What mercy did you show the unfortunate Giuliana whom you strangled in her bed? What mercy did you ever show to any that you ask for mercy now?"

He looked at me with dazed eyes, and from me to Galeotto. He shuddered and turned a greenish hue. His knees were loosened by terror, and he sank back into the chair from which he had risen.

"At least . . . at least," he gasped, "let me have a priest to shrive me. Do not . . . do not let me die with all my sins upon me!"

In that moment there came from the ante-chamber the sound of swiftly moving feet, and the clash of steel mingling with cries. The sound heartened him. He conceived that some one came to his assistance. He raised his voice in a desperate screech:

"To me! To me! Help!"

As he shouted, I sprang towards him, to find my passage suddenly barred by Galeotto's arm. He shot it out, and my breast came against it as against a rod of iron. It threw me out of balance, and ere I had recovered, it had thrust me back again.

"Back there!" said Galeotto's brazen voice. "This affair is mine. Mine are the older wrongs and the greater."

With that he stepped behind the Duke's chair, and Farnese in a fresh spurt of panic came to his feet. Galeotto locked an arm about his neck and pulled his head back. Into his ear he muttered words that I could not overhear, but it was matter that stilled Farnese's last struggle. Only the Duke's eyes moved, rolling in his head as he sought to look upon the face of the man who spoke to him. And in that moment

Galeotto wrenched his victim's head still farther back, laying entirely bare the long brown throat, across which he swiftly drew his dagger.

Copallati screamed and covered his face with his hands; Sforza-Fogliani, white to the lips, looked on like a man entranced.

There was a screech from Farnese that ended in a gurgle, and suddenly the blood spurted from his neck as from a fountain. Galeotto let him go. He dropped to his chair and fell forward against the table, drenching it in blood. Thence he went over sideways and toppled to the floor, where he lay twitching, a huddle of arms and legs, the head lolling sideways, the eyes vitreous, and blood, blood, blood all about him.

CHAPTER XIII

THE OVERTHROW

THE sight turned me almost physically sick. I faced about, and sprang from the room out into the ante-chamber, where a battle was in progress. Some three or four of the Duke's gentlemen and a couple of Swiss had come to attempt a rescue. They had compelled Galeotto's six men to draw and defend themselves, the odds being suddenly all against them. Into that medley I went with drawn sword, hacking and cutting madly, giving knocks and taking them, glad of the excitement of it; glad of anything that would shut out from my mind the horror of the scene I had witnessed.

Presently Confalonieri came out to take a hand, leaving Galeotto on guard within, and in a few minutes we had made an end of that resistance — the last splutter of resistance within those walls.

Beyond some cuts and scratches that some of us had taken, not a man of ours was missing, whilst of the Duke's followers not a single one remained alive in that ante-chamber. The place was a shambles. Hangings that had been clutched had been torn from the walls; a great mirror was cracked from top to bottom; tables were overset and wrecked; chairs were splintered; and hardly a pane of glass remained in any of the windows. And everywhere there was blood, everywhere dead men.

Up the stairs came trooping now our assembled

forces led by Landi and the Pallavicini. Below all was quiet. The Swiss garrison, taken by surprise at table, as was planned, had been disarmed and all were safe and impotent under lock and bolt. The guards at the gate had been cut down, and we were entirely masters of the place.

Sforza-Fogliani, Copallati, and the two servants were fetched from the Duke's chamber and taken away to be locked up in another room until the business should be ended. For, after all, it was but begun.

In the town the alarm-bell was ringing from the tower of the Communal Palace, and at the sound I saw Galeotto's eyes kindling. He took command, none disputing it him, and under his orders men went briskly to turn the cannon of the fortress upon the square, that an attack might be repulsed if it were attempted. And three salvos were fired, to notify Ferrante Gonzaga where he waited that the castle was in the hands of the conspirators and Pier Luigi slain.

Meanwhile, we had returned with Galeotto to the room where the Duke had died, and where his body still lay, huddled as it had fallen. The windows of this chamber were set in the outer wall of the fortress, immediately above the gates and commanding a view of the square. We were six — Confalonieri, Landi, the two Pallavicini, Galeotto, and myself, besides a slight fellow named Malvicini, who had been an officer of light-horse in the Duke's service, but who had taken a hand in betraying him.

In the square there was by now a seething, excited mob, through which a little army of perhaps a thousand men of the town militia with their captain, da Terni, riding at their head, was forcing its way. And they were shouting "Duca!" and crying out that the castle had been seized by Spaniards — by which they meant the Emperor's troops.

Galeotto dragged a chair to the window, and, standing upon it, showed himself to the people.

"Disperse!" he shouted to them. "To your homes! The Duke is dead!"

But his voice could not surmount that raging din, above which continued to ring the cry of "Duca! Duca!"

"Let me show them their Duca," said a voice. It was Malvicini's.

He had torn down a curtain-rope, and had attached an end of it to one of the dead man's legs. Thus he dragged the body forward towards the window. The other end of the rope he now knotted very firmly to a mullion. Then he took the body up in his arms, whilst Galeotto stood aside to make way for him, and, staggering under his ghastly burden, Malvicini reached the window, and heaved it over the sill.

It fell the length of the rope and there was arrested with a jerk to hang head downwards, spread-eagle against the brown wall; and the diamond buttons in his green velvet doublet sparkled merrily in the sunshine.

At that sight a great silence swept across the multitude, and availing himself of this, Galeotto again addressed those Piacentini.

"To your homes," he cried to them, "and arm yourselves to defend the State from your enemies if the need should arise. There hangs the Duke — dead. He has been slain to liberate our country from unjust oppression."

Still, it seemed, they did not hear him; for though to us they appeared to be almost silent, yet there was a rustle and stir amongst them, which must have deafened each to what was being announced.

They renewed their cries of "Duca!" of "Spaniards!" and "To arms!"

"A curse on your 'Spaniards'!" cried Malvicini. "Here! Take your Duke. Look at him, and understand." And he slashed the rope across, so that the body plunged down into the castle ditch.

A few of the foremost of the crowd ran forward and scrambled down into the ditch to view the body, and from them the rumour of the truth ran like a ripple over water through that mob, so that in the twinkling of an eye there was no man in that vast concourse — and all Piacenza seemed by now to be packed into the square — but knew that Pier Luigi Farnese was dead.

A sudden hush fell. There were no more cries of "Duca!" They stood silent, and not a doubt but that in the breasts of the majority surged a great relief. Even the militia ceased to advance. If the Duke was dead, there was nothing left to do.

Again Galeotto spoke to them, and this time his words were caught by those in the ditch immediately below us, and from them they were passed on, and suddenly a great cry went up — a shout of relief, a pæan of joy. If Farnese was dead, and well dead, they could, at last, express the thing that was in their hearts.

And now at the far end of the square a glint of armour appeared; a troop of horse emerged, and began slowly to press forward through the crowd, driving it back on either side, but very gently. They came three abreast, and there were sixscore of them, and from their lance-heads fluttered bannerols showing a sable bar on an argent field. They were Galeotto's free company, headed by one of his lieutenants. Beyond the Po they, too, had been awaiting the salvo of artillery that should be their signal to advance.

When their identity was understood, and when the crowd had perceived that they rode to support the holders of the castle, they were greeted with lusty cheers, in which presently even the militia joined, for these last were Piacentini and no Swiss hireling soldiers of the Duke's.

The drawbridge was let down, and the company thundered over it to draw up in the courtyard under the eyes of Galeotto. He issued his orders once more to his companions. Then, calling for horses for himself and for me, and bidding a score of lances to detach themselves to ride with us, we quitted the fortress.

We pressed through the clamant multitude until we had reached the middle of the square. Here Galeotto drew rein, and, raising his hand for silence, informed the people once more that the Duke had been done to death by the nobles of Piacenza, thus to avenge alike their own and the people's wrongs, and to free them from unjust oppression and tyranny.

They cheered him when he had done, and the cry now was "Piacenza! Piacenza!"

When they had fallen silent again — "I would

have you remember," he cried, "that Pier Luigi was
the Pontiff's son, and that the Pontiff will make
haste to avenge his death and to reëstablish here in
Piacenza the Farnese sway. So that all that we have
done this day may go for naught unless we take our
measures."

The silence deepened.

"But you have been served by men who have the
interest of the State at heart; and more has been done
to serve you than the mere slaying of Pier Luigi
Farnese. Our plans are made, and we but wait to
know is it your will that the State should incorporate
itself as of old with that of Milan, and place itself
under the protection of the Emperor, who will appoint you fellow-countrymen for rulers, and will
govern you wisely and justly, abolishing extortion
and oppression?"

A thunder of assent was his answer. "Cesare!
Cesare!" was now the cry, and caps were tossed into
the air.

"Then go arm yourselves and repair to the Commune, and there make known your will to the
Anziani and Councillors, and see that it is given
effect by them. The Emperor's Lieutenant is at your
gates. I ride to surrender to him the city in your
name, and before nightfall he will be here to protect
you from any onslaught of the Pontificals."

With that he pushed on, the mob streaming along
with us, intent upon going there and then to do the
thing that Galeotto advised. And by now they had
discovered Galeotto's name, and they were shouting
it in acclamation of him, and at the sound he smiled,
though his eyes seemed very wistful.

He leaned over to me, and gripped my hand where it lay on the saddle-bow clutching the reins.

"Thus is Giovanni d'Anguissola at last avenged!" he said to me in a deep voice that thrilled me.

"I would that he were here to know," I answered. And again Galeotto's eyes grew wistful as they looked at me.

We won out of the town at last, and when we came to the high ground beyond the river, we saw in the plain below phalanx upon phalanx of a great army. It was Ferrante Gonzaga's Imperial force.

Galeotto pointed to it. "That is my goal," he said. "You had best ride on to Pagliano with these lances. You may need them there. I had hoped that Cosimo would have been found in the castle with Pier Luigi. His absence makes me uneasy. Away with you, then. You shall have news of me within three days."

We embraced, on horseback as we were. Then he wheeled his charger and went down the steep ground, riding hard for Ferrante's army, whilst we pursued our way, and came some two hours later without mishap to Pagliano.

I found Bianca awaiting me in the gallery above the courtyard, drawn thither by the sounds of our approach.

"Dear Agostino, I have been so fearful for you," was her greeting when I had leapt up the staircase to take her hand.

I led her to the marble seat she had occupied on that night, two years ago, when first we had spoken of our visions. Briefly I gave her the news of what had befallen in Piacenza.

When I had done, she sighed and looked at me.

"It brings us no nearer to each other," she said.

"Nay, now — this much nearer, at least, that the Imperial decree will return me the lordships of Mondolfo and Carmina, dispossessing the usurper. Thus I shall have something to offer you, my Bianca."

She smiled at me very sadly, almost reproachfully.

"Foolish," said she. "What matter the possessions that it may be yours to cast into my lap? Is that what we wait for, Agostino? Is there not Pagliano for you? Would not that, at need, be lordship enough?"

"The meanest cottage of the countryside were lordship enough so that you shared it," I answered passionately, as many in like case have answered before and since.

"You see, then, that you are wrong to attach importance to so slight a thing as this Imperial decree where you and I are concerned. Can an Imperial decree annul my marriage?"

"For that a papal bull would be necessary."

"And how is a papal bull to be obtained?"

"It is not for us," I admitted miserably.

"I have been wicked," she said, her eyes upon the ground, a faint colour stirring in her cheeks. "I have prayed that the usurper might be dispossessed of his rights in me. I have prayed that when the attack was made and revolt was carried into the Citadel of Piacenza, Cosimo d'Anguissola might stand at his usual post beside the Duke and might fall with him. Surely justice demanded it!" she cried out. "God's justice, as well as man's. His act in marrying me was a defilement of one of the holiest of sacraments, and for that he should surely be punished and struck down!"

I went upon my knees to her. "Dear love!" I cried. "See, I have you daily in my sight. Let me not be ungrateful for so much."

She took my face in her hands and looked into my eyes, saying no word. Then she leaned forward, and very gently touched my forehead with her lips.

"God pity us a little, Agostino," she murmured, her eyes shining with unshed tears.

"The fault is mine — all mine!" I denounced myself. "We are being visited with my sins. When I can take you for my own — if that blessed day should ever dawn — I shall know that I have attained to pardon, that I am cleansed and worthy of you at last."

She rose, and I escorted her within; then went to my own chamber to bathe and rest.

CHAPTER XIV

THE CITATION

WE were breaking our fast upon the following morning when Falcone sent word to me by one of the pages that a considerable force was advancing towards us from the south.

I rose, somewhat uneasy. Yet I reflected that it was possible that, news of the revolt in Piacenza having reached Parma, this was an army of Pontificals moving thence upon the rebellious city. But in that case, what should they be doing this side of the Po?

An hour later, from the battlements where we paced side by side — Bianca and I — we were able to estimate this force, and we fixed its strength at fivescore lances. Soon we could make out the device upon their bannerols — a boar's head azure upon an argent field — my own device, that of the Anguissola of Mondolfo; and instantly I knew them for Cosimo's men.

On the lower parapet six culverins had been dragged into position under the supervision of Falcone — who was still with us at Pagliano. These pieces stood loaded and manned by those soldiers to whom I had assigned the office of engineers.

Thus we waited until the little army came to a halt about a quarter of a mile away, and a trumpeter with a flag of truce rode forward accompanied by a knight armed cap-à-pie, his beaver down.

The herald wound a challenge; and it was answered from the postern by a man-at-arms, whereupon the herald delivered his message.

"In the name of our Holy Father and Lord, Paul III, we summon Agostino d'Anguissola here to confer with the High and Mighty Cosimo d'Anguissola, Tyrant of Mondolfo and Carmina."

Three minutes later, to their infinite surprise, the bridge thudded down to span the ditch, and I walked out upon it with Bianca at my side.

"Will the Lord Cosimo come within to deliver his message?" I demanded.

The Lord Cosimo would not, fearing a trap.

"Will he meet us here upon the bridge, divesting himself first of his weapons? Myself I am unarmed."

The herald conveyed the words to Cosimo, who hesitated still. Indeed, he had wheeled his horse when the bridge fell, ready to gallop off at the first sign of a sortie.

I laughed. "You are a paltry coward, Cosimo, when all is said," I shouted. "Do you not see that had I planned to take you, I need resort to no subterfuge? I have," I added — though untruthfully — "twice your number of lances under arms, and by now I could have flung them across the bridge and taken you under the very eyes of your own men. You were rash to venture so far. But if you will not venture farther, at least send me your herald."

At that he got down from his horse, delivered up sword and dagger to his single attendant, received from the man a parchment, and came towards us, opening his visor as he advanced. Midway upon the bridge we met. His lips curled in a smile of scorn.

"Greetings, my strolling saint," he said. "Through all your vagaries you are at least consistent in that you ever engage your neighbour's wife to bear you company in your wanderings."

I went hot and cold, red and white by turns. With difficulty I controlled myself under that taunt — the cruellest he could have flung at me in Bianca's hearing.

"Your business here?" I snarled.

He held out the parchment, his eyes watching me intently, so that they never once strayed to Bianca.

"Read, Saint Mountebank," he bade me.

I took the paper, but before I lowered my eyes to it, I gave him warning

"If on your part you attempt the slightest treachery," I said, "you shall be repaid in kind. My men are at the winches, and they have my orders that at the first treacherous movement on your part they are to take up the bridge. You will see that you could not reach the end of it in time to save yourself."

It was his turn to change colour under the shadow of his beaver. "Have you trapped me?" he asked between his teeth.

"If you had anything of the Anguissola besides the name," I answered, "you would know me incapable of such a thing. It is because I know that of the Anguissola you have nothing but the name, that you are a craven, a dastard and a dog, that I have taken my precautions."

"Is it your conception of valour to insult a man whom you hold as if bound hand and foot against striking you as you deserve?"

I smiled sweetly into that white, scowling face.

"Throw down your gauntlet upon this bridge, Cosimo, if you deem yourself affronted, if you think that I have lied; and most joyfully will I take it up and give you the trial by battle of your seeking."

For an instant I almost thought that he would take me at my word, as most fervently I hoped. But he restrained himself.

"Read!" he bade me again, with a fierce gesture. And accounting him well warned by now, I read with confidence.

It was a papal brief ordering me under pain of excommunication and death to make surrender to Cosimo d'Anguissola of the Castle of Pagliano which I traitorously held, and of the person of his wife, Madonna Bianca.

"This document is not exact," said I. "I do not hold this castle traitorously. It is an Imperial fief, and I hold it in the Emperor's name."

He smiled. "Persist if you are weary of life," he said. "Surrender now, and you are free to depart and go wheresoever you list. Continue in your offence, and the consequences shall daunt you ere all is done. This Imperial fief belongs to me, and it is for me, who am Lord of Pagliano by virtue of my marriage and the late lord's death, to hold it for the Emperor.

"And you are not to doubt that when this brief is laid before the Emperor's Lieutenant at Milan, he will move instantly against you to cast you out and to invest me in those rights which are mine by God's law and man's alike."

My answer may, at first, have seemed hardly to the point. I held out the brief to him.

"To seek the Emperor's Lieutenant you need not

go as far as Milan. You will find him in Piacenza."

He looked at me, as if he did not understand. "How?" he asked.

I explained. "While you have been cooling your heels in the ante-chambers of the Vatican to obtain this endorsement of your infamy, the world hereabouts has moved a little. Yesterday Ferrante Gonzaga took possession of Piacenza in the Emperor's name. To-day the Council will be swearing fealty to Cæsar upon his Lieutenant's hands."

He stared at me for a long moment, speechless in his utter amazement. Then he swallowed hard.

"And the Duke?" he asked.

"The Duke has been in Hell these four-and-twenty hours."

"Dead?" he questioned, his voice hushed.

"Dead," said I.

He leaned against the rail of the bridge, his arms fallen limply to his sides, one hand crushing the Pontifical parchment. Then he braced himself again. He had reviewed the situation, and did not see that it hurt his position, when all was said.

"Even so," he urged, "what can you hope for? The Emperor himself must bow before this, and do me justice." And he smacked the document. "I demand my wife, and my demand is backed by Pontifical authority. You are mad if you think that Charles V can fail to support it."

"It is possible that Charles V may take a different view of the memorial setting forth the circumstances of your marriage from that which the Holy Father appears to have taken. I counsel you to seek the Imperial Lieutenant at Piacenza without delay. Here you waste time."

His lips closed with a snap. Then, at last, his eyes wandered to Bianca, who stood just beside and slightly behind me.

"Let me appeal to you, Monna Bianca . . ." he began.

But at that I got between them. "Are you so dead to shame," I roared, "that you dare address her, you pimp, you jackal, you eater of dirt? Be off, or I will have this drawbridge raised and deal with you here and now, in despite of Pope and Emperor and all the other powers you can invoke. Away with you, then!"

"You shall pay!" he snarled. "By God, you shall pay!"

And on that he went off, in some fear lest I should put my threat into execution.

But Bianca was in a panic. "He will do as he says," she cried as soon as we had reëntered the courtyard. "The Emperor cannot deny him justice. He must, he must! Oh, Agostino, it is the end. And see to what a pass I have brought you!"

I comforted her. I spoke brave words. I swore to hold that castle as long as one stone of it stood upon another. But deep down in my heart there was naught but presages of evil.

On the following day, which was Sunday, we had peace. But towards noon on Monday the blow fell. An Imperial herald from Piacenza rode out to Pagliano with a small escort.

We were in the garden when word was brought us, and I bade the herald be admitted. Then I looked at Bianca. She was trembling and had turned very white.

We spoke no word whilst they brought the

messenger — a brisk fellow in his black-and-yellow Austrian livery. He delivered me a sealed letter. It proved to be a summons from Ferrante Gonzaga to appear upon the morrow before the Imperial Court which would sit in the Communal Palace of Piacenza to deliver judgment upon an indictment laid against me by Cosimo d'Anguissola.

I looked at the herald, hesitation in my mind and glance. He held out a second letter.

"This, my lord, I was asked by favour to deliver to you also."

I took it, and considered the superscription:

These to the Most Noble Agostino d'Anguissola, at Pagliano.
> *Quickly.*
> *Quickly.*
> *Quickly.*

The hand was Galeotto's. I tore it open. It contained but two lines:

Upon your life do not fail to obey the Imperial summons. Send Falcone to me here at once.

And it was signed — "Galeotto."

"It is well," I said to the herald. "I will not fail to attend."

I bade the seneschal who stood in attendance to give the messenger refreshment ere he left, and upon that dismissed him.

When we were alone I turned to Bianca. "Galeotto bids me go," I said. "There is surely hope."

She took the note, and, passing a hand over her eyes, as if to clear away some mist that obscured her vision, she read it. Then she considered the curt summons that gave no clue, and lastly looked at me.

"It is the end," I said. "One way or the other, it is the end. But for Galeotto's letter, I think I should have refused to obey, and made myself an outlaw, indeed. As it is — there is surely hope!"

"Oh, Agostino, surely, surely!" she cried. "Have we not suffered enough? Have we not paid enough already for the happiness that should be ours? To-morrow I shall go with you to Piacenza."

"No, no," I implored her.

"Could I remain here?" she pleaded. "Could I sit here and wait? Could you be so cruel as to doom me to such a torture of suspense?"

"But if . . . if the worst befalls?"

"It cannot," she answered. "I believe in God."

CHAPTER XV

THE WILL OF HEAVEN

IN the Chamber of Justice of the Communal Palace sat that day, not the Assessors of the Ruota, but the Councillors in their damask robes — the Council of Ten of the City of Piacenza. And to preside over them sat, not their Prior, but Ferrante Gonzaga himself, in a gown of scarlet velvet edged with miniver.

They sat at a long table draped in red at the room's end, Gonzaga slightly above them on a raised dais, under a canopy. Behind him hung a golden shield upon which was figured, between two upright columns each surmounted by a crown, the double-headed black eagle of Austria; a scroll intertwining the pillars was charged with the motto "PLUS ULTRA."

At the back of the court stood the curious who had come to see the show, held in bounds by a steel line of Spanish halberdiers. But the concourse was slight, for the folk of Piacenza still had weightier matters to concern them than the trial of a wife-stealer.

I had ridden in with an escort of twenty lances. But I left these in the square when I entered the palace and formally made surrender to the officer who met me. This officer led me at once into the Chamber of Justice, two men-at-arms opening a lane for me through the people with the butts of their pikes, so that I came into the open space before my judges, and bowed profoundly to Gonzaga.

Coldly he returned the salutation, his prominent

eyes regarding me from out of that florid, crafty
countenance.

On my left, but high up the room and immediately
at right angles to the judges' table, sat Galeotto, full-
armed. He was flanked on the one side by Fra
Gervasio, who greeted me with a melancholy smile,
and on the other by Falcone, who sat rigid.

Opposite to this group on the judges' other hand
stood Cosimo. He was flushed, and his eyes gleamed
as they measured me with haughty triumph. From
me they passed to Bianca, who followed after me with
her women, pale, but intrepid and self-contained,
her face the whiter by contrast with the mourning-
gown which she still wore for her father, and which it
might well come to pass that she should continue
hereafter to wear for me.

I did not look at her again as she passed on and up
towards Galeotto, who had risen to receive her. He
came some few steps to meet her, and escorted her to
a seat next to his own, so that Falcone moved down to
another vacant stool. Her women found place behind
her.

An usher set a chair for me, and I, too, sat down,
immediately facing the Emperor's Lieutenant. Then
another usher in a loud voice summoned Cosimo to
appear and state his grievance.

He advanced a step or two, when Gonzaga raised
his hand, to sign to him to remain where he was so
that all could see him whilst he spoke.

Forthwith, quickly, fluently, and lucidly, as if he
had got the thing by heart, Cosimo recited his
accusation: How he had married Bianca de' Cavalcanti by her father's consent in her father's own

Castle of Pagliano; how that same night his palace in Piacenza had been violently invested by myself and others abetting me, and how we had carried off his bride and burnt his palace to the ground; how I had since held her from him, shut up in the Castle of Pagliano, which was his fief in his quality as her husband; and how similarly I had unlawfully held Pagliano against him to his hurt.

Finally he reminded the Court that he had appealed to the Pope, who had issued a brief commanding me, under pain of excommunication and death, to make surrender; that I had flouted the Pontifical authority, and that it was only upon his appeal to Cæsar and upon the Imperial mandate that I had surrendered. Wherefore he begged the Court to uphold the Holy Father's authority, and forthwith to pronounce me excommunicate and my life forfeit, restoring to him his wife Bianca and his domain of Pagliano, which he would hold as the Emperor's liege and loyal servitor.

Having spoken thus, he bowed to the Court, stepped back, and sat down.

The Ten looked at Gonzaga. Gonzaga looked at me. "Have you anything to say?" he asked.

I rose imbued by a calm that surprised me.

"Messer Cosimo has left something out of his narrative," said I. "When he says that I violently invested his palace here in Piacenza on the night of his marriage, and dragged thence the Lady Bianca, others abetting me, he would do well to add, in the interests of justice, the names of those who were my abettors."

Cosimo rose again. "Does it matter to this Court

and to the affair at issue what caitiffs he employed?"
he asked haughtily.

"If they were caitiffs it would not matter," said I.
"But they were not. Indeed, to say that it was I who
invested his palace is to say too much. The leader
of that expedition was Monna Bianca's own father,
who, having discovered the truth of the nefarious
traffic in which Messer Cosimo was engaged, hastened
to rescue his daughter from an infamy."

Cosimo shrugged. "These are mere words," he
said.

"The lady herself is present, and can bear witness
to their truth," I cried.

"A prejudiced witness, indeed!" said Cosimo with
confidence; and Gonzaga nodded, whereupon my
heart sank.

"Will Messer Agostino give us the names of any of
the braves who were with him?" quoth Cosimo. "It
will no doubt assist the ends of justice, for those men
should be standing by him now."

He checked me no more than in time. I had been on
the point of citing Falcone; and suddenly I perceived
that to do so would be to ruin Falcone without helping myself.

I looked at my cousin. "In that case," said I, "I
will not name them."

Falcone, however, was minded to name himself, for
with a grunt he made suddenly to rise. But Galeotto
stretched an arm across Bianca, and forced the
equerry back into his seat.

Cosimo saw and smiled. He was very sure of himself by now.

"The only witness whose word would carry weight

would be the late Lord of Pagliano," he said. "And the prisoner is more crafty than honest in naming one who is dead. Your Excellency will know the precise importance to attach to that."

Again His Excellency nodded. Could it, indeed, be that I was enmeshed? My calm deserted me.

"Will Messer Cosimo tell Your Excellency under what circumstances the Lord of Pagliano died?" I cried.

"It is yourself should be better able to inform the Court of that," answered Cosimo quickly, "since he died at Pagliano after you had borne his daughter thither, as we have proof."

Gonzaga looked at him sharply. "Are you implying, sir, that there is a further crime for which Messer Agostino d'Anguissola should be indicted?" he inquired.

Cosimo shrugged and pursed his lips. "I will not go so far, since the matter of Ettore Cavalcanti's death does not immediately concern me. Besides, there is enough contained in the indictment as it stands."

The imputation was none the less terrible, and could not fail of an effect upon the minds of the Ten. I was in despair, for at every question it seemed that the tide of destruction rose higher about me. I deemed myself irrevocably lost. The witnesses I might have called were as good as gagged.

Yet there was one last question in my quiver — a question which I thought must crumple up his confidence.

"Can you tell His Excellency where you were upon your marriage night?" I cried hoarsely, my temples throbbing.

Superbly Cosimo looked round at the Court; he shrugged, and shook his head as if in utter pity.

"I leave it to Your Excellency to say where a man should be upon his marriage night," he said, with an astounding impudence, and there were some who tittered in the crowd behind me. "Let me again beg Your Excellency and your worthinesses to pass to judgment, and so conclude this foolish comedy."

Gonzaga nodded gravely, as if entirely approving, whilst with a fat jewelled hand he stroked his ample chin.

"I, too, think that it is time," he said, whereupon Cosimo, with a sigh of relief, would have resumed his seat but that I stayed him with the last thing I had to say.

"My lord," I cried, appealing to Gonzaga, "the true events of that night are set forth in a memorial of which two copies were drawn up, one for the Pope and the other for Your Excellency, as the Emperor's vicegerent. Shall I recite its contents — that Messer Cosimo may be examined upon them?"

"It is not necessary," came Gonzaga's icy voice. "The memorial is here before me." And he tapped a document upon the table. Then he fixed his prominent eyes upon Cosimo. "You are aware of its contents?" he asked.

Cosimo bowed, and Galeotto moved at last, for the first time since the trial's inception.

Until now he had sat like a carved image, save when he had thrust out a hand to restrain Falcone, and his attitude had filled me with an unspeakable dread. But at this moment he leaned forward turning an ear towards Cosimo, as if anxious not to miss a single word that the man might utter. And Cosimo, intent as he was, did not observe the movement.

"I saw its fellow at the Vatican," said my cousin, "and since the Pope in his wisdom and goodness judged worthless the witnesses whose signatures it bears, His Holiness thought well to issue the brief upon which Your Excellency has acted in summoning Agostino d'Anguissola before you here.

"Thus is that memorial disposed of as a false and lying document."

"And yet," said Gonzaga thoughtfully, his heavy lip between thumb and forefinger, "it bears, amongst others, the signature of the Lord of Pagliano's confessor."

"Without violation of the seal of the confessional, it is impossible for that friar to testify," was the answer. "And the Holy Father cannot grant him dispensation for so much. His signature, therefore, stands for nothing."

There followed a moment's silence. The Ten whispered among themselves. But Gonzaga never consulted them by so much as a glance. They appeared to serve none but a decorative office in that Court of his, for they bore no share in the dispensing of a justice of which he constituted himself the sole arbiter.

At last the Governor spoke.

"It seems, indeed, that there is no more to say, and the Court has a clear course before it, since the Emperor cannot contravene the mandates of the Holy See. Nothing remains, then, but to deliver sentence; unless . . ."

He paused. and his eyes singularly sly, his lips

pursed almost humorously, he turned his glance upon Galeotto.

"Ser Cosimo," he said, "has pronounced this memorial a false and lying document. Is there anything that you, Messer Galeotto, as its author, can have to tell the Court?"

Instantly the condottiero rose, his great scarred face very solemn, his eyes brooding. He advanced almost to the very centre of the table, so that he all but stood immediately before Gonzaga, yet sideways, so that I had him in profile, whilst he fully faced Cosimo.

Cosimo at least had ceased to smile. His handsome white face had lost some of its supercilious confidence. Here was something unexpected, something upon which he had not reckoned, against which he had not provided.

"What has Ser Galeotto to do with this?" he demanded harshly.

"That, sir, no doubt he will tell us, if you will have patience," Gonzaga answered, so sweetly and deferentially that of a certainty some of Cosimo's uneasiness must have been dissipated.

I leaned forward now, scarce daring to draw breath lest I should lose a word of what was to follow. The blood that had earlier surged to my face had now all receded again, and my pulses throbbed like hammers.

Then Galeotto spoke, his voice very calm and level.

"Will Your Excellency first permit me to see the papal brief upon which you acted in summoning hither the accused?"

Silently Gonzaga delivered a parchment into Galeotto's hands. The condottiero studied it, frowning. Then he smote it sharply with his right hand.

"This document is not in order," he announced.

"How?" quoth Cosimo, and he smiled again, re-assured completely by now, convinced that here was no more than a minor quibble of the law.

"You are here described as Cosimo d'Anguissola, Lord of Mondolfo and Carmina. These titles are not yours."

The blood stirred faintly in Cosimo's cheeks.

"Those fiefs were conferred upon me by our late lord, Duke Pier Luigi," he replied.

Gonzaga spoke. "The confiscations effected by the late usurping Duke, and the awards made out of such confiscations, have been cancelled by Imperial decree. All lands so confiscated are by this decree revertible to their original holders upon their taking oath of allegiance to Cæsar."

Cosimo continued to smile. "This is no matter of a confiscation effected by Duke Pier Luigi," he said. "The confiscation and my own investiture in the confiscated fiefs are a consequence of Agostino d'Anguissola's recreancy — at least, it is in such terms that my investiture is expressly announced in the papal bull that has been granted me and in the brief which lies before Your Excellency. Nor was such express announcement necessary, for since I was next heir after Ser Agostino to the Tyranny of Mondolfo, it follows that, upon his being outlawed and his life forfeit, I enter upon my succession."

Here, thought I, were we finally checkmated. But Galeotto showed no sign of defeat.

"Where is this bull you speak of?" he demanded, as though he were the judge himself.

Cosimo haughtily looked past him at Gonzaga. "Does Your Excellency ask to see it?"

"Assuredly," said Gonzaga shortly. "I may not take your word for its existence."

Cosimo plucked a parchment from the breast of his brown satin doublet, unfolded it, and advanced to lay it before Gonzaga, so that he stood near Galeotto — not more than an arm's length between them.

The Governor conned it; then passed it to Galeotto. "It seems in order," he said.

Nevertheless, Galeotto studied it awhile; and then, still holding it, he looked at Cosimo, and the scarred face that hitherto had been so sombre now wore a smile.

"It is as irregular as the other," he said. "It is entirely worthless."

"Worthless?" quoth Cosimo, in an amazement that was almost scornful. "But have I not already explained . . ."

"It sets forth here," cut in Galeotto with assurance, "that the fiefs of Mondolfo and Carmina are confiscated from Agostino d'Anguissola. Now I submit to Your Excellency, and to your worthinesses," he added, turning aside, "that this confiscation is grotesque and impossible, since Mondolfo and Carmina never were the property of Agostino d'Anguissola, and could no more be taken from him than can a coat be taken from the back of a naked man — unless," he added, sneering, "a papal bull is capable of miracles."

Cosimo stared at him with round eyes, and I stared, too, no glimmer of the enormous truth breaking yet upon my bewildered mind. In the court the silence was deathly until Gonzaga spoke.

"Do you say that Mondolfo and Carmina did not belong — that they never were the fiefs of Agostino d'Anguissola?" he asked.

"That is what I say," returned Galeotto, towering there, immense and formidable in his gleaming armour.

"To whom, then, did they belong?"

"They did and do belong to Giovanni d'Anguissola — Agostino's father."

Cosimo shrugged at this, and some of the dismay passed from his countenance.

"What folly is this?" he cried. "Giovanni d'Anguissola died at Perugia eight years ago."

"That is what is generally believed, and what Giovanni d'Anguissola has left all to believe, even to his own priest-ridden wife, even to his own son, sitting there, lest, had the world known the truth whilst Pier Luigi lived, such a confiscation as this should, indeed, have been perpetrated.

"But he did not die at Perugia. At Perugia, Ser Cosimo, he took this scar which for thirteen years has served him for a mask." And he pointed to his own face.

I came to my feet, scarce believing what I heard. Galeotto was Giovanni d'Anguissola — my father! And my heart had never told me so!

In a flash I saw things that hitherto had been obscure, things that should have guided me to the truth had I but heeded their indications.

How, for instance, had I assumed that the Anguissola whom he had mentioned as one of the heads of the conspiracy against Pier Luigi could have been myself?

I stood swaying there, whilst his voice boomed out again.

"Now that I have sworn fealty to the Emperor in my true name, upon the hands of my Lord Gonzaga here; now that the Imperial ægis protects me from Pope and Pope's bastards; now that I have accomplished my life's work, and broken the Pontifical sway in this Piacenza, I can stand forth again and resume the state that is my own.

"There stands my foster-brother, who has borne witness to my true identity; there Falcone, who has been my equerry these thirty years; and there are the brothers Pallavicini, who tended me and sheltered me when I lay at the point of death from the wounds that disfigured me at Perugia.

"So, my Lord Cosimo, ere you can proceed further in this matter against my son, you will need to take your brief and your bull back to Rome and get them amended, for there is in Italy no Lord of Mondolfo and Carmina other than myself."

Cosimo fell back before him limp and trembling, his spirit broken by this shattering blow.

And then Gonzaga uttered words that might have heartened him. But after being hurled from what he accounted the pinnacle of success, he mistrusted now the crafty Lieutenant, saw that he had been played with as a mouse by this Imperial cat with the soft, deadly paws.

"We might waive the formalities in the interests of justice," purred the Lieutenant. "There is this memorial, my lord," he said, and tapped the document, his eyes upon my father.

"Since Your Excellency wishes the matter to be

disposed of out of hand, it can, I think, be done,"
he said, and he looked again at Cosimo.

"You have said that this memorial is false, because
the witnesses whose names are here cannot be admitted to testify."

Cosimo braced himself for a last effort. "Do you
defy the Pope?" he thundered.

"If necessary," was the answer. "I have done so
all my life."

Cosimo turned to Gonzaga. "It is not I who have
branded this memorial false," he said, "but the Holy
Father himself."

"The Emperor," said my father, "may opine that
in this matter the Holy Father has been deluded by
liars. There are other witnesses. There is myself,
for one. This memorial contains nothing but what
was imparted to me by the Lord of Pagliano on his
death-bed, in the presence of his confessor."

"We cannot admit the confessor," Gonzaga thrust
in.

"Give me leave, Your Excellency. It was not in
his quality as confessor that Fra Gervasio heard the
dying man depone. Cavalcanti's confession followed
upon that. And there was in addition present the
seneschal of Pagliano who is present here. Sufficient
to establish this memorial alike before the Imperial
and the Pontifical Courts.

"And I swear to God, as I stand here in His sight,"
he continued in a ringing voice, "that every word
there set down is as spoken by Ettore Cavalcanti,
Lord of Pagliano, some hours before he died; and so
will those others swear. And I charge Your Excellency, as Cæsar's vicegerent, to accept that memorial

as an indictment of that caitiff Cosimo d'Anguissola, who lent himself to so foul and sacrilegious a deed — for it involved the defilement of the Sacrament of Marriage."

"In that you lie!" screamed Cosimo, crimson now with rage, the veins at his throat and brow swelling like ropes.

A silence followed. My father turned to Falcone, and held out his hand. Falcone sprang to give him a heavy iron gauntlet. Holding this by the fingers, my father took a step towards Cosimo, and he was smiling, very calm again after his late furious mood. "Be it so," he said. "Since you say that I lie, I do here challenge you to prove it upon my body."

And he crashed the iron glove straight into Cosimo's face so that the skin was broken, and blood flowed about the mouth, leaving the lower half of the visage crimson, the upper dead-white.

Gonzaga sat on, entirely unmoved, and waited, indifferent to the stir there was amid the Ten. For by the ancient laws of chivalry — however much they might be falling now into desuetude — if Cosimo took up the glove, the matter passed beyond the jurisdiction of the Court, and all men must abide by the issue of the trial by battle.

For a long moment Cosimo hesitated. Then he saw ruin all about him. He — who had come to this court so confidently — had walked into a trap. He saw it now, and saw that the only loophole was the chance this combat offered him. He played the man in the end. He stooped and took up the glove.

"Upon your body, then — God helping me," he said.

Unable longer to control myself, I sprang to my father's side. I caught his arm.

"Let me! Father, let me!"

He looked into my face and smiled, and the steel-coloured eyes seemed moist and singularly soft.

"My son!" he said, and his voice was gentle and soothing as a woman's caress.

"My father!" I answered him, a knot in my throat.

"Alas, that I must deny you the first thing you ask me by that name," he said. "But the challenge is given and accepted. Do you take Bianca to the Duomo and pray that right may be done and God's will prevail. Gervasio shall go with you."

And then came an interruption from Gonzaga.

"My lord," he said, "will you determine when and where this battle is to be fought?"

"Upon the instant," answered my father, "on the banks of the Po with a score of lances to keep the lists."

Gonzaga looked at Cosimo. "Do you agree to this?"

"It cannot be too soon for me," replied the quivering Cosimo, black hatred in his glance.

"Be it so, then," said the Governor, and he rose, the Court rising with him.

My father pressed my hand again. "To the Duomo, Agostino, till I come," he said, and on that we parted. My sword was returned to me by Gonzaga's orders. In so far as it concerned myself, the trial was at an end, and I was free.

At Gonzaga's invitation, very gladly I there and then swore fealty to the Emperor upon his hands, and then, with Bianca and Gervasio, I made my way through the cheering crowd and came out into the sunshine, where my lances, who had already heard the news, set up a great shout at sight of me.

Thus we crossed the square, and went to the Duomo, to render thanks. We knelt at the altar-rail, and Gervasio knelt above us upon the altar's lowest step.

Somewhere behind us knelt Bianca's women, who had followed us to the church.

Thus we waited for close upon two hours that were as an eternity.

And kneeling there, the eyes of my soul conned closely the scroll of my young life as it had been unfolded hitherto. I reviewed its beginnings in the greyness of Mondolfo, under the tutelage of my poor, dolorous mother who had striven so fiercely to set my feet upon the ways of sanctity. But my ways had been errant ways, even though, myself, I had sought to walk as she directed. I had strayed and blundered, veered and veered again, a very mockery of what she strove to make me — a strolling saint, indeed, as Cosimo had dubbed me, a wandering mummer when I sought after holiness.

But my strolling, my errantry, ended here at last at the steps of this altar, as I knew.

Deeply had I sinned. But deeply and strenuously had I expiated, and the heaviest burden of my expiation had been that endured in the past year at Pagliano beside my gentle Bianca who was another's wedded wife. That cross of penitence — so singularly condign to my sin — I had borne with fortitude, heartened by the confidence that thus should I win to pardon and that the burden would be mercifully lifted when the expiation was complete. In the lifting of that burden from me, I should see a sign that pardon was mine at last, that at last I was accounted worthy of this pure maid through whom I should have won to grace, through whom I had come to learn that Love — God's greatest gift — is the great sanctifier of man.

That the stroke of that ardently awaited hour was even now impending I did not for a moment doubt.

Behind us, the door opened and steps clanked upon the granite floor.

Fra Gervasio rose very tall and gaunt, his gaze anxious.

He looked, and the anxiety passed. Thankfulness overspread his face. He smiled serenely, tears in his deep-set eyes. Seeing this, I, too, dared to look at last.

Up the aisle came my father very erect and solemn, and behind him followed Falcone with eyes atwinkle in his weather-beaten face.

"Let the will of Heaven be done," said my father.

And Gervasio came down to pronounce the nuptial blessing over us.

THE END